UNDER THE COVER OF DARKNESS

Arnoth rose to his feet, pushed a button on the far wall by the cell door, and the room darkened to black. Sierra heard him walk back to the bed and lie down.

"That was simple." She knew that she'd just said differently, but she didn't want to sleep. She shouldn't have asked how to shut off the light. Now she couldn't see him at all.

She wasn't sure, but she thought Arnoth sat up again. "Is it possible for you to maintain silence, woman?"

He was very near. A faint red light came from beneath their sealed door, and she saw a dark outline right above her. "Why do you ask?" Her heart beat in static leaps.

"Our captors' monitors are limited, aren't they?"

"The Tseir can't see in the dark, if that's what you mean."

"Good."

Sierra wondered why he'd asked. What an odd question! "I don't see . . ." He leaned over her, he bent close to her, and his lips touched her cheek.

Sierra froze. He kissed her face, her chin. His mouth brushed over hers. His tongue ran along the line of her lips. Her heart opened and poured itself in a torrent of emotion. She wrapped her arms around his neck, her fingers entwined in his hair, and she kissed him back.

Her lips parted beneath his, offering him entrance, offering him anything he wanted. She heard a low, stifled moan. And then, for a wild moment, she didn't care if their captors knew what they were doing or not.

Happy Reading!

THE WHITE SUN

STOBIE PIEL

LOVE SPELL BOOKS ⬥ NEW YORK CITY

*To Jo-ann Power—your talent for storytelling is only
surpassed by the gift of your friendship.
Thank you.*

LOVE SPELL®

January 1999

Published by

Dorchester Publishing Co., Inc.
276 Fifth Avenue
New York, NY 10001

ISBN 0-505-52292-6

The name "Love Spell" and its logo are trademarks of Dorchester
Publishing Co., Inc.

Printed in the United States of America.

The walls are high, the gates are strong, thick set
The sentinels—but true love never yet
Was thus constrained . . .
—*Epipsychidion,* P. B. Shelley

Prologue

"I am Arnoth of Valenwood. This fleet is under my control. Your feeble response was no match for the skill of my warriors. Surrender or die."

The giant auditorium fell into a deadly hush. A thousand Tseir commanders stared up at the screen, horrified at the image of this dark man taunting them from the depths of distant space.

The supreme commander rose to her feet and addressed the assembly from an elevated podium. Looming behind her, the image on the vidscreen focused on the young man's mocking smile. "After many cycles of research, we have discovered the fate of our Franconia-based fleet. From the residuals of battle communications, we deciphered this shocking transmission.

"Here, behind me, you see the perpetrator of Franconia's destruction. Arnoth of Valenwood is the most dangerous foe the Tseir have ever encountered."

The supreme commander fell silent, allowing her words to resonate over the Tseir assembly. "Since Franconia's mysterious defeat at Candor, rumors of this vile crime, and our inability to contain the resistance, have reached other systems now under our control. Incidents of rebellion have doubled since."

The supreme commander paused. "Allow me to draw your attention to the moon of Valenwood." She turned toward the giant screen, which switched from Arnoth's face to a diagram of the Franconian solar system. With a pointer, she indicated Franconia's moon.

"Four hundred years ago, this small moon harbored a devious, sensual race of people who first discovered the precious material, obsidian, from which our spacecrafts are constructed. We mounted a full-scale mission to the moon of Valenwood. It was one of the first Tseir colonies, and still provides us with raw obsidian for our reproduction facilities."

The supreme commander stopped, gazing left, then right, over the assembly. "Herein lies a shocking reality. At the time of our Valenwood mission, this man, Arnoth, was our captive."

A low murmur emanated through the Tseir. "Lax discipline allowed for his escape, although his mate was exterminated at that time."

The murmuring became confused. The commander switched the screen image back to Arnoth's face. "Arnoth of Valenwood's long life span can be explained. The Ellowan have a unique capacity to heal themselves and others, as well as the ability to halt life functions. In essence, Arnoth of Valenwood is the same twenty-six-year-old Ellowan that he was four hundred years ago."

The supreme commander turned to a uniformed man beside her. "I introduce to you Drakor, head of our military. He has communicated with the surviving Tseir of Franconia's main world, and has located Arnoth of Valenwood on the planet of Keir, an outer system world beyond Franconia.''

Drakor rose and addressed the assembly. ''Arnoth has lived on the planet of Keir since the fall of Valenwood, where he has commanded a small, insignificant band of Ellowan terrorists. Our informants tell us that he bonded with his dead mate's sister, then gave her to a Candorian ambassador.''

The supreme commander moved to center position again, and Drakor gave way. ''Here we find good news. The Candorian ambassador and Arnoth's mate were disposed of by our forces.''

Drakor eased back to the podium to continue his speech. ''However, the ambassador's death made it necessary for our Franconian forces to invade Candor sooner than intended. As we learned from this transmission, Arnoth sabotaged our mission.''

Once again, the supreme commander placed herself between the military man and the assembly. She braced her arms on the podium. ''Arnoth has not stopped his assault against Tseir supremacy since destroying our forces in Candor. Once again, he has wreaked havoc, leading an effort against our 'supervised' Keiroit allies. With rogue leaders, he led an insurrection and installed a Keiroit called Rurthgar as ruler. Keir is now in enemy hands.''

Drakor nodded. ''We have learned that the Galaxy Intersystem, a union of terrorists, is sending a formidable fleet to Franconia. For this reason, we have withdrawn our forces from that system. New information indicates that Arnoth has returned to his home world of Valenwood, a moon orbiting Franconia long considered barren and lifeless.''

Drakor adjusted the screen and Arnoth's image faded. Instead, a golden-brown desert appeared. ''This is a section of the moon. Valenwood still appears lifeless. However, it is rich in obsidian, our most valuable resource, and several Tseir missions there have ended mysteriously. The ships disappear, and our guards do not return. We believe that a contingent of Ellowan survived the first attack and live underground on Valenwood.''

The supreme commander again took the podium, this time for good. "That will be all, Drakor. Return to your duties.''

The military commander bowed, then left the stage, exiting the auditorium. The supreme commander switched the screen image once again to Arnoth. She zoomed in until Arnoth's mocking face filled the screen. The Tseir murmured in fear and anger. The supreme commander pointed her finger at the image.

"This is our enemy, fellow Tseir. Arnoth of Valenwood threatens our empire. We must deal with this vile threat and prove to our colonies that any rebellion is doomed to bitter failure. We must strike Valenwood before the Intersystem fleet arrives. We must seize Arnoth and take him prisoner, proving that no one makes a mockery of the Tseir and survives.''

At the rear of the auditorium, Sierra Karian stared up at the huge screen, at the dark man whose very image taunted the Tseir. The Tseir had found their enemy, and now they fixated on his destruction.

The Tseir audience rose and applauded in unison. Sierra rose, too, and tried to clap with the same methodical rhythm of the Tseir. It wasn't easy. Her nature was far from methodical. Impersonating a Tseir was a greater trial than she had ever imagined.

As she clapped, she studied Arnoth's face. The Ellowan were truly a beautiful people, dark-haired and sensual-looking. She knew this from researching their race, but in Arnoth, she saw something beyond beauty. She saw pride and strength and a haunting sweetness beneath the mocking visage.

Also, he had the most beautiful brown eyes she'd ever seen. *All men should have such lashes.* Sierra sighed as she applauded.

The supreme commander raised her hand to silence the crowd, but Sierra didn't notice. The Tseir applause halted at once. Only Sierra continued to clap. Sierra cringed as the Tseir audience turned toward her. She snapped her hands to her sides and maintained a blank expression like that of the other Tseir.

Even the Tseir commander had noticed her out-of-sync applause. Sierra felt the dark gaze from across the huge room and offered a weak smile. The commander turned her attention from Sierra and resumed her speech.

"We will send the Third Command to Valenwood to take Arnoth prisoner."

"What then?" Sierra spoke up, then instantly regretted her question. Junior commanders never questioned their superiors. Every Tseir turned to stare at her.

"Who are you?"

Sierra hesitated, contemplating deceit. She noticed a familiar Tseir from her regiment nearby and she sighed. "I am Sierra, Twelfth Command."

"You have questioned inappropriately, Sierra of the Twelfth."

"Yes."

"For what purpose?"

Because I want to know, you idiot. Sierra resisted her natural impulse toward a blunt reply. "I have studied the Ellowan, and wondered if this Arnoth would fall for such a trap. The Ellowan are devious in the extreme."

"That is true. You have studied the Ellowan?"

That's what I said, fool. "It was my first program."

"The Third Command's Ellowan experts were lost in the Candor reversal."

When Arnoth blasted them to molecules . . . "A tragedy, Supreme Commander."

15

"For this reason, we have no remaining experts on their race. Expert knowledge is required. You, Sierra, qualify for this mission."

No! Sierra cringed. She couldn't leave the Tseir home world, not when she'd come so far. Not for a minor mission like capturing a rebel leader as brash and reckless as Arnoth of Valenwood. But no junior commander defied orders from the High Command.

"My knowledge of the Ellowan is sketchy at best, Commander."

"Are you questioning my assignment, Sierra of the Twelfth?" Shock and potential outrage sounded in the commander's voice.

"No! I mean, no." Sierra swallowed hard. "It's just that there must be better-suited commanders, with far more experience and knowledge than . . ."

The supreme commander held up her hand. "Is there anyone here who has studied the Ellowan?"

Sierra held her breath and looked around. No Tseir responded, and her heart fell.

"You are alone in having researched the Ellowan, Sierra. You will accompany the mission leader to Valenwood."

Sierra forced herself to bow in acknowledgment. Curse her loose tongue! She shouldn't argue the matter. Every Tseir knew that much. But Sierra couldn't stop herself. "What about my current assignment?"

"What is your current assignment, Sierra of the Twelfth?"

"I'm in weapons development. We're handling the new blasters stolen from the Nirvahdi outpost."

"That task will be reassigned. Many Tseir have this capability."

"But . . ."

"Resume your post, Junior Commander."

Meaning, pipe down or be demoted . . . Sierra sighed.

16

She had worked hard to become a junior commander. Following the vast assortment of Tseir rules was exhausting.

The supreme commander moved to end the assembly. "Colice of the Third Command will head the mission to Valenwood. Sierra of the Twelfth will accompany her as Ellowan adviser. The assembly is adjourned."

Sierra sighed miserably as she followed the Tseir from the assembly hall. The huge doors hissed open, revealing the white sky of the Tseir home world. Metallic buildings devoid of beauty stretched endlessly across the red surface of the planet.

Sierra stood on the docking platform, waiting for the Twelfth's shuttle back to her station. No other Tseir spoke to her as they filed from the assembly hall. A pang of longing for her own world struck her, for companionship, for laughter.

Her head itched. Sierra resisted the impulse to scratch beneath her pale blond wig. All Tseir wore wigs, because they had been cloned so often they no longer grew hair. Only a few still even had eyebrows. Sierra's small breasts were concealed beneath large pads. Her breasts were itchy, too.

To outward appearances, she resembled the buxom Tseir females. In truth, she was their worst nightmare. An itchy nightmare.

Until now, everything had gone her way. Her mission's success had seemed assured. Where every other Intersystem agent had failed, she had succeeded and now held a command position within the Tseir empire.

As soon as she had reached the Tseir home world, Sierra had learned the operation of their cloning facilities. The Tseir reproduced each other, fully formed, as adults. They used the same facilities to reproduce spacecraft and weapons. Now that Sierra had learned how it worked, it should be simple to sabotage.

Unless she was stationed on some outer galaxy world like Valenwood. Hunting down a man who didn't have the sense to obliterate any traces of his battle transmissions.

Chapter One

"I am Arnoth of Valenwood. Four hundred years ago, I was prince of this land."

Arnoth stood deep in the caverns of Valenwood, addressing the remnants of the Ellowan society. The rough-hewn hall was filled with people jostling for position, remarking on his arrival with enthusiasm.

"It is my desire to repay my duty to my people by assisting you to restore your lives on the surface of Valenwood."

A young woman stepped forward. Her face was painted with blue and red streaks, a warrior's design. She wore only a rough-stitched loincloth and a narrow band of leather covering her breasts. She held a hand-carved spear in her right hand.

"I am Helayna Nidawi. I lead the Stone People, who you call Ellowan. 'Ellowan' means the People of the Elf

Wood. We are no longer the People of the Wood, but of the Stone Caverns.''

His companions, Dane and Aiyana, had mentioned Helayna when they'd told him of the surviving Ellowan. Arnoth understood now why Aiyana's eyes had glittered when she'd spoken of Helayna. Her resemblance to his first mate was obvious, but Elena was dead, and any attraction to this woman was merely physical. Of this he was sure.

Helayna was tall, her hair straight and blond, her eyes blue and clear. Arnoth guessed Aiyana's intentions. She'd expected him to meet Helayna and love her as he had loved Elena.

"Aiyana told me of you, Helayna."

"She told me of you, also." Helayna studied his group. "Where is Aiyana? What happened to her Dane?"

"Aiyana and Dane returned to the system of Candor, where she lives as his mate. We defeated the Tseir's attempt to overtake that system, and Dane was admitted to a league of planets called the Intersystem."

"What of the Tseir? It has been many cycles since we have seen Tseir ships in the sky."

"The Tseir have retreated from Franconia, leaving their stations in this system unguarded. Representatives of the Galaxy Intersystem are sending a fleet to protect us. When they arrive, you may live aboveground without fear."

Helayna studied Arnoth intently. "If you are prince, why have you waited until now to return to us?"

Arnoth hesitated. When he'd returned from the victory at Candor, he'd intended to travel to Valenwood. Instead, he had returned to Keir. Only the pressure of his Ellowan companions had finally persuaded him to return to Valenwood.

"Until Aiyana discovered your existence, we believed no one had survived the Tseir attack. I have lived on the planet of Keir since Valenwood's destruction. The Tseir had cloned the amphibian natives of that world and seized control of their main swamp. When I returned from Candor, I helped their rightful ruler regain power of that world.''

Helayna fingered her spear. ''You did this by battle?''

''I did.''

Helayna's eyes narrowed with interest and admiration. ''That is honorable.'' She approached Arnoth and looked into his eyes without wavering. ''Aiyana says you are a warrior.''

''I am now.''

Helayna glanced at Arnoth's Ellowan companions, then returned her piercing gaze to him. ''Who are these people with you?''

''These are my brethren. They are Ellowan, too. When the Tseir destroyed Valenwood, these men and women were off-world. They escaped destruction, and we lived on Keir, where we led a resistance against the Tseir. If you agree, they wish to resume their lives here on Valenwood.''

Beside Arnoth, his friend Morvin nodded vigorously. ''We've been away a long time, Helayna. The planet of Keir is cold and lonely. You have no idea how joyous we were to learn of your people's existence.''

Helayna paid no attention to Morvin. Her gaze remained fixed on Arnoth. ''And you, prince of Valenwood, what do you want?''

''If you wish it, I will assist you in restoring the Ellowan society aboveground, where you may lead fuller lives, free of Tseir domination.''

''Do you intend to remain on Valenwood with us?''

Arnoth hesitated. ''I will remain until I have fulfilled my duty to your people.''

''What duty?''

''According to Aiyana, you are descended from the

21

Nidawi clan of priestesses. I will teach you the role of high priestess, then find a successor to my title. When you are bonded to the new prince, he will become king, and my duty will be fulfilled.''

Helayna's mouth dropped; she looked both horrified and disgusted. ''You mean . . . you want me to become a breeder?''

''To continue the Nidawi line, you must produce heirs.''

''I am a warrior, not a breeder.''

''If you move your society aboveground, there will be no need to restrict your population growth, Helayna. You can be both breeder and warrior.''

''You expect me to take a mate? Who?''

''Whoever you wish.''

''Am I free to choose my own mate?''

Arnoth glanced around the cavern. Torches illuminated the hall, shining warm light on Helayna's Stone People. Though dirty and primitive, they were Ellowan. ''I see no reason why not.''

''Very well, then. I choose you.''

He should have expected this. And been prepared. Instead, Arnoth just stood, mouth agape, speechless. Beside him, Morvin chuckled. Also, the Candorian lingbat, Batty, issued a polite cough from his position on Arnoth's shoulder.

''Well, sir . . . Maybe you won't be returning to Keir as soon as you thought you would.''

Arnoth glanced at the lingbat. The creature's small, pointed ears twitched, his round eyes looked suspiciously wide and overly innocent. ''My plans haven't changed, Batty.''

''Looks like hers have.''

Helayna studied the lingbat. ''This is the same creature that accompanied Aiyana and her Dane when they visited the Stone People. Why is he with you now?''

"Batty returned with me to Keir and there he took a mate."

The lingbat hopped from Arnoth's right shoulder to his left, bouncing once on the top of his head. "I came along with your prince to Valenwood because I knew the location of your caverns' secret entrance."

Arnoth welcomed the lingbat's interruption. He had to think of a way to dissuade Helayna without alienating the Stone People. "Thank you, Batty. I know you would have preferred to remain on Keir with your new mate."

"Not a problem, sir. She Who Leaps High is gestating. Dwindle Bat females can be"—Batty paused, looking pained—"*testy* at that time."

"I'll be sure to have you back by the time your litter is born. And not before."

"Thank you, sir."

Arnoth reluctantly turned his attention back to Helayna. "It isn't my intention to take a mate again, Helayna."

Helayna's fine brow creased. "It wasn't my intention to take a mate, ever. I am leader of the Stone People. Mating with one of them is impossible for me without losing my authority. You are prince. You are warrior. I will mate with you."

The woman was stubborn. Dane had hinted at this, but Arnoth hadn't understood at the time what danger Helayna's temperament presented. He considered another angle. "My biological function has been dormant for nearly four hundred years. This makes me incapable of mating."

"This process is known to us. Aiyana was dormant, too, but mating with Dane restored her. Mating with me will do the same for you."

Yes, but Aiyana loved Dane. . . . Arnoth restrained his annoyance. "Mating isn't a simple act."

"I know that. It involves copulation, resulting in male

23

seed entering the female's womb.... Resulting in the heirs you wish of me. It sounds simple to me."

Batty chirped. "It's simple. And pleasant. You'll like it, sir. I know I do." Batty hesitated, craning his neck to look into Arnoth's face. "But you've been mated before, haven't you? I know you never spawned any young, but you've had two mates. You must know."

Arnoth eyed the bat in growing irritation. "Aiyana and I didn't engage in a formal mating. Our bond was for formality's sake only."

"What about the other one, Aiyana's sister?"

Arnoth's heart turned to stone. "I will never mate again."

Helayna set her spear to one side. "As I see it, it is your duty. But perhaps you prefer an endless life."

"No." Arnoth felt numb. He once again stood amid his own people, something he'd feared he'd never do, and joy still eluded him. *I have lived too long.* Deeper in his mind came another thought. *I haven't lived at all.*

Arnoth sighed. The breath came from the depths of his soul. *I want it over.* "If that is what you wish, I will mate with you, Helayna. As you say, it is my duty."

Helayna accepted his gloomy agreement without hesitation. "How is the mating performed? Is there ritual, or do we simply engage in copulation?"

Arnoth's numbness deepened. His first mating with Elena had been arranged by their parents. It was duty, but he had loved her. When Elena died, he had been joined with Aiyana. Grief bonded them. He loved her like a sister and willingly released her when she fell in love with Dane.

Arnoth looked at Helayna. She was young and beautiful and strong. Perhaps he would come to care for her. But he would never love her. Maybe that would be easier than loving.

"There is ritual. We speak our promises, and the union

is made. At copulation, the union is formalized.''

"Do we copulate before witnesses or in private chambers?''

Arnoth remembered when copulation had been involved in so many of his thoughts and fantasies. Now, it sounded cold and emotionless, devoid of magic and love. This wasn't the Ellowan way. Looking around at the painted faces, he wondered if that way was lost forever.

"In ages past, the copulation of prince and priestess was done before an audience. That practice eventually gave way to privacy.''

Arnoth didn't want to discuss the matter any more. The thought made him tired. "There's no need to engage in the act until you enter a fertile period.''

"I am fertile now.''

Wonderful. "It might be wise to wait a cycle, until you are accustomed to your new role.''

"I prefer to get it over with now.''

Arnoth sighed. "Then we will mate at dawn.''

Arnoth stood on a plateau overlooking the desert. To the southeast, he saw the gold and blue haze of the ocean. There, ages ago, he'd lived in a white tiled city, prince of a sweet land. He closed his eyes and saw himself standing alone at the edge of the sea, watching the sun rise as the amber whales lifted their heads from the water and sang.

The amber whales were gone. Their presence in the sea had been the first thing he checked for when he landed on Valenwood. Fish remained, but the mammals were gone. Arnoth drew his attention from the south and looked northward. Once, a green forest had stretched endlessly, the first home of the Ellowan race.

Only the desert dwellers had survived the Tseir devastation. They'd followed their king, Hakon, into the tun-

nels and survived. The Ellowan society hadn't flourished,
but it had endured.

"You're a lucky man, Arnoth." Morvin came up behind Arnoth and slapped his shoulder.

Arnoth eyed his old friend with misgivings. "Why do
you say so?"

"You've had three of the most beautiful mates a man
could ask for. True, you and Aiyana didn't exactly have
the kind of relationship you might have had, but still . . ."
Morvin patted Arnoth's shoulder. "You've got a chance
to start over, my friend. Don't let this one pass by."

"I don't want another mate."

"I know. And I know you blame yourself for Elena's
death. Let the past rest, Arnoth. The Tseir have left Franconia, and we have a chance to live again. To *live*."

Arnoth didn't answer. But the death that followed life
seemed more appealing to him. "I'm tired, Morvin. I feel
old."

"You *are* old. But you look young. Apparently, the
lovely Helayna thought so, too. She's a tough female,
and I'd say she's set her heart on you."

Arnoth frowned and raked his fingers through his long
hair. "I don't want her heart."

"Then take her body."

"I don't want her body, either."

Morvin's eyes widened. "Are you crazy?"

"Maybe."

"You'll change your mind tonight."

"Maybe."

"You deserve a real life, Arnoth. Don't prevent yourself from enjoying it."

"A real life . . ." Arnoth looked from the northern
plains back across the desert. "Will we find that here?"

Morvin followed Arnoth's dark gaze. "It's not what
you remember, I know. It's not what I remember, either.
Maybe Valenwood won't ever be the way we remember

it, but it has beauty now, Arnoth. It has Helayna, and her people."

Arnoth didn't respond. The sun faded beneath the horizon and the first stars appeared in the sky. Arnoth watched the golden orb of Franconia brighten on the northern horizon. "This land feels like a graveyard."

"Our people survived, Arnoth. They're strong; they're healthy. They're ready to follow you; they're ready to become Ellowan again."

"As Helayna mentioned, they are no longer 'People of the Wood,' Morvin. There is no wood."

"A few shrubs."

Arnoth glanced at Morvin doubtfully. Morvin smiled. He had been with Arnoth since his escape from Franconia, and since he and Aiyana arrived on Keir. Morvin was older, but he was ready to live again. Arnoth wasn't.

Arnoth turned his gaze back to the sky. Stars burst across its dark expanse. "Not stars . . . Morvin, those are ships."

Morvin looked up. "The Intersystem fleet?"

"If so, they're sooner than we expected."

"I don't like it. That's a Tseir formation. Could they be returning to Franconia?"

Arnoth watched the vessels. "They're not headed for Franconia. They're coming here."

"For obsidian?"

"That's a war fleet, Morvin."

Morvin groaned. "Not again."

"Again."

Arnoth turned and ran like a hunter back to the Stone Cavern entrance. Morvin followed close behind. "Why would they send soldiers here again?"

Arnoth reached the entrance and touched the hidden panel. The cave wall slid inward, and they barred it shut behind them. "I don't know. Even if they had learned about this culture, why would it matter to them? They left Franconia.''

Morvin caught his breath. ''Maybe leaving was a ruse.''

''For what purpose?''

Outside the cavern, the roar of space vessels shook the ground as they set down. ''We'll find out soon. If they're landing here, it's a good guess they know the entrances.''

''Then our people are in danger. Again.''

Helayna's warriors positioned themselves around the main entrance, waiting. Arnoth and his Ellowan companions poised rifles. The Stone People were concealed deep in the caverns. The Tseir had to pass the warriors to reach the others.

The main entrance shook, then rumbled. Morvin hissed. ''They're breaking through, Arnoth.''

Batty squeaked and dug his claws into Arnoth's shoulder. ''I'll never see She Who Leaps High again. My first litter . . .''

''You can still retreat to the caverns, Batty.''

''No, sir. My place is with you.''

The entrance crumbled. Tseir guards lined the tunnel wall, but they didn't enter. They wore red helmets, their faces concealed by white visors, and were armed with weapons Arnoth had never seen before. He glanced at Morvin. ''What are they doing?''

The guards gave way for their leader. A buxom, red-haired commander appeared, cloaked in red. ''People of Valenwood, you are under the control of the Tseir empire. Should you choose to battle us, all will die. Surrender, and you will be spared.''

Morvin's mouth dropped. ''Surrender? Since when has that been a Tseir option?''

Arnoth shook his head. Helayna crouched beside him. ''What do we do? Do we fight?''

"Wait."

The Tseir commander motioned to her guards. "We know that you lurk in these crevices. Our instruments reveal your presence."

Morvin leaned toward Arnoth. "They can't hope to storm this place."

"Unless their weapon capacity has changed. Those guards are armed with something I've never seen."

"Looks like canisters."

Arnoth smiled. "Let's find out." He placed Batty on Morvin's shoulder, then moved soundlessly from his position, creeping closer to the entrance. "Tseir, you flirt with death if you seek our surrender. You've entered an endless cavern of wolves."

The commander turned toward Arnoth's voice. She motioned behind her, and another Tseir female stepped forward. The second woman wore a shorter red cape, but she was taller than the other, blond and thin. Strange, because even across the hall, Arnoth noted that her breasts were inordinately large for her slender body.

The subcommander made her way through the guards. She caught her foot on a rock and tripped. Arnoth stared in amazement. The Tseir were always in control, always poised, sure-footed. Nothing flustered them. They never tripped.

The subcommander coughed nervously, then straightened herself. She positioned herself beside the commander and bowed awkwardly. They spoke quietly together; the commander nodded. Arnoth guessed the awkward Tseir was advising her commander as to a proper response to his threat.

The commander addressed Arnoth's position. "Nothing is endless, Ellowan. And nothing is beyond the reach of our death gas."

Arnoth waited, then shrugged. "If this substance is so

29

powerful, then gas us and be done. Tseir are not known for mercy. Why the speech?''

Again, the commander turned to the other female. Arnoth noticed that the other Tseir gestured as she spoke. She didn't stand perfectly still; she shifted her weight from foot to foot. Perhaps the Tseir had cloned a faulty model.

''We have no use for this primitive cavern, Ellowan.''

''Then why are you here?''

''We offer you a choice. We have reason to believe you harbor a vile criminal. Arnoth of Valenwood will be surrendered to us, or you will all die.''

They came for him. Arnoth considered his response. If the Tseir only wanted him, it might be possible to save the others. ''You want this Arnoth alive, I assume.''

''That is our purpose here.''

''And should he surrender to you, what prevents you from annihilating his race as you attempted to do four hundred years ago?''

The commander waited for the other female's answer before speaking. The blond woman seemed impatient. She waved her arms, then faced Arnoth's position herself.

''Look, Ellowan. The Tseir don't care about your people. We want Arnoth. While we can surely destroy whoever you've got hidden up there, there's no way we can gas out all your caverns. . . .''

The commander gasped. ''Sierra! Demoted to Thirteenth Command.''

The impatient Tseir's shoulders slumped. She bowed her head miserably. ''Yes, Colice.''

Arnoth considered the Tseir display. He'd dealt with their cloned race for centuries. He'd never seen anything like this. The Tseir lusted, they were cruel, but they weren't disobedient. Ever. He eased back to Morvin and Helayna.

"Helayna, get your warriors back into the caverns. Don't let them see you."

Morvin grasped Arnoth's arms. "You're not trusting that red-caped demon, are you?"

"No, but we've got nothing to lose."

"Nobody move!" Arnoth looked back toward the Tseir. The subcommander seized a canister from a guard and pointed it in Arnoth's direction. "We want Arnoth, and we want him now. Otherwise, we'll finish you all right here."

"Sierra . . ."

The subcommander turned toward her leader. Her impatience made her seem young. "If you want him, you'll get him." She faced Arnoth's position again. "I don't have time for this, Ellowan. All of you, out where we can see you. Here's what I'll do. I'll allow a group of you through that gate."

She pointed toward a gate at the rear of the cavern. "Females only. How's that? When you're assured your people are safe, Arnoth can give himself up."

"What makes you think Arnoth is here at all?"

The subcommander rolled her eyes. "Don't toy with me, Ellowan. I'm not in the mood. You're Arnoth."

Arnoth's eyes widened. A faulty model, but a perceptive one.

"No argument? Good. I don't feel like debating your identity. I recognized your voice from the . . ."

"Sierra!"

The subcommander caught herself. "I had a hunch. So what's it going to be? Will you surrender or not?"

Arnoth considered her bizarre offer. "And if I don't?"

The subcommander puffed an impatient breath. "We'll kill you all, and the Third Command will have to do with a dead Arnoth rather than a live one. Reasonable?"

Arnoth heard the woman's superior speak: "Sierra, demotion to Twenty-fifth Command if this fails."

Sierra nodded at her commander's threat. "Fair enough."

Morvin gripped Arnoth's arm. "You're not giving yourself up, Arnoth. I won't let you."

Arnoth looked at the remnants of his people. He felt only a detached sense of duty to them. The place in his heart that once loved had grown cold and dormant over a long stretch of time.

Arnoth shifted his gaze to the Tseir at the tunnel entrance. One thing remained in his heart. He remembered Elena's death, her throat cut by a Tseir female's hand. He remembered holding her, his one chance to save her granted by his gloating enemy.

He had entered the healing trance, bonding his mind to hers. To heal her, he had to have her compliance. *Do you desire life?* He remembered waiting what had seemed like eons for her answer.

Broken and shattered, her spirit crushed, Elena had replied *No*. There, in a black cell, Arnoth had released her. *I will face my enemy, and die at their hands. But I will die fighting.* "My life means nothing. Morvin, see that our people learn the old ways." Arnoth paused. A tremor of regret touched his cold heart. "If you make contact with Aiyana again, tell her I'm sorry. She wanted more for me. I didn't want it for myself."

Helayna positioned herself beside him. "You're giving yourself up?"

"Morvin will assist you, Helayna."

Helayna plainly considered surrender dishonorable. She fingered her spear and frowned. "We should fight."

"Your people couldn't withstand an all-out Tseir assault, Helayna. They would just keep sending troops until you're all dead. I'm not worth that. You deserve better than I can give. Allow me to do this last thing for you, that I may at least die in peace."

Morvin's fingers clenched. "The Tseir won't give you

32

peace, my friend. And they won't let you die."

"There is nothing they can do that I haven't endured already."

Morvin looked down at the Tseir woman who seemed so odd. She was balancing the canister in the crook of her arm and scratched her head. "I wouldn't count on it."

Arnoth rose to his feet, showing himself to the Tseir. "If you uphold your word and allow my people to leave this hall, I am your prisoner."

The subcommander looked up at him and nodded. "They can go." She paused, then glanced at her superior. "Can't they?"

The commander hesitated. "Yes."

Arnoth motioned to Morvin. "Take them, and secure them deep in the caverns. Block exits and put out patrols. The Intersystem Fleet will arrive soon." Arnoth looked for Batty, but the lingbat had disappeared. "When the fleet arrives, see that the lingbat is returned to Keir."

Helayna showed no emotion, but tears glistened in Morvin's eyes. "It will be done."

Arnoth kissed Morvin's forehead, handed him his rifle, and then touched Helayna's hand. "Farewell."

Helayna led her group down into the cavern. The Tseir remained at the tunnel and made no false movements. Arnoth watched the group pass through the gate. He waited until he knew they had reached the tunnel shafts.

Then he gave himself up to his enemy.

Sierra waited impatiently while the Ellowan leader climbed down from the rocks. She glanced back at Colice, wondering if her success meant her rank would be restored.

"Looks like we've got him, Commander."

Colice shifted her dark gaze to Sierra. "You took a grave risk, Sierra of the Thirteenth. It must be reported to the supreme command immediately upon our return.''

Nope, no rank restoration. Sierra stared at her feet. She saw only the toes over the swell of her massive padded breasts. Until this mission, everything had gone so well. Curse Arnoth and his flamboyant display of rebellion!

Twelfth was the lowest rank to have access to the Tseir's restricted facilities. Sierra sighed. *Well, I'll just have to work my way back up.* She lifted her gaze to the approaching Ellowan.

He walked toward the Tseir guards without fear. Arnoth was taller than Sierra expected. She'd thought the Ellowan were slight, delicate humanoids. But this didn't include Arnoth. He moved with innate grace, but he was muscular as well as agile.

The front portion of his long dark hair was tied back, revealing a proud, impassive face. A chiseled face. More beautiful in person even than on the Tseir screen. He wore leggings and a loose brown tunic, bound at the waist. A gray cape fell over his wide shoulders.

Sierra watched as he drew near. *Where is your fear? Don't you know what they'll do to you?* Sierra didn't want to concern herself for Arnoth's fate. His own recklessness had brought him here. His fate was his own doing. She had more important matters to attend to.

The guards moved to surround him. Arnoth stopped and they moved in to bind him. He didn't resist. Sierra wondered if he had something planned. Something suicidal. The cursed fool would probably destroy himself for the sake of removing a minor fleet of Tseir.

''He should be checked for explosive devices, Commander.''

''Well-considered, Sierra of the Thirteenth.'' Colice motioned to a guard. ''Use the subparticle manipulator to check him.''

Sierra cringed. The manipulator disturbed nerve endings and caused pain in its subjects, even on its lowest

34

setting. She endured a wave of remorse at the suggestion. She took a step toward Arnoth, then caught herself. Her whole mission was forfeit if sympathy gave her identity away.

Sierra steeled herself as the guard produced the manipulator and engaged it over Arnoth's skin. She watched as his handsome face contorted with sharp pain. But he didn't flinch or cry out. He endured the pain as if it were nothing.

The guard finished the probe, then stepped back. "He is unarmed, Commander."

Colice went to Arnoth. "Let this brief pain foreshadow your future, Arnoth. You are at Tseir mercy from now unto eternity . . . and you spoke of our mercy with stunning accuracy."

Arnoth held her eyes without wavering. "I expect no more."

Colice's anger glimmered. The Tseir thrived on the emotion of others; it fed their need to control when they provoked reactions in their victims. Maybe Arnoth knew this. Maybe he now played them like fools, denying them what they craved most.

Sierra stood back as the guards led Arnoth forward. He glanced at her as he passed. She looked into his brown eyes, and her breath caught in her throat. Those beautiful eyes showed no hope, no fire. Just boundless courage and eternal pride.

He would never be beaten, because he had nothing the Tseir could take. He would endure pain. Nothing would touch him. Sierra swallowed, but she couldn't look away. She'd never seen anyone without hope before. She would never forget the sight, not as long as she lived.

Arnoth seemed to sense her shock, and his brow furrowed slightly. He looked away and walked on, leaving Sierra stricken. *I can't let him die,* Sierra clasped her

Stobie Piel

hand to her head. *What am I thinking? I'm not responsible for him.*

Colice eyed her doubtfully, ready to issue a new order. Sierra snapped her hand from her forehead to her side. "Headache. It's . . . dusty in here."

"Report to my ship, Sierra. You will be reassigned there."

Sierra sighed, then followed Colice from the Ellowan caverns. Golden light filtered through the sky. Valenwood was still tonight; no creatures chirped or rustled the dark sky.

Another world, laid low by Tseir domination. Sierra's resolve strengthened. If by her life or her death she could prevent another such conquest, she would do it.

Arnoth sat in a small holding cell, guarded and bound. A narrow metal cot provided the only seat in the room. He wondered why they kept him alive, and what purpose his life could serve the Tseir now. They wanted something, something he would never give. But he had to find out what it was before he could deny them.

The narrow door hissed open and the peculiar Tseir subcommander started to enter. Too fast. She bumped into the opening door before it cleared the passage. Arnoth shook his head, fighting a hysterical urge to laugh.

She sighed, rolled her eyes, then proceeded into his room. Outwardly, she looked like a Tseir female. They were large women, straight-backed, with shoulder-length, one-toned hair. None were dark. They were uniformly large-breasted.

Her red cape was askew. She adjusted it, but on this particular Tseir, everything seemed out of place.

"Greetings, Tseir. Does my torture begin now, or will I be sport at your home-world coliseum?"

She looked annoyed. "You might have considered your fate before . . ." She caught herself and stopped.

"Never mind. I'll be demoted out of existence if I'm not careful."

"Tell me, did the cloning unit malfunction when they produced you?"

Her bright eyes widened dramatically. Her fluid, quick expressions separated her even farther from the controlled Tseir. "You know we're clones?"

"A friend of mine deduced that from your uniform behavior and appearance, among other things. Had he encountered you, he might not have come to that conclusion."

"I'm a clone, too." She sounded proud. "Not that it's any of your concern."

"Does the clone have a name? Sierra, wasn't it?"

"Sierra Kar . . ." She stopped and coughed. "Sierra of the Twelfth."

"Thirteenth."

Sierra sighed heavily and nodded. "Just so." Sierra seated herself beside him on the narrow cot. She crossed one leg over the other and massaged her ankle.

She looked young, but Arnoth wasn't sure in what way. Her light blond hair obscured her face, but it was a delicate face, with fine, soft lips, a narrow, slightly upturned nose, and inquisitive, arched brows above her bright eyes.

Her brows were darker than her hair by several shades. Strange, because most Tseir had few, if any, eyebrows or lashes. Most looked painted on. Sierra's looked real, and well-formed.

Arnoth's amusement at the aberrant Tseir female changed to anger at himself. He didn't hate her. She was part of the most evil race in the Galaxy, and he didn't hate her.

"You have graced me with your presence, Tseir. Perhaps you'll tell me the reason."

"I'm your guard." She sounded humiliated and depressed by the admission. "Can you imagine? How much lower can I get?"

"I doubt you want my opinion."

"Nope."

" 'Nope'?"

"It means, 'no.' "

"A new Tseir phrase?"

She chewed her lip before answering, then attempted a casual shrug. "We have many phrases."

Arnoth leaned back against the wall. Sierra sat back, too. Her skin color didn't match her hair. Her flesh wasn't pale and colorless like most Tseir. He saw tones of pink and gold. Freckles wouldn't have surprised him, but on closer examination, her skin was flawless.

Arnoth looked away. *Clones don't have freckles.* "Is it permitted for you to tell me where we're going?"

Sierra shrugged. "Your room is monitored, so I should find out if I'm wrong . . . but we're going back to the home world."

"Which is . . . ?"

"Unwise of me to reveal to you."

"Is the journey long?"

"Yes." This seemed to discourage her even more. "Especially if you're in the thirteenth class."

"You seem fixated on your demotion, Tseir."

She glanced over at him, woefully. "It's not easy to climb the ranks to Twelfth."

"How many classes are there?"

"Twenty-five command classes. Guards are in another grouping, naturally. And the military divides itself—"

"Sierra of the Thirteenth!" A voice boomed through a wall monitor, and Sierra jumped to attention, a pained expression on her small face.

"Reporting, Commander."

"Demoted!"

The pained expression intensified. "To . . . ?"

"Fourteenth Command."

"For saying too much?"

"Correct. Resume guard duties."

Sierra sank back onto the cot beside Arnoth. She propped her elbows on her knees and cupped her chin in her hands. "I can't believe it. Fourteenth . . ."

"Tell me, what duties does a fourteenth commander face?"

"I don't know. Probably swabbing decks with my tongue."

Arnoth tried not to smile. He didn't want to smile. "Just how many models like you are there?"

"We're not models." Sierra glanced toward the monitor. "Exactly. And conversation isn't in my best interest."

"Apparently not."

Sierra yawned and leaned her head back against the metal wall. Her neck was long and slender. Her pulse made a slight motion in her throat. Her skin looked soft. Arnoth forced his vision elsewhere, and he sat, trying not to contemplate the captivating woman.

Her skin looked so soft. Arnoth pondered his reaction to the Tseir, Sierra of the Fourteenth. It was short of loathing, so it wasn't normal.

Maybe they had poisoned him somehow. The worst fate he could imagine was to find a Tseir female appealing, right? Arnoth glanced back at Sierra. Her eyes were closed. Her thick brown lashes cast small shadows over her cheekbones.

He didn't like her hair. It looked coarse and rough, reaching just to the line of her jaw. The blunt end distracted from her delicate face. *Good.*

His gaze traveled lower. Her arms were slender, in contrast to her full chest. Her hands were narrow, the fingers tapered, and they rested folded on her lap. One fingernail looked chewed. Her red cape fell from one shoulder, but she didn't adjust it.

Because she was asleep. Arnoth stared in amazement. Sierra of the Fourteenth had fallen asleep on duty. Twenty-fifth class loomed over her slender shoulders.

Arnoth heard footsteps in the corridor outside his cell. He heard guards. He heard the commander speak. "Sierra, is the cell secure for entry?"

No answer came from the sleeping blonde. Her breaths came even and deep. Peaceful. "Sierra? Is the cell secure?"

Ellowan don't touch Tseir. Arnoth debated his action as the door panel engaged. As a guard, she could be worse. "Tseir!"

No response. He leaned closer to her ear. "Tseir!"

She started at his hiss, bumped her head, and opened her eyes just as the door slid open. She recognized the situation immediately and hopped to her feet, standing poised as the commander entered the room.

"Sierra, your reply wasn't noted."

"I replied, Commander. Secure."

The commander eyed the young Tseir suspiciously but didn't argue. "Is the prisoner contained?"

Sierra glanced at Arnoth. "He is."

Arnoth detected a faint hint of sarcasm in Sierra's voice. He half expected her to add, "Can't you see for yourself?" But she maintained a blank expression.

"Your shift is over, Sierra. Report to Level Three for rest duties."

Rest duties? Sierra cast a forlorn glance over her shoulder as she left his cell. Arnoth endured a pang of regret at her departure. The commander stood in her place. The difference was astounding.

"I am Colice, First Commander of the Third Fleet."

"Your numerical labels are confusing, Tseir. Espe-

40

cially when they alter as often as with my previous guard's title.''

"Sierra is a junior commander. Some commanders are more polished than others.'' Colice's gaze scraped over him. "You are at our mercy, Arnoth of Valenwood. It would be wise of you to remember that fact.''

"I look forward to my death, Tseir.''

"You won't die, Ellowan. We have something much better in mind for you.''

"Torture, then.''

"We can do better than that.''

Arnoth caught her lustful gaze. "If you're referring to any kind of sexual contact, that *is* torture, Tseir.''

"A time will come when you will do whatever we ask, Ellowan. You'll respond without question, without resistance.''

"A man whose mind has been altered might as well be dead. Your threat means nothing to me.''

Colice's face contorted in anger. "We will find your weakness, Ellowan. And when we do, we will use it to destroy you.''

Arnoth smiled, a taunting rebellion. "You murdered my mate. You can't kill her again. You can't hurt her, so you can't hurt me. There is nothing worse you can do. I endured, and I fought you. I will fight you forever.''

"All things have a weakness. We will find yours.''

"I had many weaknesses, Tseir. All are gone.''

"It's a shame you don't have another mate.''

Arnoth folded his arms behind his head. "Isn't it? That would make my destruction so simple. You could dismember her before my eyes, kill her, destroy her.''

His light tone worked well. Colice's face flushed red. "They said you are a ruthless man. I see that it is so. But all living creatures have weaknesses. And we Tseir are experts at finding weakness.''

41

"Your culture has thrived on it. But it won't work with me."

Arnoth closed his eyes, still smiling. His final vengeance would be to deny them. Death didn't frighten him, pain didn't frighten him. Nothing moved him at all. Arnoth felt strong and impenetrable.

"Guard!" Colice spat the word. Arnoth enjoyed her fury. "The next shift is yours. At completion, summon Sierra of the Fourteenth to relieve you."

Arnoth's smile faded. *Sierra of the Fourteenth.* No, he was wrong. Something frightened him, after all. Deep in his soul, Arnoth knew Sierra was a threat he'd never imagined.

Sierra lay on her back staring at the white metal ceiling. She hated living in barracks. But even those of the Twelfth Command shared living quarters. *If only I'd made it to Ninth. . . .* Ninth was out of the question now. Curses!

Sierra rolled over onto her side and stared at the Tseir sleeping on their bunks across from her. They slept on their backs, suffering no dreams, no nightmares. No sleeplessness.

She closed her eyes and tried to summon sleep. It didn't come. Instead, she thought of Arnoth in his cell, bound and destined for a fate grimmer than death.

He'd brought it on himself. The Tseir must be handled delicately. The humiliating defeat at Candor had made them tighten their control on their other systems. Perhaps Arnoth of Valenwood should have considered that.

Sierra squirmed onto her back again. His victory had shaken the Tseir. She couldn't feel sorrow for that. And he had saved an Intersystem world from extinction. The Candorians were wise and gentle people. Their system harbored worlds with young civilizations, newly introduced to the Galaxy community.

Arnoth had saved them. Sierra wished she could ask him how he had done it. If only the rooms weren't monitored! But he was a prisoner, and every move he made was recorded. If only he'd had the sense to scramble his interstellar messages.

He had been too eager and too proud. But Arnoth's opinion might have more weight than she had first imagined. He wasn't as stupid as she'd thought he would be. His fearlessness had made him seem primitive, initially. But it was the fearlessness of a man who had lost everything, not of one who knows no better.

Sierra considered what she knew of Arnoth of Valenwood. He had been prince, heir to the Ellowan kingship. The king had been an off-worlder, from a race of barbarians. But the Ellowan made him king. Arnoth had mated with the king's granddaughter.

And the Tseir had murdered her. So he'd mated with her sister. Sierra's brow furrowed as she contemplated what she'd learned from the supreme commander's speech. Apparently, Arnoth simply handed his second lifemate to another man, the Candorian ambassador. Both had been killed by the Tseir.

Sierra drummed her fingers on her chest. What kind of man hands his wife over to another? He'd sacrificed himself for the remnant Ellowan, so Sierra knew he was honorable.

Why did he wake me? Sierra sat up in bed. The man had reason to hate all Tseirs. Why had he not watched another humiliating demotion? She wanted to know, and she wanted to know now. But her next guard shift didn't start for several hours. She was exhausted. Falling asleep on duty should have been an indication. Sierra jammed herself back into her bed.

And why do they want him alive? She hadn't heard a convincing answer yet. What kind of example could Arnoth be? If they tortured and murdered him it would

43

prove nothing. In fact, if he bore it as he had endured the manipulator, his heroism would become almost legend.

What could the Tseir do with their most annoying enemy? Sierra's breath caught as the answer crystallized in her mind. She knew what they wanted. They would make him a Tseir.

Sierra's skin felt suddenly cold. The Tseir knew his death wouldn't serve their purpose. They would hold him up, somehow, as a renegade who had conformed to Tseir domination, who now served them. Joined them.

Could they intend to clone him? It might be possible. No, it would take too long. Many Arnoths would have to be created before they lost his spirit, or his ability to reproduce. That wouldn't work. And by the time a dormant Arnoth was created, the clone wouldn't resemble him closely enough.

So they had to transform the real man. Sierra thought of his dark, hopeless eyes. He had nothing to lose. The Tseir would never bend him to their will. They were searching for weakness, and Arnoth had none.

Hope was a weakness and love was a weakness. He'd given away love when he'd handed his mate to another man. He'd left his hope for his race on Valenwood. So he had nothing.

Sierra didn't want to care, and she wasn't sure why she did. True, he was beautiful. He was brave, and intelligent. She didn't think he was kind, but maybe once, when he'd been prince of a prosperous land, maybe then he'd been kind.

He must have loved his first wife. Maybe he'd loved the second one, too, but she'd betrayed him with a lover. . . . Maybe because he couldn't make love while averting the aging process, she had chosen another. Maybe he'd loved her, and it had broken his heart.

Who cares who he'd loved? Sierra gave herself a firm

mental shake. It didn't work. She wondered what he looked like in love. Even without hope, his brown eyes sparkled. In love . . .

Self-restraint would be a good thing here. I could learn from the Tseir.

And since when had she cared about love? She remembered infatuated boys from her days at the Intersystem Academy. Nothing more than irritation. She remembered an old friend declaring his love. An embarrassment.

Love never proved anything. It certainly wouldn't prove her worth. A brilliant tenure at the Academy hadn't proven anything, either. It just meant that she was capable. It meant she warranted a dangerous mission among the Tseir. And here was her chance to prove she was more than the favored daughter of the Intersystem prime representative.

Unless Arnoth of Valenwood got in her way, Sierra had every intention of seeing her mission through to a brilliant conclusion.

"Sierra of the Fourteenth, report to First Commander, double-quick."

Sierra emerged from the dressing unit and groaned. She was late. She'd waited until the other Tseir departed so she could wash her real hair. All Tseir wore wigs. Only Sierra had actual hair beneath. The itching eased, but Fifteenth Command loomed large.

Sierra made her way to the commander's station, hesitated outside the doorway, then pushed the entry panel. She heard Colice's voice through the panel monitor. "Admitted."

Colice was waiting. Sierra sighed. "Fifteenth, Commander?"

"Fifteenth what, Sierra?"

Sierra's eyes brightened. "Nothing. Reporting in, Commander."

"We have come across something strange."

"What?"

Colice held up a metal box and passed it to Sierra. "Look in through the grid."

Sierra looked in. Something looked back. She gasped and dropped the cage. "It's alive!" She bit her lip. "Or was alive." She picked up the cage and looked in again. Large, round eyes blinked. Sierra breathed a sigh of relief.

"What is it?"

"It appears to be a rodent of some sort. A guard discovered it hanging from a vent last night. He swatted it down, knocked it out, and turned it over to me."

"Poor thing." Sierra held the cage to the light, illuminating the animal. "It's very small. How did it get onto our ship?"

"That is the question, Sierra. Could this creature be some sort of Ellowan weapon?"

Sierra eyed Colice doubtfully, resisting an impulse to laugh. "A weapon?" She peeked in the cage. "It has wings. I don't see much for fangs, though. It's cute, in a peculiar way. Maybe it's a pet."

Colice grimaced. "Do the Ellowan keep rodents as pets?"

"I didn't think they had creatures like this at all. Maybe it's from Keir."

"Its presence on our ship is unexpected."

Sierra kept her expression straight, but a giggle bubbled in her chest. The Tseir hated the unexpected almost as much as the unknown. "What do you want me to do with the creature?"

Colice turned back to her monitor. "Kill it."

Sierra felt sick, but argument would raise suspicions.

46

"Yes, First Commander. Shall I resume guard duties over the Ellowan now?"

"Yes. Anything you learn about the Ellowan will aid our progress."

"What information are you looking for?"

"His weaknesses, Sierra."

"I haven't seen any sign of weakness, Commander."

"Every man has a weakness. Arnoth has learned to hide his, to conceal his nature. Once, he was a man of lust, of deep conviction. Our records from Valenwood mention him as a negotiator for peace. He sacrificed himself for his mate's sister, the woman he later married. We must learn what matters to him now."

"So we can use it against him." Sierra's voice betrayed regret. Colice's eyes narrowed.

"Do I detect disapproval, Junior Commander?"

Sierra swallowed. "Not at all! It's just that I haven't noticed any weakness. I'm hoping we find something. Otherwise, we'll never bring Arnoth under our control."

"All creatures can be controlled, Sierra. Remember that."

Sierra bowed. "With your permission, Commander, I will dispose of this rodent."

"Do so."

Sierra hurried from the room and took the cage to a waste disposal unit. She would stuff the creature into it quickly, and it would be obliterated. Sierra opened the cage. The little rodent shook violently, terrified. Its eyes were wide and round; it blinked.

"I'm sorry."

The rodent scrambled into the corner of the cage, its claws scraping on the slippery metal. Sierra tilted the cage, and it slid backwards. *I hope it bites me. I deserve it.*

Sierra closed her eyes and grabbed the rodent. It squealed and struggled, but she held fast. She picked it up and started to put it in the disposal. She felt its tiny heart racing. It knew she was going to kill it. Sierra's eyes puddled with tears.

She looked at her victim. It looked back. "You're so small. It's not your fault that you got caught on our ship." Sierra sniffed. "But I can't keep you." She drew a quick, tight breath. "It will be over quickly."

She pushed open the waste lid. A sucking, grinding noise sounded from below—the sound of disintegrated matter shot into space. The rodent gulped, then froze. Its small legs stiffened, its claws dug into her hand.

Sierra closed the lid. "I can't do this. . . ." The rodent looked up at her as if wondering whether her indecision was part of its torment. Sierra held it close to her large chest, then scratched gently behind its pointed ears. She lowered her chin to its head. Her tears dripped from her cheeks to its fur.

"I can't kill you. You're so small."

Sierra looked around. She peeked out of the waste unit room to check for guards. Then she opened the disposal and stuffed the cage in. It clattered loudly as it fell, then dissolved.

The rodent craned its neck and looked at her. Sierra smiled, then brushed her tears away with her free hand. "Now what? What am I going to do with you?"

The rodent exhaled a surprisingly full breath. It squirmed around in her hands to face her. "I am small, mistress. You can hide me."

Sierra squealed and flung the rodent up and across the room. It flailed its leathery wings and righted itself before banging into the wall. It shook its head and staggered to its feet.

Sierra sank to her knees, her mouth agape. "I'm sorry! You scared me. You . . . talk?"

The rodent nodded. It actually nodded. Like a human. "I do, mistress. True, it's not the norm for lingbats . . ."

48

"Lingbats?"

"I am a lingbat, from the planet of Candor."

"Candor! Then you belong to Arnoth!"

"I don't belong to anyone, as such. I'm more of a guide, you might say."

"I see." She didn't. But the lingbat seemed inclined to offer more of an explanation than Sierra wanted. Better to stick to pertinent facts. "Go on."

The lingbat hopped closer to her. "A lingbat is a flightless winged rodent." He held up his wings as evidence. "Now, my sire uses his wingspan for gliding. Since living among the Dwindle Bats, I've adopted a fair glide myself."

"Dwindle Bats?"

"A fine, albeit tiny, race of bats evolved in the beauteous, lush swamps of the planet of Keir. I went there with my first human companion—that would be Dane, the ambassador from Candor, although of course he was Thorwalian . . ."

Sierra shook her head. "I see. Go on."

The lingbat sighed. "That's where I met She Who Leaps High. My mate . . . I had to see her again. So when the prince came back to Keir, I went with him."

"You followed him here."

"Not exactly. As soon as I knew what you people wanted, I knew he'd give himself up. He's that sort. So I eased out of the caverns. . . . You'd be surprised how few humans notice a lingbat in motion."

"I didn't notice you."

"No one did." He looked proud. Puffed up. "Figured I'd find a way to help him. Done it before, for my Dane."

"You saved this Dane?"

The lingbat's eyes wandered to one side. Apparently, he realized he was talking to a Tseir and had said too much. He attempted a careless shrug. "Oh, once or twice. Long time ago."

49

"Saving Arnoth won't be so easy."

"The journey's not over yet." The lingbat eyed the waste disposal. "Although it was close."

"If you can talk, why didn't you say something before now? I almost killed you."

The lingbat's round eyes widened rounder still. "You're a Tseir! From what I've heard, nothing I could say would make a difference to your kind."

"That's probably true. For the most part." Sierra chewed her lip. "But I like animals." She hesitated. Telling this talkative rodent too much would be a mistake. "I don't want to kill you. But I can't disobey my commander, either. So you'll have to hide, and hide well."

"Under your cape, mistress?"

Sierra glanced down. She saw her breasts, and nothing else. "I could make you a pocket. Just a moment . . ." A rodent wouldn't think about human physiology. She tore out a portion of her padding and made a hole. "In here."

The lingbat climbed onto her lap, up her shirt, and into the brassiere pocket. "Don't talk unless it's safe. Many places on this ship are monitored, including Arnoth's cell."

"I'd like him to know I'm here, just to reassure him."

"I'm sure it would come as a great relief, but you can't tell Arnoth anything. I'm in enough trouble already."

"Just so long as I can keep an eye on him, mistress."

"I'm his guard, and you're with me, so you can watch him when I do. But I don't think there's much you can do to help him."

"That remains to be seen."

Sierra rose to her feet and adjusted her red cape to cover her left breast. "Do you have a name, lingbat?"

"In the language of battery, I am He Who Flames With Courage. Humans seem to have difficulty with formal names. You can call me Batty."

"Batty. I am Sierra Kari . . . Sierra of the Fourteenth Command. Please remember if you're caught, I'll be Sierra of the Twenty-fifth. It's important that I reach Twelfth again, you see. I can't explain why, but it is. So if you'd be so good as to not get me into trouble, I'd appreciate it."

Batty looked up from her breast. "You spared me, mistress. I don't know why, but it doesn't matter. I am now at your service."

Chapter Two

Arnoth finished a small bowl of Tseir grain, then drank what appeared to be wine. Apparently, flavor wasn't a consideration to clones. Yet the mixture was immediately nourishing. He could live on it, though he wouldn't enjoy it.

His guard stood at the door, looking at nothing. Unlike Sierra, the man hadn't spoken a word since assuming duties. Outside in the corridor, Arnoth heard guards shifting command. Sierra would arrive soon. He wondered if she'd make it through the doorway unscathed this time.

Maybe the Tseir reassigned guards, and he wouldn't see her again. Maybe she'd failed "rest duties" and been demoted below the level of guard. Arnoth wondered how the bumbling Sierra had made it this far.

The door panel buzzed. "Sierra of the Fourteenth, reporting for duty."

The way she said *fourteenth* sounded woeful. But beneath her depressed manner, Arnoth sensed abundant energy. Unusual, because the Tseir weren't energetic. They sought energy from others.

The guard engaged the panel, and the door opened. Sierra waited an extra moment before entering. She hopped over the threshold and glanced back at the door suspiciously as it closed behind her.

The guard didn't seem to notice anything odd about the Tseir woman. He just bowed and departed. Sierra watched him go, then seated herself beside Arnoth.

"I trust you slept well, Ellowan." She didn't look at him. She seemed to avoid looking at him. Arnoth waited until she glanced his way before answering.

"If you really want to know, the bed is hard and narrow and too short for my body."

Sierra sighed and nodded. "You should see the barracks' bunks." She caught herself and shook her head. "The Ellowan are known for being overly sensual." She eyed him more closely. "Although I don't see any evidence of that in you."

"Neither of us represents our respective races accurately, Tseir."

"No."

Sierra's face formed an odd, surprised expression. She fidgeted, twisting her torso as if a bug had invaded her clothing. She scratched at her left breast, adjusting it nearer the center while Arnoth looked on in amazement.

She noticed his attention and offered a polite smile. "Itchy."

"I see."

"Well, Ellowan, is there anything you'd like to share with me? Weaknesses, foibles, needs, that sort of thing."

A transparent, bizarre attempt to gain information. She didn't look as if she expected an answer. "Nothing comes to mind."

"You've been married a few times, I gather."

"A few."

Sierra's gaze intensified. "Why did you give up your second mate?"

"Because she loved another man."

"So you let her go, just like that?"

"Since I found them in bed together, I saw no alternative."

"You could have killed them!"

"True. He was in a particularly vulnerable position, asleep with my mate."

"Why didn't you?"

"I liked him."

Sierra's brow furrowed. "This is odd beyond comprehension. The peculiarity of the Ellowan race hasn't been exaggerated." She paused. "Would this be the Candorian ambassador called Dane?"

"How do you know his name?"

Sierra bit her lip, then looked toward the ceiling, casually. "Tseir know many things."

Sierra of the Fourteenth wasn't an accomplished liar. Strange, because Arnoth considered it a natural Tseir trait. "It was Dane who absconded with my second lifemate, yes. Why do you ask?"

"Just wondering . . ." She looked back at him. The color of her eyes varied between blue and gray. He'd never noticed a Tseir's eyes before. But Sierra's were piercing and quick. She didn't stare; her gaze wandered as thoughts flitted across her mind. "Did you love her?"

"I did."

"Did you grieve at her death?"

Arnoth hesitated. Aiyana wasn't dead. But apparently the Tseir thought she was. He recalled Dane mentioning something about having died twice. The Tseir probably believed that Dane and Aiyana had been killed when their shuttle was destroyed. He would leave them with that illusion lest his friends be threatened, too.

"I grieved."

"About both of them?"

"Yes."

"You cared for the man who took your woman?"

She wasn't relenting on this subject. Arnoth decided to expand on his answer to silence her. "Aiyana and I were never lovers. We performed the life-halting ritual together, prolonging ourselves for the purpose of fighting the Tseir. In this state, an Ellowan doesn't reproduce."

"No sex. I see." She fell silent, but her brow furrowed. "I take it she changed her mind over this Dane."

"She did."

"So she lived a bit before she died?"

"I presume so."

"That's good. . . ." Sierra's voice trailed off. She seemed to mean it. Arnoth wondered why she cared about Aiyana's fate. She looked back at him, her face thoughtful. "What about you?"

"What about me?"

"Don't you want to live again, too?"

"It appears I'm more likely to die than live."

"True. Do you have to mate to . . . well, unprolong yourself?"

"Now, why would I be fool enough to tell you that?"

"Fair point." Sierra fidgeted, then bit her fingernail. The one he'd noticed the day before. Her teeth were very white and even. Her lips looked soft.

Arnoth snapped his gaze away from the Tseir's lips. Poison. Somehow, they'd poisoned him. Maybe it was something in the air.

The monitor buzzed, startling him. "Sierra of the Fourteenth, report to First Commander. Bring the prisoner."

Sierra puffed a breath of air. It elevated a portion of her coarse, blond hair. "I suppose you'll be questioned."

She reached to unhook his manacle from the wall. She

55

leaned across him and he noticed a soft, warm scent. A woman's scent. She lifted his gray cape from a hook and started to put it over his shoulders. Arnoth recoiled and she stopped.

"What's the matter? Colice just wants to question you."

"I will do that myself."

Her eyes wandered to one side. "What?"

"The cape." Arnoth rose and looked into her small, surprised face. "Ellowan do not touch Tseir. Ever."

One brow angled. "You're a prisoner. You'll be touched."

"Not willingly."

"Very well." She dropped the cape and backed away. "I have no desire to touch you, either." She sounded offended, but she didn't taunt him as another Tseir would. "I guess I've found your weakness. I'll report to Colice that touching infuriates you. No doubt you'll be strapped down and touched until you scream. How's that for torment?"

Arnoth placed the cape over his shoulders. "Willingly, Tseir. Whatever you do to me, I can bear. But I will not willingly touch you."

"I never asked you to."

"Ellowan don't touch Tseir."

"You keep saying that. I heard you the first time."

Sierra marched to the door and engaged the panel. "Exit." The door hissed open and she looked back at him, waiting. Arnoth's pulse moved in an erratic beat. For one sick instant, he had imagined caressing her. To see if her skin was as soft as it looked, to know if she was warm or cold.

Her lips twisted to one side. She held up a slender finger, the one she chewed when nervous. "Get moving, Ellowan, or else!" She took a step toward him, her small face alight with cunning as she aimed her finger at him.

Arnoth refused to soften his manner. He fixed a cold glare in return, then walked to the door.

She backed away dramatically as he passed by. "Proceed to the left. Should you try anything, Ellowan, just remember this finger remains poised. One wrong move, and I'm willing and able to touch you."

She chuckled behind him. Arnoth's anger faded, leaving instead a nagging discomfort. Tseir didn't tease. They didn't have the imagination.

"The temptation to touch you grows stronger, Ellowan. Walk faster."

Arnoth glanced back over his shoulder. A tiny smile played on her lips. Something tugged at his memory, as if he'd seen her before. But not this way . . .

Her short, pale hair was wrong for her face. It should be soft and long and fall along her neck, down her back. Arnoth forced his attention away from Sierra and down the corridor.

Poison.

Sierra lagged behind Arnoth. Batty scratched at her chest. She adjusted her red cloak. She eased her shirt open and looked down. "What's the matter?"

"Hot." Batty gasped for air.

"Hush!" She spoke too loudly. Arnoth heard her and glanced back over his shoulder. His brow angled doubtfully. She lifted her chin and scratched her collarbone, fanning herself. "I'm a little warm." She waved him forward. "Proceed."

Sierra waited until Arnoth headed up the hall, then returned her attention to the lingbat. "Stop that! And stop wiggling. You're lucky to be alive."

"Just so."

"I'll get you water as soon as I'm alone. But stop squirming. Someone will notice. And you're tickling me."

"Sorry, mistress."

"Behave."

A guard passed by and Sierra smiled weakly, then hurried to catch up with Arnoth. She skittered in front of him, then stopped at Colice's door. "In here."

Arnoth entered before her, and Sierra followed. Colice was standing by her table. Sierra noticed that the commander wore a more revealing gown than usual. She fought an urge to groan. Tseir females wielded the power of command for sex.

Sierra had once made the mistake of entering a commander's chambers unannounced, and found the woman carnally engaged with a guard. It wasn't a memory she wished to see repeated.

"Seat yourself, Arnoth of Valenwood. We have no wish to see you strained."

"I prefer to stand."

Sierra started to sit, but Colice issued a dark look of warning, and she straightened beside Arnoth. "I just thought, if he wasn't sitting . . ."

"Sierra, dismissed!"

At least it wasn't *demoted*. Sierra hesitated. She wanted to know what Colice intended to say to Arnoth, especially dressed like that. But defiance wasn't in her best interests.

"I'll wait outside, Commander."

Sierra left the room and positioned herself outside the door. She rested one foot against the wall and leaned back. The hall was empty. She eased her cloak back and checked Batty.

"Are you all right?"

"Ssh! I'm listening. Lingbats have superior hearing."

Sierra rolled her eyes. "Don't let me interrupt you."

The lingbat didn't notice her sarcasm. He leaned to one side, straining to overhear Colice's conversation with

58

Arnoth. Sierra's impatience grew. "What are they saying?"

"Hold a bit, mistress."

Sierra didn't speak as the lingbat listened. He nodded, then chuckled, then listened more. Sierra puffed a breath. "Well?"

"Your commander isn't getting far. Fishing around for information. You got a lot more out of him this morning."

"Did I?"

"Ssh."

Two guards passed down the hall and Sierra nodded to them. They bowed and walked on. The lingbat peeked out from her shirt and checked the hall. "She just called him sexless."

"She may have a point there."

"Dane said otherwise."

Sierra frowned. "Well, he should know. He bedded Arnoth's mate."

"That's right." Batty sighed in apparent admiration. "Thought those two would go at it over the female, but the prince just gave her up. Dane said he was crazy."

"I've noticed that."

"I thought the prince would wake up once he was mated to that Ellowan female."

"Another one?"

"Helayna. . . ." Batty issued a choking noise, and Sierra guessed he'd said too much.

"Don't worry, Batty. I won't say anything."

Batty peeked up at her, assessing her sincerity. Apparently he trusted what he saw. "Helayna was the leader of the Valenwood Ellowan."

"The ones in the caverns?"

"That's right. Morvin—he's one of the prolonged Ellowan, second to Arnoth in command—he said Helayna looked like Arnoth's first mate, and he had a chance for

59

happiness. They were supposed to mate, but you Tseir interrupted them.''

Sierra's brow knit as she considered this. So Arnoth had yet another woman. ''Was she beautiful?''

Batty eyed her doubtfully. ''Not by lingbat standards, but Morvin considered her a good mate.''

''Was her hair blond?''

''Like yours.''

Sierra sighed. ''Well . . .'' Sierra scratched her temple, beneath the wig. ''I think I remember her. She was the one wearing almost no clothes.'' Her frown deepened. ''Men seem to like that kind of woman.''

''She wanted him, anyway.''

''Naturally.'' Sierra sighed again. Maybe this Ellowan female explained Arnoth's hopelessness. He'd given up a chance at love. He was about to mate, and the Tseir prevented him. She imagined him beside the sparsely clad woman; Arnoth dark and strong and beautiful, graced by his lovely blond mate.

Sierra's lips curled in irritation. ''Who cares whom he loves?''

''Mistress?''

''Nothing.'' She felt sullen, annoyed.

''They're coming!'' Batty dove back into her breast pad and disappeared. She plucked her cape casually over her chest.

''Sierra! Escort the prisoner to his cell.''

The door hissed open and Arnoth appeared, his dark eyes glittering. He looked pleased with himself. His lips curved in a smile.

''If you annoy her enough, Ellowan, they just may forfeit their plans and kill you.''

Arnoth shrugged. ''If that is a defeat to them, I am willing.''

Sierra gazed up at him for a moment. ''Aren't you afraid to die?''

"I've lived a very long time, Tseir. I'm not afraid of death."

"I think you're afraid to live." Sierra didn't wait for his response. She walked on down the hall toward his cell. She could imagine him happy. For some reason, it wasn't hard to picture. Her jealousy gave way to a deeper feeling. Arnoth of Valenwood deserved happiness. He had lost everything and fought, and endured.

He'd intended to live among his own people, to regain what the Tseir had stolen. It was a noble effort. He'd made a mistake when issuing his interstellar transmission. And for that one oversight, his chance at love and happiness was forfeit.

"It's not my problem." She spoke aloud. Arnoth caught up to her.

"Are you talking to me, Tseir?"

"No. To myself."

"That's something else I've never seen a Tseir do—engage in conversations with themselves."

"If you continue to pester me, Ellowan, I will touch you." She glanced up at him, her eyes narrowed in a threatening fashion. "Slowly."

Her threat worked better than she expected. His jaw tightened and he distanced himself from her side. A guard opened Arnoth's cell and the Ellowan walked in before Sierra. She followed and seated herself on his cot.

"Did Colice tell you what they're going to do with you once we get back to the home world?"

"Only in vague threats and insinuations. I don't think she has any idea." Arnoth stretched his arms behind his back, then sat down beside her. Too close. He nearly touched her before moving to the far end of the cot.

Sierra decided not to mention the brush with touching. His touch would be gentle, she felt certain of that. She peered casually at his hands. Long, powerful fingers, strong, clean wrists. An odd heat filled her loins.

"You have pretty hands."

He glanced at her, then at his hands. "Thank you."

"Tseir men have short, stubby fingers and broad hands."

Arnoth appeared uncomfortable. Maybe he thought she was trying to seduce him. "I hadn't noticed."

"Your fingers look . . . musical."

His brow raised in surprise, though he tried to hide the reaction. Sierra noticed. "Do Ellowan play music?"

He didn't answer immediately Sierra wondered why. "We did once."

"Not now?"

"Not recently."

"What sort of music?"

For some reason, this subject disturbed him. "Not another weakness, Ellowan? You have many, it seems. Perhaps a new torture presents itself. You'll be strapped down and touched, while we play out-of-tune music until you beg for mercy."

He didn't want to smile. Sierra knew that. His lips pressed together, but his eyes twinkled. "I shudder to think what you would do with a harp, Tseir."

"A harp. Is that like a lyre?"

"Similar."

Sierra smiled, wishing she could tell him what she could do. Wishing she could show him. "You'd be surprised, Ellowan."

"Don't tell me Tseir value music. Or did your people clone musicians, too?"

"No musicians."

"Good. I don't think I could stand that."

"Music isn't something that can be cloned."

"Nor humor, or so I believed. Yet you . . ."

Sierra glanced at the monitor and bit her lip. "You mistake humor. I am always serious."

"That is the humorous element, Tseir."

Sierra breathed a small sigh of relief. She didn't want to even consider that he might suspect her identity.

"For a man facing an uncertain fate, Ellowan, you are calm."

"I keep my panic inside."

Sierra assessed him carefully. Curse those twinkling eyes! Her insides fluttered. Something about him made her ache. It almost hurt. He was like a wall, and beyond that wall lay an infinite promise. A blissful unknown.

Arnoth's expression changed. Almost as if he guessed her thoughts. Sierra forced her attention to the floor. Her thoughts had always been too easy to read. Fortunately, the Tseir weren't a perceptive race.

"When do we reach your home world, Tseir?" His voice sounded stilted. Sierra peeked at him. If he guessed she found him intriguing, why didn't he use that against her? He enjoyed taunting Colice. Why not herself as well?

"Soon, I suppose. I haven't checked our position. By my next shift, we'll be landing." Sierra sighed. "You'll be transferred to the supreme commander's facility, and I'll go back to my duties. Assuming I still have duties."

"Will I see you again?"

Sierra endured an odd pang, but she shrugged casually. "I doubt it."

Arnoth didn't respond. Sierra wondered why he'd asked in the first place. Surely one Tseir guard was the same as the next.

"You won't like the home world."

Arnoth smiled, and her pulse churned. "I wasn't expecting to find a haven, Tseir."

"To each his own, I suppose."

"That's true. I knew someone once who considered the swamps of Keir a paradise."

The lingbat stirred beneath Sierra's padding. Probably sighing. "What is your haven, Ellowan?"

63

"What is forever gone."

"Valenwood? But that's not gone. It's a little barren, but it can be restored."

Arnoth shook his head. "Not to the world I knew. The land was devastated, but it can grow back. My people, also. But it will never be the way it was. The Ellowan Wood grows as shrubs, but where are the giant trees? Life still exists in the ocean, but where are the amber whales?"

"Amber whales? What are those?"

"Giant creatures that filled our largest ocean. They were golden in color, and they sang. It was said at the dawn of the Ellowan race, the amber whales gave us music. It was their gift to our people, that we might live in bliss."

"And they're gone?"

"Yes."

Sierra felt his sorrow like a part of her. She had never known this kind of pain. "You mean the people you knew, and loved, will never return."

Arnoth glanced at her, surprised by her empathy. Sierra glanced at the monitor, hoping she hadn't said too much. "That is true. Thanks to your race, everything I loved is gone."

"Don't you think there might be a life worth living beyond your memories?" Sierra longed to hear him agree; she longed to see his eyes brighten with sudden hope. Instead, he looked away.

"No."

Sierra endured a rash impulse to touch him, even to kiss his face in a gesture of comfort. Tears swarmed her eyes. *Curses! I can't cry!* She hopped to her feet and paced around the cell.

Motion helped. Her nerves calmed, her tension eased. Sierra stopped and looked back at him. *He's not in the Intersystem. He's reckless, he got himself into this. I am not responsible for him.* But there was something relaxed about the set of his shoulders that appealed to her.

"I suppose after four hundred years, you're fairly comfortable with yourself."

His brown eyes widened at her remark. "I'm used to this body. I've been in it for a while."

Sierra nodded and gazed around the room. Curse the Tseir for using no decoration to divert the eye! Her gaze shifted back to Arnoth. The tie that held back his hair had loosened. A portion fell along the side of his face. "You have pretty hair."

"I know."

"I guessed you harbored great conceit when I first saw you."

Sierra fidgeted. She fiddled with her cape. *I can't stay in this minuscule cell with him....* "If you don't fix your hair, Ellowan, I will do it for you! And that involves touching!"

His eyes shifted to one side at her sudden outburst. "My hair?"

"It's coming loose."

Arnoth noticed his loose strand of hair. He removed the binding and his hair fell forward, around his face. Sierra groaned out loud. He looked up at her, and her face burned with embarrassment.

She expected a biting remark. Instead, Arnoth of Valenwood looked hurriedly away. Sierra chomped on her lip and turned her back to him. *I have lost my mind. You'd think he'd stripped in front of me. It's just hair, fool!*

"Are you finished?" she snapped at him. She hadn't intended to snap.

"Not quite."

This is the oddest moment in my life. Except for the talking rodent.

Batty was curiously still inside her breast pad. She

wondered how much the lingbat guessed of her secret heart.

"Finished."

Sierra peered over her shoulder suspiciously. Arnoth's hair was in place. He looked somewhat less sensual with his hair back. It wouldn't be so easy to run fingers through bound hair; it wouldn't fall softly around his perfect cheekbones.

She twitched. "Tseir men wear their hair to the level of the ear."

Arnoth frowned. "Ellowan men do not."

"Yours is too long." He had only tied the front part back. The rest hung along his neck, over his shoulders. "Much too long."

"Yours, Tseir, is too short."

Sierra resisted a strong impulse to yank off her wig. "Mine is the proper length for a junior commander."

"It's ugly."

She felt stung. He'd criticized her wig, and she felt insulted. Never mind than that she hated it, too. She longed to demean him in turn. Unfortunately, he was perfect. In looks. "You are rude, Ellowan."

Arnoth rose to his feet and bowed. "Forgive me, Tseir. Your race attempted to annihilate mine, but rudeness remains inexcusable."

"That's right." Sierra lifted her chin. "Should you make that mistake again, I will touch you . . . and hum." She waited while he resisted furthering their conversation. "While I cut your hair."

His mouth looked tense, as if he held back a smile. "Your presence is torture enough."

He seated himself. Sierra sat beside him at the far end of the cot. "It wasn't my choice to guard you. If you desire another guard, perhaps I can arrange that."

"Something tells me your capacity to arrange anything would result only in a demotion."

"You may have a point there. But I could try."

He hesitated. "I don't care who guards me."

Sierra's suspicions rose. Why didn't he agree? Why didn't he attempt to rid himself of her, if her presence was such torture? "I think you like me."

A shrewd guess. Sierra had found Arnoth's sore spot. His eyes turned black with anger. "You are Tseir."

"You like me."

His jaw hardened, his hand clenched into a fist. "You are Tseir."

"I know that." Sierra studied his dark expression. It truly caused him pain to feel anything for her. "Never mind. I trust, given the opportunity, you would gladly see me dead." She wasn't sure she believed this, but it appeased Arnoth.

"I would."

"Or demoted."

"That is also a pleasure." Arnoth's voice softened. The tension between them relaxed.

Sierra checked the time grid on the monitor. "My shift nears its end, Ellowan. You will be relieved of my presence soon." She paused. "And I, of yours."

The monitor buzzed. "Guard Seven-forty reporting for duty."

Sierra sighed. Her frustration refused to abate. "Admitted, Seven-forty. Assume duties."

The door hissed open and the guard entered. He took position in the corner, saying nothing. Sierra glanced at Arnoth. He didn't look at her. He deliberately avoided looking at her.

"You are a trial, Ellowan. It will please me to see you delivered to the supreme commander's division."

She didn't let him answer. Sierra smacked the door panel and left. Her heart beat with unusual fury. *Who cares if he likes me?* She stomped down the corridor toward the barracks. She stopped at a food unit and engaged the panel for biscuits.

Sierra took a bite of a biscuit, then sighed. She missed real food, food that grew from a clean earth, juice that came from real fruit she could pick from a tree outside her own bedroom window. From her father's prized garden.

I miss Nirvahda. She hadn't missed home in a long while. She hadn't missed her father. She had fixated on her duties and never looked back. Why now? Sierra glanced back down the hall to Arnoth's door.

It had been so simple. Easy. Until Arnoth of Valenwood. Now she had dropped to Fourteenth Command and an uncertain future. Now she cared about something as much as she cared about her mission.

She cared about Arnoth.

That will change once I'm back on the home world. I won't see him again. Sierra's appetite waned and she set aside the biscuit. A small cough from within her shirt reminded her of the lingbat's presence. She looked around, waited until three guards passed around the corner, then shoved the biscuit into her breast pad.

She felt Batty chewing, felt crumbs fall to her stomach. Sierra's heart lightened. She wasn't alone. She had a rodent companion. She wasn't sure why that made her feel better, but it did.

Sierra made her way along the hall to the fore of the vessel, where a long, narrow viewport revealed the stars. The three guards sat around a table, drinking flavorless wine. They weren't wearing their helmets, and were off-duty. All three looked alike, with rigid, expressionless faces, pale eyes, and pale hair.

The guards glanced up at her, then spoke quietly among themselves. She knew what they were thinking. They expected her to approach them and request their "presence" in private chambers.

Sierra ignored the guards. She wondered why the Tseir thought so much about sex. It was their favorite pastime, and they found more and more bizarre ways of enjoying its pleasures. As if the normal exchange between lovers wasn't enough. Few Tseir women settled for one man at a time. And they never loved.

Sierra sighed. Maybe they had the right idea. Love might be painful. Not that she loved Arnoth. That would be foolhardy in the extreme. Even if he knew her real identity, she doubted he would welcome her affection. His fate wasn't likely to provide an opportunity to find out, either.

She wished she didn't care. She wished the ache would go away. It had started in little pangs. Now it just sat in her stomach. Reminding her.

"Commander, you look lonely."

Sierra startled at the guard's voice. He stood right behind her, too close. A brave man. Guards didn't generally approach commanders. "I'm not."

The guard glanced pertinently at his companions. "We'll satisfy your itch."

Sierra grimaced. "I don't have an 'itch.' That's reserved for the higher command. Now, leave me alone."

The guard shrugged. "One commander's as good as another." He hesitated, and his gaze moved along her body, stopping at her bottom. "Wouldn't mind trying you out, though." He placed his large, squat hand on the flare of her hip and slid to the center of her bottom, pinching.

Sierra jerked back. "Do that again and die, guard!"

He lifted his hands. "Just thought you needed it."

"I do not! Make your way to the barracks, guard, or I will report you."

"For what?"

"Does it matter?"

Sierra eased a small breath of relief when he accepted

69

her response. He motioned to his companions, and they left the hall together. Sierra turned her attention back to the viewport. The Tseir ship moved in a cluster with the smaller fighter vessels in support.

They didn't expect any attack, but should one happen, they were ready. Tseir were never unprepared. Sierra wondered how Arnoth ever defeated them in battle.

She opened her shirt enough to see the lingbat finishing his biscuit. "You can come out a little, Batty. We're alone. The view hall isn't monitored."

Batty stuck his head from her shirt and breathed deeply. "Thank you for the biscuit, mistress. Not much flavor, but filling. Tell me, are there insects on your home world?"

"Why do you ask?"

"I'd like something tasty for a change."

"Oh." Sierra eyed him doubtfully, then shrugged. "There are insects. Quite a few. They like the noxious air near the dump sites."

"Good, good."

"How did Arnoth defeat our fleet at Candor?"

Her question surprised the lingbat. He looked nervous. "Well, now . . . of course, the prince is a clever human. . . ."

"And you can't tell me. Never mind. I shouldn't have asked." She looked back out the viewport. "It's just that it seems . . . impossible."

"Not for the prince."

"Apparently not. But he only removed one fleet, Batty. And there are so many . . ." Her voice trailed away while the lingbat looked up at her, a thoughtful expression on his small, scrunched face.

"What will happen when we reach your world, mistress?"

"I don't know."

"How will we save the prince?"

70

Sierra glanced down at the lingbat. "What makes you think I want to save him?"

Batty adjusted his frail wings as if they were stiff. "I've studied humanoid function for quite a while now, mistress. I recognize the signs."

"Of what? And I'm not exactly humanoid."

"If you say so."

"I do. And pipe down." Sierra paused. "I couldn't save him even if I wanted to. As soon as we land, he'll be transferred to the Supreme Command. I'm not in that division. My usual assignment is in weapons development. Meaning, I study the weapons we seize from other cultures and learn how to process them."

Batty's face scrunched even more as he considered her words. "Still, you're all I've got, mistress. The prince is my human now. He needs me. He needs you, too."

"He's mean and rude and I don't know why I should lift my smallest finger to help him."

Batty peered up at her with big, knowing eyes. "You don't have to know why. You'll do it. I know, because I've seen humans in your condition before. You'd be surprised what lengths my Dane went to for his mate."

"You mean Arnoth's mate."

"She was Dane's. If you'd seen them together, you'd know. The prince knew right from the start. I noticed that he kept leaving them alone together."

"Noble." So Arnoth encouraged his mate's affection for another man. Sierra wondered if she would be that noble herself. "Look, Batty, I'll do what I can for him. But that won't be much. I've got my own position to consider."

"Positions change, mistress. Priorities change. I think yours have changed already."

Sierra's eyes narrowed to fierce slits. "They'd better not, rodent. A lot depends on my success. A lot more than Arnoth of Valenwood."

71

*   *   *

Sierra missed her second shift. Arnoth lay on his back staring at the ceiling. From the sound of the ship's engine, he guessed they had entered orbit around the Tseir home world. He hadn't seen her since she stomped from his cell, calling him a "trial."

He didn't miss her. He felt certain he'd exaggerated the look and texture of her skin because of the low Tseir lighting. In daylight, she would be as coarse and plain as every other Tseir female.

Her hair was ugly. Just as he'd told her. Arnoth resisted an element of regret at that comment. She actually looked hurt. And she hadn't exactly insulted him. She looked as if she wanted to, but she just said his hair was long. Which it was. And pretty. Which he knew.

Arnoth wished Sierra had attempted a blatant seduction. Enough Tseir women had propositioned him through his lifetime for him to believe lust was a weakness to their race.

He didn't see evidence of lust in Sierra. What he detected was worse. She seemed . . . infatuated. Smitten. Tender. Arnoth closed his eyes and drew a taut breath to clear his senses. There was something sweet about her. Sweet and bright. And clumsy.

Maybe she'd been demoted to deck swabbing, after all. Or maybe she really didn't want to see him again.

Arnoth sat up in bed and clasped his hands to his forehead. "Why am I thinking about this?"

He got up and walked around the room. The guard ignored him. "I'm assuming we'll be landing soon."

The guard didn't respond. Arnoth sighed. *I miss her because she talked. Too much is better than nothing.*

The monitor buzzed. "Guard Seven-forty, bring prisoner to landing shuttle."

The guard lifted his heavy canister, then engaged the door panel, and it opened. "Move, Ellowan."

72

"Good talking with you." Arnoth started into the aisle. Guards assembled along the corridor, but he didn't see Sierra.

"This way." The guard gestured to the right hall.

Arnoth walked in front of the guard. As he passed, the female commanders assessed him with undisguised interest. They looked at his groin before his face. Sierra never looked at his groin.

The guard led him around a corner and through a long narrow passage. It opened into a shuttle bay, where the Tseir commanders waited. Sierra stood beside Colice. Not demoted. Her legs were longer in proportion to her body than the other Tseir woman.

She turned to Colice, and Arnoth noticed that her bottom was small and firm. Well shaped. He'd never noticed a Tseir woman's bottom before. He didn't want to notice it now.

He still disliked her hair. She didn't look at him as he approached. He couldn't take his eyes from her. She scratched her oversized left breast and fidgeted.

Colice stepped forward. "We have arrived, prince. It may be time to reconsider your response."

"I will not serve Tseir. I will not touch Tseir. I will die first."

"Perhaps the supreme commander can change your mind."

"Your commander has nothing more than you, Tseir. You've searched for my weaknesses, no doubt to use them to convince me to do your bidding. You have failed."

Arnoth's gaze moved to Sierra. He noticed a bruise above her eye. If someone had struck her . . . "What happened to you?"

She looked pained and sighed before answering. "I fell off my bed during rest duties. While sleeping." She peered up and to the side, humbled by the admission. "They are very narrow beds, you see."

"Positioning yourself accurately must have been a severe trial."

She nodded, but she said nothing more. Arnoth forced his attention back to Colice. "I have been imprisoned by Tseir before. There is no greater darkness."

"There is death, Ellowan. That is eternal darkness."

Arnoth smiled as she radiated anger. "Is it? Do we know what follows death? Perhaps I will release life for bliss beyond imagining. Perhaps I will take a new form. Perhaps I will dance with angels. The unknown intrigues me."

Sierra's brow furrowed at this, as if she contemplated the possibilities, too. But his words inflamed Colice to greater anger.

"Into the shuttle, Ellowan. Your death is not yet at hand."

Sierra didn't travel in the same shuttle. When they landed on the Tseir home world, Arnoth looked for her, but he didn't see her. Guards surrounded him, armed, silent, as they led him into the open air.

If air it could be called. The Tseir hadn't learned to control the waste of their production plants. The air stank with rough fumes from chemicals, with acrid smoke. Arnoth stood on the docking platform and looked around.

Black hovercrafts, copied from Ellowan designs, moved around endless metallic buildings. Buildings were elevated above the ground on high platforms, some with many levels reaching toward the cloud coverage.

The sky was white with no streaks of color. The ground beneath was red, the same shade as the Tseir commanders' cloaks. The air was neither warm nor cold, and there was no breeze.

"Welcome to Dar-krona, Ellowan. Here, we produce

in a day what it took your ancient Ellowan a year to manufacture.''

"Yes, but for each vessel we crafted, we saw that it took nothing from our planet. Your massive production has wreaked havoc with whatever environment existed here once.''

"When this planet ceases to be habitable, we will move to another. Perhaps Valenwood. The Candor Moon was considered for that purpose, because of the rings that made manufacturing simple.''

Colice wouldn't tell him this if she'd expected him to ever leave. "I trust you're not attempting to garner my admiration, Tseir.''

"We don't care about your admiration, Ellowan. Just your compliance.''

"You've wasted a trip, Tseir. I will never give you what you seek.''

"That is for the supreme commander to evaluate. We will take you to her now.''

Arnoth glanced around again. "Where is my guard? Sierra.''

Colice's brow furrowed. "Sierra has reported to her station. But it interests me that you ask.''

A flicker of warning engaged in Arnoth's mind. "I tired of her constant 'persuasion.' Ellowan don't touch Tseir.''

The sexual intimation stirred Colice's mood. "Sierra attempted to seduce you?''

Arnoth hesitated. Loose words might see his bumbling guard demoted again. He wasn't sure why it mattered. "Is that considered a crime or an accomplishment?''

Colice smiled. "A right. I am pleased Sierra exerted her authority over you. She showed promise in her previous assignment. Some Tseir don't fare well in space. Sierra may have been affected by the transitions involved in interstellar travel.''

"That could explain it." Could it? Could a malfunction in Tseir neurosystems have made a normal Tseir
woman transform into the bungling, tender Sierra?

"The supreme commander is waiting, Ellowan. I have
alerted her to our arrival. Understand that your audience
with her may well be your last chance at survival."

"Survival, Tseir, is overvalued. But you should know
that better than anyone."

Colice led Arnoth into a large elevated building. Every
room looked the same, though some were larger than
others and different functions were performed within. Arnoth noticed many levels of commanders. Not all commanders were female, though they outnumbered the
males.

The supreme commander stood at the end of a long,
low room, her red cloak splayed on the floor behind her.
Despite her posture and attire, she resembled every other
Tseir woman Arnoth had seen. She was a large woman,
blond, with a broad face and dark eyes. Tseir had either
pale eyes or dark, nothing in between.

Except Sierra, with her fluid expressions and blue-gray
eyes. And though Sierra was tall, she was fine-boned.
Delicate.

Arnoth stopped and waited for the supreme commander to approach him. Colice knelt in honor to her
leader, bowing her head. Arnoth waited without reaction.

"Colice, Third Command, is this the Ellowan prisoner?"

Arnoth rolled his eyes at the formality. *No, I'm an imp
from Candor's gas planet. . . .* "Who else?"

Her dark eyes turned to black, but her expression
didn't change. "I am Extrana, supreme commander of all
Tseir, director of Dar-krona."

"An impressive title, Tseir. What do you want from
me?"

76

Extrana's eyes shifted to Colice. Colice rose to her feet and bowed again. "I have warned the Ellowan that his choices are limited. Serve us or die. He prefers death."

"I do."

Extrana's jaw muscle twitched. "That is not an option, Ellowan. You will recant your minor victory at Candor and align yourself with our Tseir fleet."

"The victory at Candor troubles you a great deal, Tseir. It is a source of pride to the victors. Why would I choose to refute that glory?"

"By your vain and foolish words, I see your life has no meaning to you."

"Not much. Or perhaps something means more."

"What?"

Arnoth allowed himself a smile. "Defeating you, Tseir. Knowing that, whatever happens to me, your defeat at Candor haunts you. You wonder how it happened, how one man destroyed your fleet. You wonder if it will happen again. What will happen when other systems learn of Candor's success?"

His defiance sealed his fate. It was worth the end, to see the fury on the supreme commander's features. She turned her twitching, red face to Colice. "Did you find no weakness, nothing we can wield to force his compliance?"

"We found nothing, Supreme Commander. The Ellowan are a sensual, emotional race. If he had a mate, I believe we could use her to gain whatever we wanted."

"Unfortunately, you've killed both my mates. A shame."

His light tone infuriated the Tseir. "There must be a way. We must have his compliance."

"You won't get it, Tseir."

The supreme commander regained control over her expression. "If we can't get it from you, Ellowan, we will get it from your spawn."

77

"My spawn?"

"You have learned that the Tseir are clones. We can clone you, too."

"What makes you think my clone will agree any more than I will?"

"It takes several repetitions to deaden the defiant impulses. We clone you, then your copy, until we get . . ."

"An empty shell. Like yourselves."

"You're wrong, Ellowan. We contain powerful elements."

"Lust, I've noticed. Greed, ambition, deceit. You harbor the innermost, basic aspects of humanity. Fear, survival, appetite. You obsess over details and see no outer shape. Yes, those are powerful elements, but they are empty."

"We lack nothing."

Arnoth knew now. He knew why he failed, four hundred years before, to reason with his enemy. He knew why reason wouldn't touch them now.

"You lack love, Tseir. You lack individual values and dreams and hopes. You want nothing more than satisfaction of base appetites and your own survival. But you have taught me something, here at the end. The Ellowan were lost in dreams, we lived without life, our longings ruled our souls. Life is somewhere in the middle between us, between the reality of the present and the forever unknown. You fear the unknown, you fear reality. I never did."

"You will die, Ellowan, knowing our victory is assured."

"Nothing is assured, Tseir."

"Perhaps we will prolong your life enough to witness our final victory. The setting for battle may interest you. The Galaxy Intersystem has engaged a prime fleet in the system of Franconia, your own system. We will annihilate them, and your Valenwood, and we will then expand

78

our empire over all the significant worlds of the Galaxy. With the combined strength of the conquered Intersystem, we will be invincible.''

''Unless they annihilate you first.''

''We are much stronger than you know, Ellowan. We conquered a flight ship from the world of Nirvahda, and from its wealth of power and weaponry, we now arm our own craft with fusion lasers. Little remains but the actual battle for supremacy.''

''Then what did you want with me?''

''From your minor victory at Candor, you have become a hero to the resistance. There is nothing more effective than to see a hero fall, to face that fallen idol in battle.''

''They don't believe in me, Tseir. They believe in themselves. You wouldn't understand that. But your words hide another mystery. Why the proposition? Why not clone me and be done with it? Why the search for my weaknesses?''

''Cloning is a less desirable solution. Clones aren't exact copies for us, and the process of eliminating your more difficult qualities takes time.''

''You don't want to take the risk. But you'll have to, Tseir. I have no weakness for you to use.''

Extrana turned to the guards, clutching a horned scepter in her broad hands. She had short, stubby fingers . . . no fingernail chewed or uneven. Arnoth considered the scepter hideous, a craven image. The horns supported a blood-red globe which reflected an evil light.

''Take him to the cloning facility. Prepare him for immediate reduction.'' Extrana cast a dark glance toward Arnoth. ''Cloning isn't without agony, Ellowan. The best procedure involves the removal of your right hand.''

''One piece at a time. Grim.''

Arnoth smiled, sneering at their efforts to frighten him. Extrana called to the guards, who appeared in unison to surround him. She issued orders, but Arnoth didn't listen. He lifted his hand and looked at his palm. *"You have pretty hands."*

He saw his own fingers on a golden harp; he heard echoes of his music. On Valenwood, it was said that if a man and woman played music well together, they would be well-mated. If not, the match was doomed to fail.

Maybe the old seers were right. Elena never had learned the harp, though she had practiced on the king's flute until her temper flared and she'd flung it across the room.

Arnoth didn't notice where the Tseir guards led him. He walked blind, remembering. He saw the last king of Valenwood, and he recalled Hakon's last words before Arnoth left to negotiate with their enemy. *"One day, you will be king. Bend, and you will never break, Arnoth."*

"I will never break."

He closed his eyes as he walked and he saw Elena. She lay in his arms, near death. *"Do you desire life?"* The interminable wait for her answer. *No.*

"I release you."

He saw Aiyana when she fell in love with Dane, when the force of life rang through her like music from a harp. He saw Dane, laughing and pleased with himself, indignant and unafraid. "Fare well, my friends."

Arnoth's memory faded. He opened his eyes and saw a large window to the white sky and the red earth. The guards opened a door at the end of the hall, and he continued through it.

Only one thing remained. Sierra. Did she know the end her commanders had ordered for him? Did she care? Was she capable of caring? He wanted to see her, just once. He wanted to see her, to touch her skin, to be sure it was as smooth as he remembered.

"Ellowan don't touch Tseir."

A Tseir technician met him at the door and overheard his quiet words. "You'll be touched, Ellowan. And the last touch you'll feel will be Tseir."

"Mistress!"

Sierra stifled a scream as she left the weapons lab. She looked around, then up. Batty hung from a grid. He looked desperate and terrified.

"Batty! What are you doing up there? I thought you went to find Arnoth."

She checked the hall, then held up her hand. Batty dropped and she caught him. She stuffed him under her cloak just as a guard came around the corner.

"Report in, Guard Ninety. You may bring in the next rifle shell."

The guard went into the lab, and she drew a quick breath. "What is it, Batty? I'm working here."

Batty gasped and caught his breath. "You've got to help me, mistress."

"Why? Is it Arnoth?"

Batty nodded vigorously. "They've got him, and he stood up to them. I was hiding on the ceiling, overhearing everything. Of course, I couldn't alert him to my presence, or those females of yours would have overheard."

"What did you hear?"

"He stood up to them—"

"You said that." Sierra fought her impatience. Her heart beat erratically. "What did they do to him?"

"Nothing, yet. They said they were going to clone him."

"Is that all?"

"After they cut off his hand."

Sierra's face drained of blood. Her knees quavered. "His hand?"

Batty nodded, his eyes round and damp. "They said

81

they'll keep him alive, partly, while his clone defeats the other fleet.''

''Then they really mean to battle the Intersystem.'' Sierra shook her head. ''They've got the fusion lasers. They could do it.''

''Can you help the prince, mistress?''

Sierra's heart swelled in a sick wave. ''Batty . . . I'm almost at the point where I can stop this madness. I had to decipher a Nirvahdi pistol for them to get back my Twelfth rank.''

The bat looked confused. ''Then you can't help him? Maybe later . . . after they cut off his hand.''

''His hand.'' Sierra's stomach contorted. His hands. His long fingers, his gentle hands. ''If I do, all will be forfeit. The fleet, everything . . .'' She paused and closed her eyes. ''His hand. Arnoth.'' Her voice faded to a whisper.

I can't let them hurt you. Her mission was forfeit. Arnoth of Valenwood mattered more. ''Where is he, Batty?''

''They took him to a room on the next platform, mistress. They're preparing him now.''

''Then we don't have much time.''

Sierra slipped back into the lab. Several Tseir technicians were at work with the Nirvahda equipment. She picked up a pistol and examined it. ''This pistol should reveal the workings of the larger rifle. I suggest you work on that.''

''You directed that before, Twelfth Commander.''

''So I did. I just wanted to make sure you understood.''

''Yes, Twelfth Commander.''

Sierra placed the pistol back on a pile of equipment and waited for their attention to return to their work. Then she picked it up again and slipped it beneath her cape.

No one noticed her theft. Sierra held her breath and left the lab. She had to walk slowly as she left the laboratory, as she made her way down the platform to the elevating grid. Tseir don't walk fast; they almost never run.

She had to wait for two guards and a junior commander to join her on the grid before lowering it to the bottom level. A shuttle passed by, and she had to wait for it to leave before proceeding to the cloning facility.

Her heart beat so fast that she felt dizzy. *I've got to save him. How am I going to get him out of there?* Her mind raced for an answer, but none came. She opened her cloak. "Batty, how can we get out of here?"

I'm asking a rodent.

"Steal a shuttle, mistress. It works every time."

Sierra looked around. The shuttle bay was nearby. "It's possible." She paused, and a grimness settled around her heart, an emotion she'd never known before. "Batty, if something happens to me, get him to the shuttle bay. Over there, just beyond this building. You might get off the planet. Send a code . . . Nirvahda seven-nine."

"Got it. What's it mean?"

"It doesn't matter. Just remember it."

"I will, mistress."

Sierra stopped at the elevating grid to the cloning facility. "Maybe you should sneak into the shuttle bay, to keep watch. If this works, I'll bring him there. We'll have to work fast."

"And if it doesn't?"

"It has to work, Batty. There is no other way."

Chapter Three

"Blood retrieved. Next test."

A female Tseir technician set aside a vial of Arnoth's blood, then ran an image scan. Arnoth watched impassively as an image of his skeletal system appeared on the technician's monitor.

He was bound to the lab wall, his hands shackled. The fixture that held his right hand served also as a cleaver. A large, sharp blade was poised above his wrist.

Arnoth revealed no fear, no emotion. Pain didn't frighten him. He expected nothing from his life. Since Valenwood fell and Elena died, he had expected nothing at all. He'd taken joy in life, despite his losses. In his long friendship with Aiyana, in his alliance with the amphibious Keiroits, in his meeting with Dane. In the music of his harp.

Arnoth resisted the pang of regret. There was much of

life that had eluded him. But few men live full lives. Why should he be favored by fate?

The technician approached him, casting a lustful gaze over his body. She touched his chest and ran her short finger down to his waist. "I trust your spawn will be as strong as you, prince. Perhaps he will be more agreeable to the pleasures of the flesh."

"You'll have to clone me more than once for that to be even a remote possibility, Tseir."

The technician withdrew her hand and backed away. "You've probably lost the ability to pleasure a woman over your endless, dormant years."

"Probably."

She engaged the cleaver. "It's said Ellowan heal themselves." The technician paused to laugh. "Think you can heal a missing hand?"

Arnoth didn't answer. The pleasure Tseir took in others' pain never ended. He wondered if they felt pain themselves. Probably only dull pain, an echo of feeling.

"I'll be taking both your hands, Ellowan. Pain is worse the second time."

Arnoth kept his expression straight. His whole race had died. His mate, his friends. They'd died in pain, slowly. Why should his fate be any different?

The technician elevated the cleaver. The lab door hissed open. Sierra appeared in the doorway. The technician turned and Sierra yanked a pistol from her cape. The technician leapt aside. "Guard!"

Sierra fired, and the technician crumpled to the ground. She whirled and engaged the door panel, closing it behind her. She was shaking. From across the room, Arnoth saw her hands tremble.

"Sierra . . ."

She darted across the lab, then stopped in front of him.

Tears glistened in her wide eyes. She fixed her gaze on his hands, then closed her eyes in relief.

She cared. Arnoth's pulse moved in dizzying, shocked leaps. She was Tseir, but she cared. "Sierra . . ."

She looked back toward the door. "Quiet! This room is monitored. They may not notice . . ." An alarm sounded, the monitor buzzed. "Then again, they might."

Her hands shook violently as she freed him from the shackles. She didn't touch him. "Follow me."

She started across the room, but Arnoth heard guards racing down the hall outside. "They're coming. Sierra, there must be another way out of here."

She stopped, staring at the door. "No." She poised her pistol. "If I shoot them, you might get out. There's a shuttle bay to the left. You must hurry."

The guards burst open the door. Sierra jumped in front of Arnoth and fired. The first guard fell. Arnoth leapt toward her. A second guard appeared in the doorway and fired a rifle. The blast struck Sierra's chest, hurling her backwards. She fell at Arnoth's feet.

Wild fury erupted in his heart. He ran toward the guard, stooping to seize Sierra's pistol. He shot before the guard aimed his gun. Another appeared, but Arnoth shot the man before he reached the lab entrance.

More would come. "Sierra . . ." Arnoth looked down at her. The rifle blast had split her chest, but her fingers clenched. She was alive.

Ellowan don't touch Tseir.

Arnoth looked at the door; he looked back at Sierra. He could escape. Maybe he could reach a shuttle. She'd sacrificed herself for him, and she was dying. Arnoth went to the door and engaged the panel. It slid shut. He fired the pistol into the grid, freezing the mechanism.

"That should hold them."

Arnoth knelt beside Sierra. She lay on her back, her head twisted to one side. Blood soaked her torn uniform, darker than her red cape. Her skin was as smooth as he remembered.

Ellowan don't touch Tseir. They'd destroyed his world, they'd murdered his mate. All he wanted was an end to their festering empire. And Sierra had sacrificed herself for him.

Arnoth bowed his head. He laid his palm over her forehead, his other hand over her throat. He closed his eyes, and he felt the essence of her life.

It surged beneath Sierra's soft, torn flesh. It leapt and crashed and bounded in youthful abandon. It acted on impulse, filled with emotion and hope. It longed and wanted and cared.

Arnoth's trance deepened, he blended with her, reaching inside her for what she was. She rose to meet him, even as she fought death. He was the greatest Ellowan healer that had ever lived. Ancient power flowed strong in his veins. There was nothing short of death that he couldn't cure.

Do you desire life?

She answered before the question finished. *Yes.*

Then yield to me. I will heal you.

She yielded with complete trust, with an eagerness to learn that he had never encountered before. Her essence raced to do his bidding, learning before he had finished the lesson. He taught her vessels to realign, her nerves to mend, her flesh to knit itself together. He taught her bones to rejoin, to bond, to unite.

Her body had been shattered by the blast, but it was eager for life, for wholeness. Arnoth lifted from his deep trance and waited.

Sierra opened her eyes and looked at him. Her soft lips parted in wonder. "You touched me. Ellowan don't touch Tseir."

Arnoth fought a surge of emotion. "You saved me. Tseir don't save Ellowan."

87

Her lips curved in a small, weary smile. "That's true."
She struggled to sit up. "We have to get out of here."

She leaned on his shoulder, dizzy. "You're too weak,
Sierra. Your body is healing, but it's not complete."

Sierra tried to stand. She sank back to her knees, and
Arnoth eased her down beside him. "I'll help you."

She shook her head. "No time. You have to get out
of here. The lingbat is waiting by the shuttle. If you go
now, you might make it."

"The lingbat?"

"He'll help you. I'll be all right. You must go."

"I can't leave you."

She pushed him, trying to make him stand up. "I'll
say you attacked me. Go."

"Sierra, you'll face a lot worse than demotion."

She looked up at him, tears streaking her cheeks.
"Please go."

He shook his head. He'd felt her life; he saw her courage. He couldn't leave her. "There's still a chance, Sierra. Come with me. I'll get you to the shuttle."

"This room is monitored . . ."

"Then we move fast."

Arnoth helped her to her feet. She swayed and he
caught her. Her skin was warm to his touch. He led her
to the door.

"What happened to the grid?"

"I shot it."

"Wonderful. How are we going to get out?"

Arnoth shrugged, then aimed the pistol at the grid. He
shot again, and the door ground open. "After you."

Sierra eyed him doubtfully, then peeked out into the
hall. "All clear."

"Let's go."

Arnoth took her hand and they moved silently down
the hall. From below, the elevating platform creaked as

it rose. "They're coming. There are stairs down the other hall."

Sierra ran, though she stumbled. Arnoth ran beside her. She bounded down the narrow staircase, skipping several with each leap. Arnoth followed. She shoved open the lower door just as the guards stormed onto the elevating platform.

"Good timing. If we run . . ."

Arnoth nodded. "We run."

They ran together, their steps echoing on the metal walkway as they raced toward the shuttle bay. They might succeed.

Sierra stopped at a tall, narrow door. "In here." Her hands trembled as she engaged the door panel. It opened, and she breathed a sigh of relief. She entered the shuttle bay and Arnoth followed.

"Sierra, wait . . . They know. They'd know I'd go here."

She bit her lip and hesitated. "There's no other way out."

The shuttle bay was dark. Too dark.

"Sir! It's a trap! A trap!"

Batty squealed from the high ceiling. Sierra whirled around and grabbed Arnoth's hand. "Get out of here!" She shoved him back toward the door, but the door opened and three guards stood in the passage.

Arnoth pulled her back, then along the wall toward the shuttles. "Not that way, sir!"

More guards appeared before them. Arnoth turned toward the center, dragging Sierra with him. She stumbled and fell. They were surrounded. There was no escape.

The guards moved in around them, separating them from the shuttle, from the doors. The main shuttle entrance hissed open, letting in the light from the white sky. Sierra winced, but Arnoth looked into her face. Her skin was soft in the daylight, too. Soft and perfect. Tears glistened on her cheeks as she peered up at him.

"I'm sorry. I seem to have bungled freeing you, too."

He couldn't respond. His throat tightened and he took her hand. Her fingers wrapped around his, tight as she steeled herself against her fate.

The supreme commander entered the shuttle bay with Colice, surrounded by guards. Arnoth aimed the pistol, but he knew there was no use.

"If I shoot, they'll kill us both." Why did it matter? He was ready for death. They would die anyway. But Sierra wasn't ready for death. He'd felt that as he healed her. She wanted life. As much life as she could get.

Arnoth tossed the pistol aside. "I am your prisoner. Again."

The guards closed in, and the supreme commander approached them. His escape attempt and capture seemed to have confirmed the Tseir's sense of control. Extrana smiled, her dark eyes glittering with evil delight.

Arnoth's blood ran cold. He didn't care what they did to him. But when one of their own turned against them, what evil punishment could they devise? He moved Sierra behind him. It was no use, but he couldn't resist the impulse to protect her as long as it was in his power.

The supreme commander motioned to Sierra. "A junior commander . . ."

Sierra positioned herself in front of Arnoth. He realized with a strange, cool thrill that she intended to protect him, just as he offered his own futile protection to her.

"Sierra of the Twelfth, Commander."

Arnoth glanced down at her. "Twelfth? What happened to Fourteenth?"

Her lips curved in a faint smile. "I earned my way back."

The supreme commander gestured to the guards. "Take her and kill her."

Arnoth grasped her shoulders, holding her back. He

had to stop them. The supreme commander noticed his defense and her eyes narrowed. "Guard, bring the female to me. Restrain the Ellowan."

Sierra turned to look at him. He saw no fear. "It's all right, Arnoth. I am prepared to die." She glanced up at the ceiling, indicating the lingbat. "For you, there may be a way."

She wanted him to find another method of escape. She expected Batty to help him. She still hoped. Arnoth's shock vibrated through his soul.

The guards seized her and pulled her away. Arnoth reached for her, but they surrounded him, holding him back. They dragged her forward, then shoved her to her knees before Extrana.

She didn't look humble. Every muscle in Arnoth's body drew tight in helpless fury. Extrana still smiled. Her reaction made no sense. One of her own commanders had betrayed her, yet she was neither shocked nor shaken.

"Sierra . . ." Extrana leaned toward Sierra, her face mocking and cruel. "Did you think to succeed where so many others have failed?"

Many others? How many Tseir had turned on their leaders? Yet Arnoth had seen no evidence of unrest in the Tseir.

Sierra didn't bow or turn her head. She looked up at Extrana without remorse or fear. "I failed, Tseir. But think how far I'd come. '*Sierra of the Twelfth*.'" Her voice mocked the Tseir. Arnoth wondered if she had malfunctioned and willed her own death. "How many others have reached Twelfth Command, Tseir?"

Extrana's expression hardened, her back straightened to an imperious height. "Those who promoted you will be questioned."

Sierra glanced toward Colice. "You've got some explaining to do, Tseir." Her tone remained light, taunting. Arnoth heard an echo of his own voice in hers.

91

Colice looked nervous. She licked her lips. "Sierra served in the weapons division. Her work furthered the Nirvahda research."

Extrana's hard face spread into an evil smile. "Nirvahda . . . Yes. A Nirvahdi . . ."

The name *Nirvahda* meant nothing to Arnoth. But it meant something to the Tseir, and to Sierra. Her slender shoulders tensed.

"Much is explained by this, Colice. I will refrain from issuing a demotion."

Extrana reached out to touch Sierra's blond hair. Sierra winced and turned her head. Arnoth cringed as the Tseir fingered Sierra's hair, then tightened in the strands. Arnoth's fist clenched when Sierra gasped in pain.

Extrana yanked, and Sierra's hair came off. Arnoth's mouth dropped. A wig. The binding that had tied her own hair back was released, and a coiled river of dark hair spread over her shoulders, along her neck, down her back.

Extrana threw back her head and laughed. "Nirvahdi! How many such spies does your fool leader think to throw our way? How many already lie dead in our pools?"

"When one fails, another comes forward. We will never stop, Tseir. Who but a Nirvahdi can stop you? Who knows your race better than we who created you?"

"Created you?"

Sierra didn't look back, but Extrana smiled at Arnoth's question. "The Tseir profit from the designs of others, Ellowan. Ages ago, the Nirvahdi race designed cloning facilities."

"They weren't intended for this. . . ."

"The Nirvahdi had enemies, even then."

Arnoth began to understand the twisted history of the Tseir. "The enemies . . . Your 'ancestors,' I presume."

"They were wise enough to know how the Nirvahdi

could profit. Their goal was to secure the Nirvahdi world.''

Sierra straightened and staggered to her feet. ''You failed. After so long, you never did.''

''Only because your system lies at the heart of the Intersystem. When we devastate your pathetic fleet, we will conquer Nirvahda as we have conquered every other world.''

Arnoth angled his brow. ''Except Candor.''

Extrana glared at Arnoth. He smiled. ''Yes, Candor was the result of your trickery, Ellowan. You will pay the price. We have confiscated Nirvahdi weaponry, and with their power, we will destroy them.''

''I'm sorry I won't live to see you fail, Tseir.'' As he spoke, Arnoth's gaze went to Sierra. She stood, silhouetted against the white sun, fragile and powerful before Extrana. Her long hair fell in loose curls down her back. He couldn't let them hurt her.

Extrana looked at Sierra, then back to Arnoth. ''We haven't failed yet. Nothing is infallible, but we will handle all unexpected elements. We always have been before.''

''Except Candor.''

The commander stiffened. ''Bring him closer, guards.''

The guards shoved Arnoth forward, until he stood beside Sierra. He didn't look at her, but he felt her beside him. Her shoulder touched his.

''Candor will be your ultimate doom, Ellowan. Yes, your victory made you a hero. But only a hero can demoralize and devastate the Intersystem as we intended.''

''My clone will enjoy the effort, no doubt.''

He couldn't look at Sierra. He wanted to see her. For that reason, he had to keep his eyes fixed on Extrana.

''Our first tests indicate that you aren't suitable for cloning. The result of your prolonged life span.''

"An unfortunate turn of events."

"You *will* serve us, Arnoth of Valenwood."

"You have nothing, Tseir. My mind hasn't changed."

Extrana glanced at Sierra. "Hasn't it? Is there nothing you value, Ellowan?"

"There is nothing."

"Shall we test your resolve?"

Arnoth tensed, but he forced himself to remain impassive. Extrana looked from him to Sierra, her eyes narrow and suspicious. "You were not in league, the two of you?"

Sierra didn't respond, so Arnoth restrained his answer.

Extrana's expression turned into a gloating smile. "A turn of events that might prove . . . interesting." She nodded to a guard. "Take the Nirvahdi woman."

Arnoth clenched his jaw as the guard pulled Sierra aside. Extrana smiled, prolonging the moment. Sierra didn't react. "She must be checked for concealed weapons. The particle manipulator . . ." Extrana paused, returning her gaze to Arnoth. "On full force."

"No . . ."

"I believe you endured this simple examination without flinching, Ellowan. Of course, that was on the lowest setting. We will see if the Nirvahdi is as strong."

Extrana stepped back and motioned to the guard. Arnoth yanked his arm free from his guard, but Sierra shook her head. *Don't.* He heard her silent demand. *If you do, they have your weakness.* Arnoth saw her thoughts, saw her quick mind working. He had to make them think he didn't care.

"I know nothing of Nirvahda. It will be an interesting test." His words caught in his throat, but he kept his expression blank.

She was already weak, her body still mending itself from the rifle blast. She couldn't handle this brutal pain. He'd barely endured it himself, on a low force.

Black rage built and throbbed in Arnoth's soul as he watched. She stood, slender and innocent, from a distant world. She didn't struggle or cry as they engaged the manipulator over her soft skin.

She closed her eyes and clenched her fists at her side. Her jaw tightened as she grit her teeth. Her small face contorted with pain, and he saw tears beneath her lashes, dripping onto her smooth cheeks.

The guard passed the manipulator device over her chest and thus her wound. A broken cry burst from her lips and she doubled over. Arnoth jerked to free himself, but she collapsed, unconscious. The guard chuckled and ceased the procedure.

"She is unarmed, Commander."

The commander turned to Arnoth. "Well, Ellowan? What do you think of our test?"

Arnoth swallowed hard, fighting hatred. "It doesn't appear thorough, Tseir. Much could escape such a hasty examination. Perhaps she collapsed to prevent a deeper probe."

"Ruthless words, Ellowan. I wonder if you mean them. We will grant you an opportunity to learn otherwise."

Extrana gestured to Sierra's body. "Take her to the First Division holding cell. Imprison her with the Ellowan."

Colice hesitated. "Together, Commander?"

Extrana met Arnoth's eyes, challenging his cold resolve. "Together."

Sierra emerged from sleep, then resisted awakening as she remembered her capture. The pain of the particle manipulator had faded. That was something. She felt no pain at all. Even after being shot and tortured.

Sierra opened her eyes. She lay on a narrow bed. Not a bunk, above and beneath other bunks, but a single bed.

She angled her head and looked around the room. Arnoth sat on the floor beside the bed, his back to her, his head bowed.

The binding in his hair had come loose again. Sierra wondered if he slept in his uncomfortable position. Arnoth sighed and raked his fingers through his hair. He was not asleep. Sierra hesitated, then tapped his shoulder.

Arnoth started and turned. "Sierra ... Are you all right?"

Sierra nodded. "Why didn't they kill me?"

"I'm not sure." He knew. And he didn't want to tell her.

She didn't argue. She didn't want to know. "I'm assuming it wasn't a merciful decision on the Tseir's part."

"Probably not."

Sierra glanced around the room, then sighed. "This is typical of the Tseir. They confine us together and only give us one bed. I suppose I shall have to register a complaint."

Arnoth eyed her doubtfully. "I don't think they'll listen to your complaints, Sierra. You're a prisoner."

"Sierra of the Twelfth, demoted to prisoner. Of course, now I'm free to complain ... This room, for instance. It looks exactly like your cell on the ship."

"I noticed that."

"No imagination. They've reproduced one holding cell, which was stolen from another world. A little variety might be pleasing." She elevated her voice to reach the Tseir listening on the monitor. Sierra started to sit up. She felt dizzy and sank back onto the bed. "That's odd. I don't hurt anymore. But I'm ... rather fuzzy."

Arnoth smiled at her description. "I taught your body to mend itself rapidly. It's trying, although the Tseir made its efforts more difficult."

"The particle manipulator. I'd never actually experienced it." Sierra cringed as she remembered their first

96

meeting. "I'm sorry about putting it on you. I thought you were just a crazy rebel, and that you'd attempt to blow up the fleet in an act of suicide."

"Not a bad idea. But I'm afraid I didn't think of it at the time."

Sierra didn't like his response. He didn't value his own life. "That's why I reminded them to check you. The guards are checked daily, whenever they enter or leave a weapons lab. I didn't realize it hurt so much."

She saw no anger or blame in Arnoth's dark eyes. He sat close to her, his face near hers. A surge of self-consciousness passed through her. Sierra forced her gaze to the ceiling.

"The pain was greater because of your injury, Sierra. But the Tseir don't feel pain the way we do. The sensitivity of a clone appears to be lacking."

The ceiling offered little of interest. Her eyes shifted to Arnoth again. He was so close. And he had touched her. A tendril of her hair fell over her eye, blocking her view. She blew it aside. It fell back, and she shoved it back behind her head. For a reason she didn't understand, he smiled.

Probably because he knows I want to look at him. Sierra's cheeks burned with embarrassment. She cleared her throat. "You endured it better than I. The screaming on my part was excessive."

Arnoth laughed. He rested his elbow on her cot, inches from her. Her gaze traveled the length of his arm, from his shoulder to his beautiful hands. His gaze followed hers. Sierra endured another wave of intense embarrassment.

His brow rose doubtfully as his vision fixed on her body. Sierra's embarrassment eased as she wondered what caught his attention. She looked at her chest. The padding had ripped from the rifle blast, making it appear that she had one large breast and two small ones.

A short giggle erupted before she could stop it. She struggled to sit up. ''I guess I won't need these anymore.'' Sierra reached down her shirt and pulled out the padding. She tossed the padding toward the corner of the room and lay back down.

Arnoth didn't seem to know what to say. It occurred to Sierra that this might be considered a delicate matter, best conducted in privacy. But they had no privacy. ''They were itchy.''

''I like it better this way.''

''Do you?'' Sierra looked down. ''There's not much there anymore.'' She stopped and sighed. ''Never really was.''

That, too, might be a delicate matter. She coughed. ''But it provided a good spot to hide your lingbat.''

Arnoth seemed equally relieved by the change of subject. ''Ah, yes. Batty. How did he get here?''

''On our ship, of course. He followed you. Well, actually, he guessed what you'd do and managed to sneak on board the commander's vessel.'' Sierra paused. ''I hope he's all right now. Maybe the Tseir didn't know where his voice came from.''

Arnoth glanced toward the monitor and sighed. ''They know now. How did you find him?''

Sierra hesitated, feeling guilty for exposing the rodent. ''I didn't. The guards found him and brought him to Colice. She ordered me to kill him. I almost did.''

''I take it he talked you out of it.''

''He didn't talk at all, until I decided to hide him. I almost killed him then, too. When he first spoke, I flung him across the room.''

''Maybe the bat needs my attention, too.''

''He's a sturdy little creature.'' Sierra sighed and yawned. Her eyes drifted shut. With her eyes closed, she couldn't see Arnoth. And he was so close. She peeked at him, to refresh her memory.

He was looking at her, too. More closely than he had before. "It seems I overlooked something." He focused on her forehead.

"What?"

He smiled and laid his hand over her forehead. Just above her eye. His touch was gentle, just as she knew it would be. Their eyes met and Sierra's heart stirred fiercely. She could hear its rapid beat. Maybe he could hear it, too, because he looked suddenly tense.

"Close your eyes."

She obeyed without hesitation. His hand felt cool, then warmer. His warmth entered her, her brow tingled, then numbed. He withdrew his hand and she sighed. His touch was even sweeter than she'd imagined.

She glanced at him. His eyes fixed on her mouth. Her pulse surged, and she swallowed. Her chest rose and fell with tight breaths. He was closer now than before, because he had leaned over her to heal her bruise.

He touched the side of her face, as if he resisted but had no choice. The ache inside her intensified almost to pain. If he kissed her, she would kiss him back, and she would never let go.

He didn't kiss her. He pulled his hand back and turned his back to her, leaning against the bed. Sierra squirmed to the edge of the bed, her hand almost touching the back of his shoulder. She longed to touch his hair. It just hung there, unsuspecting. . . .

With one finger only, she touched the end of his hair. She closed her eyes in sudden bliss. Hair has no nerves. Maybe he wouldn't notice. She held her breath and touched a little more. His shoulders tensed. She slipped her finger back to her chin and snapped her eyes shut.

She knew he looked back at her, probably suspiciously. She casually opened her eyes and offered an innocent smile. His brown eyes looked darker than normal, almost black.

"Is it better?" Good, she sounded innocent, too.

"What?"

"My head."

Arnoth glanced at her forehead. "The bruise is fading. You heal quickly. A Nirvadhi trait, perhaps." He paused, but he seemed anxious to continue conversation. Probably afraid she'd finger his hair again if left to her own devices.

Which she might.

"What is a Nirvahdi?"

"A person from the world of Nirvahda."

"That much I guessed. Where is your world?"

"At the center of the Intersystem, closer to the galaxy center than your system. There are many suns near each other at the center. Many are inhabited. The Nirvahdi race founded the Intersystem Council. We were the first to develop space travel."

"I imagined that beings long evolved would cease to be humanoid."

"No. We are as human, and as frail, as we ever were. But Nirvahdi learn from our mistakes. We learned to tend our planets as we tend ourselves. Ages ago, we were a people of many tribes and many wars. But the wars eased, and we became one. Did Valenwood have such a past?"

"No, our people treasured and respected peace."

"And whales taught you to sing."

Arnoth smiled. She loved his smile. He looked young when he smiled. Maybe he always looked young. But he seemed ageless. Probably because he *was* ageless.

"If life was so blissful, why did you advance at all? Much of Nirvahdi technological progress came from the need to protect ourselves from attack. First, from each other, and later, from more aggressive systems."

"We advanced because we wanted to fly. We wanted to know what lay beyond our world, then what lay beyond our sun. We learned of other races because we wanted to learn their gifts, and add their music to our own.''

Tears started in Sierra's eyes. She wasn't sure why. ''Instead, you met the Tseir.''

''Yes. But we found many other races more pleasant. Our last high priestess found her mate on a world of barbarians. And he became our greatest king.''

''This king . . . you married his granddaughter.''

Arnoth's face clouded. ''I did.''

It sounded romantic. A blissful love affair among a peaceful people, who valued music and loved new experiences and worlds. Sierra frowned, then realized she was frowning and straightened her face into a casual expression. She hoped he hadn't noticed.

''How did you bruise your head?''

Sierra glanced at him. He'd deliberately changed the subject. Which was probably just as well. She didn't want to hear about his beloved mate and the joy he would never feel again.

''I told you how I hurt myself, didn't I?''

''I assumed you invented that unlikely explanation for the sake of the Tseir.''

''No. I fell off my bunk.''

He smiled, then looked away. ''So you really are clumsy.''

''Not at all!'' Sierra's lips tightened angrily. ''Perhaps I'm not quite as graceful as an Ellowan . . .''

A stilted chuckle cut her off. ''I assume Nirvahdi doors open swiftly so as not to get in your way. Your race would never survive otherwise.''

''Ha! At least I'd have the good sense to scramble my interstellar communications!''

Arnoth eyed her doubtfully. ''What are you talking about?''

''Your glorious victory at Candor. Annihilating the

101

Tseir fleet would have been a bit more effective had you not left your transmission floating for any probe to recover.''

A slow smile grew on Arnoth's face. ''My transmission . . . So that's what all this is about.'' For a reason Sierra didn't understand, his smile turned into a laugh.

''What's so funny?''

Arnoth glanced toward the wall monitor. ''In other circumstances, I might tell you. But not here.'' Arnoth closed his eyes, still smiling. Sierra suspected he relived a pleasant memory. ''So, he got me into trouble, after all. I should have known. . . .''

''Who?''

''Can't tell you that either.''

Sierra fidgeted on the bed. She propped herself up on one elbow, looking at the back of Arnoth's head. She couldn't see his face. ''There is much I can't tell you, too.''

''Then we're even.''

Sierra rolled onto her stomach and propped herself on both elbows, her chin in her palm, drumming her other hand on the flat pillow. ''Do you think they'll kill me slowly, expecting your better nature to sacrifice yourself on my behalf?''

''Only if they think I have a better nature.''

''I suppose there's not much chance of that.''

''No, there isn't.''

''I wouldn't want you to, anyway.'' *But it might be a touching gesture.* ''All Nirvahdi are prepared for death.''

''I assumed that, or you wouldn't be here impersonating a Tseir commander.''

''I would have succeeded, if not for your lax battle procedure.'' Sierra wasn't sure why she felt angry. But she did.

''Next time I'll be more careful.''

''There won't be a next time, Ellowan.''

102

Arnoth glanced over his shoulder at her, probably wondering why she sounded so irritated. *Because you don't care if I live or die.* Sierra felt foolish. *What's he supposed to do? Declare his undying affection? That's what the Tseir want.*

"I'm sorry. It's been a long day."

"You need sleep, Sierra."

She sighed. "Yes, I probably do. Tseir snore rather loudly, so I never sleep very well. I've often wondered if it's a clone trait."

"Aiyana snored, too." Arnoth smiled at the memory of his second mate. "But not loudly. I never dared tell her. I wonder if Dane had the courage? Probably."

Sierra studied his tender expression, tenderness on behalf of yet another woman. Not herself. "You said you weren't intimate."

"I said we weren't lovers. We often slept together."

Sierra winced. "Must you tell me these things? I don't care who you sleep with."

One dark brow raised. "Then you shouldn't probe into matters that are none of your concern."

Arnoth was annoying. She had almost forgotten that fact while studying his beautiful hair, and because of his touch. He was obnoxious whether he thought she was Tseir or not. "I see you're not only rude to Tseir. Perhaps it's a general Ellowan trait."

"Perhaps."

Sierra sat up, crossed her legs, and pointed her finger at him. "And you're vague. 'Perhaps.' What does that mean? Not much . . ."

"You talk too much."

Her hair fell forward as she leaned toward him. She'd forgotten how to manage the heavy length, how to fix her curls back so they didn't intrude on her activities. She rolled her eyes and shoved it behind her head, tying it together in a knot.

She returned her attention to Arnoth. His expression had changed. She wasn't sure how exactly. But he looked more sensual than normal. Sierra's impulses threatened to take over.

"If you insult my hair now, Ellowan, you'll wake up without any yourself!" She felt like arguing. Even fighting. How satisfying to punch his shoulder! To pull his hair . . . Her fingers twitched.

"I see the Nirvahdi are an unusually aggressive race."

"We are not!"

"Why are your fists clenched?"

Sierra straightened her fingers like small spikes. "I don't believe they are."

There was something intoxicating about this argument. Sierra wished it could be a physical entanglement. "It's the frustration of dealing with the Tseir and not being able to fight back, and being demoted all the time."

"What are you talking about?"

"Why I want to hit you." She bit her lip, too late.

"As I said, aggressive."

Their discussion had stooped to new lows. Sierra relinquished her adversarial posture and giggled. "I wonder what they'll do if we kill each other before they get the chance?"

"Scrape us off the walls and toss us into their death pools, no doubt."

Sierra's mood altered. "Many lie there already, Ellowan. Dead Nirvahdi, my predecessors, corroding in those stagnant red pools. They're not water, those pools. They're run-off chemicals from the manufacturing plants. The Tseir finally found a use for them. Burial."

Sierra rolled onto her side, her head cradled on her arm. So much had been kept inside, for so long. Fear, and sorrow, and anger. It came out too easily in Arnoth's presence.

He touched her cheek, then slid his hand into her hair.

To her neck. Every nerve came alive and held itself ready. For what, she didn't know. But ready. He sifted her hair, gently, a comforting gesture. He meant to calm her, to reassure her. Because he was a gentle and tender man, despite his ruthless exterior.

She didn't feel calm.

"Why did you come here, Sierra? Extrana admitted the Tseir haven't defeated your planet."

He kept touching her. Sierra didn't remember why she came to the Tseir's world. She wet her lips, trying to focus her thoughts. His fingers idly stroked her neck. She felt so warm, her pulse raced.

"Why? Oh, well . . . It seemed like the thing to do." She swallowed and cleared her throat, and still felt tense. "I thought I could succeed where others failed."

"Why?"

Sierra noticed Arnoth's doubtful tone. Apparently, he considered her incapable of doing anything successfully. His soft touch sent little shivers down her neck, across her chest . . . all over.

"Why what?"

He twirled a portion of her hair. It teased her cheek. "Why would you consider yourself a likely candidate for such a dangerous mission?"

She glared, despite his sweet touch. "Until you came along and bungled everything, I was doing well enough. I'd reached the Twelfth Command, and I was about to . . ."

He clapped his hand over her mouth. "Tell the Tseir your plans . . . Maybe we should change the subject."

It was his fault. She didn't bungle anything until she met him. No, not when she met him. When she first saw his face at the Tseir assembly. She'd spoken up, too loud, and gotten herself into trouble. Sierra considered biting his palm. Either bite, or perhaps lick. Just taste a bit . . .

It was a frighteningly sensual image. Running just the

105

tip of her tongue along his palm. He released her before she had the chance. Which was probably a good thing, considering they were monitored. *What possessed me to even consider such an act?*

Sierra flipped over on her back, folding her hands over her reduced chest. It felt odd, not to have large, padded breasts.

"What made you think you could succeed, if so many others have failed before you?"

"I thought we were changing the subject."

"If you'll consider what you say before saying it, which would make for a change, you should be able to answer me."

Conversation was less stressful than thinking about doing odd things to Arnoth's palm. "I believed in the plans laid out by my predecessor. He believed we had a way of . . ." Sierra glanced toward the monitor. "Well, of doing something against the Tseir."

"I take it he failed."

"He failed."

"Then what makes you think his plans were viable?"

"He made a mistake, he was rash. And he was a man. Men don't rise to command as easily as women."

"I've noticed that. What was his mistake?"

Sierra sighed. This wasn't a good memory. She didn't want to share it with Arnoth. "He left Nirvahda in anger, and he took the place of the person who should have gone."

"You."

"I was prepared. I knew what to do with his plans."

"He went instead . . . To protect you?"

"I believe that was his intention." Sierra frowned. "He was chosen over me for the mission, though I was the best candidate."

"Why was he chosen, then? Because you're a woman?"

"No. The first scouts were women. It was because . . ." Sierra stopped and looked at the monitor. "I can't tell you. But it was a stupid reason."

"Why was he angry?"

She didn't want to tell him this, either. "Because I said I didn't love him."

"I should have known. You have all the elements of a heartbreaker."

"I do not."

"You're beautiful, selfish, and you don't know what you're doing."

"I do!"

Arnoth's eyes darkened. "To a man."

"I don't do anything to any man, ever. Which is what I told him. If men want to engage in ridiculous fantasies, that's their problem. It's not my responsibility in any way."

"Then maybe you should cut your hair."

"When you cut yours." Sierra met his eyes without wavering. "I like my hair."

"I like it, too."

"Thank you. I like yours as well."

"I know."

That feeling stirred again. In such unexpected moments! And it was getting stronger. *I feel like fighting again.*

"You need to sleep, Sierra." Arnoth swallowed, visibly. His breaths seemed strained. He turned his back to her and leaned on the bed.

He had touched her hair. Run his fingers through it, doing just as he pleased. Sierra endured a dizzying swirl of images. She would play with his hair, ease it back, and she would kiss his neck. Soft kisses, tasting his skin, teasing him until he kissed her back.

It's the tension of being imprisoned alone with a man who is more than moderately attractive. And it's all his mystery and secret pain, and those cursed brown eyes that look so hopeless, yet still twinkle. That's why I want to kiss him.

Sierra cleared her throat. "I'm not sleepy."

Arnoth sighed. Sierra suspected he was struggling for conversation material. "If you weren't selected for this mission, why are you here?"

"Never mind."

"Do you know what happened to your predecessor?"

"Not exactly. When I arrived, I learned the whereabouts of those who went before. Three women had taken Tseir positions, all disguised as I was."

"Do you mean their chests were padded?"

Sierra squirmed uncomfortably. "Well, quite frankly, they didn't have the need. Actually, only one was Nirvahdi. The others were from other Intersystem races. But there are Nirvahdi more . . . substantial than myself in that particular area."

"I see."

"It was a mistake for them to attempt the mission together. They were caught because they socialized even though they were assigned to separate divisions. It was deemed suspicious. Tseir don't form friendships, so their effort to congregate was out of place."

"So they were exposed as spies."

"That's right. Their fate was grim. They were imprisoned, and attempted to escape." Sierra paused. "Perhaps that was for the best. In the attempt, they were blasted by gas canisters and killed instantly. Because they were all dead, it was impossible for the Tseir to clone them."

"What happened to your would-be lover?"

"I know he was captured and imprisoned. There is no Tseir record of his execution, though the murder of the women is recorded in grotesque detail. I assume he lies in the chemical pools beyond the city." Sierra sighed. "I suppose I'll end up there, too."

Arnoth didn't respond. He glanced at the monitor. She guessed that he wanted to speak, but he couldn't risk being overheard. Sierra longed to know what he would say.

"Why didn't you love him?"

"I don't know. What an odd question!"

"Was there someone else?"

Not then. Sierra bit her lip to restrain a rash declaration. "I had a mission to accomplish, Ellowan. I wasn't interested in frivolous pursuits."

"You would have been wiser to stay on your planet, Sierra. Using your beautiful body for something more interesting than impersonating a clone. Where you could indulge in every sweet pleasure the flesh offers. . . ."

Arnoth's voice trailed into slow, horrified shock at his sensual outburst. Sierra just stared, lips parted.

Arnoth turned his back to her, looking stiff and tense. "Sleep."

"Good idea." Sierra lay flat on the bed, eyes wide as she envisioned the scene he described. She'd never considered her body beautiful. Just functional. "Sweet pleasure" never occurred to her . . . until now. She peered at him from the corner of her eye.

"Where are you going to sleep?"

"On the floor. You need the bed for recovery."

"It's narrow. I don't suppose the Tseir will provide extra blankets."

"I have my cape."

"My shirt is torn."

"I know." His voice sounded suspiciously low and raw. Almost like a groan.

"It's much too large, the shoulders hang too low. Without my pads, I have nothing to hold it up."

"Tie it at the waist, woman, and stop tormenting me with this discussion."

"That won't work. It's not the waist part that's torn. . . . I was thinking . . ."

"What?" Now he sounded annoyed.

"Well, your shirt isn't torn . . ."

Arnoth sat up and looked at her, eyes narrow. "So?"

Sierra sat up, too. "So, I thought we might trade."

"Why would I want a torn red shirt?"

"You'd look good in red." Appealing to his vanity might work. Arnoth's lip curled at one corner.

"Would I?"

His sarcasm indicated that her appeal to his conceit had failed. "Look." Sierra indicated the torn portion of her shirt. Just above her right breast. "This wouldn't be embarrassing on you. But I have to keep adjusting it so personal bits of me don't show."

His dark eyes flicked to her exposed skin. His jaw tightened. "Trade."

Arnoth tore off his shirt and handed it to her. Sierra didn't take his shirt. She stared at his chest and shoulders, the way his hair fell over his smooth dark skin. She could put her palm over his chest and feel his heart. . . .

"Well?"

Sierra caught herself and snatched the shirt from his hand. "I have to give you mine. Turn your head and close your eyes."

He obeyed. Sierra removed her shirt and pulled his over her head. "This is much nicer."

"Wonderful."

The sleeves were too long. She rolled them up, feeling satisfied. His shirt was warm from his skin. His scent gently lingered as if he surrounded her. Sierra closed her eyes and breathed, feeling a peculiar bliss.

"Aren't you forgetting something?"

She opened her eyes and looked at him. "What?"

Arnoth placed his hand over his bare chest, in exactly the same place she imagined putting her own hand. "You want me to touch you?'' She saw his surprise and realized her error. ''Oh! Of course. You want my shirt.''

She flipped the shirt to him and watched him put it on. She breathed a sigh of relief when she saw that it fit. Although he had to roll up his sleeves, too, because they were too short for his arms.

''I was right. You look good in red. It's your hair . . . I suppose you know that.''

''I've never worn anything red in my life.''

''In four hundred years?''

''In four hundred years.''

''Well, it suits you.''

''Wonderful.'' Arnoth buttoned the shirt and lay back.

Sierra didn't speak for a long while. Her thoughts wandered back to his mention of ''pleasures of the flesh.'' She peeked down at him. His eyes were closed, but he wasn't sleeping. She noticed his lashes. They were long and black and actually cast shadows on his cheeks.

''I admired your eyelashes when I saw you on the screen.''

He looked up. She leaned over the edge of the bed, looking down. They were imprisoned. They would probably both die. But it didn't matter just now.

''What screen?''

''When Extrana told the assembly about you. They had retrieved your Candor communication, when you ever-so-brilliantly announced your name and the name of your world. '*Arnoth of Valenwood.*' Good thinking, that.''

''You may not understand this, but it was necessary at the time.''

Sierra's hair slid from its knot and spilled over the edge of the bed. It almost touched him. But not quite, so she didn't move it.

''Anyway, they had your image, and they played you taunting them. '*Surrender or die.*' Very dramatic.''

"It worked. Unfortunately, they didn't choose the wiser option."

"Apparently not. I suppose you can't tell me here how you beat them."

"That would seem unwise."

"True." Sierra hunted for something else to say. She liked looking at him. "Well . . . Good night, Ellowan. I shall sleep now."

"That should provide a welcome silence."

So, he didn't want to talk. "Fine." She positioned herself back on the narrow bed, brows furrowed. "I wonder how the lights go out in here?"

Arnoth rose to his feet, pushed a button on the far wall by the door, and the room darkened to black. Sierra heard him walk back to the bed and lie down.

"That was simple." She didn't want to sleep. She shouldn't have asked about the light. Now she couldn't see him at all.

She wasn't sure, but she thought he sat up again. "Is it possible for you to maintain silence, woman?"

He was very near. A faint red light came from beneath their sealed door and she saw a dark outline right above her. "Why do you ask?" Her heart beat in static leaps. She wasn't sure why. Maybe it was because she couldn't see him.

"The Tseir monitors are limited, aren't they?"

"The Tseir can't see in the dark, if that's what you mean."

"Good."

Sierra wondered why he'd asked. What an odd question! "I don't see . . ." He leaned over her, bent close to her, and his lips touched her cheek.

Sierra froze. He kissed her face, her chin. His mouth brushed over hers. His tongue ran along the line of her lips. Her heart opened and poured itself in a torrent of emotion. She wrapped her arms around his neck, her fin-

112

gers entwined in his hair, and she kissed him back.

Her lips parted beneath his, offering him entrance, offering him anything he wanted. She heard a low, stifled moan. For a wild moment, she didn't care if the Tseir knew what they were doing or not. She wanted to pull him over her, draw him inside her, and they would dissolve into each other.

He broke the kiss and moved away, back into darkness. Her heart beat so fast that she couldn't speak. She couldn't comment, anyway, because then the Tseir would know he'd kissed her.

He'd kissed her. Arnoth of Valenwood, who felt nothing, who refused to love again, who cared nothing for anyone, had kissed her. The most perfect kiss she'd ever imagined. Her whole body tingled.

"Sleep well, Sierra. We probably won't live through tomorrow, so you might as well enjoy the rest."

He sounded so calm. Sierra forced herself to breathe. "I don't care if I live through tomorrow. I lived tonight."

Arnoth lay in darkness and ached. Not just sexually. His whole cursed body burned. *Why did I do it?* Madness. Dane called him crazy. Maybe he was right.

He'd felt glimmers of desire throughout his long dormancy. It had been hard to sleep next to a beautiful woman and not feel desire. But the self-control of the ritual had kept him from acting on it, from seeking resolution. Dane hadn't believed him, taunting him about his resistance.

The harder you resist, the harder you'll fall. Arnoth frowned in the darkness. He remembered Dane's infuriating, lyrical tone.

The unexpected. He'd known Aiyana, he'd known she would be a temptation, if he allowed it. So his resistance was simple. Sierra was different. He hadn't expected to be tempted by a Tseir female. Then he didn't expect her

113

to transform before his eyes into . . . a goddess.

She didn't look Ellowan. She didn't look like anyone he'd ever seen. Ellowan didn't have curly hair. And she was taller than an Ellowan woman.

And Ellowan didn't trip. They didn't talk so much.

No one talked so much. Except a lingbat.

He wore her shirt. It wasn't as soft as his own, but it carried her soft, woman's scent. That didn't help dampen his desire. He wondered what he'd done wrong. Touching her had been his mistake. Not saving her, but touching her neck because he wanted to comfort her.

Her hair had felt alive to his touch. Her neck was so soft that he wondered why the Tseir's red shirt didn't chafe her skin. Her life vibrated inside her, in a swift, warm pulse. . . . It had grown swifter beneath his touch. So quickly!

I kissed her. He'd half expected Sierra to kiss him first. He knew she wanted to, because her thoughts were easy to read. Everything showed on her little face. He knew her outburst of anger had come from desire. He knew she wanted to fight because she wanted him.

She wanted to lose control so she could surrender to whatever impulse moved her, caring nothing for the consequences of her act. Nirvahdi people must be the most impulsive in the galaxy. They flung themselves into space, without thought of the consequences, then handled the conflicts as they arose.

They created clones, then dealt with their creation after disaster had struck. No forethought. But so much passion. . . .

Her hand slid from the bed, hanging just above his left shoulder. She was asleep. Her fingers were curled slightly. He heard her soft, even breaths. She was sleeping on her stomach, her face turned toward the wall.

Arnoth touched her hand, then eased it back on the bed beside her. She made a smacking, grumbling noise, then rolled over onto her side. Apparently this position wasn't comfortable either, because she rolled onto her back.

Silence again. He had turned out the lights so he couldn't see her. But her image remained clear in his mind. He saw her leaning over the edge of the bed, looking down at him as her dark hair fell around her face.

Her hair was the same color as his own. Longer and curlier. And he knew everything she was thinking as if he watched it emerge in her thoughts, then hop in abandon to a new thought. She looked so beautiful, peeking down at him, her hair around her face.

That was when he'd decided to kiss her. He hadn't really acknowledged it to himself before, but that was the moment. A weak moment. He'd turned out the lights to stop himself, and then he'd found himself leaning over her, knowing the darkness concealed them. Cloaked in shadow, there was nothing to stop him.

It's knowing we can't escape. We probably won't survive tomorrow. If he'd thought they could escape the Tseir, he would never have kissed her. He would have kept his distance. His desire was a man's primitive impulse. Arnoth cleared his mind. He was locked in a small room with a beguiling, peculiar woman. He'd kissed her, only because he couldn't think of anything else to do.

Nothing he could hide from the Tseir, anyway.

Making love was out of the question.

Never.

Arnoth closed his eyes, shutting out everything in the dark room. Sierra rolled over again, from her back onto her side. She grumbled in her sleep, then rolled again. . . .

She jerked, squealed, and tumbled off the bed.

Onto Arnoth.

She braced herself on his chest and propped herself up. "I was thinking. . . . Maybe you should take the bed."

115

"Maybe."

He pictured her eyes narrowing at his vague response. He would have said more, but his throat was so constricted. His whole body was tight. He wondered if she noticed.

She caught her lower lip between her teeth. She hesitated a moment, then scrambled off him, onto the cold metal floor. "I'm sorry."

"You are a torment beyond anything the Tseir could invent."

She nodded, woefully. "I know." She peeked over at him, her small face knit in shame. "I didn't hurt you, did I? Break anything?"

"You're not that heavy."

"Good." She waited for him to get up and move to the bed. "Nirvahdi beds are wide and low. I haven't gotten used to these."

"That is obvious."

"I'm lucky you were there to break my fall."

"That was fortunate."

"I'll just sleep here, shall I?"

"Good idea."

Arnoth forced himself to move. Her body fit so perfectly above his. He liked the way her legs straddled his thighs when she sat up. True, her knee had jabbed him in an unfortunate area. . . .

He sat on the edge of the bed and she took his spot on the floor. He passed her the flat pillow and the thin blanket. She gave him his cape.

She lay on her back, looking up. Her dark hair spread around her face and shoulders. His shirt opened at her throat, her skin almost glowing in the blackness, revealing her long neck, her chest. . . .

Arnoth rolled his eyes and repressed a groan. He sank to his knees beside her, bent and scooped her into his arms. She stiffened but didn't resist.

He propped her up in his arms and kissed her again. She relaxed, and her fingers made their way to his hair. He tasted her soft mouth, then slid his tongue between her teeth. She touched her tongue to his, tentatively, then sucked very gently.

Her hair fell over his arm to his thigh. He kissed her face, her forehead, then tilted her back so that he could finally kiss her neck. Her pulse raced beneath his lips. Her breath came in small gasps.

He pressed his mouth to hers to quiet her. Her tongue swept to taste him, dipping at the corner of his lips. His arms tightened around her, drawing her closer to his body. Her breast touched his rib cage. She squirmed deeper into his arms, then onto his lap. She wrapped her arms around his neck, kissing his face, his mouth. A small, low moan erupted from her throat.

A moan that could be heard on the Tseir monitor. . . .

Arnoth pushed her back. He caught his breath, his heart pounding. *Madness*. The woman had no restraint. He ached. He leapt to his feet, dropping her to the floor. He stood above her, looking down, shocked by his own weakness.

"Should you drop on me again, woman, the Tseir won't get a chance to kill you. I'll do it myself first."

Chapter Four

The monitor buzzed and Sierra leapt to her feet. *I'm late!*
She wasn't in a bunk, but on the floor. She stumbled and
fell back onto the bed. Onto Arnoth. Again.

He woke with a start and groaned. "You are a men-
ace."

Sierra hopped to her feet. "I forgot where I was. I
thought I'd overdone rest duties. . . ."

"You're imprisoned, woman. Which in other circumstances might be a good thing. Prison is probably where
you belong."

Sierra placed her hands on her hips and glared at him.
He sat up and rubbed his hand over his eyes. His hair
looked messy, and his red shirt was crumpled from sleep.
He was so rude. Maybe his kiss had been a dream.

But his anger afterwards wasn't. He'd actually threatened to kill her if she dropped on him again. He hadn't
meant that. He'd meant if she *tempted* him again, but he

couldn't say that because the Tseir would overhear it, and know. She knew that.

As if she'd kissed him first! Arnoth of Valenwood had nerve. She longed to point that fact out to him, and to remind him who'd initiated the whole encounter.

"The Tseir are coming."

Arnoth yawned. How infuriating! "I guessed that from the monitor."

"We'll probably be killed."

"You, maybe. They want me for their fleet, remember?"

"How lucky for you!"

Sierra turned her back to him and faced the door. The door hissed open. Extrana entered the room, followed by Colice and two guards.

"I want another cell, and I want it now."

Extrana glanced at Colice, then back at Sierra. "The temptation must be strong between you, if you demand to be separated."

Sierra's jaw firmed, her eyes narrowed. "It's strong, all right. If you don't move me, I'll kill him, and you'll lose your precious figurehead."

Arnoth rose to his feet behind her. "This torture you devised, Tseir, is much worse than I imagined. Confining me with this demonic female was crueler than usual for your kind."

Sierra refused to look at him. He meant it. Well, she meant it, too. Their anger appeared to confuse Extrana.

"You saved the Nirvahdi female yesterday. You healed her, and you took her with you when you attempted to escape. And you, Sierra, tried to free him."

"A mistake on my part. We're trained for compassion." The Tseir might believe this. Sierra cast a dark glance over her shoulder to Arnoth. "I overdid it."

"I healed the woman because I needed her to escape.

119

Given the opportunity, I would gladly reverse the procedure.''

Sierra rolled her eyes. ''You'd probably forget to cover your escape, anyway, Ellowan. Maybe leave a trail . . . That seems to be your usual method.''

''Ah, but I wouldn't trip over my own feet doing it. . . .''

''Cease!'' Extrana held up her hand. ''This exchange is irritating.'' She looked between them. ''Perhaps you need more time.''

Arnoth stretched and assumed a languid posture. ''Or a gag.''

Colice watched them suspiciously. ''Their affection has dwindled rather than increased, Supreme Commander. Perhaps we should have kept them apart instead.''

''It is possible that Sierra attempted to free the Ellowan for the sake of her fleet. Perhaps the fear of our endeavor is great. She doesn't want us to use the resistance hero against them.''

Sierra wondered how this development would affect her future, and her life. She glanced at Arnoth. He didn't look at her. He looked bored and a little annoyed.

''I have no more inclination to serve you than I did, Tseir. Do what you will with this female. The Ellowan aren't part of the Intersystem. It means nothing to me.''

Sierra's lip curled into tight irritation. ''The first requirement for Council Membership is good sense. You would not be approved.''

'' '*Good sense*'? That term must have a different meaning on your world, woman. I haven't seen any evidence of its existence in you.''

Maybe he meant it. Maybe he was just trying to convince the Tseir he didn't care. Maybe a little of both, Sierra thought. Extrana didn't seem certain, either.

''We could torture her, to gauge your reaction.''

Arnoth shrugged. "The Ellowan healing technique is tiring, Tseir. I trust you won't injure her to a level that requires any work on my part."

Sierra's mouth dropped. "That *would* be an inconvenience, wouldn't it?"

Arnoth nodded, though he kept his eyes on Extrana.

Extrana fingered her scepter. "Perhaps you both need proof of the hopelessness of your situation. Colice, summon Drakor."

Sierra's brow furrowed. "Drakor? The military commander?"

"Drakor is our highest-ranking male Tseir. Have you met him, Sierra?"

"I've seen him. But I wouldn't recognize him. He always wears his helmet, with his visor down."

"Today, you will see the man beneath the visor."

"That should be thrilling beyond words. One Tseir is much like another."

"This Tseir may interest you more than the rest, Nirvahdi."

The door slid open behind them and Drakor entered the cell. He looked like every other Tseir guard. He wore a uniform, white pants, a red shirt, a red cape. Because of his rank, his cape was longer than those worn by the guards.

He wore a red helmet with a white visor. Sierra waited. "I assume it is Drakor, although I see little to differentiate him from any other guard."

"It is Drakor, Sierra. But perhaps you know him by another name." Extrana motioned to Drakor. "Remove the helmet, Drakor."

He lifted his helmet from his head and Sierra's heart stopped. "Koran!" She shook her head wildly. "It can't be. You're dead!"

Arnoth moved to her side, studying Drakor intently. "He looks like you. He's Nirvahdi."

121

Tears swarmed Sierra's vision. "He was. . . . What have you done to him?"

Arnoth touched her shoulder. "He's a clone, Sierra. He's not the man you knew."

Drakor's eyes looked blank; his face showed no expression at all. Extrana smiled. "The Ellowan is correct. Your Nirvahdi spy died, but not before we took elements from his living body."

Sierra closed her eyes, blotting tears. What they had almost done to Arnoth, Koran had endured. She looked at him and remembered the man he was when she last saw him. On his knees, eyes shining, begging her to marry him. He'd said he'd loved her all his life. He'd said she filled every dream.

She'd told him he was her dearest friend. . . .

Sierra touched the clone's face. Like Koran, he had shoulder-length, curly hair. Lighter than her own, soft brown. His eyes were a muted gray, his face sweet and young. "There must be some trace of Koran in you."

Something flickered in his eyes, then disappeared. "This woman isn't Tseir, Supreme Commander. She is the saboteur you mentioned."

"Like all saboteurs, she was captured."

"But not killed? This seems unwise."

"We have other purposes for Sierra. Drakor, you may leave now."

Drakor bowed and departed. He hesitated in the doorway a moment, then glanced back. For a second, no more, Sierra saw a vestige of her old friend in the clone's eyes. It vanished, and he went about his duties.

Sierra brushed away tears, her chin firmed angrily. "Why did you bring him here? We know you clone people."

"I wanted you to see, Sierra. Drakor is a third-generation reproduction. The second, of course, retained too many of your Koran's unfavorable qualities." Extrana took a step toward Sierra, her face glowing evilly.

"Rest assured that Koran's tender memories of his previous life are erased now. He retained only his basic knowledge of Nirvahdi command. From his knowledge, we reproduced your fusion laser. An amazingly destructive weapon."

"And you intend to use Arnoth the same way."

"Drakor will maneuver our fleet, but Arnoth will be its commander."

Arnoth laughed, a harsh sound in the strained atmosphere. "I don't think so, Tseir. You'll have to reproduce me more times than three to remove my hatred for your race. It is part of my flesh, part of my core."

"We won't need to reproduce you at all. If you agree to our assignment."

"Never."

Sierra shifted her weight uneasily. "What about me?"

"It is most certain you will be cloned, Nirvahdi. You hold knowledge equal to Drakor's original."

Colice assessed Sierra. "Sierra made an impressive Tseir. With a few alterations, your clone might elevate to the Final Third."

"I was well on my way."

Arnoth eyed her doubtfully. "A source of great pride, no doubt."

Sierra nodded. "It wasn't easy, to be sure."

Arnoth leaned his wide shoulder against the metal wall. Impossibly casual. Impossibly sure of himself. "You don't offer much, Tseir. You expect me to display affection for this female, with the certainty she will later be dismembered and killed."

Sierra winced at his assessment, but Extrana tapped her scepter. "We could keep her alive, so as to offer you hope."

"Thoughtful. I don't want a one-handed woman."

"You don't want any kind of woman." Sierra fought

123

a surge of irritation. "And my clone wouldn't agree, one-handed or not."

Extrana's eyes narrowed as she looked between Arnoth and Sierra. "You wear each other's shirts."

Sierra looked down at the shirt she'd commandeered from Arnoth. "So we do."

"Why?"

Sierra tried to think of a good reason. She glanced at Arnoth. "Well . . ." Sierra's face paled when she saw he had no explanation, either.

A guard spoke to Colice, and she nodded. "This matter was covered in the morning's report, Commander. They exchanged shirts in the night. The reason was not substantial."

"It was! My shirt was torn and showed . . . well, too much."

Extrana considered this. "You feel no affection, El-lowan, yet you gave her your shirt?"

"Only to quiet her, Tseir. For a few moments of silence, I would have given her my boots and cape and anything else she asked for."

Sierra's lip curled to one side. "Oh, would you? I hasten to remind you, Ellowan, that it was you who . . . elevated our conversation to . . . new heights." By kissing her. Sierra watched as Arnoth took in her meaning.

"This bickering may well conceal desire. We are not fools, Ellowan."

To Sierra's surprise, Arnoth nodded. "She's beautiful. Yes, in other circumstances I could think of some interesting ways to make use of that delectable little body."

Sierra gaped, astonished. Extrana's eyes darkened. "An interesting admission, Ellowan."

"I don't see any point in denying the obvious."

"I do!" Sierra caught herself and shook her head. "You have lost your mind."

Extrana kept her attention on Arnoth. "You desire the Nirvahdi?"

Arnoth looked casual and somewhat bored. "Desire is a gentle term, Tseir. I haven't been dormant so long that I've forgotten how much pleasure a woman can bring to a man."

Sierra glanced between Extrana and Arnoth, her eyes narrow as she considered Arnoth's purpose for this "disclosure." He waffled between intense dislike and irritation to a casual announcement of lust. Why?

"Yet you claim to bear her no affection?"

Arnoth looked genuinely puzzled. "What has affection to do with sex?" He shook his head, as if the Tseir were fools. "But, unfortunately, in my condition, sex remains impossible." He sighed.

Sex might be impossible, but kissing obviously wasn't. Sierra seated herself on the bunk and watched Arnoth facing Extrana. She began to understand his purpose. He was keeping them off-balance. First, he'd indicated no interest in her.

But showing no interest might encourage the Tseir to abandon their scheme and kill Sierra anyway, attempting to convince Arnoth by some other method. So Arnoth had teased them with possibility. *In other circumstances* he might desire her.

Enough to keep the Tseir on their course, and Sierra alive.

At least, Sierra hoped that was Arnoth's intention. Otherwise, he was simply crazy.

"We will give you more time alone, Ellowan. Perhaps you will relinquish your dormant state to sample this Nirvahdi's lush pleasures."

Sierra rolled her eyes. "I don't have 'lush pleasures.' "

Arnoth and the Tseir ignored her comment. But Arnoth successfully kept the Tseir confused, and Sierra alive for another day. She should be grateful. Instead, she wanted to fight.

"And even if I did, I wouldn't share them with him."

Arnoth chuckled, increasing Sierra's annoyance.

Extrana glanced at her report, then back at Arnoth. "There is one other thing. Your communication device . . ."

"Communication device?"

"It is disguised as a winged rodent."

Sierra peeked up, wondering if Arnoth had thought of a way to protect Batty, too.

"I don't know what you mean, Tseir. I have no such device."

"Don't toy with me, Ellowan! Colice saw this creature on the ship. Prisoner Sierra was instructed to do away with it. She obviously realized its importance and refrained from exterminating it. It alerted you to our guards in the shuttle bay."

"I have no such device."

"We have put out a search on it. Don't expect to recall it to your aid, Ellowan. It can't come near this facility without being apprehended."

Arnoth shrugged. "You waste time in peculiar ways, Tseir. But don't let me stop you."

Extrana gazed around the little room. "Perhaps you were dissuaded from the full expression of lust by your sleeping arrangements. Ellowan are sensual. Our records indicate that you designed entire chambers for sexual purposes."

Sierra glanced up at Arnoth. "Did you?"

He hesitated. "Our private chambers were . . . comfortable."

Extrana frowned at his evasive reply. "Your people considered sexual union an art form. Ellowan males taught young women to pleasure them as a matter of course . . . in unique ways."

Arnoth looked a little strained, then cleared his expression while Sierra watched intently. "That was before my time, Tseir."

"Nonetheless, you hold sensuality in high regard."

Arnoth shrugged. "It whiles the hours."

"We'll see how you while yours, given the chance, Ellowan."

Arnoth glanced at the monitor. "The Ellowan never equipped our private chambers with monitors, Tseir. Such devices aren't conducive to lovemaking."

Extrana eyed the monitor. "The monitor is necessary, Ellowan, as you well know. But we will cover it to preclude viewing. Guard! Conceal the monitor, then bring a larger mat to this room, and remove the bunk. In fact, double the mat by two, so that it offers comfort."

This sounded good to Sierra. "Maybe I'll finally get some sleep."

The guard covered the monitor with black tape, then left the cell to follow Extrana's orders. Sierra shook her head. "Maybe he should bring flowers and wine, too."

"You scoff, Nirvahdi, but you haven't experienced the Ellowan's hard body in yours."

Sierra grimaced in embarrassment. "No, I haven't. And I'm not going to."

"We'll see. There was a time when Ellowan men took females like yourself and taught them every pleasure, until the female functioned solely for sexual satiation."

Sierra angled her brow doubtfully. "Nirvahdi females are not thus disposed."

Extrana laughed. "Ha! On your world, wars have been waged over females, over sex."

"In the distant past, Tseir. My ancestors fought over many things. Sex has no particular appeal to us."

"That remains to be seen. Look well, Sierra. This handsome Ellowan will be your doom."

Sierra glanced at Arnoth. He *was* handsome. There

127

was no getting around that fact. He was so handsome that she ached when she looked at him. "He already *is* my doom."

Extrana left the cell and Arnoth turned his attention back to Sierra. She looked grumpy and depressed. "In what way am I your 'doom,' woman? In fact, if not for my efforts . . ."

Her gaze shot to him, her face tight with displeasure. "I'd be happily dead by now." She rose from the bunk and moved toward him, her hands clenched into fists at her side. "But, *no* . . . Now, I'm captured and set up to be some sort of bizarre sexual sport for you, *should* you decide to use me!"

"Would you really prefer death?"

"Yes! No." She turned away.

"I have looked inside you, Sierra. I felt no denial of life in you."

"I wasn't thinking."

"No. You were feeling. That is real."

Sierra tapped her foot, glaring at the monitor. "I do not like the restrictions of this confinement." She glanced back over her shoulder. "There is much I would like to say."

Arnoth repressed a smile. "I thank you for restraining yourself, for your sake and mine."

Sierra seated herself on the bunk again. She didn't look at him, but she fidgeted. Arnoth waited.

"Did you really train women for sex?"

He should have guessed that was preying on her mind. Arnoth sat down beside her. "Training" Sierra was a curiously compelling image, so he banished it from his mind.

"My ancestors were sensual, as the Tseir noted. In times past, a man chose a woman to his liking and . . ."

He hesitated, clearing his throat. "Guided her as to what gave him pleasure."

Sierra studied him intently. Arnoth endured a flash of memory—Sierra seated on his lap, kissing him without restraint.

"What about her pleasure?"

Arnoth couldn't resist a smile. "Most often, that *was* his pleasure, Sierra. To teach a woman of her own body is a man's greatest joy."

Sierra hopped up from the bunk and paced around the room. She looked flushed. Arnoth wondered if she knew anything about the desires in her body. She kissed as if surprised, as if untaught, but eager.

He knew exactly how he would teach her, had the circumstances between them been altered by time and fate. He would start with the lightest touch on her soft skin, at the top of her head, and he would work to the tips of her small, neat toes.

With his tongue.

Arnoth jumped up from the bed, too, and paced in opposition to Sierra. They stopped in the middle of the room and looked at each other. For a second only, Arnoth felt sure they were thinking the same thing.

Sierra's eyes widened and she proceeded to a swifter pace. She hurried to one wall, pausing, and back again. Arnoth paced, too. He'd never endured this kind of desire.

Restraint fans the flames. That phrase was written in the Ellowan mosaics, which featured painstaking accounts of sexual union. It was the first thing a man learned when studying the art of increasing pleasure.

But this was forced restraint. He had no choice. If he allowed his desire a release through their union, his life would lurch from dormancy and claim its full expression. Then the Tseir could clone him.

They could use Sierra against him, just as they'd used

Elena. Arnoth stopped in the middle of the room. Sierra kept walking. He couldn't let it happen. He'd never had a problem in the past. Maybe his desire had reached the breaking point because he was far from other Ellowan, from Aiyana, who'd helped him control the innermost functions of his body.

It was necessary to engage another person, to balance, to control. Arnoth eyed Sierra. She was all he had. But it would mean touching her. He debated the alternatives. In his present condition, he wouldn't last another night. Not if the Tseir gave them only one bed. Of course, he could sleep apart from her. But in this small room, there was no "apart."

The door slid open and two guards entered bearing mats. Sierra stood out of their way as they removed the bunk and positioned the mats. "Most generous."

The guards didn't respond, but Arnoth noticed that they both lingered near Sierra, who didn't notice their attention. The malice so evident in the commanders was different in the guards. They operated like beasts, well trained, disciplined, yet emanating a sense of continued violence.

They knew no mercy, and their lust was strong. They would tear at a bound woman until she neared death. . . . Arnoth closed his eyes. The past was gone. He couldn't change it now. Maybe he couldn't do anything about the future, either, but it was still unmolded. Sierra couldn't face Elena's ending.

The guards left and Arnoth seated himself cross-legged on the mat. "Come here."

Sierra turned toward him, her hands on her hips. "You've changed your mind? Well, I haven't. You can just keep your 'training' to yourself!"

Arnoth repressed a grin at her assumption. "I have no intention of subjecting you to my instruction, woman. I have need of you."

130

"In what way?"

"Sit, and I will tell you."

Sierra hesitated, then seated herself facing him. Her posture remained stiff, as if she was ready to spring should his intentions prove erotic. "What do you want?"

"There is ritual involved. . . ." Arnoth glanced at the monitor. Perhaps the Tseir couldn't see, but they could hear whatever was said. "If you would trust me in this, our lives would be easier."

She chewed her lip. "What do you want me to do?"

"Allow me to touch you." Her eyes narrowed suspiciously, but he cut her off before she could argue. "It is necessary in order that I regain . . . maintain balance."

"Do I touch you, too?"

Arnoth swallowed. This might be more difficult than he imagined. "Where I touch you, you touch me, also."

"Very well. Touch as you please." She paused. "If I dislike the spots you choose, I will strike you."

"The spots I require are inoffensive."

"Am I sitting correctly?"

"Relax."

Her shoulders lowered, but she still looked tense.

"Breathe deeply."

She did. Arnoth waited until Sierra seemed comfortable, then placed the fingertips of one hand upon her temple. She peeked up at him. "Do I do this to you, too?"

"Yes."

She drew a quick breath, then touched his temples, too. Her fingers trembled. Arnoth felt every rapid breath she took. He tried to sink into his trance. Instead, he felt the warm, swift life in her fingertips.

It didn't help that she stared at him with piercing intensity. "Now what?"

"Close your eyes."

Her chin firmed. "There's no need to snap at me. I didn't ask to do this, you know. But it seems to be your way to insult me for things I had no part in doing, which were totally your idea. . . ."

She referred to their kiss. Arnoth attempted to collect himself. "I wouldn't say that, woman. You know your part." She'd teased him. Hanging over the bed, her eyes sensual and warm, filled with promise. He had to kiss her. But that was before he realized the danger. Now, he could control those impulses.

Sierra's fingers twitched, but she didn't withdraw them. "It's likely you imagined . . . whatever you imagined, and took it to extremes."

"If I'd taken it to extremes . . ." Arnoth stopped himself. He would have made love to her until morning. . . . He withdrew his hands from her temples and drew a constricted, calming breath. Sierra sat back and studied him intently.

"Are we finished?"

"We haven't begun."

"You're snapping. I see no reason to sit here, *helping you,* because you asked me to, and be snapped at."

She started to move, but Arnoth caught her arm. "I'm sorry. The ritual is stressful." No, it was sitting close to her that was stressful. Sierra settled back on the mat.

"Well? What's stopping you? Hurry up!"

"If you would maintain silence—"

"Ha! We know what happened the last time you ordered me to 'maintain silence'!"

She wasn't making it easy.

"Sierra, please . . . I need your help. Quietly."

"Oh, very well. Proceed."

Arnoth replaced his fingers upon her temples. She did likewise.

"What's the purpose of this, anyway?"

"Never mind." Arnoth closed his eyes and tried to find peace and spiritual balance. He had to meet her, and retreat.

"I don't feel anything."

Arnoth opened his eyes. "You're not supposed to feel anything."

"Oh." She closed her eyes. Her fingers weren't trembling now. They felt warm. She moved them slightly, as if feeling his skin.

"No moving."

"It was an accident."

He didn't believe her, but he didn't argue. Arnoth tried to deepen his breathing. After a moment, it worked. His muscles relaxed. Sierra's breaths slowed, too. He adjusted his pressure on her temple.

"You're moving. You said I couldn't move."

"Sierra . . ."

"Sorry." A long silence followed. "I won't talk anymore."

His pulse quickened. "That is a challenge for you, I know, but I appreciate the effort."

The pressure of her fingertips increased slightly. Arnoth recognized the combative gesture. "Aggressive."

She puffed an impatient breath. "*You're* talking."

Arnoth dropped his hands and groaned. "This is impossible. I should have known."

She looked hurt but defiant. "I believe you lured me into this ridiculous act for the sole purpose of insulting me."

What remained of his patience crumbled. "No! I need you!"

Her eyes widened in surprise, and Arnoth caught his breath. "I need your help." He spoke slowly and clearly, so she wouldn't misunderstand his outburst.

She smacked her fingertips back to his temple. "I won't say a word. If you ask it, I won't breathe."

She jammed her eyes shut. Arnoth smiled. "It is necessary that you breathe."

He placed his fingers back upon her temple. Again.

Sierra remained true to her word. She didn't speak, and her breaths came slow. Despite her unexpected cooperation, Arnoth's own respiration refused to slow or deepen. He adjusted his position, yet still he felt his merciless heart beating all the way to his groin.

He'd performed this ritual for almost four hundred years. It had been as easy as taking food. He imagined Aiyana before him, respectful of his distance, understanding his pain. He blocked Sierra's penetrating gaze and soft lips from his mind and focused on Aiyana's cool image.

It worked. His pulse slowed. His breathing deepened. His essence congealed and reached out. Everything he was turned outward, releasing demands, releasing needs, releasing the desire for satisfaction.

The purgation continued, and grew. Arnoth's trance fluctuated and he felt his release alter, almost imperceptibly at first, then develop. His essence soared—toward a penetration, toward satisfaction.

He found a softness, yielding, inquiring . . . then giving in turn.

"I knew I couldn't do this with you!"

He sat back and shoved himself up from the mat. Sierra stared up at him, shocked. "What did I do?"

He pointed his finger at her. "You know."

She shook her head, and as his annoyance faded he found he believed her. She looked hurt. Her chin quivered. "I didn't do anything."

Nothing consciously, anyway. She'd just turned a ritual of control into a subtle dance of sexual energy.

Arnoth resumed pacing.

"Does this mean I failed to help you?"

He stopped and glared at her, though he knew it wasn't her fault. "Not only did you fail to help me, you've made matters worse."

Her eyes filled with tears. She bowed her head to hide

her sorrow. Remorse claimed his heart and he sat back down beside her. He touched her shoulder. "I'm sorry, Sierra. I shouldn't have attempted this with a non-Ellowan."

"No, you probably shouldn't." She refused to meet his eyes. "It might have been helpful if I'd known what you wanted."

"It doesn't matter now."

Tears dripped down her cheeks. She brushed them angrily away, but more came. Arnoth ached with pity. "It's not your fault." He touched her damp face. "I'm not worth your tears, little one."

"I'm not crying about you."

Her pride pierced his heart. Arnoth eased a strand of hair from her cheek. "I understand."

She sniffed. "It's been a distressing day."

"I know." Arnoth slid his hand across her slumped back and stroked her hair. "The Tseir, Drakor . . . He was your friend. The one who loved you."

"He was." Sierra attempted to dry her wet cheeks, but her eyes still glistened. "I guess it's obvious what happened to him. He was a very gentle person. Sensitive. He must have been so scared. . . ." Her voice caught on a sob.

Arnoth had no choice. He drew her into his arms and cradled her head on his shoulder. "It's over now."

"For him." Sierra peeked up into his face, her eyes wide and young. "I'm afraid of being cloned, Arnoth. I knew it could happen, but somehow I never really believed it would happen to me. I've never had anything bad happen to me before, I've never made mistakes. . . . Everything I did worked."

Arnoth didn't argue. Apparently, she'd overlooked slamming into doors and tripping and her demotions.

"Koran came to Dar-Krona to find a way to demobilize the Tseir. I suppose that's no secret to them. But we

135

also wanted to learn whether there's anything redeemable about their race.''

"There was a time I wondered that, too. Because of my fool's hope, my world was lost." ˙

"Why is that your fault?"

"When the Tseir made war on Valenwood, I convinced our king to allow me time to negotiate. They took me prisoner, they killed my wife, and they annihilated my world. There is nothing redeemable in the Tseir."

Sierra reached to touch his face. "You blame yourself."

"My judgment was flawed."

She smiled faintly. "But noble."

"Nobility counts for nothing when your world is destroyed."

Sierra rested her cheek on his shoulder. Her hand found its way to his chest. "Your world regains life, Arnoth. Not the life you knew, but there *is* hope."

Arnoth glanced down at her. For nearly four hundred years, he had suffered the agony of his bitter mistake. It had deadened his heart and deprived him of a real life. Nothing penetrated his sorrow, nothing relieved the darkness.

Sierra leaned against him, her fingers playing with his red shirt. Her hair touched his sleeve. His heart beat too fast. Not the slow, even pace of a dormant man's, but the erratic pulse of desire. He had no right to want. Not here, not now. Not with her.

Sierra seemed comfortable in his arms. Too comfortable. "You may be right about the Tseir. I learned they are cruel, insensitive, and driven to control others. Spontaneous acts confuse them. Because of this, they rely heavily on rules, on titles, on formality. But they aren't all the same. Maybe because they originate from real people."

"Evil, ambitious people."

Sierra sighed. "Most were evil. But not all. Koran wasn't evil or ambitious. Maybe he wasn't exactly a strong-willed person, but he was kind and enthusiastic and filled with emotion."

"You did care for him."

"I did. Just not the way I care for . . ." She stopped, gulped, then jerked upright. Her small, beautiful face revealed embarrassment. Her cheeks turned bright pink. There was no doubting the end of her statement.

Arnoth had no idea what to say. He wanted to tell her he could never love again. Though she tempted him, though he found her beautiful and sweet, that part of him capable of love had died long ago. He wanted to warn her that loving him would make all her other mistakes seem like nothing.

He couldn't say a word. He couldn't reject her affection because he couldn't help wanting it.

"The way I care for . . . my planet, my people, and my family." She spoke in a rushed voice, her cheeks still pink. "That is what I meant."

"I understood that."

"Good."

She exhaled a quick breath of relief. She believed she had fooled him, that he didn't know how she felt about him. He saw no point in correcting her.

In other circumstances, if he could be another man, he would take great pleasure in teasing her until she admitted she adored him. He would give her everything she wanted and teach her things she'd never imagined, and give her every sweet pleasure.

Arnoth leapt from the mat and went to the window. His heart slammed in his chest, his blood pulsed to his groin, deepening his arousal. A fantasy swarmed his brain, refusing to surrender. He saw himself, deep inside her, moving as she moaned her surprised pleasure.

Waves of heat spread through him. He felt desire all

137

the way to his toes. He kept his gaze fixed out the window. Tseir hovercrafts moved, all at the same speed, all busy making reproductions. Reproductions intended for war.

He tried to remember their danger. He tried to focus on a way to prevent another mass destruction.

"You are a very nervous man. The Ellowan obviously have fragile nerves."

Arnoth glanced back at Sierra. She sat cross-legged on the mat. "Our nerves are strong, woman. But when subjected to this level of torment . . ."

"You crack. I know." Sierra smiled, pleased with herself, then flopped back onto the double mat. "Well, it's comfortable, at least. I might as well have a good night's sleep."

"It's not night, Sierra. It's probably midmorning."

"Days on Dar-Krona are short." Sierra looked out the high, narrow window. "But not that short. I would guess, just before noon."

"On my world, that's termed 'midmorning.' "

Sierra's lip curled. "It's going to be a long day, if I'm to spend it stuck with you." Her small face changed, as if she were scheming. She tapped her lip, then smiled slowly. She got up and went to the monitor.

"Tseir! This is your prisoner calling, formerly known as Sierra of the Twelfth, Thirteenth, Fourteenth, resumed to Twelfth again."

The monitor engaged. *"Prisoner message received. Colice of the Third Command responding."*

Sierra uttered an impatient *huff*. "I'm aware of that, Colice. . . . I can't possibly make love with this Ellowan—" Sierra paused to wave her arms in Arnoth's direction, apparently forgetting the view screen was blocked, "—in this condition."

"Clarify, prisoner Sierra," came the voice.

"I'm filthy. I stink. I need to make use of your cleans-

ing facilities.'' Sierra paused, then chuckled. ''And so
does he. Or I won't touch him. He's disgusting. That ratty
hair of his needs a good washing.''

Arnoth braced at this deliberate slight. He had no idea
what Sierra was up to, but she seemed pleased with herself. It would probably get them both killed.

''And we need to be fed. Have you ever made love on
an empty stomach?''

Silence. *''These demands will be considered.''*

The monitor switched off. Sierra cast a superior glance
at Arnoth, then sat on the mat. She lay back, her hair
splayed around her head. She crossed one leg over her
raised knee and folded her arms behind her head.

''I do not require bathing facilities.''

Sierra eyed him doubtfully. ''You do.''

''What was all that about 'making love'?''

Sierra's face formed a devious expression. ''You
won't find out looking like that.''

''I look''—Arnoth paused to collect himself,—''the
same as always.''

''Exactly.''

''Why do you want to bathe?''

Her eyes twinkled. A tiny smile appeared on her soft
lips. ''It whiles the hours.''

She meant to tease him. No, to torment him. Arnoth
suspected she had no idea how well it worked. He ached.
He remembered the large, tiled baths of Valenwood, a
favored place of seduction. He would lave her skin with
scented oils. . . .

''They'll never allow it.'' *Perfect!* Now he sounded as
nervous as she'd said.

The door slid open behind him, and Arnoth started.
Sierra chuckled.

''Jumpy, aren't you?''

He refused to respond. Colice entered the room, accompanied by four guards. ''You will be allowed to

139

cleanse, prisoner Sierra. Food will be administered once you both are free of debris."

Sierra hopped up. "Good!"

"The supreme commander instructs that you bathe together."

Arnoth tensed, but Sierra seemed to have foreseen this suggestion. "Then the supreme commander has gone too far." Sierra settled back onto the mat. "I do not remove grime and 'debris' in the presence of anyone."

The monitor buzzed. "Proceed as the prisoner demands, Colice."

Arnoth breathed a muted sigh of relief. "I have no interest in cleansing, Tseir."

Sierra stood up and straightened her shirt. *His* shirt. "He thinks bodily filth is appealing. I do not."

"You will bathe, Ellowan."

Arnoth had no actual reservations about bathing. It might help, if the water could be administered cold. "I accede to your demands, Tseir. In this, and in nothing else."

Colice stood back and motioned to the guards. "Take prisoner Sierra to the commanders' cleansing station. Watch her closely while she performs bathing duties, so that she makes no escape attempt."

The guards responded too quickly. Arnoth knew why. If he had the chance to watch Sierra bathe, he'd take it. Given the chance, the guards would vent their lust on her. He had to think of something, fast. . . . "Are you a virgin?"

Sierra stumbled as she crossed the room, steadied herself by seizing Colice's shoulder, then stared at him in utter astonishment.

"What?" Her voice was a tiny squeak.

He already knew the answer, but he had to have her response. "Are you a virgin?"

"Oh, *that's* not a personal question!"

Arnoth restrained impatience. "I know the nature of the question, Nirvahdi." He tried to stress *know*, to alert her to the necessity of answering, but apparently, Sierra missed his intimation.

"I don't think that's any of your business."

"I *need* to know."

"Do you?" She glanced at Colice and made a face. "He *needs* to know. Can you imagine?"

Colice seemed disoriented at the personal, woman-to-woman nature of Sierra's remark. "You will respond to his inquiry."

Sierra rolled her eyes and groaned. "Very well. I am a virgin. And I will stay a virgin until I die." She paused. "Why do you ask?"

"I don't touch women who aren't virgins."

"Well, aren't we picky? Probably because they don't know any better, and will tell you how wonderful you are. . . ."

"Precisely." Arnoth turned his attention to Colice as she strained to understand the significance of his sudden question. She glanced at the guards, her face knit thoughtfully. The monitor buzzed.

"*Colice, you will accompany the guards while prisoner Sierra cleanses.*"

Arnoth repressed a smile at Extrana's order. She wasn't supreme commander for nothing. Sierra obviously missed the purpose behind his query. She glared at him in suspicion and irritation.

"Can we go now?"

Colice nodded. "Proceed."

Colice stood outside the door while Sierra bathed. The Tseir woman had abruptly ordered the guards to wait outside. Braving punishment, they argued for entering the cleansing chambers, too. Sierra considered this as she engaged a warmer setting.

141

Perhaps the Tseir guards' unrestrained pursuit of violent sex explained Arnoth's sudden demand to know the state of her virginity. *I don't touch women who aren't virgins.* The Tseir wouldn't risk making her less desirable in his eyes, and they knew their guards' natures. Hence, Extrana's order.

"Makes sense."

But how did he know what her answer would be? How could he have been certain she was a virgin? Sierra chewed her lip. Because he was Ellowan, and Ellowan knew matters of sensuality. And her kiss must have been . . . virginal.

Sierra adjusted the water's pulse to a stronger force and washed her hair. The Tseir had stolen plumbing from an inner-galaxy world, but Sierra had to admit that it was a favorable addition to their own unimaginative designs.

Sierra loved bathing. She'd often been chastised for taking too much time at "cleansing duties." She wondered if Arnoth was reluctantly enjoying his bath. Sierra frowned. Probably not. He would rinse himself dutifully, and take no pleasure.

Bathing together might have been interesting. She would like to see his beautiful hands running over his body. . . . The water suddenly felt too warm. Sierra adjusted it for a cooler spray.

Colice tapped on the unit door. "Allotted cleansing time complete, prisoner Sierra."

Sierra chuckled. The Tseir expected prisoners to abide by their rules, too. "Just a little longer, Colice. I'm enjoying myself."

Colice hesitated. "Cleansing units are functional devices." She hesitated again. "In what way do you take pleasure?"

"I don't know. It's warm; it feels good. It's relaxing."

A long pause followed. "I feel nothing during cleansing duties."

142

Sierra didn't respond. She felt pity. She disengaged the unit and pressed a button that delivered a towel tray. She dried herself, wrapped the towel around her body, and left the unit.

Colice pointed at a folded uniform. "We have provided new clothing."

"I prefer Arnoth's shirt."

"Why?"

"It's soft."

Sierra seized Arnoth's crumpled shirt, turned her back to Colice, and pulled it over her head. "I will take the new pants, however."

She pulled on the white pants and secured the waistband, then replaced her old shoes. "Have you given Arnoth new clothes?"

"They will be provided for him also."

"I hope he's still wearing a red shirt."

"Why?"

Sierra bit her lip. "No particular reason."

"Red is a strong color, to indicate power."

Sierra sighed. "I suppose that's why he's never worn it before. Arnoth has power within."

Sierra found Arnoth already finished with his bathing, seated on the mat and looking irritable. His hair hung damp over his shoulders. Over her large, red shirt. Sierra smiled.

"Your skin is lighter than I thought, Ellowan. You must have removed several layers of grime."

Arnoth's mouth curved into a frown. "My skin is no different than it was."

He was right, but Sierra liked tweaking his vanity. She toweled her damp hair, then fluffed it, wishing she had a mirror. She sat next to him, bent forward, and flipped the curly mass forward, shaking it fiercely.

"Stop that! You're spraying droplets everywhere."

143

"It is necessary, or it won't dry right."

Arnoth rose from the bedding and positioned himself across the room. "Now what?"

Sierra tossed the towel aside and adjusted her hair to fall to one side. Her wet hair left a damp spot on her shirt, just above her breast. The shirt clung to her flesh. Sierra snapped it off her skin to dry it.

Arnoth's eyes looked wide, but he turned quickly away. Sierra rose and tapped the monitor. "Tseir . . . I believe you mentioned administering food. . . ."

"*Consumptives engaged.*"

Sierra glanced back at Arnoth, who shrugged. "I think that means we're going to be fed."

Arnoth frowned. "From what I've tasted of Tseir food, what's the point?"

"It keeps you alive." Sierra stopped and sighed. "I would give much for a Nirvahdi banquet. You would like that, Ellowan, since you're such a *sensual* being. We have maintained meals from every facet of our history, even into the most distant past."

"Fascinating."

Sierra suspected that despite Arnoth's dry tone, her world interested him. "Some have rich sauces, others spicy. Followed always by sweet and fluffy cakes and pies. I prefer the spicy foods myself."

Arnoth didn't answer.

"What was Ellowan food like?"

"Based on fruits, nuts, and grain."

Sierra rolled her eyes. "From that lavish description, I can almost taste it."

Arnoth cast her a dark look, but he didn't respond.

"You seem to have something on your mind, Ellowan. What is it?"

His brow furrowed. "Nothing I can consider while you're talking."

"Forgive me for interrupting you."

Sierra ground her teeth together. She was tired of trying to make friends with Arnoth. The monitor engaged,
and a guard appeared with a cart bearing food. Tseir
food. Sierra sighed.

"Well, at least there's a lot of it. Thank you."

The guard hesitated, as if surprised to receive her
thanks. He departed without a word and Sierra positioned
herself by the cart.

"Dar-Krona used to grow fruit trees, but the pollution
in the environment has rendered their produce poisonous.
A shame. Now all is manufactured. Cloned, in essence."

"Appetizing." Arnoth eyed the tray and took a portion
of flat bread. He ate it without enthusiasm.

"What time is it now?"

"Midafternoon."

Sierra sighed, then stuffed a chunk of dry cheese into
her mouth. "How long do you think they'll keep us here
together?"

"Until I crack, or they give up."

"They're wasting their time. You cracked a long time
ago."

Midafternoon passed slowly into evening. Arnoth stood
at the narrow window, staring as the white sky altered to
darker shades of gray. Sierra peeked over his shoulder.

"Bleak, isn't it?"

"The sight of the Tseir landscape doesn't inspire the
thoughts of an artist, I'll say that." Arnoth glanced down
at her. He was still contemplating something. His brow
furrowed slightly.

"Well?"

"How well do you know the geography of Dar-
Krona?"

"Why?"

Arnoth drew a restrained breath. "Just answer the
question."

145

"You take your role of prince too seriously, *prisoner Arnoth.*"

"And you have spent so much time among the Tseir, you're beginning to sound like them."

"Demoted!"

Sierra burst into laughter, clutching her sides at what she considered her vast wit. Her eyes watered. She peeked up at him. His face looked a little strained, as if he repressed humor.

"Dar-Krona, Sierra. How well do you know it?"

"Well enough. Why do you ask?"

"You should know better than to question me in this."

"Or in anything. A fish's charm exceeds yours."

"Thank you. Could you find your way around, outside the perimeters of the main city?"

"I suppose so. But there isn't much there. The toxic pools, but those are so foul that it's impossible to linger in the vicinity." She eyed the covered monitor. "Perhaps the Tseir should consider the results of their pollution and seek a way to combat it, before it's too late."

"It's good of you to consider their climate, woman. What else exists outside the city, beside the acid pools?"

"Most of the terrain is flat and unadorned. A few dried shrubs, dead trees. There are a few hills. Those have caverns, where the Tseir abandoned the useless items from past conquests. Things they deem unworthy of reproducing. There are waterways, but those are generally tarnished from the reproduction plants."

"But they get water from somewhere."

"From underground, most of it. Far from the city, the water is more or less pure. Drinkable, anyway. There are a few nut trees left in the hills, which I suppose are edible."

Arnoth frowned. Sierra wondered why her description displeased him. He seemed to be expecting something more. "What else do you want to know?"

146

"These hills—you say there are few."

"Compared to Nirvahda."

"I see . . ." Arnoth fell silent, still pondering. Sierra longed to know what he was thinking.

"I suppose it's no good asking why it interests you."

"No."

"I thought not."

Arnoth resumed a slow, thoughtful pace back and forth across the room. Sierra took his position at the window. The gray darkened to black. A small nervousness surfaced inside her, almost excitement. She had no idea why.

"It's night."

"I see."

"I'm hungry again."

"How could you be hungry? You devoured half that cart before they took it away."

Sierra's chin firmed. "I'm hungry. Tseir!"

The monitor buzzed. "*Consumptives engaged.*" Colice sounded weary. Sierra smiled in satisfaction.

"I wonder if I should demand another round of cleansing duties?"

"No!"

Sierra's eyes widened at Arnoth's outburst. "Why do you care if I bathe again?"

"Your shirt . . . hair is barely dry now."

She felt her hair. "I suppose you're right. I guess not."

Arnoth looked relieved as he began pacing again. "You're bored."

"You've got that right." Sierra moved from the black window and paced beside him. He folded his hands behind his back. Sierra repressed a smile and folded hers back, too. His head was bowed, as if in deep thought. Sierra bowed her head and furrowed her brow.

Arnoth stopped and sighed, not noticing her. Sierra stopped beside him and sighed, too. He noticed and his eyes darkened. Sierra tried not to smile. She fought to keep her expression innocent.

"Stop that."

"Stop what?"

"You know." His voice was a low growl. Sierra tilted her head to one side.

"I don't know what you mean."

He began walking again. She walked, too. Exactly mimicking his stride and his expression. She knew he was attempting to ignore her.

The guard returned with another food cart, forcing Sierra to abandon her torment of Arnoth. She turned her attention to the stale bread and wine. "Good, they didn't forget the cheese." She loaded a flat plate with bread and flavorless cheese, took a goblet of wine, and seated herself cross-legged on the mat.

"This cheese—" Sierra paused to swallow, "—isn't exactly tasty, but it's not bad." She waved her hand at Arnoth. "You should try some." Her voice sounded sticky. She took a drink of the wine to clear her throat.

"I'm not hungry."

"Good. All the more for me."

Sierra finished her meal, then approached the monitor. "Oh, Tseir! I require the private chambers."

Arnoth shook his head, but Sierra detected a small smile on his lips.

The monitor engaged. Sierra caught the end of Colice's sigh. "*Colice of the Third, engaged to direct prisoner Sierra to the private chambers.*"

"Thank you. Prisoner Arnoth requires the same."

"*Guards engaged.*"

Sierra cast a triumphant glance Arnoth's way, then waited by the door. Colice appeared, looking weary. "Follow me."

* * *

148

Sierra returned before Arnoth. The room felt empty without him. When he held her in his arms, she'd experienced bliss. So much bliss that she almost told him so. Sierra cringed at the memory. *"The way I care for you."*

It was possible that she loved him. In privacy, she had to admit this. If love made the heart ache, and race, and spin, if it made breaths short and the fingers tingle . . . Then she loved him.

Maybe those things would pass, and the sight of his face wouldn't make her ache anymore. Maybe she wouldn't live long enough to find out.

Sierra heard footsteps outside the cell and positioned herself by the door. Her lips curved into a smile. . . .

The door slid open and Arnoth entered. He didn't trip or bump into anything. "What took you so long?"

He jumped. He gasped. Sierra chuckled as he whirled to face her. He seemed to grow, to darken, as he moved closer to her.

"You do it on purpose, don't you?"

She widened her eyes to their most innocent expression. "What?"

"You hid by the door, woman, intending to startle me."

She slanted her brow in a cocky posture. "Not at all. You're just high-strung."

He looked as if he wanted to strangle her. He even leaned toward her. He stopped himself and crossed the room. "I'm beginning to think this was all a ruse."

"What?"

"You . . . the Tseir. You're probably allied, and this is a setup to drive me crazy."

"Crazier."

He didn't argue, to Sierra's disappointment. "Did you make use of the mouth purifier?"

"If you mean the instruments to clean my teeth, yes. Once I divined their purpose."

149

Sierra seated herself on the mat, looking up at him. "Clever, isn't it? It's a Nirvahdi invention." She paused. "We have very clean mouths."

"And very active."

Sierra wondered what he meant. Maybe he meant kissing. She blushed. Arnoth watched her, shaking his head. "Talking, woman. I've never met your like. You could drown out a lingbat."

"I hope Batty is all right."

"I think we can count on it."

Sierra noticed a strange expression on Arnoth's face, as if he was trying to tell her something but couldn't, because the Tseir would overhear. She tried to figure out what it was but failed.

Arnoth seemed tense. Probably because she'd startled him. Sierra endured a wave of remorse. "Do you want to try your ritual again?"

"No!" He cleared his throat. "No. That won't be necessary."

"You think I'll bungle it again."

"That, too."

Sierra frowned, but she couldn't argue. She wasn't sure how she'd failed the first time, so it was no good avoiding the same mistake on a second try. She peered up at him. He looked tense. Their eyes met and held briefly, but he turned away to stare at the door.

Apparently, the door held no interest, because he turned his ponderous attention to the window instead. His hair hung loose around his shoulders. Almost black, shiny. Sierra sighed. She remembered how it felt entwined with her fingers, as he'd kissed her. . . .

Then insulted her and threatened her life. Sierra felt restless. He wouldn't kiss her again. She wasn't sure why he'd done it in the first place. Her gaze wandered from his hair to his shoulders. Arnoth of Valenwood had impressive shoulders. No question about that.

She wished she could see more of his skin. It was beautiful, darker than her own, smooth. She hadn't had enough time to explore it last night. She'd been so surprised that he'd kissed her at all, her attention had focused solely on his lips.

Sierra liked the relaxed set of his body. His motion came easily, in perfect control. She endured a pang of envy. Arnoth of Valenwood never tripped. She felt certain of that. Her gaze traveled lower to his bottom. She liked that, too. Firm, decidedly well-formed, meeting strong thighs and hard calves.

Sierra swallowed. An admirable sight. Any woman would think so. Her reaction to his appearance wasn't extraordinary. She wondered how his Aiyana had slept beside him and not sampled the touch of his skin. No woman could resist exploring the lines of his muscles, or fingering his shiny, dark hair.

And his eyes . . . A world of emotion stirred in those brown eyes. Emotion that would intrigue the dullest female, and send a more imaginative woman into a frenzy of expectation. How could any woman resist the impulse to delve into his heart, to indulge in a search for its hidden treasures?

And it would be treasure. In love, Arnoth would be tender and skilled, because he would know what she wanted. He would teach her of her body's pleasures. . . . Sierra wasn't sure how, but she knew it would be pleasant.

I'm fantasizing about him. He threatened to kill me, and I'm dreaming of his body. This is pathetic.

Sierra's cheeks warmed. She hoped he wouldn't notice. He didn't. He just stared out the window as the cold blue lights illuminated the metallic walkways of Dar-Krona, reflecting on the dull surfaces of buildings. A depressing sight, and one Sierra had always avoided. Yet it offered seemingly endless fascination to Arnoth.

151

Her restlessness surged. She pushed herself up from the mat and went to the window beside him. Neither spoke, though she thought he tensed slightly. Hovercrafts moved in perfect unison, to and from technical facilities.

"Where are we?"

His voice startled her. Sierra eyed him doubtfully. "We're in a holding cell."

Arnoth frowned, irritated. "I'm aware of that, Sierra. I meant, where is this cell located?"

"If that's what you meant, you might have been clearer to begin with."

His jaw clenched, but he didn't respond.

"To the left are the research labs. That's where I earned my way to Twelfth."

"Admirable."

Sierra ignored his tone. "Off to the right are the re-production units, where you were almost cloned."

"Then the shuttle bays are just beyond. Not far . . ."

"That's right. Only the ground shuttles and hovercraft are stored there, though. The flight ships are outside the city." Sierra paused. "Why do you ask?"

"No reason."

She didn't believe that for a second, but she knew better than to ask. "Across the walkway is the command center auditorium, where, incidentally, I first saw your face." Sierra realized her wistful tone and cleared her throat. "Unfortunately, I spoke up inappropriately, drew Extrana's attention, and got stuck on a mission to retrieve you."

Arnoth looked over at her, his eyes narrow. "Do you mean it wasn't your choice?" He sounded insulted.

"No, it wasn't my choice. I had more important matters to consider, far more important than dealing with you."

"Indeed." He sounded even more insulted. Sierra liked the progress of this conversation. She liked affecting him, any way she could. If it meant angering him, well, so be it.

"You have caused me no end of trouble, prisoner Arnoth."

"Have I?" His mouth curled to one side. "Why did you speak up 'inappropriately'?"

Sierra hesitated. "I'm not entirely sure. An impulse."

"Motivated by what?"

Her patience crumbled. "I liked your eyes!"

His brow rose. The slightest of smiles flickered on his lips. "And you announced this in the Tseir auditorium?"

"No, I did not. I was distracted . . ." Her cheeks burned. "So I clapped out of sync."

"I'm not surprised."

Her eyes narrowed to slits; her lips tightened. "And I issued an inappropriate question having to do with their plan to capture you. In doing so, I revealed my knowledge of the Ellowan, and they . . ."

"What knowledge?"

"I had researched your race, among many others, during my tenure at the Intersystem Academy."

"Why?"

"I don't know. We were learning of the known races, those who refused entrance into the Intersystem. Apparently, your people had been contacted long ago and refused to join the alliance."

"Ellowan don't 'join.' We learn of others, but we do not follow the dictates of anyone."

"Yes, that's what I learned. You're stubborn."

"Independent."

"Irritating."

This is what she wanted. The tension between them increased. Sierra's pulse quickened. Her gaze fixed on his mouth. She dampened her lips with a quick dart of her tongue. She realized suddenly that she was leaning toward him. She straightened and brushed a tight wave of hair from her cheek.

"The desire to strike you increases."

"I see that." His voice sounded curiously raw.

"I am not certain what provokes this urge." She wasn't. "The Tseir are also irritating, yet I've never contemplated striking them." Sierra's face puckered thoughtfully. "I feel it in all parts of myself. It is a physical wish."

He exhaled a strained breath. "I would appreciate it if you restrained yourself."

"I suppose I must." She spoke regretfully. "I've never hit anyone before. Never even imagined it." She would make a fist and slam it into some portion of his body. She studied his face. "Not your face." Her gaze lowered. "Perhaps your chest."

"If it would please you, go ahead."

"You'd let me hit you?"

"You'll probably miss anyway."

Sierra made a tight fist. "I wouldn't miss."

His brow tilted. Deliberately baiting her. "You'll probably hit yourself by mistake."

Sierra drew her fist back, aiming. She faltered. "Would you hit me back?"

"No."

"I think I shall hit you, to relieve myself of the desire."

Arnoth lowered his hands to his side. "You have my permission."

Sierra frowned. "Somehow, that reduces the urge."

Her fist relaxed and she touched his chest with the tips of her fingers. She felt his heartbeat, strong and demanding. "You are afraid!"

"I'm locked in a cell with a lunatic. Who wouldn't be?"

She flattened her hand on his chest. His muscles

154

tensed. She liked the feeling. She looked up into his face. His brown eyes burned. She knew now. "I want . . ."

Arnoth clapped his hand over her mouth. *I want you.* She would have said it, and the Tseir would have heard everything on the monitor. She stared up at him, over his hand. She felt the heat of him through his palm.

His palm. She parted her lips, feeling his skin. She touched her tongue to the smooth surface and licked. Madness. He quivered, but he didn't release her. She placed her hand over his and clasped it firmly. Her eyes locked on his, she ran her tongue from his wrist to the tip of his central finger.

He was astonished. His mouth opened and he sucked in air. Sierra felt possessed by something she didn't understand. She slid her mouth over his finger and sucked. Arnoth's whole body clenched.

He jerked his hand from her grasp and seized her shoulders. *Oh, no! He's really going to kill me this time!* Arnoth pulled her from the window. "You have lost your mind."

Sierra's eyes watered with hot, stinging tears. "I have."

Arnoth stared at her, shocked. So shocked that he trembled. Visibly. Sierra was shaking, too. She couldn't stop.

"It may please you to remember, woman, that we are in a well-lit room. Outside, it is night. *Dark.*"

He meant that any Tseir passing by could see into the cell. He meant that she'd risked both their lives for the sake of desire. For the taste of his skin. Sierra hung her head in shame. Her hair fell forward, concealing her misery from his eyes.

"You're overtired, Sierra. Sleep now."

He sounded so calm, restrained as always. Despite her embarrassment, Arnoth's tone irritated her. She pushed her hair back. "Overtired? How could I be overtired? It's far more likely that I've cracked under the strain of confinement.''

"Whichever explanation pleases you."

His tone was decidedly patronizing. "I will sleep now, but only because it provides relief from your company."

"Relief is exactly what you need."

His voice sounded suspiciously raw. Sierra peeked at his face to gauge his expression, but Arnoth turned away. Her gaze fixed on his hands. She'd licked his palm, she'd sucked his finger. *What was I thinking?* She shook her head. "Not much."

He glanced over his shoulder. "Are you talking to me?"

"Myself."

"Ah. A habit of yours. I'd forgotten."

"Arnoth of Valenwood, good night."

With as much dignity as she could muster, Sierra placed herself on the double mat, rolled onto her side, and faced the wall. He shut off the light.

"Sierra of the Twelfth, Thirteenth, Fourteenth, back to Twelfth again, demoted to prisoner . . . good night."

Chapter Five

She thought she was dreaming. She had to be dreaming. Arnoth was kissing her neck. Sierra held very still, fearing to wake and lose the magic of her illusion. His lips caressed the back of her neck; his fingers softened her hair.

She didn't remember falling asleep. But it must have happened. Now his hand seemed to be on her shoulder, sliding to her side. His sweet kiss persisted, too good to be real. Little shocks of fire surged through her veins.

Sierra longed to move, to join this dream Arnoth, to kiss him back. But if she did that, it might end. She bit her lip hard to keep silent. His breath felt warm on her neck. His hand slid around her rib cage and settled beneath her right breast.

She felt his tongue on her skin. As if he wanted to taste her the way she had tasted him. Naturally, she would dream something like this. Wishful thinking. That he wanted her the way she wanted him.

His fingers touched the swell of her breast; the passion of his kiss intensified. Sierra's heart slammed, and her pulse raced. A peculiar, demanding ache pooled between her legs. She swallowed and tried to slow her breathing.

It didn't work. His lips played on her neck and she gasped. Sierra felt sure she heard him chuckle. As if in response to her quick breath, his hand cupped her breast, his fingers brushing over the sensitive tip.

Sierra's eyes shot open. She would never dream this. She'd never *think* of this. But it felt good. The demanding ache turned liquid. *If I'm not dreaming, then this is real.*

She tried to form her thoughts into a cohesive structure. If she spoke, he'd stop. Maybe *Arnoth* was dreaming, moving in his sleep.

In which case, the only honorable thing to do would be to wake him. Honor didn't come easily. He toyed with her nipple. It tightened into a hard peak. Her stomach fluttered into a spiral of nerves. Even lying down, motionless, Sierra felt dizzy.

His tongue teased her neck. She couldn't stand it. If he woke and stopped, she would hold him down and kiss him until she found relief. If relief was to be found at all. . . .

Sierra exhaled a shuddering breath and rolled over toward him. He met her, caught her face in his hands, and moved above her. Sierra wrapped her arms around his shoulders, preventing him from moving away.

"Oh, thank you! You're not asleep." She drew a hungry breath, then kissed him again.

Arnoth chuckled, low in his throat. "Hush, little one."

"Oh . . . right." He kissed her neck, her face. Sierra surrendered to perfect bliss. She didn't care if the Tseir heard. But, for Arnoth, she forced silence. She fingered his hair greedily, fearing the moment would end without warning, as it had the night before.

Arnoth's body felt hot against hers. His heart pounded, and his breath came as if he'd been running. He kissed her mouth. His tongue slipped between her lips, and Sierra met it hungrily, sucking fiercely. He lay half on top of her, his hair around her face. Something hard and hot pressed against her thigh.

Sierra recognized male arousal. She twisted her face away to see him in the darkness. He remained a dark shadow in the night. "You said that didn't work!"

"It seems I was mistaken." He stopped further words with a kiss. A demanding kiss. Sierra's muscles felt weak, shaky.

He moved, grinding his hips against hers. The pressure touched something Sierra had never noticed before. The place where she wanted him most. She arched beneath him, hoping he would touch it again. He did. Their bodies rubbed together in a primal rhythm. Sierra's senses spiraled, interwoven with Arnoth's.

His male extremity bulged beneath his leggings, as if attempting to free itself. Sierra longed to see his face. Were his brown eyes twinkling; did they shine with love? Or were they blinded with desire? A less pleasant thought.

He'd failed in his ritual. Sierra understood now what he'd been trying to control. This. Because she desired him, she had failed to help him. And now he was giving in to something he didn't want.

Arnoth buried his face in her hair, kissing her neck, his loins hot against hers. Sierra touched his hair more gently, soothing him. Her own body burned with a desire she'd never imagined. But tears stung her eyes and emerged from beneath her lashes.

I don't want to stop. Her mind raged in denial, but her heart refused. "Arnoth . . ." He didn't hear her. He kept

159

kissing her, moving his male length against her as she writhed beneath him. A hot, wild need was growing inside her.

If he does this, they can clone him. He will die. "Arnoth." Her voice was nearly a groan, but she fought for control. "Wake up."

"I'm awake." His voice was a groan, too.

"No. You're not." She pushed him back, away from her. It hurt. Her tears spilled to her cheeks. She'd never wanted anything more than to hold him this way.

Arnoth froze above her. If he came to his senses and resumed his passionate lovemaking, Sierra wouldn't stop him. She would welcome him into her body and give him whatever he wanted. He didn't move. He seemed shocked. Sierra longed to see his face, to see what was in his eyes.

Her heart throbbed, and her breaths came tight and painful. Moments eased by, and still he didn't move. She did nothing, balanced between the desire to influence his decision and to set him free.

Arnoth moved away and lay back beside her. Sierra fought an anguished sob. She held her breath until it passed. She looked over at him. From the faint light of the Tseir night, she saw that he lay on his back, staring at the ceiling. She wanted to touch him, but she stopped herself.

The silence deepened. Sierra wondered if he'd fallen asleep, after all. But Arnoth touched her face, so gently she barely felt his fingers. "Thank you."

He said nothing more. Sierra took his hand, but she found no words. She kissed his hand and let him go.

Arnoth fought his dream. He knew where it would lead. Asleep, he was powerless to affect its course. He found himself walking along the ancient, tiled corridors of Valenwood. Entering the prince's sleeping chamber. His own room, long ago. Before he had wed, before he'd lost his world.

He fought, even asleep. He didn't want to open the door, but it opened anyway. He walked inside, though he knew what lay beyond. The bedchamber opened wide before him. His long, low bed, beneath a king's canopy. A room built for sex.

She stood by the bed, young and sweet and innocent, the offering of an alien lord. Dimly, in the dream, Arnoth knew he had walked these corridors before, and found the same vision. An alien female with long, curly hair and tilted, surprised eyes.

She knew why she was here, in the prince's chambers. She was an offering, a symbol of friendship between two worlds. It was the Ellowan way. The way of Valenwood's history. Arnoth tried to stop the image. It hadn't been that way in his lifetime, but ages before, a prince would take sexual offerings and form alliances through pleasure and love.

"It is a fantasy." He spoke aloud, fighting to remind himself that he dreamt. But he couldn't break through the barrier of sleep. His old fantasy came real. The woman was Sierra, and she wanted him, too.

She wore a long, soft gown, the color of nectar fruit. A warm shade of pink. Her skin was freshly bathed and softened with scented oil. She was an offering of sex, and he couldn't refuse her. She held out her arms, though she quivered with fear.

Though he knew it wasn't really himself, Arnoth smiled, reassuring her. He crossed the room and took her into his arms. When he felt her pulse, he knew with ecstatic shock that she quivered not with fear, but with desire.

She drew back to look at him. He saw more than desire in her eyes; he saw love, ripe and for him alone. "Whatever you wish of me, I will do. Whatever you want, it is yours, for I am yours.''

He wanted to teach her slowly, to bring her gently to erotic life. But her words fueled his need, and his need was so much more desperate than he had realized. His staff was swollen near bursting. Near pain. He wanted hours to please her. Instead, he found himself lowering her to the bed beneath him.

He pulled her gown up to her waist; he bared her round pink breasts. She wore nothing underneath her gown. He positioned his aching length between her soft thighs. His staff met damp curls, a warm and slippery woman's entrance.

His blunt, hard tip pressed against her moist opening. He groaned with the force of primal lust. Her legs wrapped around his, angling her firm bottom for his entry. His staff pulsated, and her woman's mound throbbed, too. It was delicious sex, pure and untarnished. He drove himself deep inside her and her soft flesh squeezed tight around his length.

He meant to take time, to love her to sweet exhaustion. No, he hadn't meant for this to happen at all. Arnoth fought his dream with a last, desperate effort, but his silent mind took him where his waking mind refused to go.

Life demanded its entrance in sexual release. His body quaked, driving, seeking. Met by softness, a yielding femininity. What he sought, he found. She met him with sweet vigor, seeking, too. And giving in turn.

''No . . .''

Arnoth tried not to move, but she moved around him. His control shattered and he thrust into her. His desire erupted and poured into her, through her, until she became his. He would never let her go.

Arnoth woke with a start. His heart slammed; his blood burned. A sheen of perspiration covered his body. He was panting for air, as if he'd been running. "A dream. It was only a dream."

But a productive dream. Arnoth jerked upright in bed. His body had seized its fulfilment in sleep. A true fulfilment. Shock radiated through him, his fate sealed. No longer dormant, he was once again a fully living man.

Sierra slept peacefully beside him, unaware that he'd made primitive love to her in his dream. Unaware that he'd taken her like a beast, mindless with desire. His hands were shaking. If the Tseir learned, if they tested him again . . .

Arnoth felt around for the towel that Sierra had used to dry her hair. He cleaned away the evidence of his release. His shaking refused to abate. He'd prevented this for four hundred years. It had stolen his power in sleep. Desire crept over him, and he couldn't stop it.

He'd forgotten his old fantasy, but now it burned in his mind. He'd seen an image of an alien race, a race that once attempted to enlist the Ellowan in . . . in a galactic union. Arnoth closed his eyes and drew a long breath. *Of course. Those were the Nirvahdi.*

They'd sent images of their people. Young and old, male and female. Images of their buildings and flight craft. Even pets. The Ellowan refused to join their system, and the communications failed. But they kept the records in the library of Valenwood.

There Arnoth, at the age of fourteen, had found an image of a lush female with dark, curly hair. The image hadn't been clear—he couldn't really see her face—but his adolescent imagination had filled in the rest.

What he'd imagined was . . . Sierra. He'd fantasized about her, lusted for her in his dreams. He imagined arranging a tryst with her alien father. And she would be given to him, so that the Ellowan would open negotiations with the galaxy system. An unlikely scenario, he knew. But at fourteen, he didn't care.

163

Arnoth clasped his head in his hands. *I should have known.* No wonder he couldn't resist her. She'd come from his youthful fantasies, a dream he'd forgotten ages ago. But his subconscious mind remembered, and took full advantage.

What am I going to do now? Arnoth tried to ignore the life that flowed through his veins, but his cells and fibers celebrated the change. His blood moved with a new, energetic pulse. Arnoth tried to make sense of this unexpected development.

If nothing else, it eased his pent-up, burning desire. For the time being. He could make it through the night, anyway. If he didn't think about that cursed dream. If he didn't remember touching her.

He hadn't intended to touch her. She lay sleeping, her back to him. He'd waited for what seemed like hours, standing in darkness, before lying beside her. He'd fought to regain control, but all that filled his mind was the image of her lips on his palm, her eyes aglow with lust as she trailed her little tongue to his finger. And suckled.

Sierra outdid his old dream. Mindless sensuality, probably unintentional. Spontaneous. She had no idea what she did to him. He'd stopped her, and she'd looked ashamed. Embarrassed. He'd hurt her, because she fueled the dormant life in his veins.

Fueled it to the point of combustion. Liquid combustion. Arnoth slid the towel beneath the mat. He could dispose of it in the morning, when the Tseir allowed him the private chambers. No one would know. Sierra wouldn't suspect, because she was innocent. The Tseir were too dull of wit to imagine the power of an aroused man's dream.

No, they expected shouts of conquest, groans and grunts. Not soft moans and whispers.

Sierra didn't know what motivated her actions, so

164

she'd tripped into them. As she tripped into everything else. Arnoth's heart warmed with affection. That proved impossible to resist, too. She'd suckled his finger because her lithe, soft body had ached for fulfillment. Instinct.

Arnoth considered this. Maybe he should have given her a release. To quiet her. To still her mindless need. His loins tightened at the thought. Apparently, his cursed body was eager to make up for the time lost over four hundred years.

It wouldn't work as he imagined. Sensual union would engage her innocent heart. Too late. She loved him already. He had to protect her from her own misguided illusions. He was no man for her. He was cruel and ruthless, without the capacity to love. He would take her as he had in his dream, to satisfy himself.

Arnoth lay back beside her, his decision made. He had to save her first from the Tseir, then from himself. Then he'd return her to her sweet world, to the world he remembered from the library images. He'd thought it a beautiful planet, maybe even more beautiful than Valenwood.

Valenwood. The Tseir turned their attention now to Nirvahda, to their oldest enemy, their creators. With their combined stolen weaponry, and their swollen fleet and cloned warriors, the Tseir might have the power at last to fulfill their quest for domination.

Valenwood wasn't the target now. Arnoth knew with grim certainty, the next Tseir target would be Nirvahda.

Sierra woke to find Arnoth sleeping beside her. He looked content. In sleep, perhaps Arnoth escaped the darkness of his life. He looked young asleep, young and sweet. Sierra wondered what he had been like as a boy. Maybe Arnoth himself had forgotten. She felt certain she would have liked him.

More than liked him. Sierra sighed. She glanced at the

monitor. The Tseir couldn't see, because of the black tape. They could hear, of course, so she'd have to be careful not to startle him.

Sierra held her breath and snuggled closer to him. She inhaled his warm, masculine scent and closed her eyes in bliss. She nuzzled the base of his throat. He murmured in his sleep, then put his arm over her. Her pulse leapt in expectation. The monitor was covered; they could kiss in the light of day. As long as they were careful to make no noise.

Sierra pressed her lips against his throat, feeling his pulse surge as he woke. She smiled and slithered higher to kiss his mouth. For an instant only, he kissed her back. His arm tightened, and he started to roll her onto her back. Sierra ran the tip of her tongue between his lips, but Arnoth jerked back, his dark eyes flaming . . . and angry.

"What are you doing to me?"

"I'm . . ." His anger both hurt and infuriated Sierra. Her eyes stung with tears, but her chin firmed into an angry ball. "Nothing. Nothing at all."

The door hissed open and Extrana entered the room, accompanied by four guards. Colice followed just behind. Sierra's heart stopped, then jumped into dizzying heights of fear. She scrambled to the far side of the mat, away from Arnoth. He didn't move or speak.

"It's too late for that, Nirvahdi. Your desires have made themselves known."

"I was cold." Her voice shook; she felt small and strangely alone.

Extrana laughed, an ugly sound. "Did you think to fool us by your quiet rutting?"

Sierra gasped, then struggled to her feet, facing Extrana. Still, Arnoth didn't move or deny the Tseir's accusation. *"What?"*

166

"You were concealed in darkness. You did well to quiet your howls."

"What 'howls'?" Sierra paused. "That is disgusting."

"You woke as lovers, Nirvahdi. We saw everything."

Sierra rolled her eyes and gestured at the monitor. "You didn't see anything. The tape . . ."

"The tape is translucent. It covers nothing. A clever trick, don't you agree?"

Sierra's face went white. Until this morning, they'd made no mistake. They'd said nothing, done nothing to alert the Tseir to their attraction. Until she woke and kissed him. For the brief, exquisite bliss of cuddling in his arms, Sierra's life was now forfeit. And Arnoth's. "No . . ."

Tears rolled down her cheeks. She couldn't stop them. She wrapped her arms tight around her body, a futile shield against fate. "It didn't mean anything."

"Sex is your weakness, Nirvahdi. To the Tseir, it is power. We use it. You are at its mercy."

"I am not." She was. She'd proven that this morning, by betraying Arnoth's life for a moment of pleasure. To feel love.

"You were near rutting, until the Ellowan realized the danger. Your passions in the night must have been strong indeed."

Arnoth rose slowly. He walked past Sierra, ignoring her. "You're wrong, Commander."

Sierra glanced at him doubtfully. " 'Commander'?" Normally, he addressed all Tseir as *Tseir*, with scorn in his voice. She heard no scorn now.

"You mistake what you saw this morning, and misunderstand the nature of our encounter."

"You can't expect me to believe you, Ellowan."

"Confining me with this female was indeed clever. Brilliant, in fact. But not in the way you think."

Sierra peered at Arnoth. He was up to something. He'd

thought of a way to save them, to confuse the Tseir. Her confidence soared. Her fear abated as she waited for his plan to unfold.

"What do you mean, Ellowan? Your affection for this female is your weakness."

To Sierra's astonishment, Arnoth laughed. "My lust is weakness, Commander. It threatens my dormant state, as you well know. I desire neither a fertile life nor death."

Extrana looked confused. Sierra felt the same. She touched his arm, but he moved away, impenetrable. "Arnoth?"

"Explain yourself, Ellowan. Your words make no sense."

"You have won, Tseir. I am no longer your prisoner, but your ally."

Sierra went weak, astonished. He wouldn't surrender. Colice glanced between them.

"What about prisoner Sierra? Don't you wish to bargain for her life?"

Arnoth glanced at Sierra. Her face drained of blood; her pulse slowed like ice water. "Her fate doesn't concern me."

Sierra shook her head in disbelief. She couldn't speak. She barely breathed. Hurt replaced the warmth of desire, and stabbed through her.

Extrana fingered her scepter. "You were ready to mate with her. Yet you claim to care nothing?"

"Mating, Tseir, has the unfortunate effect of rendering me . . . vital. I do not wish vitality. I prefer my dormant state, and the endless life."

Extrana seemed convinced, but Colice eyed him doubtfully. "We saw you, Ellowan. You were kissing prisoner Sierra."

Sierra's ears hummed, and pain engulfed her. In this room of enemies, only Colice seemed sympathetic.

Arnoth didn't look at her. "The Nirvahdi tempted me.

168

As no doubt she's tempted many men. Maybe she thought to save herself by enticing me. But I am a warrior. I prefer the role you offer.''

Extrana ran her palm over her scepter's red globe. ''It will be done. Our victory is assured. Prove yourself, Ellowan, and the power of the galaxy will be yours.''

Colice chewed her lip, an unusual action for a Tseir. ''What of prisoner Sierra? What will we do with her?''

Extrana turned slowly to Colice. ''You have questioned inappropriately, Colice of the Third.''

Colice hesitated. ''I know.''

''For what reason?''

''Because I want to know.''

Sierra stared at the Tseir female in astonishment.

''Demoted to Fourth, Colice.''

Colice bowed her head. ''Yes, Supreme Commander. Will you answer my question?''

''Fifth!'' Extrana paused, glancing maliciously at Sierra. ''The Nirvahdi will be cloned immediately, then killed.'' She turned her dark gaze to Arnoth. ''Unless you have objections, prince? We might be persuaded to alter that choice at your word.''

Sierra held her breath. Her heart took no beat. Now was his chance to save her.

Arnoth glanced at her, his expression cold. ''I have no objections, Commander. Do with her what you will.''

Sierra stood perfectly still, staring at him while the room swirled around her. She swayed, but she didn't fall. She saw no emotion on his face; he didn't meet her eyes. Her shock took her beyond pain. The guards surrounded her, but she didn't struggle when they took hold of her.

''What do you want done with her, Commander?'' The guard sounded greedy. He wanted the sport of her. Sierra was too numb to care, too shocked to feel.

''She must be reproduced immediately.''

The guard's grip intensified. ''And then?''

Extrana reached her short, pudgy hand and fingered Sierra's hair. "Then you all may have use of her for the day. At nightfall, she dies."

Beyond hope, beyond catastrophe, Sierra still hoped for Arnoth's defense.

"If you would spare me the sight, Commander . . . Ellowan are sensitive to violence."

He had to be joking. Or maybe she was still dreaming. But when the guards pulled her toward the door, Arnoth made no move to stop them.

Colice stepped toward Sierra, then stopped. "Prisoner Sierra did well as a commander. If you kept her alive . . ."

"Cease!" Extrana's face reddened with anger. "Your sympathy is shocking and weak, Colice. Demoted to Sixth, with rehabilitation for nonconformity."

"Yes, Commander."

"Guards, remove the Nirvahdi to the reproduction facility at once and engage technicians for the procedure. You, Prince, will be taken to our First Session. You will be attended at all times, to assure your loyalty."

"I agree."

Sierra went limp, but she reached for him. "No . . . Arnoth, it will destroy you."

Extrana waved her hand at the guards. "Remove her at once!"

Sierra shook her head. "What have you done to him?"

Arnoth finally met her eyes. She saw no trace of her lover. She saw a dangerous man, a ruthless man. The man he had warned her he was, the man the Tseir believed him to be. "You have done it, Nirvahdi. What I am, I am because of your temptation."

Tears swarmed her vision. "I didn't mean to hurt you . . . I didn't know." Her voice broke, and she started to cry. If she'd caused his destruction . . . Sierra's thoughts

170

cleared, her panic eased . . . then she deserved whatever came.

She straightened and forced her gaze away from Arnoth. Her tears ceased. "I'm sorry." She walked to the door and waited for the startled guards to surround her again. "I am ready. Do what you will. I have no fear."

Arnoth watched her go. He watched the door slide shut behind her. Four hundred years of practice had made him a resourceful man. A warrior. But even a warrior had to have perfect timing. And he couldn't surrender to anguish, lest his timing be forfeit. He banished the image of Sierra's stricken face from his mind and turned to Extrana.

"Let us hasten away, Commander. I would learn of my new duties."

Extrana motioned to Colice. "Report to rehabilitation, Colice. Double-quick."

Colice hesitated while Extrana's black eyes widened in outrage. For an instant, Arnoth saw the unthinkable. A Tseir on the verge of defiance. But Colice's shoulders slumped and she bowed. "Yes, Commander."

Extrana straightened and turned back to Arnoth. "Follow me." She smiled, an evil expression. "Understand that we don't trust you, Ellowan. Many guards will accompany us to the session hall."

"I'm counting on it."

Surrounded by guards, twenty at least, Extrana led Arnoth from the holding cell. Their pace was slow as they walked along the metal walkways toward the auditorium and the session hall within. Beneath the walkways flowed odorous, red brine, fouled with poisons and chemicals. The air stank with bitter fumes.

To the left, Arnoth saw a multistoried building where Sierra had earned her way to Twelfth. To the right, the

171

low, flat shuttle bays. Just ahead, on a higher platform, the guards led Sierra to the cloning facility.

She walked straight and steady, her head high. She didn't look down or try to see him. She faced her doom without fear, as she had been trained to do. As she steeled herself to do.

Every nerve in Arnoth's body came alive. A warrior . . . But even the greatest warrior needs an ally.

Hovercraft moved just above the walkways, transporting Tseir to and from their labors. They moved in precision. Except one. It angled, then righted itself. Arnoth cast a furtive glance at his guards. None noticed the hovercraft's peculiar trajectory.

It came from the left, the research labs. It flew too low and scraped on a walkway. Arnoth cringed. The unusual noise caught Extrana's attention. She held up her hand and stopped. "What is this?"

She had no time for speculation. The hovercraft lurched forward toward their group. "It's out of control! Guards, prepare to shoot!"

The guards aimed their canisters, uncertain. The hovercraft plunged toward them, scattering the guards. Extrana stumbled back.

Arnoth had one chance. If he failed, all was lost. Sierra was lost. The hovercraft rose, then dove toward him. He whirled, and broke free from his guard.

Extrana struggled to her feet. "Weapons on stun! Fire! Apprehend the traitor!"

Already a traitor . . . The guards fired, and blasts of purple energy shot around him. Timing. The hovercraft whizzed near, low to the ground. Arnoth caught the side of the craft, then vaulted through the opening shell.

"Sir! I'm no good at braking, sir! Take the controls."

Batty clung to the speed lever, his small body straining with the controls. Arnoth lowered himself to the helm and took over. "Perfect timing, Batty. Well done."

Batty squirmed into the viewport. "You were right, sir. Operating this craft wasn't so hard. Of course, I did it once before, for Dane. Didn't have to take that one far, though. I couldn't have maneuvered this without your instruction."

Arnoth wondered how the lingbat issued so many words in so short a time. He angled the craft upward. "Now comes the hard part, Batty. Brace yourself."

Batty cranked his small head around. "They're shooting, sir. Not the purple stuff now."

"What color are the blasts?"

"Blue."

"They're shooting to kill. Hold on."

Arnoth reversed, spun back, then forward and up. The blasts went wild. He aimed for the reproduction facility. He saw Sierra's guards on the highest walkway, looking down from the ramp, confused by the bedlam below. They shoved her along the high walkway toward the entrance. If they got that far, his rescue would be in vain.

The hovercraft was a reproduction of an Ellowan vessel. A vessel perfected by his own design. He knew its limits, and its strengths. "Batty, down on the floor. There's a cord. Disengage it."

"Sir?"

"Do it!"

The lingbat scrambled to the floor and snapped at wires with his teeth. "Done, sir!"

"I hope you didn't get the brakes." Arnoth gunned the speed lever, and the hovercraft jerked forward in a burst of energy. "Up here, Batty. Keep the lever down, full throttle."

"But how will we get Mistress Sierra?" The bat's voice was a squeak as he clamored back onto the control panel, panting.

"Leave that to me. Just do as I tell you."

"What about the brakes, sir?"

"We don't need brakes."

Arnoth shoved the shell open. The hovercraft spiraled toward the guards, toward Sierra. If only he'd found a way to warn her, to prepare her. He saw her now, standing amid the guards, staring, mouth agape. He waved his arms to alert her. The guards engaged their rifles to kill.

"Now, Batty!"

The craft dropped. Arnoth leaned from the shell. The guards scattered, avoiding the craft's impact. Sierra didn't move. She knew.

"At the count of five, Batty, Lift."

Arnoth heard a squeak. He hoped it meant "yes."

She held up her arms. He reached for her. He caught her by the wrists just as the craft soared upward. Arnoth dug his knees into the edge of the craft, using all his strength to haul Sierra into the craft. He pulled her over the rim, and she fell headfirst behind Batty. Arnoth jumped in after her and yanked the shell down.

A blast of blue fire exploded at the back of the hovercraft. It jerked but maintained elevation. Arnoth seized the controls and Batty collapsed, panting, on the seat beside Sierra's upturned bottom.

"Mistress?" The lingbat hopped up on her bottom and jumped. "Are you alive? Didn't bust your head, did you?"

A muffled voice came from the upside-down Sierra. "Not my head." Arnoth laughed. He laughed. He hadn't laughed this way in ages. A deep, hearty pleasure filled his soul.

"Right yourself, woman. I have need of your navigation skills."

Sierra groaned, then squirmed around until she sat upright in the seat beside Arnoth. She looked at him, eyes wide and shocked. She looked at Batty. Then she smiled. Her smile became a laugh. It was the sweetest sound he'd ever heard.

The sky of Dar-Krona was a white fog of fumes, always. The noxious cloud formation swallowed the shuttle, but Arnoth didn't slow the craft.

Sierra eyed the control panel. "Where are we going?"

"Up."

"That's very comforting. If you head west, then south, you'll reach the hills. I assume we're going to hide."

"That's right."

Batty hopped onto the control panel. "If you'd like a break, sir, I could probably manage the lever again." He flexed his wings and flapped. "Bit of a strain, though."

"Your activity has made a larger lingbat of you, Batty. She Who Leaps High will be impressed."

Batty puffed up with Arnoth's praise. "I considered that possibility myself."

Sierra made a spot for the lingbat beside her seat. "You need to rest, Batty. You must be exhausted. I didn't realize that lingbats were such capable pilots."

Batty sat forward, then bounced onto her shoulder. "Not normally, mistress. As a matter of fact, I am the only known pilot in the history of battery."

"You did it very well."

"A few tense moments, but nothing the prince and I couldn't handle. Of course, I knew you were both counting on me."

Sierra looked at Arnoth. "Were we?"

He met her gaze and smiled. "Batty and I had a conversation yesterday, during cleansing duties."

"Clever, wasn't it, sir? Meeting you there. I assumed they'd have to wash you sometime. True, I was guessing when I picked a chamber to lurk in, but I noticed where they sent the guards. Figured they'd send you there, too."

"Brilliant."

"Thank you, sir. I thought so, too."

Sierra's head moved back and forth, following their

conversation. "This is odd beyond comprehension. I wonder if I'm still dreaming."

"Were you dreaming, too?"

Sierra's brow angled doubtfully, and Arnoth blushed. A product of his restored life, perhaps. He hadn't blushed in four hundred years. Maybe longer.

Not since he was caught with a stolen library image under his pillow. . . . His blush intensified.

"Are you ill?"

"Under strain. Where do we go, woman?"

"I don't know. Is that why you asked me about the geography of Dar-Krona?"

"Of course. We can't escape the atmosphere in a hovercraft, and Batty and I couldn't think of a way to steal a flightship."

"Even if you had, it wouldn't have worked. They're automated."

"The Ellowan models can be reconfigured. But it takes time."

Sierra tapped her lip as she considered where to go. "Our escape must have shocked them. They weren't expecting it."

She cranked her head around to look out the tiny rear port. "See, they're not following us. Isn't it lucky their sky is so polluted? They couldn't see us once we broke through the clouds."

She faced the front again. "And they aren't prepared to track us down on their own planet. Isn't that ironic? They can travel the galaxy, but they don't know their own planet."

She didn't pause long enough for Arnoth to comment. "It would have been easier for them if we had tried to take a flight ship. This entire sector is controlled by the Tseir."

Arnoth wanted to ask how much area a sector encompassed, in Nirvahdi terms, but she didn't give him a chance.

"If we had enough of a start . . . If you can reconfigure a shuttle, and we could get off the planet, there might be a way. But we'd have to get back into the city."

"If what you say is true—"

"Of course it's true! If we can get off the planet, with enough of a jump on any Tseir pursuit, we can send a message. . . ."

Batty chirped. "Nirvahda seven-nine!"

Sierra patted Batty's head while Arnoth watched in confusion. "What good will that—"

"It summons a rescue ship." Sierra sighed. "I might as well tell you now, since the Tseir aren't listening. . . . My mission here wasn't exactly approved by the higher-ups. In fact, it was forbidden. They felt, since Koran disappeared, that it was too dangerous for me."

"They were right."

"Not so! If not for you, I'd have succeeded, and he would have to agree. . . ."

"*He?* Who?"

"My father." Sierra drew a long breath. "Never mind about him. There is a Nirvahdi rescue ship regularly stationed just outside the sector. The first agents couldn't get off the planet in time to send the signal, and apparently Koran didn't try. We'd have to be quick." She didn't seem to draw a breath as she spoke.

Arnoth sighed. "The Nirvahdi have elevated rapid speech to an art form."

Batty nodded vigorously. "Impressive, isn't it, sir?" He paused, smacking his lips. "What are you going to do about food? I can forage, so I'll manage all right. True, most of the specimens I've located so far are so hard-shelled that I can barely bite through to get to the tender insides, but I can subsist on them indefinitely. Oh,

177

sir! How I long for the worm-based slugs of the Keir swamp!''

Arnoth opened his mouth to speak, but Sierra cut him off. ''I'd suggest hiding out in the hill caverns, and we can figure out a way to seize a shuttle. The Tseir use the caverns to dump the stolen items they don't have use for. There are shrubs with berries there. Nuts, too.''

''Nuts, mistress?'' Batty smacked his lips again. ''I can eat nuts.''

''Good. Water will be more difficult, unless we're lucky enough to find a spring handy.''

''Lingbats require a large amount of water, because of our speedy metabolisms.''

''Nirvahdi, too.''

Arnoth leaned back in his seat. ''I've had nightmares like this. Trapped between two talkative aliens.''

Sierra's mouth was open, to continue speaking, no doubt. She considered his comment and frowned. ''You've had dreams about aliens?''

An innocent question. Arnoth's face burned with embarrassment.

''What on earth is the matter with you? You're flushed.'' She placed a cool hand on his forehead. ''I think you have a fever.''

Arnoth cleared his throat. ''I'm fine. Ellowan react in this manner during stress.'' And after incredibly erotic dreams.

Her blue-gray eyes narrowed to slits. ''If I didn't know better, I'd think you were blushing.''

Arnoth forced a condescending expression. ''That hardly seems likely.''

''True.'' Sierra's gaze softened. ''You saved me. I haven't thanked you yet.''

''No, you haven't.''

Her soft lips curved into a smile. She leaned toward him and kissed his cheek, close to his ear. ''Thank you.''

Her whisper sent shudders of desire through his veins.

A low, rumbling snore emanated from the seat beside her. Batty had fallen asleep. Sierra giggled, then touched the lingbat's head. "Poor little fellow. Hauling on those levers must have been an incredible strain."

"If not for his efforts, we'd be dead."

Sierra turned back to him, still leaning close to his shoulder. "You wouldn't have let me die, Arnoth of Valenwood. And you know it."

His insides constricted; his throat clenched. "I wasn't eager to serve the Tseir fleet against your world."

"My world? What are you talking about? The Tseir plan to engage the Intersystem fleet when it travels to your system, not mine."

"A ruse, Sierra." She sat close to him. He felt her breath, her warmth. His pulse quickened. "My guess is that's the story put out by the top commanders, to prevent leaks of their real intentions."

Sierra's mouth dropped. "Why didn't I think of that?"

"You're not ruthless. I am. If I was Tseir, that's what I'd do."

"When you gave me up to them, I almost believed that."

"Then you'd be wise to believe it now."

Sierra laid her hand on his tense shoulder. Her lips curved in an agonizingly sensual smile as she leaned close to his ear. Arnoth held himself taut, dreading her intentions. Her little tongue flicked out to taste his earlobe. A tiny puff of deliberate air followed.

He stiffened so fast that his loose pants strained over his erection. The hovercraft lurched as his hand clenched around the gear. "Sierra, you're just making this harder."

"I noticed that."

A low groan rumbled in his throat. "Please . . . behave."

She sat back. "I will. For now. But in darkness . . ." She clicked her tongue as she settled back in her seat. Arnoth allowed himself a quick glance from the corner of his eye. Sierra had transformed overnight. No longer innocent. Her teasing had turned deliberate, and so effective that he thought he might haul her onto his lap here, forgetting everything.

He tried to remember his vow. He had to protect her. If they gave in to passion, he would hurt her far more than he had already. He was no longer dormant, but that would have happened if he'd stayed on Valenwood, if he'd mated with Helayna. He could have forced himself into copulation. Maybe.

That was the trouble. He didn't have to force himself to desire Sierra. She was a young man's fantasy come to life. Worse still, a four-hundred-year-old man's fantasy. . . .

Sierra had never felt so happy in her life. She was escaping with Arnoth, and they'd have to hide out for a while, at least. Alone, except for Batty, and he'd be off foraging for bugs much of the time. They'd bathe in springs, they'd sleep. . . . She wasn't sure where they'd sleep, but together.

Sierra sighed. Bliss. She glanced over at him. Arnoth didn't look as happy as she felt. A tremor of unease surrounded her heart, but she shoved it away. Maybe he feared Tseir pursuit. He'd relax when they found a suitable hiding spot.

"If you flew lower to the ground, I could see where we are."

Arnoth hesitated. Apparently, he wasn't as eager to land as she was. "I'm reluctant to leave the cloud cover."

"Well, we can't stay up here forever. Just lower a bit so I can see."

Arnoth lowered the craft, and Sierra looked down. The ground below was red, broken up by jutting brown rock formations. "We're over the plains. Most of Dar-Krona's surface is like this. A red desert." Sierra shielded her eyes against the hazy white sun. "Go to the left a little. The mountains should be just there."

"You mentioned caverns."

"Natural formations, and quite beautiful, really. The Tseir could have made a lot of them. They didn't, of course. They just use them to store useless items. The stuff they can't destroy, and don't know what to do with." Sierra paused. "In essence, we're hiding out in a garbage dump. But it should be interesting."

Arnoth seemed tense. Sierra touched his thigh to comfort him. He tensed more, and his jaw tightened. She moved her hand away. *I want to be with you.* She longed to hug him, to kiss his face, to lie in his arms and say whatever she wanted.

"We're free, you know."

He looked over at her. His expression sent a chill of fear into her heart. "Are we?"

"I am!" Sierra contained her emotion and forced herself to smile. "You're strained. You said so. Ellowan are exceedingly high-strung."

He didn't argue, but he sighed. Sierra's happiness faded. "What's wrong, Arnoth? Are you angry?" She didn't let him answer. She was afraid of what he would say. "I know I've been difficult. Perhaps I didn't use terribly good sense at all times. . . ."

He huffed, looking as if he wanted to comment, then sighed again. "It doesn't matter, Sierra." He looked away, out the viewport. "Are those the hills we're looking for?"

How dare he change the subject! Her heart was beginning to ache. She'd never felt this way before. It frightened her; it threatened to leave her empty and alone.

181

Sierra forced her gaze to the terrain below. Jagged hills lined the plains.

"Yes. The largest caverns are in the central hills. Go there."

Arnoth angled the hovercraft, but he didn't speak. Sierra decided to let his mood shift before pressing the subject. "We should hide the craft, then hide ourselves in another place."

"That is my intention."

Arnoth lowered the craft toward the hills, scouting for the cavern entrances. Sierra noticed a gaping black hole in the hillside. "There's one! It's a large one, too. There should be tunnels where we can hide indefinitely."

"An obvious hiding place. We'll find another."

Sierra frowned. He didn't want to stop. Well, they had to stop sometime. She could wait.

Arnoth guided the hovercraft along the hillside, along the middle range. "There's another entrance, smaller."

Sierra eyed it and shrugged. "They'll have stored the small stuff in there. Maybe that's for the best. They'd put the plumbing thefts in the larger caves."

"Plumbing thefts? Only the Tseir would steal plumbing."

Sierra chuckled. "They stole a lot of it, too, until they found something that could work on this planet." She leaned to look out the viewport. "I wonder what they put in here?"

"You'll soon see." Arnoth landed the craft and opened the shell, but he didn't get out. "You and Batty find a place to stay. . . ."

"What about you?" Her voice sounded shrill.

He didn't meet her eyes. The cursed ache grew until tears threatened. "I'm going back to the larger tunnel to hide the craft."

"You're coming back, aren't you?"

A moment's hesitation revealed his inclination to stay

as far from her as he could get. Sierra swallowed, not breathing.

"I need to hide the craft, then I'll return here." He still didn't look at her. "Stay underground, Sierra. The Tseir may send patrols."

"What if they see you?"

"They won't."

The conversation felt strained, but Sierra didn't want to let him go. She hated the uncertainty, not knowing his heart.

"We can't linger out in the open like this, Sierra. Go."

Sierra's eyes burned with tears, but she scrambled out of the craft. Batty woke, shook his small head, and hopped to her shoulder. "We'll see what we can find for food and water, shall we, sir?"

Arnoth nodded, then pulled the shell down. He didn't wait. The craft elevated and sped away, leaving Sierra standing on the red ground alone.

"Mistress?"

Not alone. She had Batty. "What, Batty?"

"The prince said we shouldn't stay out here."

"I know." Sierra drew a long breath. "Let's see what's in there."

Batty smacked his lips. "Should be bugs inside, don't you think? Good-sized, plump varieties. The crawling specimens . . ." Batty stopped and sighed. "I've been without for too long. I'm letting my imagination wander, and I'll just be disappointed."

Sierra's eyes puddled with sudden tears. "I know what you mean. Imagination is a dangerous thing."

The cavern opened through a thick, jagged entrance, forming a narrow passage into the mountain. After a short tunnel, the cavern opened into a deep hollow, the ceiling graduated upwards. Giant stalactites hung from the ceiling, glittering with half-hidden crystals.

Remnants of other societies lay strewn across the ground, propped carelessly against the rough walls. Mysterious artifacts, instruments Sierra didn't recognize, all products of Tseir conquests.

"There used to be an ocean on Dar-Krona. It formed some of these caverns. Beautiful, aren't they?"

Batty tensed on Sierra's shoulder. His small claws dug into her flesh. He quivered, then sprang. Sierra watched in horror as he launched himself across the ground, then dove onto an unsuspecting grub. She heard a chomping noise and grimaced.

Batty hopped up and down, almost as if engaging in a victory dance. Sierra clapped her hand over her mouth to keep from laughing. "How was it, Batty?"

"Delicious!" Batty bounded back to her feet but made no move to return to his shoulder position. "Didn't expect a species of that quality, mistress. As thick as it was long and tender, with just enough of a skin to give it a 'pop' before—"

"Ugh!" Sierra stopped herself. "It sounds . . ." *Revolting beyond words.* "Maybe you'll find more deeper in the tunnel."

Batty looked thoughtful and grave. "That's likely, in fact, mistress. Your instincts are very good for a human." He paused. "Maybe I should fetch a few for yourself and the prince."

"No! No, thank you. I'll take a walk and see what else I can find."

"I'll sniff out water while I'm on the hunt, then."

"Good idea."

The lingbat headed off deeper into the tunnel, and Sierra wandered around the cavern. *If this is home, I might as well make it comfortable.* Home. With Arnoth. Sierra's heart took a little jump. She wondered what her father would think of him. And what would Arnoth think of Nirvahda?

And why was she engaging in this sort of futile speculation?

Sierra shook herself, then puttered around the cavern. The Tseir had stolen items that could conceivably be weapons. She found a wooden totem, decorated by loving hands. An artifact she recognized as Zimdardri, the most recent conquest of the Tseir. The Intersystem had warning of the attack beforehand, and managed to remove the population, but all their possessions were lost when the Tseir destroyed their planet in the aftermath of attack.

Just as they had done in the first wave of ''colonization,'' when they'd invaded Valenwood. Arnoth's planet was among the first secured, because it was in an unprotected sector. A sector which had refused communications from the Intersystem. So they'd brought it upon themselves.

Sierra wondered where the Tseir stored the stolen Ellowan artifacts. Maybe Arnoth would find something he valued in the cavern. Sierra resisted the impulse to begin an immediate search. Food was more important. She wouldn't find food in the rubble.

The light of dull gold caught her eye. She fished through the rubble and found a heart-shaped instrument on a pedestal. ''A Zimdardri lyre.'' She touched the strings, then tightened them. Arnoth had mentioned harps. Maybe he could play this. She dusted it off and set it aside.

They would need a place to sleep. Unfortunately, it was unlikely that they would find anything of comfort. But there had to be something she could use to make a suitable bed. Sierra set her hands on her hips and scrutinized the area.

Maybe she'd be wiser to let Arnoth devise sleeping arrangements. The way he was behaving, he'd probably choose the far side of the cavern, if he stayed in the same quarters at all. If possible, he was colder since their escape than he'd been in confinement. But he'd kissed her; he'd woken her in the night to kiss her and more.

When Sierra thought about the *more,* her pulse surged and warmed. She wanted to feel that way again. Maybe after he ate . . .

Sierra found a small canvas bag among the rubble, then headed off in search of a meal that would change Arnoth's mind on the subject of romance.

She found twelve nuts and twenty-four berries. No water. So much for enticing Arnoth of Valenwood with a surprise meal. Sierra's shoulders slumped as she surveyed the landscape of Dar-Krona. Curse the Tseir for wreaking havoc with their environment!

Low shrubs yielded nothing. *What if we're reduced to eating Batty's grubs?* Sierra tasted one of the berries. Sour. Her lips contorted into a puckered *o.*

"Didn't I tell you to stay out of sight?"

Sierra jumped. The berries flew in all directions. The nuts scattered as she whirled around. Arnoth stood on a boulder looking down at her, his hands casually on his hips.

"Look what you've done! That was our supper."

Arnoth ambled down from the boulder and gazed at the scattered remains of their meal. "A feast."

"You said Ellowan lived on a diet of nuts and berries."

"And fruit and bread, and a large quantity of fish."

"Healthy. I suppose that's why you're so . . ." She caught herself. "Not fat." The white sun shone behind his beautiful head, its pale light golden on his dark skin. Sierra's stomach fluttered at the sight. "Did you hide the hovercraft?"

"It's hidden."

A foolish question. Sierra felt nervous, though she

wasn't sure why. She should be used to his presence. "That's good."

She knelt to gather her nuts and berries, stuffing them back into the canvas bag. Arnoth knelt beside her and helped. Their hands met, then their eyes. "I missed you."

An even more foolish comment. Worse, Arnoth didn't respond. He looked pained and rose to his feet. "We can survive on these indefinitely."

Sierra felt sick. Everything between them seemed wrong, and she didn't know why. "Did you spot any Tseir?"

"If I did, I wouldn't be out here, would I?"

"I suppose not." He was still irritating. Sierra frowned. "Why *are* you out here?"

Arnoth hesitated, but Sierra knew. She jammed the last berry into the bag and stood up. Her fingers were stained dark purple from the berry juice. She sucked her finger vengefully and eyed him with growing annoyance. "I know why you're out here. You thought I'd trip and fall off a cliff, or bumble into the Tseir, right?"

A smile was her answer. "Not at all."

Sierra flung her hair over her shoulder. "I don't think one massive cavern is big enough for both of us." She stomped on ahead of him, but Arnoth caught up with her in time to grab her arm when she stumbled.

Sierra yanked herself free and faced him angrily. "I never do that when you're not here!"

Something threatened to explode, just beneath the surface of her awareness. Her control wavered. She dropped the bag. She took a step toward him. Fire raged inside her, through her. He looked surprised, maybe even uneasy. As if he suspected her intentions, but couldn't believe them. . . .

Sierra seized his hair in her fist. She pulled his head down, twisting her wrist to pin him close. She pressed her mouth firmly against his, wrapped her other arm around his neck, and kissed him with all the passion he'd created inside her.

She felt him try to withdraw, to stop her. She twisted her wrist a little more as a warning. She slid her tongue between his closed lips. Her mouth moved softly on his, and he started to kiss her back. *I've won. . . .*

Arnoth caught her waist in his hands and eased her back. "Sierra, don't do this."

The look on his face stopped her heart. She knew what he would say before he said it. "I don't want to hurt you."

She hung her head, shame radiating through her. She turned away, but he caught her shoulder, gently, and turned her back. For an instant, she hated his gentleness. "We have to get back to the cavern. The Tseir might send a patrol at any time."

"That thought didn't trouble you a moment ago."

"Let me go."

Arnoth dropped his hands. "We need to talk."

A yawning pit formed inside her, an emptiness that ached and twisted. She knew what he would say, and loathed to hear it. "I see no need—"

"There is a need."

Sierra hated his expression. It meant the end of the world. "I don't want to talk."

"It's necessary."

He would force her to stand there and listen. . . . Sierra lifted her chin and eased past him. "Talk to yourself."

"I can't love you."

Her whole body seemed to turn in upon itself. A heat pierced her, aimed at her core. She longed desperately to hide from him, but it was too late. Tears clouded her vision; her throat constricted too tightly for speech.

With a bitter flash of empathy, she remembered speaking those same words to Koran. Maybe he'd endured this same physical misery. She'd had no idea how much it hurt. It wasn't simply saying, "No, you can't have sweets tonight." It was the end of the world.

Sierra stared at her feet, trying to muster what pride she still retained. Arnoth touched her shoulder. Again, that cursed gentleness, the cold sympathy. It cut like a blade of ice into her tender heart.

"What happened between us was my fault."

Sierra peeked up at him. "I know that."

A trace of impatience flickered in his eyes. He was trying to be calm and reasonable as he delivered this sentence of heartbreak, and she had interrupted him.

"You may not know why it happened."

Sierra drew a long, tight breath. "But you'll tell me, whether I want you to or not."

"Since you persist, I have no choice."

She held herself very still, refusing to look at him or respond. *Persist, indeed.*

"The ritual I attempted was intended to still sexual impulses."

"I guessed that. You failed."

"I failed." Now Arnoth looked away. "Without another Ellowan to maintain dormancy, my life resurged. And you were . . ."

Sierra caught her breath, her mouth opened in astonishment. "I was the nearest woman handy!"

He nodded. "Our confinement proved too much to endure."

Sierra's fists went to her hips. "I see. It had nothing to do with me."

"No."

"Why are you telling me this?"

"So you'll understand what happened between us."

"So I won't think it means anything."

"I don't want you to hope for something I can't give."

"You are the vainest man in the galaxy." Arnoth's dark brow elevated and he started to speak, but Sierra cut him off as she stepped toward him. "And let me tell you, Arnoth of Valenwood, I've seen quite a few incredibly vain men in my life. Nothing, *no one* compares to you."

"I'm not vain. This has nothing to do with—"

"Ha!" Sierra poked his chest fiercely. "Did it ever occur to you that I feel no more for you than you do for me?"

"No."

"No, of course not. You think I'm pining for you."

"Your feelings are easy to read, Sierra. I know you care for me, too much for your own good."

"Is that so?" Anger replaced pain, for the moment. "I'm not surprised. You're vain, so you would think that."

Arnoth's solemn expression changed into annoyance. "Are you saying you don't?"

"I'm saying you don't know squat about what I feel."

" 'Squat?' "

"Diddly squat."

Arnoth looked confused, and Sierra didn't explain. "As long as you understand—"

"I understand, all right. You're afraid I love you, and you don't love me, and you don't want to break my heart. Is that it?"

"In essence."

"Well, don't worry. I had the misfortune of being the nearest warm body to yours. It was purely physical. Any other woman would have suffered the same fate."

"I wouldn't call it 'suffering.' "

"No, you probably think I was fortunate."

Sierra looked up into the white sky. It looked empty and dismal, where a moment ago, it had been an exotic setting for her first love. "We need to hide. I found no water, but maybe Batty's had more luck."

"The lingbat discovered a spring deeper in the tunnel,

as well as several juicy bugs that he offered to share.''

Sierra smiled, but her face felt tight. ''That was good of him. We may end up accepting his offer.''

Sierra headed back toward the cave, Arnoth walking just behind her. They didn't speak. She felt numb, empty. But they had to go on, and stay together, and find a way to free themselves. At the entrance to the cavern, Sierra stopped.

I was happier in prison.

Chapter Six

"Maybe you'd like to tell me how you defeated the Tseir. A good story might help to while away the endless hours."

Sierra sat cross-legged on the stone floor of the cavern, watching as Arnoth examined the Tseir's junkpile. She ate a berry and contemplated saving the last for him. *"I can't love you."* Sierra popped the last berry into her mouth, then fingered the final nut.

"Do you want this?" She held up the nut, expecting Arnoth to say no.

"Thank you." He took the nut, broke it open, and ate it. Sierra eyed him resentfully.

"I was still hungry."

An unwilling smile crossed his face. "That doesn't surprise me. We'd have to find a lot more than nuts and berries to satisfy your appetite. Batty and I will have to be on our guard."

Sierra refused to engage in his teasing behavior. Her heart hurt, and she didn't want to like him. "Candor, Arnoth. How did you beat them?"

"I didn't."

"You did. The Franconian fleet was destroyed."

"It was, but it wasn't my victory."

"But the transmission—"

"Was a clever device to confuse the Tseir, to make them believe they'd been sabotaged." Arnoth seated himself on the stone floor, a safe distance away.

"Then what happened?"

"They destroyed themselves, with a little provocation from a surprisingly resourceful Thorwalian."

"The man called Dane? But I thought he was dead."

"The Tseir thought so, too. He and Aiyana survived, and live happily on Candor. They have a daughter, and named her Elena for my first wife. Aiyana sent a message to Keir asking my permission."

"And you gave it? It wasn't painful to you?"

"It would please Elena, I think."

Sierra studied his face. No emotion showed in his dark eyes, no twinkling and no despair. "You loved her." She heard her own wistful emotion and bit her lip. *"Your feelings are easy to read."*

"That was long ago."

"And you can never love anyone that much again." *Why do I speak when silence is so much safer?*

"I can never love anyone at all." He spoke with emphasis, reminding her of what she already knew too well.

"Batty says you were about to take another mate on Valenwood. Did you love her?"

"I didn't know her well enough to love her." Arnoth didn't meet her eyes. He was hiding something, reluctant to talk.

"But you were going to marry her. Perfect sense."

"Helayna is the last Nidawi priestess. It was my duty as prince. Nothing more."

"Did you kiss her?"

Arnoth glanced at her, his brow raised. Sierra refused to look away in embarrassment. She fixed her gaze on his face, keeping her face expressionless.

"I didn't get the chance. You abducted me, if you recall."

"I'm sorry. In ever so many ways." Sierra scrambled to her feet and paced around the cavern. Anger warred with sorrow. She didn't want him to think so, but she did care for him. She would have given anything for his love, to see his brown eyes sparkling for her.

Sierra noticed the Zimdardri lyre. Her "gift" for Arnoth. She started to kick at it, then stopped herself. "By the way, I found this." She pointed at the small harp. "I thought it might please you, if that's possible, which I doubt."

Arnoth glanced at the lyre. "Where did you find that?"

"On the moon of Gloriah." Sierra glared. "I found it here, of course. The Tseir must have originally thought it was a weapon, then realized it was just for music." Sierra reached down and plucked a string vengefully. "Of course, I could probably use it as a weapon."

"I know. You would play until I screamed for mercy."

"The thought is tempting." Sierra studied his downcast expression. She paused. "When you kiss, it seems . . . warm."

"You mistake desire for affection."

"I see. So . . . when you seem loving, it's just . . ."

"Sex." He didn't look at her. His long fingers toyed with a nutshell.

"That wasn't clear at the time."

"Only because you are innocent."

194

"Is that why you only kissed me in darkness, because you didn't want to see me?"

He winced, almost as if in pain. "Sierra, this conversation—"

"Is necessary." Sierra positioned herself in front of him. "It may be that I deserve this."

He glanced up at her. "Why?"

"Because of what I did to Koran. I didn't think so at the time, but I was heartless. I wasn't as crazy as you, and I didn't lead him on by kissing him and . . . more. But I can see now that it must have caused him pain."

"Love is painful."

"In no way have I mentioned love."

He started to smile, but Sierra glowered, and his expression straightened. "You don't need to mention it, Sierra. It shows."

A hot wave of infuriated embarrassment surged through her, settling mercilessly in her cheeks. "I see." Her voice came as a satisfying growl. "You think I love you."

"Perhaps it's better termed *infatuation.*"

"Or *stupidity.*"

Arnoth didn't argue.

"Well, you're wrong. You are a trial to me. You've ruined my mission, and as soon as we can find a shuttle, and get ourselves rescued, you can return to your 'duty' and I'll return to Nirvahda, and we need never look at each other again."

Curses! I'm going to cry. Sierra clamped her lips together and narrowed her eyes to prevent tears. She seized a cracked pottery urn and marched toward the rear of the cavern. "I shall join the lingbat and make use of the spring. If you want water . . . get your own."

Arnoth sat alone amid the rubble of conquered civilizations. His own soul seemed equally ravaged. He tried to

195

banish Sierra's pain, but it refused to relent. He'd looked a sweet dream in the face and turned it away. Worse than that, he'd murdered it, willfully, just as if he'd driven into it with a rapier.

What do I fear? He feared hurting Sierra. But he had. From her stricken expression, he couldn't have done much to hurt her more. Arnoth warred inwardly with his own judgment. If he'd taken her, if he'd made love to her . . . Then what? He reminded himself that he couldn't return her love.

No matter what she said, he knew she loved him. And he had thrown it back in her face. As if it terrified him. Arnoth's heart ran cold. It did terrify him. Her sweet face, her teasing eyes, the magic of her touch.

He reeled and closed his eyes. Her love unsettled him, and he didn't know why. Or perhaps he did. He had loved before and it hadn't been perfect. He and Elena had fought; she had distrusted him, and she'd been jealous without cause. Her death was the result of her suspicions.

She gave up on her life, and Arnoth set her free. He blamed himself for her death, and for the death of their world. But he set her free. His breath came tight and short. He didn't know why. He had released Elena.

He heard an echo of his dream's ending. Never, not for any reason, would he let Sierra go.

Arnoth's heart held perfectly still in his chest. He opened his eyes and stared across the dusky cavern. He had survived Elena's death and found life—dormant life—beyond. If it hadn't been for the nature of his quest to destroy the Tseir, his mating with Aiyana might have taken a different turn.

It wasn't Elena but the need to prolong life that had kept him from being a lover. Arnoth's lips parted to allow a breath of astonished air. Until this moment he hadn't realized the full truth of his situation. He wasn't grieving.

When he'd released Elena, it had been done. He had refused to allow the Tseir victory, but he had released her.

Now they wanted Sierra's world. He knew this in the core of his being. They wanted the world that had created them. For ages, they sought power. Not for endless domination, as Arnoth once believed. No, they sought power for a purpose. To challenge, and destroy, their creators.

They cloned a Nirvahdi, Koran, and set him up as military leader. They intended to clone Sierra, too. Her world was in danger. She was in danger.

And Arnoth couldn't let her go. He knew, suddenly and with grim certainty, that it wasn't for Sierra that he feared, but for himself.

I can't let you go.

He broke her heart not for her sake, but for his own. For the first time since Elena's death, tears sprang to his eyes and fell to his face. *I can't love you, because I can't endure losing you.* The lyre Sierra gave him lay on its side, a poignant remnant of a destroyed civilization.

Arnoth rose and picked up the instrument. He knelt and positioned it against his knee, then set his fingers to the strings.

Sierra sat miserably beside the dark spring. Batty dug for grubs beside her, tossing half-eaten worms to the side in search of better varieties. After only a few minutes in his company, she already knew far more than she wanted to about the various insect specimens frequenting underground springs.

She didn't cry. Arnoth didn't love her. There was no reason he should. Only that she wanted him to. He was free not to love her. It was too much to hope that two people could feel the same way about each other. As much as she wanted to, she couldn't make herself love Koran. Arnoth couldn't make himself love her, either.

He was more likely to fall in love with his new Ellowan mate. Sierra wondered what this Helayna was like. She felt certain the young woman she'd seen in Valenwood wasn't a tripper. Not clumsy. She probably didn't talk a lot. She wouldn't bungle rituals.

Sierra wasn't poised enough for Arnoth of Valenwood. She wasn't calm and reasonable. She was awkward and excitable and nervous. He couldn't love her.

So she had lied to him, to protect her pride. She'd said she didn't love him either.

Batty poked his head out of a deep hole. "What's that noise, mistress?"

Sierra sniffed. "What noise? I don't hear anything."

"Lingbats have superior hearing. It's coming from the cavern, mistress. Sort of a humming." The lingbat paused, a peculiar, almost teasing expression on his scrunched face. "Maybe you should check it out. Could be the prince is in danger."

"Arnoth . . ." Sierra leapt to her feet. If the Tseir found Arnoth . . . She broke the pottery urn, spilling the water she'd collected over her feet. "Stay here!" Sierra poised the broken urn as a weapon and raced back up the tunnel toward the main cavern.

Halfway up the tunnel, she heard the noise Batty had heard, too. But it wasn't Tseir. It was music. Sierra stopped, frozen. The most beautiful, poignant music she'd ever heard came from the hall. *Arnoth.*

If he knew she listened, he'd stop. And she couldn't let it end. Sierra crept along the tunnel, closer. Low and sweet, yet sorrowful, his music pulled at her heart until she thought she would die from pain. His pain. Sierra closed her eyes, and the music changed. It rose and wafted, and offered something beyond her wildest dreams.

All the power and beauty she'd seen in Arnoth of Valenwood was represented in his music. Sierra stood in the dark tunnel, tears streaming down her face. *I love you.*

He was all she wanted. All she wanted to know could be found inside him. And he didn't love her back.

Sierra moved slowly up the tunnel toward the cavern, drawn despite her pride to hear him. He didn't notice as she quietly approached. When she knelt at his feet, he stopped, shocked when she placed her hands on his knee.

"I lied. I love you."

She didn't care what he would say. She wasn't afraid to hear what she already knew. He paused, looking stricken. "I can't . . ."

Her fingers tightened on his thigh. "I know. I don't care."

He touched her head. His dark eyes glistened. Tears of pity, from a gentle heart. A heart that refused to open itself. "Sierra, I can't . . ."

His voice cracked. He stood up, set the lyre aside, and left the cavern. Sierra sat alone, staring at the harp, knowing she'd opened herself to more pain than she'd ever imagined. But she wasn't sorry. *I love you.* She'd never spoken those words, never felt the transformation of passion. It was worth the pain, to know the emotion.

Maybe Koran had thought so, too.

Sierra lifted the harp and bowed her forehead to the dull metal. It felt warm with the life Arnoth had given it. Warm and strong, and more beautiful than anything. Sierra held it close to her heart and wept silently.

The tears were cleansing. The bitter pain in her heart eased, accepted what it couldn't change. She wanted to know what he knew. She wanted to be a part of him. His music echoed in her brain. Sierra sat up and studied the lyre. Similar to a Nirvahdi instrument, for which she'd won two awards in childhood.

Sierra wiped away her tears with the back of her hand. She sniffed and fingered the strings. She closed her eyes and remembered his song. It started low and quiet and slow, and rose. . . .

The strings burned her fingers. She'd forgotten the pain of playing the lyre and the time it took to condition the skin to endure the scraping. But Sierra didn't stop. She longed to create what he created. The first part came easy. It came from pain and hopelessness, and for the first time in her life, she understood those things.

Sierra replayed what she remembered twice. The next part was harder. The music increased in intensity. It echoed with power, with satisfaction and yearning. She fumbled, then tried again. The notes came easily, but the performance was lacking. Each time, she accomplished expressing the yearning, but the power eluded her.

It hadn't eluded Arnoth. Nothing eluded him. Sierra stopped, her brow furrowed in concentration. She closed her eyes tight and set her fingers back to the strings.

"You're starting in the wrong place."

Sierra gasped and jumped, and the harp clattered to the hard ground. Arnoth stood behind her. Her face burned with embarrassment, but his expression remained unreadable. He seated himself behind her, his long legs wrapped around her as he reached to replace the harp.

His arms went around her, too. Sierra sat very stiffly as he guided her hands back to the strings. "What are you doing?" Her voice shook. Her fingers tingled until they went numb.

"You do want to learn, don't you?"

"I don't know."

He smiled. Curse him! Sierra jerked around to face the harp, refusing to look into that perfect face. She relented. "I would like to learn."

"I thought so." Arnoth set his fingers on the strings. "Do what I do."

"Very well."

Sierra tried to concentrate. His fingers began low and he played slowly so that she could follow. She did. She dreaded making a foolish mistake, but it didn't happen.

She followed easily. "You can start at the top and work down, or the bottom and work up. Whichever you prefer."

"I would prefer the top down."

"I thought so."

He sounded . . . odd. Sierra had no idea why. What he did, she did, also. Their music echoed together, perfectly. It began light, then moved deeper and into a dark passage. But in the darkness of the melody there was hope unexpected, and Sierra's heart lifted unexpectedly, too. She smiled.

He took her back and forth over what they'd done, and when she followed perfectly, he took her along new patterns and new rhythms. Focused on the music they created together, her pain eased. She felt his body around hers and felt safe, and his music was around hers, too.

His fingers moved faster, yet still smoothly. Sierra tried a counter melody that rose in opposition to his, then blended into harmony, then contrasted for greater power. Everything worked. Against the strength and assurance of his song, she could play and explore, and it was bliss.

He stopped, but she didn't. He placed his hands on her shoulders, but she kept playing, delighted with what she could do that she hadn't known until now.

He rested his forehead against her hair, listening to what she did on the small harp. Very gently, he kissed her temple. Sierra stopped short. Anger flared in her tattered heart. "You can't . . ."

He touched her lips, silencing her. Sierra looked around, up into his face, into his warm, brown eyes. "I lied, too."

She opened her mouth, and her eyes widened without blinking. Arnoth didn't let her question him. He cupped her chin in his hand and turned her face to his. His mouth brushed softly against hers, and still she couldn't move or draw a breath.

201

His hand slid into her hair, and he deepened the kiss. His tongue played against her parted lips until she gasped in astonishment. He wrapped his arms around her and drew her to face him. He pulled her against his body, then lifted her.

"Where are we going?"

"Into the light. When I kiss you, I want the sun on your face."

Sierra stared up at him. "You didn't bump your head, did you?"

He smiled. It was a full smile. His brown eyes twinkled as he carried her from the cavern. He looked—Sierra swallowed hard—*in love.*

"The Tseir might see us."

"They won't see us."

Sierra wanted to ask how he knew, but he kissed her forehead and she forgot her question. Arnoth carried her along the ridge of the hill to a bed of red sand, then set her on her feet. A pocket of spiny trees enclosed the spot, and the jagged cliff hung above them.

The white sun cast long shadows across the desert, turning the pale sky warm in the afternoon. "I noticed this spot on the walk back. From above, the Tseir wouldn't notice us here." Arnoth tossed his cape over the sand, then knelt beside her. "Come here, Sierra. We don't have much time."

She was shaking. It felt like a dream. "Time for what?"

"Before the sun sets."

"You've cracked, haven't you?"

He smiled and held out his hand. She took it and knelt beside him, still watching him suspiciously. "What did you mean? About lying . . ."

That glorious smile widened. "What do you think? It means I love you, too."

Tears burst across her vision, dripping to her cheeks in a sudden rush. "You said you didn't."

"I said I couldn't." Arnoth touched her face. "But I do." He seized her hands and drew them to his lips. He kissed the backs of her fingers as they wrapped tight around his. "Sierra, I loved you when I thought you were Tseir."

Sierra shook her head, unable to accept or believe what seemed beyond hope. "No. That last nut, it had a peculiar effect on you. Maybe you should drink some water to clear your senses."

He cupped her face in his hands and kissed her mouth until she felt dizzy. "It wasn't the nut."

"What changed your mind?"

Arnoth kissed her cheek, then sat back. He ran his fingers through her hair, and it coiled around his thumb. "I thought I was protecting you."

"From what?"

"From myself, from pain."

"Oh."

"I was wrong. I was protecting myself."

"I wouldn't hurt you."

"I know. Sierra, I never thought I would love again. Not like this. Not so much." Sierra's tears started again, but he brushed them gently away and he kissed her face. "Do you know how my wife died?"

"Only that the Tseir killed her when they destroyed your planet."

"If it had been so simple . . ." Arnoth closed his eyes and Sierra kissed his shoulder. "I told you that I attempted to negotiate with the Tseir on Franconia."

"Yes. It was noble, whether you think so or not."

"I wasn't alone. Aiyana felt as I did, and went with me."

"It was noble of her, too." Sierra paused. "Did your wife go, too?"

Arnoth drew a long breath. "No. Elena felt otherwise. Like Hakon, she thought we should annihilate the Tseir while we still had the chance. She was furious when we convinced Hakon to let us make the attempt."

"I suppose she had a point. Still—"

"You don't understand, Sierra. Elena's reasons weren't what they seemed. I didn't know at the time, though maybe I should have. But I was distracted by the Tseir invasion; I wasn't thinking."

Sierra studied Arnoth's face. She loved him. She didn't know him, and she longed to understand every part of him. "What happened?"

"Aiyana and I went to Franconia, and the Tseir led us into a trap. I was able to distract them and Aiyana escaped, though she didn't leave the planet. She hid and evaded the Tseir, trying to find a way to free me."

"That was good of her. I take it she succeeded."

"She did, but too late. Elena arrived on Franconia. Unexpectedly."

"Why?"

"Until recently, I had no idea. I guessed she intended to trade herself for us. But I was wrong. Elena was convinced that I loved Aiyana, or at least desired her."

"Did you?"

"I cared for her, but like a sister. I taught her the harp, and I helped her perfect her healing technique. She told me of her scheme to abduct a Thorwalian. Their parents had died shortly after Aiyana was born, and Elena was devastated by the loss, perhaps more so than anyone realized."

Sierra thought of her own childhood. She had lived protected and adored, denied nothing. "She knew she could lose everything, because it had happened already."

Arnoth nodded. "That belief ruled her, though her grandparents raised her with boundless love. Elena took after their grandfather's people, the Thorwalians, and Ai-

yana resembled their grandmother. My parents lived in
the desert, but, as heir, I was apprenticed from early
childhood in the palace. Aiyana and I understood each
other. But between us, there was never anything more
than friendship.''

"Her sister, your wife, thought otherwise." Sierra
touched Arnoth's smooth, strong face. "She was afraid
of losing you. That's not so hard to imagine."

"She was afraid. All creatures have fear, I know. But
Elena was different. Her emotion controlled her. When
she was angry, she was consumed with fury. And when
she was afraid, nothing else mattered.''

"So when you went alone with Aiyana . . . she followed you to keep you apart, didn't she?''

"That is so. But the Tseir captured her, and they
learned she was my mate. They wanted nothing from me
then, so they didn't bother to use her against me. They
gave her to their guards. . . .''

Sierra choked back a horrified gasp. She knew what
that meant. Rape; the Tseir knew no other way. "Oh . . .
I'm sorry.''

"A Tseir commander slit her throat, leaving her near
death. They brought her to me and threw her into my
cell. I will never forget the laughter of that Tseir woman,
the evil joy she took in Elena's misery.''

Sierra squeezed her eyes shut, longing to blot the image. Instead, she kissed his hand and held it against her
heart. "You couldn't heal her?''

"I could have healed her body, but her soul was shattered. When I reached into her mind to ask her if she
desired life, she said no.''

"You couldn't convince her?''

"At that level, there is no convincing. There is only
truth. She didn't want to live. Her emotion and fear and
pain was stronger than her desire for life. Hakon knew
this. He survived the destruction of Valenwood and kept

my race alive, though Aiyana and I only learned this recently. He kept records in a book, which Dane deciphered. So I know now what I didn't know for all that time. Elena went to Franconia because she didn't trust me.''

Sierra pressed her wet cheek against Arnoth's hand. ''It's not your fault.''

''For a long time, I thought otherwise. But Dane convinced me I was wrong. Perhaps there is no blame.''

''Aside from stealing your second wife, he seems a good person.''

Arnoth smiled. ''If you spoke to him, you would think I was the interloper. From the first moment they saw each other, Aiyana belonged to Dane.''

''That's what Batty said.''

''Lingbats know.''

Sierra smiled, too. She fingered his hair, free at last to touch him as she pleased. ''Is that why you don't want to love me?''

Arnoth ran his long finger along Sierra's face; he touched her lips. ''Oh, Sierra, when I was prince, I thought I could do anything. I never doubted my strength. But when the Tseir killed Elena, I learned that all power has limits. The worst *can* happen, and I can't change it.'' Sierra kissed his finger, and his dark, sweet eyes glistened with tears. ''Don't you see? They could take you from me, and I might not be able to stop them.''

''You've done a good job stopping them so far.''

''So far we've been lucky. A lingbat who happened to be a fair pilot hid himself on board a Tseir ship. Otherwise . . .''

''You question fate too much.'' Sierra nuzzled Arnoth's neck and kissed his throat. ''But you're right. Anything can happen. They can kill us both, and clone us, and the world can end all over again. That doesn't mean I don't love you now.''

Arnoth slid his arm around her shoulder. "I know. But it will be harder this time."

"Why?"

"When she asked it, I let Elena go. Sierra, I can't let you go."

Sierra gazed into his face, and her heart ached, beyond the pain of rejection, beyond anything she'd ever known. "There will never be a need."

He kissed her mouth, so softly that Sierra thought she would die from longing. "Let us not make promises we can't keep. If we have now, and nothing else, there's nothing they can take from us when the time comes."

"I'll love you whether it's safe or not, Arnoth. I'll love you beyond death, beyond anything. I didn't think about it at the time, but I made that choice when Batty told me what they were doing to you."

"When they were about to clone me?"

Sierra touched his wrist. "You see, I could have stopped the Tseir empire. I was close to sabotaging them from within, so all their flightships would fail at a critical moment. If I'd done that, I could have signaled the rescue ship, and the Intersystem fleet could have secured Dar-Krona."

"But you didn't get that far, because of me."

"Because you matter more."

"More than your world, Sierra?"

Sierra gazed into the depths of his brown eyes, and she knew. "More than anything."

"I'm not worth it."

"You don't have to be. I love you, even when you're irritating—"

"I'm not irritating."

"And when you're rude."

"I wouldn't call it 'rude.' "

"And when you're vain."

"I can't imagine how you'd get such a ridiculous impression."

Sierra rested her cheek against Arnoth's shoulder. "Do you remember what you said when I told you that you have pretty hair?"

She waited while his brow furrowed. "Nothing significant."

"Ha! You said, 'I know.' "

"A statement of fact isn't vanity."

Sierra giggled and wrapped her arms around his waist. "You were so sure I loved you, right from the start."

He glanced down at her, his eyes narrow. "You did."

"I was infatuated."

His eyes narrowed still more. "You loved me."

"Well, in a way."

"*In a way?* You loved me, woman. You've admitted it."

"I didn't know I loved you until I heard your music."

Arnoth huffed. "It was well before that."

"Part of me loved you from the moment I first saw your face. But not until today, when I was in the tunnel, in the dark, and listening. . . . That's when I knew I loved you no matter what."

Arnoth considered this for a long while. "It was there, anyway."

Sierra looked up into the white sun. The red desert had turned to the color of flame, and a dry breeze ruffled her hair around her face. Sierra turned back to Arnoth, her heart filled with hope.

"You said we don't have much time. Why did you bring me here?"

"You said I kissed you in darkness because I didn't want to see. You were wrong. I saw your sweet face when my eyes were closed. Darkness couldn't blot your image from my mind. No, I didn't want you to see me."

"Why?"

"If I'd kissed you in the light, you would see what I felt for you."

"Then show me now."

Arnoth turned so that he sat facing her. "Are you sure you want to see?"

"More than anything."

"I want everything from you, Sierra. Do you know what that means?"

Sierra looked into his eyes, and her heart burned. "If it means I'll feel the merest speck of what I feel when you kiss me, then I can ask for nothing more."

"If I offer you tonight only, will that be enough?"

"I will want tomorrow, too."

"It may not come."

Sierra touched the back of her hand to his face, then slid her hand through his hair. "We'll worry about that tomorrow, shall we?"

Arnoth cupped her cheek in his hand and bent to kiss her. Sierra caught his hair in her fingers, gently this time. She kissed his mouth, his face, then rested her forehead on his shoulder as he stroked her hair.

"I'm so afraid I'll wake and find this is only a dream."

For a reason Sierra didn't understand, a low chuckle emerged from Arnoth's throat. "If your dreams are anything like mine, woman, it won't make much difference."

Sierra peered up at him. "Do you dream of me, too?"

"I do. And the result is quite . . . powerful."

She didn't know what he meant by this, but Arnoth was grinning. He had the sweetest smile she'd ever seen, young and fully happy. It embodied his capability for mischief, for teasing, and for true love. "You are so beautiful, you know."

"I know." He was teasing her now, his brown eyes glittering. "And you, my lady . . ." His long fingers

209

toyed with the clasp of her shirt. His shirt. "But there is much of you I haven't seen."

A warm heat suffused Sierra's neck, up to her cheeks. She'd never given her body much thought, other than to rearrange it to simulate a Tseir. Some parts needed more rearranging than others. Arnoth parted her collar, then ran his finger along the neckline, stopping at the cleft of her breasts.

Sierra gulped a breath of air, then held it tight.

"This is so much easier if you breathe. . . . Fainting for lack of air would interrupt my plans."

Sierra stared at Arnoth. An odd, thrilling feeling washed over her. "Arnoth of Valenwood, you have changed."

He caught a long tendril of her hair and kissed it. "Have I? I don't think so, little alien. I think I've become again what I was long, long ago. But then, I didn't know how precious life was. I know now."

Sierra's heart filled with happiness. This was the man she had imagined when she first saw him, the man whose happiness she felt but couldn't see. She touched his red shirt and fingered the buttons. "You make even the Tseir's handiwork beautiful. There is hope yet."

Arnoth ran his hand down the red shirt. "I'm getting used to it."

"Not for long." Sierra undid his buttons and opened the shirt, baring his wide chest. She pressed her palm over his heart and closed her eyes in bliss. She felt his pulse, strong and demanding as it fueled his desire. The white sun cast its fading light on his dark skin, on his shiny hair. Sierra moved her hand across his chest, feeling his smooth, firm skin.

"You have no idea how I longed to touch you this way."

"I know exactly. You had a hard time resisting this, woman, and you know it."

Sierra couldn't argue, but she wouldn't surrender so easily to the man's self-assurance, either. She sat back and fixed her eyes on his. She dampened her lips, deliberately, with a small lick, then pulled her shirt over her head and tossed it aside.

Arnoth's mouth opened, his eyes darkened to black. He caught his breath, and Sierra allowed herself a smile of victory. "You said you wanted to see me in the sun."

She kept her voice low, seductive. The effect was admirable. His warm gaze moved slowly to her waist. Her hair fell over one shoulder, partially covering her breast. She had never sat naked in the sun, even partly naked. Never for a man's pleasure. Yet it felt natural. Easy.

Fear slid away, replaced with power. Because he loved her, she could do anything. Arnoth's hands trembled and he looked young. Her heart opened wide and she took his hand in hers, then pressed it against her breast.

A shudder rippled through him. He started to speak, but a low moan came instead. "Whatever you wish of me, I will do. Whatever you want is yours."

Arnoth's eyes widened, as if her words surprised him. Stunned him. "I have heard those words before, but only in dream. Maybe it was more real than I imagined."

Sierra touched his mouth. "Because I have said them many times, without words. I am yours."

"It is a sweet offering." Arnoth pulled off his own shirt and dropped it beside hers. She'd seen him without a shirt before, when she'd convinced him to trade. But in the sun, without shame or fear of revealing her interest, she could study him at her leisure. Every sinew, every line.

His chest was broad and strong, defined, a warrior's body. His stomach was hard and taut, firm where it met narrow hips. A large bulge pressed against his leggings, a man's arousal. Sierra bit her lip. When he moved his hips against her, that male organ stoked a strange, dizzying pleasure. Even covered by his clothing. If freed . . .

Sierra reached out to him, almost touching before she realized what she was doing. Her hand snapped back, but he caught it and kissed it. "Do you want to touch me, little alien?"

Sierra swallowed hard. "It seems . . . brazen."

"It is brazen. Is it what you want?"

"Would it please you?"

"That remains to be seen."

Sierra eyed him intently. A smile flickered on his lips, though he kept his expression serious. She shifted her gaze back to his loins. "This desire to touch you . . . it is close to the desire I felt to strike you."

Arnoth laughed. "I noticed that."

"Did you?"

"I did, and it was a torment beyond anything I've ever endured."

"Until now." Sierra placed her hand over his concealed arousal. She felt its rapid pulse, its heat. Arnoth repressed a groan, and she beamed. She moved her hand, then ran her finger along its length, from the tip to the base.

He groaned again. "Until now."

Power surged in her veins. *I can do anything.* "It would please me to see you, all of you, in the sun, Ellowan. These leggings of yours hinder my viewing."

"Brazen." His voice sounded hoarse, but he unfastened his narrow belt and pulled off his low boots. He stood up in front of her and removed his leggings. Sierra watched, her mouth agape, her heart pounding.

She looked at his feet first. Handsome feet, well made. Up to strong, clean ankles and firm, muscular calves. And his thighs—his thighs were perfection. Every muscle hard and distinct.

His thighs met his firm, defined buttocks. Not simply something to sit on, it was something that moved his glorious body, and grew stronger with each stride. And there, standing straight and high from his body, was poised his male extremity. Darker than the rest of his body, silken yet hard. Larger than she'd imagined, and thicker. The tip was blunt and full, swollen, darker still.

Sierra felt dizzy. He wasn't moving now. Sierra's gaze shot to his face. He was watching her watching him. Smiling. As if he knew the pleasure his body gave her. Sierra blushed, and his smile widened.

"Touch me now."

Breath caught in her lungs, she obeyed, mesmerized by the sight of him, by the controlled power of his masculinity. She rose to her knees in front of him, then laid one finger on the side of his erection. She heard his harsh breath, but she couldn't look at his face.

She ran her finger down its length, then back to the rim. She hesitated, then circled her finger around the swollen tip. His stomach muscles strained, tightened. Sierra felt his pulse, swift and strong. An amazed smile formed on her lips, and she closed her palm around him.

He stood before her, allowing her to explore his size, to feel his most intimate flesh. A generous man. Sierra slid her hand along his shaft, feeling its shape, its intricacies. The base was hard, steel wrought in fire. The tip was taut and swollen, yet different in texture. When her fingers touched him there, Arnoth's breath came as a gasp. That part seemed more sensitive than all the rest, so she fixed her attention there.

It worked like magic. His hands clasped in her hair; his thigh muscles strained when she increased the friction. A bead of moisture formed at the tip of him. She caught it between her fingers and spread it over his fiery skin.

The white sun left nothing beyond her sight. She saw every pulse, every flush of his skin. Another bead replaced the first. She applied it likewise. Fierce heat raged inside her. She looked up at him and saw his face drawn with lust, consumed.

Sierra released her grasp and chewed the inside of her mouth. "I am brazen."

He nodded, but he didn't speak. Sierra wondered if she'd gone too far, but Arnoth sank to his knees in front of her. He clasped her shoulders, and his hands quivered. "Little alien, you exceed dreams."

He didn't let her speak or question his meaning. His mouth came down on hers, demanding and sensual. He seemed . . . hungry. Sierra felt ravenous, too. His tongue entered her mouth, slow and rhythmic, searching. Sierra answered, gently sucking his tongue, then eagerly. She moved closer to him so that the tips of her breasts pressed against his warm, smooth chest.

His strong arms closed around her. He bent her back and kissed her throat. "You are sweet . . ." He tasted her neck, then brushed his lips over her collarbone. "And soft." His kiss moved lower, over the swell of her breast. "And very beautiful."

Arnoth eased her back onto his cape, then bent over her. The sun formed a white halo over his dark head, a surreal image, as if his beauty replaced its center. Sierra reached for him and he lowered himself upon her. He kissed her mouth, then sat back, kneeling beside her.

Sierra started to sit up, too, but he caught her shoulder. "Stay where you are."

She lay back, waiting. Arnoth unfastened her Tseir trousers, then tugged them over her hips. His knuckles brushed along her thighs as he drew them over her feet, pulling her shoes off with the rest.

"I knew it. Perfect little toes. You would have beautiful feet."

"Thank you. I liked your feet, too."

Arnoth sat gazing down at her, as if relishing a feast before consumption. Sierra's heart raced and jumped, bounding in her chest. "I've wondered whether to start at the top of you and work down, or the bottom up."

"As you prefer, my love." Sierra watched him, warmth spreading through her.

"There is an alternative."

"What?"

Arnoth smiled, his brow rose. "You'll see."

"What?"

He chuckled, then caught her foot in his hand and lifted it. He kissed her toes, and Sierra bit back laughter. He ran his finger along the arch of her foot, and her toes curled. He kissed the soft skin behind her ankle, then trailed his fingers up her calves to the backs of her knees.

He explored her legs the way she'd explored his male organ, with the same delight. Sierra wondered what he found so fascinating, but every nerve tingled, centering at the apex of her thighs. His touch rose higher, toward that spot, and her anticipation built with great leaps. He wound his hand along the inside of her thighs, then bent to kiss her flesh. His hair trailed along her skin, firing her nerves to a fever pitch.

He neared something, the same spot he'd touched in the night. Sierra held her breath, waiting, but he sat up and positioned himself near her head. She puffed a gasp of frustration. She felt certain her head wasn't as sensitive as the spot he'd just missed. But maybe a man wouldn't realize that.

He sat behind her, cupped his hands under her arms, and lifted her so that she sat up in front of him. He was kneeling, his strong thighs on either side of her. She felt the heat of his male length against her back. The touch triggered the hidden spot that he hadn't noticed. She wasn't sure why, but that area throbbed.

She peeked back over her shoulder. "What are you doing?"

"I've gone up from your feet, and now I'm going down from the top of your head."

"Oh."

She waited. His gentle fingers playing in her hair, he kissed the top of her head. He eased her hair over one shoulder and kissed her neck. He touched her chin and kissed the corner of her mouth. As his tongue played softly against her lips, his hands slid around her waist, beneath her breasts.

She should have known. He knew her better than she did. She turned her face to his, but he didn't deepen the kiss. His hands cupped her breasts, his thumbs toying with the little peaks until they drew taut and erect to his touch.

Sierra leaned back against him. Fiery need coursed through her, coiling downward. . . . His palms replaced his fingers, making slow circles that left her aching and weak. Then his fingers again, tugging gently, then teasing, until her breath came as small moans.

He kissed her shoulder, her neck, his fingers played with her breasts, until she thought madness had overtaken her. Her back arched and he nipped her shoulder, then kissed. She felt his arousal, hard and hot behind her. She moved her bottom back against him, and he pressed harder against her.

She tilted her head to his shoulder, and the last rays of the sun of Dar-Krona fell on her face. Warmth came from a distant sun, deep into her soul. She'd imagined lovemaking in darkness, yet all light focused on her now.

His magical fingers left her breast and slid down over her tight stomach. Sierra bit her lip, hard. He abandoned another tender spot, but she trusted him to find better.

He did. His fingers eased through the soft thatch of curls covering her woman's mound, then slipped inward. Sierra held her breath, her whole body tense. Arnoth kissed the side of her neck, her chin, and his fingers played deeper. Her body had turned molten, liquid. His finger discovered a wealth of moisture, evidence of female desire.

The discovery seemed to please him more than she expected. His body drew taut behind hers as he explored her inner warmth. He parted the damp folds, delving between, sliding along the secret cleft, up. He found the tiny, sensitive bud within and Sierra cried out in astonished pleasure.

"That is the place!"

Arnoth chuckled. "It is." His touch increased its intensity, centering there, where she wanted him so much. Sierra closed her eyes and leaned back against him. He drew his finger in circles, back and forth, making the small bud pulsate with need. Her legs stiffened as she arched and moaned.

"From the top of you, or the bottom, we reach . . . this."

Sierra murmured incoherently, then reached back to grasp his hair. She kissed him, and he returned her kiss with equal passion. His finger still toyed with her; her hips writhed, her breath coming in gasps and moans. "I want . . . I want more."

Arnoth eased her to her back. "You want me."

"I want you."

He lowered himself above her, positioning his powerful thigh between her legs. It felt awkward, to lie on her back and spread her legs this way. He bent to kiss her, and Sierra forgot her position. He kept his weight off her body, but she wanted him closer. She wrapped her arms around his shoulders and arched upward, needing flesh against flesh.

Her small peak tingled; her feminine center remained hot and liquid, slippery with need. Arnoth braced his arms on either side of her, looking down into her face. "I am not worth you, Sierra. If you give yourself to me,

217

I can't promise you happiness, and you deserve happiness.''

Desire left her dizzy and weak, but Sierra smiled. ''Maybe not, but there is no one, anywhere, who can do what you do.'' She lifted her hips suggestively. ''If you leave me now, I will die.''

''Not for the world. Any world.'' Arnoth pressed his mouth against hers, his tongue moving past her parted lips, gently mimicking his intentions for their bodies. His body lowered to hers, and she felt his hard length against her thigh.

Her heels dug into the sand beneath his cape and she braced herself, but he just kissed her face, her neck. He moved his hips against her, so that his large organ rubbed purposefully over the tiny bud. She felt the slick, hard ridge sliding over her, their pulses mingling. He reached down and poised his tip against her woman's core.

Sierra's teeth sank into her lip. She forced herself to breathe. He rose up enough for her to watch what he did, so that she saw the expanse of his powerful chest, the drawn, quivering muscles of his stomach, down to the black hair that framed his thick organ. His beautiful hand gripped the base, and his dark eyes held hers as he slowly entered her body.

''Don't be afraid, little alien.'' His words came low, mesmerizing. ''I'm not going to hurt you.''

Sierra couldn't look away, or close her eyes. An enormous pressure filled her as his body entered hers. She tensed, her legs contracted, but he didn't stop. His swollen, hard tip inched between the damp folds, and she squeezed around him. Pleasure shot through her, and he moved deeper.

His eyes never left her face. Sierra watched every flush of enjoyment, every glance of lust as her woman's sheath closed tight around him. His face darkened, his eyes blazed. Her body offered an insubstantial barrier. He

218

didn't force her compliance, he just filled her, pressing against the resistance until her body opened to him.

Sierra gasped and clasped his shoulders as his length sank deeply inside her. He didn't move; he waited until she became accustomed to his size. Sierra stared up at him. "We are one."

Arnoth smiled, though his face seemed swollen with desire. "We are."

Sierra angled her hips toward him, taking him deeper inside her. For a long moment, they watched each other, neither moving. Then, very slowly, Arnoth began. In and out, with increasing rhythm. Like music. Sierra followed. What he did, she did, too.

At first, she moved with him, following his thrusts. Then she moved against him, meeting him and withdrawing to meet again. Everything worked. He took her back and forth over what they'd done, and when she followed perfectly, he took her along new patterns, to new rhythms.

His thrusts deepened, and he moved faster, perfectly smooth, bringing her close to the edge of her control. Sierra held herself still and he drove inside her. She clamped her legs around him and kept him from motion, then twisted her hips around him until his whole body shook.

Arnoth pinned her shoulders down, his beautiful face flushed with pleasure. "You, little alien, are torment beyond endurance."

Sierra squeezed around him and he groaned. They moved together, then in contrast. Against his strength and assurance, she could play and explore, and it was bliss.

He stopped, prolonging his pleasure, but Sierra didn't. She writhed and squirmed beneath him, delighted with what she could do that she hadn't known until now. She drew closer, and rapture beckoned. Her toes curled as she held tight to his strong arms.

He moved as if he had no choice, as if he couldn't stop. He moved as if it gave him all the pleasure it gave her. The ecstasy built and soared, and Sierra's body quaked around his. She cried out and arched and her pleasure splintered into a thousand fragments of sparkling light. Over and over, wave after wave of ecstasy spread through her, through him.

Arnoth drove into her, and his pleasure splintered, too. His head tipped back, his neck strained, as his body reached its shuddering release. Sierra felt the spasms of his joy as her own eased into tiny aftershocks. His thrusting slowed, his motion stilled, but she felt his wild pulse inside her.

Her breath came in astonished gasps. Her eyes opened wide. Over his head, the first stars burst into the murky sky, a crown for an ageless king. She lay looking up at him, loving him beyond anything she'd imagined until this moment.

Arnoth looked down at her. "I will never let you go."

"It's getting cold." Sierra snuggled next to Arnoth as they lay together on his cape. She didn't want to move. Arnoth reached lazily for his Tseir shirt and put it over her.

"It will be warmer in the cave."

Sierra sighed, gazing up at the dim stars. "You know, it might be beautiful here, in a peculiar way. Here, far from the Tseir city, it's pretty. Don't you think so?"

Arnoth glanced at the sky. "I think you love me very much. I can't believe this happened to me on the Tseir home world, of all places."

"It's your perfect victory over them. No matter what happens." Sierra twisted around to face him. "Does what we did here mean you're . . . unprolonged?"

"I am, yes. But not as a result of what we've just done."

"I thought you had to have sex to stop dormancy."

220

"I had to have an orgasm, to be precise."

"Then how . . . ?"

"It happened last night."

Sierra's brow furrowed. "I must have missed something."

Arnoth kissed her forehead and laughed. "I'm afraid we both missed something. It happened while I slept. And dreamt."

"What did you dream?"

"I dreamt of a woman I loved when I was fourteen. I found her in a library."

Sierra resisted a pang of disappointment. She had hoped he'd dreamt of her, but dreams unfolded beyond control. It wasn't Arnoth's fault that he'd dreamt of another woman. "You were fourteen? What were you doing in a library? I'd think at that age, you would have been practicing riflery or something warriorlike."

"A warrior I wasn't. Not then. I was overly serious, and spent too much time studying. I took my future role as king in deadly earnest. Something my nemesis never let me forget."

"Your nemesis?"

"Elena."

"You don't mean your wife, do you?"

"She wasn't my wife at that time. We were betrothed from birth, but we weren't friendly. Throughout our childhood, she was the warrior, and I, the hapless victim."

Sierra eyed him doubtfully. "I can't picture that."

"We were the same age, but she was stronger, and far more violent."

"Impossible."

"You'd have to meet a Thorwalian to understand. Elena was only one-quarter Thorwalian, but their blood ran strong in her. She tormented me from the time she could walk, and we grew up bitter enemies."

Sierra stared in amazement. "I thought you had a blissful love affair and married."

"I don't think anyone would call it 'blissful.' As we aged, the nature of our conflicts grew more imaginative, too. I stuck her in a cubicle and dropped her into the ocean, where the amber whales tossed her around until she escaped."

"Arnoth! She might have died!"

Arnoth appeared skeptical, remorseless. "The amber whales were a gentle species."

"Yes, but drowning . . ."

He shrugged, looking unconcerned. "There was air in the cubicle."

"Still . . ."

"In revenge, she locked me in a spacecraft and shot me into orbit. I learned piloting the hard way."

"It sounds like war. An amusing war, if viewed from the outside."

"Aiyana said the same."

Sierra considered Arnoth's unexpected relationship. It wasn't quite what she'd pictured. "I suppose abject loathing is better than indifference."

"The battle between us proved more alluring once we matured. We finally married as we were supposed to do and, at first, I thought that battle had turned to love."

Arnoth's voice trailed away and he sighed. Sierra rested her cheek on his arm and he played with her hair. "But maybe the battle never really ended. I thought we would find peace, but it never happened. Life became a bitter strain, until I spent most of my time at the library or at the Tribunal—it was duty, or so I told her. I kept the trouble in our marriage to myself. For that reason, even today, Aiyana has no idea of its hardships. Only the King knew, though we never discussed the subject."

"Did you still love her?"

"I don't know. I loved her for what I believed might

222

have been, but there were conditions on my love. I know it now. I didn't know it then. 'If she matured. If she gave away anger.' I didn't realize then how much a part of her nature those feelings were. But a time came when I didn't want to battle anymore.''

''So her fears grew.''

Arnoth nodded. ''It became a downward spiral. When I left her to travel to Franconia with Aiyana, the last words between us were in anger. It is a dark memory.''

Sierra kissed his arm and he wrapped his arms around her naked body. ''I am sorry.''

''In our last argument, she reminded me of something I'd forgotten. She claimed the woman in the library stood between us, and that I would never be fully satisfied with her, because my first love was given to another. Maybe she was right.''

Sierra stiffened. It was one thing to share his love with the memory of a dead wife. She felt a kinship with Elena, but this other woman . . . ''The woman you met when you were fourteen?''

''We didn't exactly meet.''

Sierra issued a puff of annoyance. ''Who was she?''

Arnoth smiled at her reaction. ''You.''

Sierra's eyes narrowed to slits. ''I wasn't alive four hundred years ago.''

''No, but the dream of you was.'' Arnoth reached out to touch her face. ''Your people contacted mine, if you remember.''

''And your people refused to join the Intersystem.''

''Ellowan don't join. But we did keep images from the communications in the Library of Valenwood. Images that included an alluring portrait of a young woman. It wasn't a clear image, I admit. But she had long, curly brown hair, and I was convinced I'd found the sweetest female in all the universe.'' A slow smile grew on Arnoth's face while Sierra waited suspiciously. "The face I imagined was yours."

Sierra's mood altered toward interest, and pleasure. "Truly?"

"And the body." His eyes moved from her face to her exposed breasts. A warm rush of expectation flooded Sierra's veins, spreading outward from her heart all the way to her toes. She glanced at his wide, bare chest, and her flesh tingled. He had been part of her, inside of her.

"That glorious image obsessed me. It became a constant fantasy. I felt certain your father would be a lord of some exotic world. . . ."

"Well, not exactly . . ." Sierra wasn't ready to tell him that her father held far greater power than a lord of an alien world. Better that they learn of each other here, alone, before she introduced him to the power of Nirvahda.

"I decided this alien lord would offer me his daughter in exchange for Ellowan cooperation. Not likely, I know. But it fueled my fantasy admirably. In ancient times, the Ellowan negotiated treaties in that manner."

"Bartering women?"

"Sex, more accurately. We were a sensual race."

"So I'd be given to you and you'd . . ."

"Make admirable use of your perfect body. I must have imagined a hundred scenarios with my alien lover. Unfortunately, I relieved the library of your image . . ."

"You stole it?"

"Coarsely put, little alien. But yes, it found its way beneath my pillow, where it became my treasure."

Sierra's eyes glistened with tears. "What happened to it? Did your affection pass?" She felt indignant at the thought.

"It didn't pass. But my nemesis discovered my theft— the library was sacred to our people—and I was exposed to the worst person imaginable. The king."

"Oh, dear! Your nemesis? Elena?"

"Yes."

Sierra shook her head, but she laughed. "What was she doing in your room?"

"I have no idea. Probably rigging it to blow up when I entered. It wasn't beyond her. But she found better ammunition in my well-worn lover's image. She took great pleasure taunting me, and informing her grandfather of my theft. She summoned him and I threw myself at her. In the fight, my picture was torn, and I lost you."

Arnoth sighed. "It was the one time I got the better of her in a fight. Normally, she wound up on top. This time, I had her pinned, and I was ready and willing to kill her, but Hakon arrived and separated us."

"There is a certain humor in this tale."

"Hakon said he spent the better part of his kingship prying Elena and myself apart, and preventing Elena from murdering his heir."

"What did he do to you? Were you punished for stealing?"

"I feared the worst when Elena displayed my theft. I sat on my bed, humiliated, but Hakon told Elena that she'd invaded my privacy, and he sent her away. Then he sat beside me and told me he'd stolen a statuette of a Thorwalian goddess from a temple when he was a boy— for similar reasons."

Sierra clasped her hands to her breast, her eyes misting with feminine tears of appreciation. "What a wonderful man!"

"I thought so, too. I admired him—I longed to be like him. Perhaps that's why I accepted Dane so easily. They are much the same."

"How did this Thorwalian become king of your world?"

"By chance, as such things often happen. An Ellowan priestess, Ariana, crashed on his planet, and he saved her.

They fell in love, got involved in a war, then escaped and returned to Valenwood. At the time, she had been betrothed to my father. He released her from their bond, and Hakon became king, with the condition that their children would marry. But my father didn't take a mate until late in life, so I was betrothed to their granddaughter instead."

"I see. So when Dane took Aiyana, did you make the same condition?"

"No. Funny you should mention that. It was Dane's solution, too. It seemed impossible at the time."

"Is it impossible now?"

Arnoth looked at her stomach. His brown eyes widened, as if the thought hadn't occurred to him. "I don't know. My body should be functional. Yours is certainly a worthy vessel."

"Worthy vessel, indeed! When will I know? Can't you use your healing skills and find out?"

"It's too soon." He looked uncomfortable, not quite as pleased at the prospect of a baby as Sierra.

"I suppose it's not the best timing for a baby."

"No."

Sierra's mouth formed a tight frown. "And I'm not Ellowan."

"That's true. But you are a very sweet dream."

Sierra fidgeted. "This girl you dreamt of . . . what did you do with her?"

Arnoth looked askance, one brow angled. "What we just did, little alien. Maybe my fantasies weren't so developed, but in essence, we . . . made love until we dropped."

"Delicately phrased." Sierra repressed a grin of satisfaction. "What did you do with her after that?"

His brow angled further still. "Made love to her again. What else?" His eyes darkened. "In fact, that might prove an admirable conclusion to this conversation."

Arnoth rolled over and eased her beneath him. He glanced over his shoulder at the western horizon. The white sun was gone, and the sky had darkened to gray. "You're right, it's getting cold. But the cavern floor is harder than this red sand. I'll bring you back there later."

Sierra braced her hands upon his chest. "You didn't discard her when you were finished with her, did you?"

"I was never 'finished.' " Arnoth stooped and kissed her forehead. "But no, in most cases my fantasy ended with her rescuing me from my prearranged betrothal with Elena. I had to travel with her to her world, to stop a war or something equally heroic. I had grand dreams, my little alien."

Sierra reached to touch his mouth. "Arnoth, you *are* grand. And if you're not heroic, no man ever was. Don't you know?"

He looked skeptical, but he smiled. "I am a warrior, Sierra. Because that's all I could be when the Tseir destroyed my world. After four hundred years, it's all I know how to be."

Sierra moved her hips beneath his. "Not all, my love. Not all."

She felt him, stiff and hard, poised to enter her. She was ready, wet and warm, and she wanted him deep inside her. Sierra wrapped her legs around his, urging him closer. "Where you go, I will follow. And when you need me, I will be there, and I'll protect you, and whatever you ask of me, I will do."

"Then take me, and let me please you, little alien. That is all I want tonight."

Chapter Seven

"Sir?"

Arnoth opened one eye and found Batty perched on his chest. "Batty?" He looked around the dark cavern. "It's still night."

"That's a truism, and no mistake, sir. Of course, ling-bats are nocturnal by nature. Thought I'd keep watch, and take my sleep during the day."

Arnoth closed his eyes. "Good idea. I'll relieve you at dawn."

Batty hesitated, then hopped from one side of Arnoth's chest to the other. Arnoth sensed that the bat wanted something. Something that didn't include his sleep. He sighed heavily.

"Yes, Batty. What is it?"

"Hate to bother you, sir, but here's the thing . . . My Dane gave me strict instructions on this subject. If I found you . . . well, not to be blunt, but"—Batty paused

and smacked his lips, as if broaching a delicate matter—
"mating, sir, he said I was to record the moment on an
image device and bring it at all costs to him so that he
could gloat and speak the words *I told you so.*"

Arnoth sat up, dislodging the bat. "You woke me to
take an image of . . . ?"

"Of yourself and Mistress Sierra. Yes, sir. Just a small
one. The thing is, I don't have an image recorder." The
bat hopped from one foot to the other. "Wondered if you
did."

"No!"

"My Dane won't be pleased."

"It's none of his business."

"Seemed to feel otherwise, sir. Said it was his right
to know."

"Oh, did he?"

"Yes, sir. He told me it wouldn't happen with the
Ellowan female, that Helayna, so I was to keep an eye
out for a likely specimen."

Arnoth stared at the lingbat in astonishment. "Please
don't tell me that's why you followed me here."

"Partly, sir."

"Well, you've gotten yourself into a lot of trouble for
one nosy Thorwalian, haven't you?"

Batty sighed. "I've thought that more than once since
we took off with the Tseir. Agreed, sir."

Sierra stirred beside Arnoth. Her long legs stretched,
then slid over his. She nuzzled his shoulder as her
breathing deepened. Her soft lips pressed against his flesh
in a leisurely fashion. Arnoth eyed the lingbat.

"It would be a shame if the Tseir sent a night patrol
and we were all captured because of you."

"It would, sir."

Sierra opened her eyes and yawned. "Is it morning?"

Arnoth glared at the lingbat. "Not quite."

"Hello, Batty. What's the matter?"

229

"Just questioning the prince on the matter of an image recorder."

Sierra propped herself up on her elbow. Her dark hair curled over her shoulder, brushing Arnoth's skin. Four hundred years of celibacy needed correction, and needed it now.

"Rodent, take the watch."

Both Batty and Sierra ignored his order. Batty hopped onto Sierra's hip, then eased upward, assuming a friendly posture. "What do you want with an image recorder, Batty?"

Batty tilted his small, innocent head to one side. "It's not what I want, it's what my human wants. That would be Dane. Fine fellow. *Fine.*" Batty paused, allowing the presumed anticipation of his disclosure to grow. Arnoth clenched his fists, imagining his fingers around the bat's thin neck.

"As I say, my Dane is a *fine* human."

"You said it, all right. Several times."

Sierra looked from Arnoth to Batty. "What does your Dane have to do with an image device?"

Batty hopped to Sierra's shoulder and looked directly down into her face. "He wants a shot of you and the prince, mistress." Sierra's eyes opened wide, but Batty's opened wider. "Now, as I say, he's a *fine*—"

Arnoth rolled his eyes and groaned. "Nosy . . ."

"Human, but he can be a bit . . . temperamental. If I don't follow through . . ."

"He'll wring your neck."

Sierra turned to Arnoth. "You said he was *wonderful,* like Hakon."

Batty leveled a dubious look in Arnoth's direction. "Did you, sir? Think he'd want that recorded, too?"

"I didn't say wonderful, precisely. And that was before this disclosure."

Sierra considered the bat's dilemma with surprising

earnestness. "We don't have an image device, Batty. If we escape Dar-Krona and reach Nirvahda, you can take a picture of us together." Sierra paused. "Well, standing together, that sort of thing . . . If we don't escape, you won't see Dane again, anyway, so you won't have to worry about incurring his wrath."

"Good point, mistress." Batty hopped down from Sierra's shoulder, then turned back, wings folded. "Don't know about the 'standing together,' though. He did request mating shots."

"Did he? The nerve!"

"And a full report. By the way, sir . . . You didn't happen to crawl on your knees and beg Mistress Sierra for anything, did you?"

"No, I did not."

Sierra chuckled. "Not exactly. He was on his knees for a bit."

"Was he? I'll add that to the report, then. Thank you, mistress. You're a good one to deal with, and no mistake! On his knees . . ." Batty uttered a chortling noise that sounded like a chuckle. "My Dane will value that part."

Arnoth tensed, but Sierra patted his knee. Her hand slid up his thigh, and Arnoth relented. Batty hopped from the cavern, and Arnoth sighed. "Well, at least our deaths will deprive that treacherous Thorwalian of taking pleasure at my expense."

"I thought you cared for him."

"I'd forgotten how infuriating Dane Calydon could be."

"Just out of curiosity, what did you do to him?"

Arnoth eyed her indignantly. "Why do you assume I did anything to him?"

"I remember what you did to Elena, sticking her in a cubicle and tossing her to the whales."

"Oh, that . . ." Arnoth's lips curved in a smile of satisfaction. "I did nothing similar to Dane." He paused.

"Except hold a rapier to his throat and force him to face our tribunal—where I had Aiyana explain their first night together in excruciating detail while he squirmed like a fish on a hook."

Sierra burst into laughter. "Oh, nothing, *really...*"

Arnoth slipped his arm around her. "It was enjoyable, I must admit."

The first light of morning broke through the murky sky, illuminating Sierra's face and tousled hair. She settled her head on his shoulder, and Arnoth's heart filled with love. He felt alive, truly alive. He remembered the young man he had been, ages ago. He remembered the hopes and passionate dreams, and they came real in his arms.

Sierra pressed a leisurely kiss on his shoulder, then his chest. Her long, soft hair tickled his skin; her lips sent fire along his veins. "I suppose I can tolerate the Thorwalian's gloating for the sake of this night."

"I would like to see you together. It must be an amusing sight. What does he look like?"

"An enormous, hulking barbarian warrior with shaggy blond hair and annoying bright blue eyes."

"He sounds rather frightening."

"Unfortunately, his giant size is accompanied by a rather boyish and youthful face, which a woman might favor, if her senses were addled beyond measure."

"In other words, he's cute."

Arnoth grimaced. "I never, ever called Dane Calydon 'cute.' "

"You did." Sierra started to sit up. "Batty!"

Arnoth clamped his hand over her mouth and pulled her down beside him. She laughed, and he laughed, too. "You are just the kind of demonic female he wished on me. I should have known. That man has a way of getting what he wants."

Sierra slid her hand down between their bodies and

clasped him in a firm grip. "As long as I get what I want, too."

Arnoth groaned when her fingers squeezed tight around him. "Whatever you want."

She moved her wrist and massaged him, and Arnoth caught his breath as hot desire flooded through him.

"You know what I want, Ellowan. You've taught me very well."

"I've barely begun." Arnoth seized her hand and pinned her wrists at her side. "We've only sampled a small portion of your sweet body's delights, little alien."

Her eyes widened in a satisfying manner. "There's more?"

"There's more."

Arnoth propped himself up on his elbow and eased a portion of her tangled hair from her forehead. He touched her lips. "We've discovered the secrets of your lips, how sweet and soft, and how perfect for kissing." He bent and touched his mouth to hers, but when she reached to pull him closer, he put her hands back to her side.

"I'm not finished." He ran his hand down her throat, pausing to feel the swift pulse beneath her delicate skin. "Your neck is particularly sensitive." He kissed her neck, too.

"I like that."

Arnoth breathed close to her ear. "I know."

He trailed his finger from the base of her throat to the swell of her breast, and Sierra's breath quickened. "I like that, too."

He drew a light circle around her firm, round breast, then moved to the other. The morning light grew stronger, revealing her golden skin, flushed with arousal. He let his hand brush her nipple and watched as it hardened into a taut peak. His own arousal doubled at the sight.

"Another sensitive spot."

Sierra caught her breath as he idly drew his finger back and forth across the little peak. "I like that, too."

He cupped her breast in his hand, feeling its weight, then bent to lave his tongue across the tip. Sierra tensed and gripped his hair. He suckled gently, and her grip tightened. He lashed his tongue across the hard little peak, and a ragged moan tore from her throat.

He moved back to look at her. Her beautiful face was alive with passion, her eyes tilted and burning. Her breath came quick through parted, soft lips, and her hair fell around her face like a raging, dark sea. She was exotic and alien, sweet and . . . his.

I will never let you go. Arnoth gazed into her eyes and knew he was a warrior no longer. He was a man, the man he was born to be. In the land of his most bitter enemy, his oldest dream had come true and lay naked before him.

He moved lower and kissed her stomach. Her muscles quivered and tensed as he tasted her flesh. She smelled warm and feminine, a sweet temptation to his senses. Her fingers eased their grip as he moved lower still, then tugged at his hair when he kissed the softness of her inner thigh.

Arnoth glanced up at her. Her eyes widened, and she chewed her lip. She had no idea what he intended. Her innocence fueled his desire. He positioned himself between her legs. She expected him to enter her, but he bent to part her exquisite pink folds with his fingers. Like a new flower opening to the sun, her sweet nectar beckoned and promised fulfillment beyond any dream.

Arnoth trailed his finger along the moist pink cleft, then circled the tiny bud. Sierra uttered a shivering moan, her legs tensing. Arnoth repeated the act, slower. She quivered and murmured his name.

He let her feel his breath close to her woman's core. Her little toes curled tight in anticipation. He tasted her so gently that he thought the restraint might shatter him.

He felt every tiny shudder, he heard every raspy moan as he licked and teased. Her legs wrapped over his shoulders, she arched and writhed, and her feminine center pulsated with furious need.

He felt the first spasms of her climax and slid his finger into her sheath. She squeezed tight around the probe, arching and twisting as the rapturous waves surged through her delectable body. She was ready: she was his. Arnoth rose above her, poised to enter her, to drive them both to mindless oblivion.

"Sir! Oh, help, help!"

Arnoth jerked up and snapped his cape over Sierra's trembling body. The lingbat bounded into the cavern just as he'd covered his own arousal with the red shirt. *I'm covering myself from a rodent* . . . "This had better be important, bat."

His ragged growl startled the lingbat, but it didn't slow the creature's bouncing advance. "Sir, they're coming!"

Sierra jumped up, heedless of the nudity Arnoth tried to conceal. She yanked his old shirt over her head and tugged on her Tseir pants. "Arnoth! Get dressed. We have to get out of here!"

"Mistress . . ." Batty choked between gasps, keeling to one side, then the other. "Mistress, there's no time. There's a hovercraft, and four guards. They landed out where you and the prince were . . ."

She turned to Arnoth, her eyes wide. "What do we do? We can't hide in here. Their instruments can detect anything alive."

Arnoth pulled on his Tseir clothing, his mind racing for a way to prevent the inevitable. Outside the cavern entrance, he heard the Tseir approach. There was no escape. They could hide, but not for long.

Sierra looked toward the entrance, then back at him. She touched his face. "Whatever happens, I am part of you and you are part of me. Nothing they can do will truly separate us, or change what we've found.''

He feared this moment, knew it would come. But now that it was here, and he was no longer a warrior, Arnoth knew he would never be defeated. ''I will not lose you. You and I will have more than a memory.''

The warrior was gone, but the man remained. His thoughts flashed to Dane, and what he had learned from the young Thorwalian. *Make no comparisons to the past, adapt to what you have, and you can always win.*

''The unexpected . . .'' Arnoth's mind worked in a flourish. He rummaged through the discarded treasures and seized the broken Zimdardri totem.

''Follow me.''

Arnoth raced toward the tunnel at the rear of the cavern. ''Batty, up to the ceiling. . . . Sierra, you stay behind me.''

She was smiling. ''I don't think so.'' She grabbed the harp and positioned herself inside the rear tunnel entrance. '' 'Aggressive,' remember?''

It was too late to stop her. Maybe he had no right, anyway. Arnoth crept to the other side of the tunnel. Batty hung upside down above them, ready. . . .

The Tseir guards entered the cavern poised for attack, canisters aimed as they spread out. ''They're in here. . . . Instrumentation shows positive.''

''In the back.''

Arnoth kept his gaze on Sierra. She gripped the harp in both hands, holding it near her chest. The Tseir came closer, moving slowly, cautiously. ''They're not armed. Dig them out!''

She looked at him expectantly. He shook his head. Above him came Batty's hoarse, raspy pants. But they were the pants of a small warrior, and not fearful.

Arnoth nodded to the lingbat. The first Tseir approached the tunnel entrance. Batty squealed and dove into the guard's helmeted face. The guards fired blind,

the blasts ricocheting off the cavern walls. Arnoth leapt
from the tunnel and knocked a guard to the ground.

Sierra jumped out after him. He whirled in time to see
her smash the small harp over another guard's head. Two
fell. The third aimed his canister to kill. Arnoth wielded
the broken totem like a club, and the Tseir crumpled to
the hard ground.

.The last guard pulled out a small device.

"He's calling the commanders! No!" Sierra didn't
wait. She drew her arm back, then flung her harp toward
the guard. The harp spun through the air and struck the
device with a whirling vengeance. It was ripped from the
Tseir's hands and shattered on the cavern floor.

The Tseir recognized defeat and raced from the cavern.
Arnoth bounded after him, but Sierra seized one of the
fallen guard's canisters. If the Tseir reached his hovercraft and escaped, they had no chance. . . .

"Arnoth!"

He turned, and Sierra threw him the weapon. He
caught it in midair and turned just as the Tseir craft elevated. He aimed the canister, his hand steady and sure
despite his desperation. The craft turned, rising. Arnoth
knew the craft—it was cloned from an Ellowan design.
He knew every inch. He aimed the canister and fired.

The blue blast struck the rear of the craft. It sputtered,
then reeled to the side, its tail on fire. The black metal
screeched, then exploded in a mass of fumes and fire.
The first battle was theirs.

Sierra ran to his side, and he dropped the canister. He
pulled her into his arms and cradled her head on his
shoulder. "We stopped them. Arnoth . . ." Sierra wiped
away her tears, then drew back to look at him. "Now
what?"

Arnoth glanced back at the cavern. "Now it's time to
take a few risks."

Her mouth dropped open. "What do you call what we just did?"

"Necessity, little alien. But we need to get off this planet. That means we need a flightship. And that means we've got to get back into the Tseir city." Sierra looked at him as if he'd lost his mind. He took her hands and kissed them. "And I think I know how."

"I don't like it. It was bad enough to pose as a commander. This helmet is worse than a wig."

Arnoth lifted his visor and studied Sierra. "It's a lucky thing you're tall enough to pass for a man."

"Lucky, indeed!" Sierra lifted her visor, too, revealing a glimpse of her beautiful little face before it clamped shut again. He heard a muted sigh from within. "No wonder they keep these things closed all the time. They won't stay up unless you hold them."

"Sir!" Batty scratched at Arnoth's hair, distracting him from his amusement at Sierra's dismay. "Cramped, sir."

Arnoth adjusted his helmet to give the lingbat more room. "When you next see Dane Calydon, you can report your complaints to him. In detail."

"I'm formulating a list, sir."

Arnoth laughed. "Good."

Sierra pointed at the bound Tseir guards. At her persuasion, Arnoth had resisted killing them. Only the giddiness of love could have stopped him. "I don't feel right leaving them."

Arnoth repressed a groan. "You've given them water. They'll survive."

Sierra positioned herself in front of the three guards, elevating her visor to see clearly. "I'm sorry about your comrade's fate." Arnoth groaned again, but he didn't stop her. "I'm not sure you bear each other much affection, but now is the time to learn. If you work together,

238

cooperate, you'll find a way out of this predicament, and become better persons for the effort.''

''Sierra, you are talking to clones.''

She cast a reproachful glance Arnoth's way. ''They are still persons.'' She turned back to the guards, gesturing as she spoke. ''You will find nuts and berries outside the cave. These are indigenous to your planet, and they're healthy, much better for you than 'consumptives.' If you move in unison, you can manage to find some. I picked those to the south, but I think you'll find more farther down the hill. Anyway, good luck to you.''

Arnoth stared in amazement, shaking his head as she lowered her visor and walked to him. He loved her. She wasn't sane, but a sane woman couldn't love him the way she did. She was crazy. Laughter burst from the depths of his ancient heart.

My friend, if you designed a woman for me, it would be this one. Despite himself, Arnoth looked forward to the day he could present Sierra to Dane, and hear the endless gloating of the man who'd known him better than he knew himself.

''Your rank is higher than mine.''

Sierra settled herself beside Arnoth in their hovercraft, holding her visor aloft as she studied the insignia on his shoulder. A frown tightened her face. Arnoth shrugged. ''As it should be, woman. I'm older than you.''

She considered that, but her brow remained furrowed. ''I can't help feeling I earned the higher rank by my promotion to Twelfth.''

''She has a point, sir.'' Batty spoke next to his ear, and Arnoth jumped.

''Not so loud, rodent.'' His words reminded him of another. ''Curses! I'm beginning to sound like Dane.''

''Noticed that, sir.''

Arnoth held up his visor, facing Sierra. She'd brought

239

more to his dormant life than sex. She'd brought humor and the deep warmth of life. He motioned to her with his finger. "Come here."

A tiny smile curved her lips and she leaned toward him. They angled their heads to kiss beneath the visors. She touched his shoulder and moved her lips against his.

"Sir?"

"Argh!"

Sierra hopped back at Arnoth's outburst, and the bat clawed at his neck as the visor dropped shut. Arnoth leaned back in his seat. His breath steamed the visor.

"It is conceivable that, at one point in time, Dane Calydon was a patient, calm man. Until he made contact with that relentless species, the lingbat."

Sierra chuckled beside him, then sighed happily. "Your restraint has weakened on many counts, sweet prince. Batty, I think you should add that to your report."

"Done, mistress. Keeping it all in my head, you understand. Lingbats have superior memories, due to advanced neurotransmitters."

Arnoth adjusted the hovercraft controls. "Wonderful."

"We're an amazing species, sir, capable of any number of wonders. That's what my sire always said."

"I don't suppose maintaining silence is among your wonders, is it?"

Batty hesitated, then exhaled a long, ashamed breath on Arnoth's neck. "No, sir."

"It was too much to hope." Arnoth reached for Sierra's hand. "Are you ready, little alien?"

She wrapped her gloved hand around his. "I am. I will follow you, wherever you go."

"I wish I had a more romantic destination in mind than the Tseir city, but we have no choice."

"We'll be together, Arnoth. That's romantic enough."

"We have to be careful not to do anything to arouse their suspicions."

"I know. I have had practice, remember? What about you? Can you impersonate a Tseir?"

"I've done it on many occasions. The Ellowan of Keir practiced elaborate sabotage at the expense of the Tseir. My impersonation skills are flawless."

Sierra shook her head and sighed. "I should have known."

"I don't know the procedures of the Dar-Krona Tseir, however. What can we expect back in the city?"

"The first thing we have to do is report to Drakor . . . Koran. He'll want to know what happened to the others. Maybe we could tell him you and I were killed."

Arnoth considered her suggestion, then shook his head. "I doubt they had orders to kill, Sierra."

"Good point. If the guards bungled the operation, they'd be punished or even killed. I don't want that."

"Death would certainly defeat our purposes. The best solution is to tell them the prisoners took refuge deep in the plumbing cavern. We couldn't get at them without killing them, so we're coming back for further instructions."

"That sounds good. The Tseir value caution."

"Sometimes I think you admire them."

"It's not admiration. I suppose I've come to understand them. They're a terribly literal people. They don't understand much. They're cruel because they don't know another way. I didn't realize it at first, until Colice asked me why I enjoyed cleansing duties. She truly didn't know. I felt sorry for her."

Arnoth huffed. "They don't deserve your pity."

"I don't know . . . They're numb inside; they don't know how to feel or to care. But Colice almost defended me, if you remember."

"Maybe. But it didn't last long, did it?"

"No. But that she did it at all . . . She risked demotion, maybe worse. It gave me hope."

241

"It's unwarranted hope, Sierra. You have a tender heart. I was kindhearted once, too."

"Your kindness is tempered with wisdom, but you're still tender."

"I'm not."

Sierra lifted her visor and smiled. "You are. And I know exactly where."

Arnoth's face warmed. He felt fourteen. And fortunate his visor shielded that fact from Sierra. He engaged the hovercraft and maneuvered it from through the plumbing rubble. Stacks of tubing and pipes filled the wide cavern. Giant pumps lay torn apart, discarded.

Sierra clucked her tongue. "Waste, waste. The Tseir could have found some use for this material. Instead, what do they do? They dump it in what might have been an interesting geographical landmark."

"They're clones, woman. Little different from machines themselves. You're expecting them to live like a real species. They're not capable of living."

"That's what you said about yourself. And you were wrong."

"Guards Sixteen-forty, and Twelve-seventy-five reporting to military commander."

Arnoth repeated the words Sierra had taught him, and Sierra held her breath. Fortunately, the Tseir guards kept their numerical titles on their uniform insignia. Most used no other name to identify themselves. Sierra wondered what the three bound guards called each other back in the cave.

"Admitted, Sixteen-forty and Twelve-seventy-five. Military commander advised of your arrival."

The entrance to Drakor's chamber slid open and Sierra followed Arnoth inside. The guard stepped back, then resumed his post outside the door. Drakor sat at a low metal desk. He rose when they entered, standing straight

242

and stiff. He wore no helmet, probably because of the low lighting and the need to scrutinize his battle plans.

Sierra studied his boyish face. He revealed no emotion, nothing of Koran's ebullient personality, yet in appearance, they were identical.

"Report, Sixteen-forty."

Arnoth stepped forward. "We made contact with the escaped prisoners, Commander. The result was negative. Two guards were disengaged on a permanent basis."

"The prisoners were armed, then?"

"They had secured weapons, yes, Commander. They took refuge in the plumbing cavern. We couldn't extract them without negative effects. Further instructions required."

"Other procedure reports?"

"We disengaged their hovercraft, limiting mobility."

"Correct procedure, Sixteen-forty. Report in for rest duties. The matter will be assessed by the supreme command and rectified."

Arnoth bowed, and they turned to leave. Sierra drew a tight breath of relief.

"Were there injuries, Sixteen-forty?"

Arnoth hesitated, then turned back. "Two guards, Commander."

Drakor stepped around the desk. "Were the prisoners injured?"

The clone's voice altered slightly. Sierra detected a trace of Koran's voice, a gentle voice. "Uncertain, Commander."

"The woman . . . did you make visual contact? Did you see her?"

"We did." Arnoth paused, and his own voice softened. "She was unharmed."

Drakor didn't respond. His head tilted to one side, as if his interest puzzled him. He returned to his desk and seated himself. "Dismissed, Sixteen-forty."

Sierra glanced back at the clone. He retrieved the battle plans and spread them across the desk. But his gaze wandered, and his puzzled expression remained.

Sierra hurried after Arnoth, but she waited until she and Arnoth stood alone before speaking. "What do you make of that? Why did he ask about me?"

"I don't know. It is possible he retains some memory of you." Arnoth paused, and his voice lowered. "Love is strong, Sierra. How can it leave no trace?"

"I'm sorry he's trapped here. I'm sorry he's caught this way, between life and death. Arnoth . . ." Sierra's throat caught with emotion, and Arnoth touched her arm.

"You must be strong, little alien. We don't have much time. The commanders will send a patrol, and it's likely the bound guards will be found. I should have killed them. What was I thinking?"

"It's one thing to kill in self-defense, Arnoth. Quite another to take a life when you can as easily spare it. Even Tseir life."

"You speak as I did . . . before the Tseir ravaged my world."

"If you're right, and they intend to ravage Nirvahda, we have to return soon to warn them. My father isn't expecting an attack. He doesn't believe they have the power or intention to challenge us. I see how that he is wrong."

"Your father? How much power does your world have?"

Sierra bit her lip beneath the visor. "Oh, well . . . Quite a bit, comparatively, I suppose. Our weaponry is generally advanced."

"Another reason the Tseir want to conquer your world. We don't have much time. I need to reconfigure a ship, and you need to cover for me. It will be dangerous, Sierra. One mistake, and our lives are forfeit."

"I have no intention of making a mistake."

"You never do."

Sierra looked around, saw that no one watched, then elbowed Arnoth in the ribs. "We'll see who bungles first, Ellowan. If I do, you can lie on your back and I will start at the top of your head and work to your toes ... with my tongue, and any other part of me that appeals to you."

Sierra enjoyed Arnoth's sharp breath, then nodded. "On the other hand, should you make *any* mistake *whatsoever . . .*"

Arnoth seized her hand and shook it vigorously. "Done! Now, quiet, woman, you're arousing me."

"Me, too."

"Sir . . ." Batty's wheezing voice sounded from Arnoth's helmet.

Arnoth tipped his hidden head back and drew a long, strained breath. "We've got to hurry. I don't know how much longer I can stand a rodent caught in my hair."

Sierra took her position outside the open docking bay while Arnoth fiddled with the circuits inside the craft. So far, it had proven an easier task than either expected. No one questioned their purpose, and since guards entered and departed the bay regularly, their presence didn't arouse suspicion.

Sierra began to relax. Arnoth had chosen a replica of an Ellowan shuttle, by virtue of its speed. It wouldn't travel far, but they only needed to reach the sector's rim for rescue purposes. If he could reconfigure the automatic pilot circuits and gain control, they would escape Dar-Krona. Everything seemed perfect. Arnoth loved her. Sierra felt certain of success.

Guards passed along the metal walkways, and the afternoon sun piercing through the murky haze and glaring on the harsh buildings. Sierra sighed. It was hotter than usual on Dar-Krona today. Hard-shelled insects hovered over the red brine beneath the walkways. She hoped

Batty wouldn't notice and expose himself for the sake of a crispy feast.

Across the walkway, Colice emerged from the rehabilitation center. She must have been further demoted, for she was dressed as a guard. Colice stood back as a hovercraft passed, then proceeded toward the commanders' barracks. Sierra endured a pang of sympathy. The Tseir woman looked so alone.

Colice rounded the corner and disappeared just as a squadron of hovercraft lowered toward the docking bay. Sierra tensed, but she didn't dare flee, lest she arouse suspicion.

The craft landed on the walkway and the guards emerged, fully armed. Drakor stood among them, giving orders that Sierra couldn't hear. The guards fanned out in different directions, canisters poised as they searched.

And if they were searching, it had to be for herself and Arnoth. Sierra waited until they spread out, then eased back into the docking bay. She took a deep breath, then darted toward the shuttle.

"Halt! Turn slowly, Twelve-seventy-five."

Sierra froze. Drakor had followed her into the bay. She squeezed her eyes shut and turned. He stood alone, only his red cape revealing his personal identity. He held a short rifle. The red switch on the top was set forward, on full force.

Sierra gripped her stolen canister, but she couldn't shoot.

"Lift your visor, Twelve-seventy-five."

She didn't know what to do. Her hands shook as Drakor stepped toward her. "Lift your visor."

If he saw her, maybe he wouldn't kill her. He would stun her and take her captive, but Arnoth would reach her first. "As you wish." She lifted her visor. Drakor didn't shoot, and he didn't move. He stood still as stone, staring at her face.

"Sierra . . ."

His soft voice pierced her heart. It was Koran's voice. "Koran."

The pilot's door hissed open behind her. Arnoth fired his canister, and Koran dropped to the ground. Sierra bit back a cry and ran to his side, kneeling as she wept. Arnoth left the shuttle and grabbed her shoulder. "We have to get out of here."

"He'll die."

Arnoth squeezed her shoulder. "Sierra, your friend died a long time ago."

She sniffed, unable to brush away her tears beneath the helmet. "I know. But he recognized me, Arnoth. He said my name. And he didn't shoot. I showed him my face, and he didn't shoot. I can't let him die."

Arnoth sighed, then looked around the bay. "Maybe we should move him, before someone sees him." He picked up the fallen clone. Koran's body looked small. Arnoth lifted him almost effortlessly.

"What are you going to do with him?"

"Hide his body somewhere."

Sierra winced at Arnoth's callousness. "You're right. You've been a warrior too long. We can't leave him."

"Sierra, he's dead already."

"He's moving." Her voice choked on a sob.

"What do you expect me to do with him?"

"You can heal him."

Arnoth groaned and started to speak. "Ellowan don't . . ."

"I know. 'Ellowan don't touch Tseir.' Well, you touched me."

"You're not Tseir, woman, although you may need a reminder of that occasionally."

"Koran isn't Tseir, either, not really. Arnoth, please . . ."

247

He drew a long, weary breath, his shoulders slumped. "Curse your pretty eyes, woman."

"You can't see my eyes."

"Yes, but I know . . . They're wide, and teary, and as innocent as they have to be to get what you want."

"Shall I lift my visor for effect?"

"There's no need." Arnoth shook his head, then carried Koran onto the shuttle. "What are we going to do with a clone?"

"We're rescuing him, too."

Arnoth sighed, but he didn't argue as he placed Koran's body on the floor of the shuttle. He started toward the helm, but Sierra caught his arm. "Aren't you going to heal him?"

"I am not finished reconfiguring this vessel. They're searching for us now, *as we speak*. I do not have time to enter a trance and heal a clone who isn't a real person, anyway."

"It will only take a minute."

"What makes you think he desires life?"

"Ask him and find out!"

Arnoth groaned. "Close that door."

Sierra pressed a button, and the shuttle door closed. She watched as Arnoth knelt beside Koran. He pulled off the helmet, revealing the boyish face beneath. Reddish brown curls fell to Koran's jawline; he looked innocent and sweet. Sierra remembered his enthusiastic declaration of love, his far-fetched promises, and she burst into tears.

Batty bounced from the viewport to examine the clone. "This specimen is smaller than other humans I've seen." He seemed to appreciate the similarity. "Of course, massive size is overvalued. I, myself, am considered small for a lingbat."

Sierra nodded as tears splattered on her visor. She pulled off her helmet and tossed it aside. "He was a good person."

248

Arnoth shook his head. "He isn't a 'person' at all." Despite his negative assessment, he placed his hand over the clone's forehead and entered the Ellowan trance.

Maybe the cloned Koran wouldn't desire life. Sierra held her breath. It was his right. Arnoth couldn't force him. For a long while, Arnoth didn't move. Sierra guessed the procedure went slowly. A look of surprise crossed Arnoth's solemn face, and he bowed his head. His hands moved, then stilled. He sat back and looked up at her.

"Well?"

Arnoth shrugged. "It's weak, and vague, but I found a desire for life."

Sierra beamed with pleasure. "I knew it! Is he all right?"

"The injury wasn't as severe as I imagined. Although it was beyond the Tseir's capacity to heal."

"In other words, you saved his life."

"Such as it is." Arnoth rose to his feet and tore a portion of cloth from Koran's red cape.

"What are you doing?"

"Unless you want him to alert his guards to our presence, I'm going to gag him and bind him."

"We're taking him with us, aren't we?"

"I suppose we have no choice."

"Good. Don't tie it too tightly. Koran isn't very strong."

Arnoth wrapped the gag around the clone's mouth, then tied his hands and feet. Sierra checked the ties, then loosened his ankles. Koran opened his eyes and looked at her, an expression of wonder on his face. She touched his cheek gently.

"You're safe. We won't hurt you."

His soft brown eyes glanced toward Arnoth, then back at her.

"Arnoth healed you, Koran . . . I'm sorry. *Drakor.*"

249

Sierra patted his arm. "We're taking you with us. You're not really a Tseir, you're Nirvahdi. And you're my friend, whether you remember me or not."

Batty hopped to the clone's shoulder and looked him straight in the eye. Koran's eyes widened, and Sierra smiled through her tears. "This is a lingbat. Batty. Your original would have found him very amusing."

Sierra caught Batty's doubtful, suspicious glance and cleared her throat. "And capable of any number of wonders."

An alarm blared outside, and Sierra jumped.

"Attention: All commanders, guards! Assume stations, ready arms!"

Sierra froze; her heart stopped. They had been discovered. Arnoth sighed. "Wonderful."

"Military commander missing, presumed dead. Prisoners suspected of infiltrating Docking Bay One-one-four, or One-one-seven. One-two-four. Posing as Guards Sixteen-forty and Twelve-seventy-five. Apprehend immediately. Secure all bays!"

"Oh, no! Arnoth, are you ready?"

"Not quite."

"Hurry!"

He looked up from beneath the control panel, his dark brow angled. "There's a good suggestion. I wish I'd thought of that."

Sierra ignored his tone and peeked out the viewport. "There are guards all over the place. Arnoth, they're checking the other shuttles. What do we do?"

He returned to his circuits. "I'll use your brilliant suggestion and hurry."

"Oh . . . they're coming to this one. Arnoth . . ."

Arnoth glanced at the door. "Sierra, I've almost got it. You're going to have to hold them off as they enter. You'll have to open it or they'll break through, and we can't enter space with a hole ripped in the hull."

250

Sierra seized the canister and positioned herself by the door. From the corner of her eye, she noticed Koran squirmming to sit up. He was shaking his head vigorously. Her heart took a strange pang. He was afraid . . . for her.

She held up the canister. "I'm good with this. Don't worry."

The Tseir surrounded the shuttle and Sierra closed her eyes.

"Sixth Command! Guards, secure entrance!"

Sierra pressed the open grid and the door slid wide, surprising the guards outside. She aimed her canister, and a guard started in. The guard was Colice.

Arnoth leapt to his feet and engaged the engine. "Ready! Close that door!"

Sierra smacked the grid and the door hissed shut. Catching Colice's red cape . . . on the inside of the craft.

The shuttle started to rise. Sierra heard Colice scream outside the door. "Arnoth! We've caught Colice!"

He looked over his shoulder. "What do you mean, 'caught Colice'?"

"I mean her cape is caught in the door and she's hanging from the shuttle!"

Batty hopped to the round side window. "She's right, sir. You've got a Tseir female hanging off the side of your ship, and no mistake."

Arnoth issued a long, agonized groan. "Only you, Sierra of the Twelfth, could catch a clone by the cape." He left the helm and looked out the round window. "You're not joking. She's hanging there like a flag."

"What do we do?"

Arnoth shrugged. "She'll burn up when we leave the atmosphere." He hesitated while Sierra gaped in horror. "On the other hand, her weight might throw off our trajectory. It might be better to cut her loose."

"We can't do that!"

Arnoth angled his head and glared. "Oh, yes, we can. Saving your friend, or copy thereof, was one thing. Saving a Tseir commander is out of the question."

Sierra placed her hand on Arnoth's arm. She widened her eyes and her chin quivered. His dark glare intensified.

"No."

Sierra's lip quivered, too. "Please."

"No! Ellowan do not touch Tseir. Ever."

"I'll touch her."

"Sierra . . ." Arnoth rolled his eyes and shook his head. A slow smile spread across his face and he bent to kiss her forehead. "This must be considered a 'mistake' on your part, little alien. I expect reward."

"You'll get it." Sierra grinned. "In any way you can think of."

"I have a vivid imagination."

"I hope so."

"You'll have to hold her cape so she doesn't drop when we open the door. And . . ." Arnoth paused to sigh. "I will pull her in."

Sierra grabbed the end of Colice's cape, bracing herself against the hull, and Arnoth opened the door. The acrid wind whipped into the shell of the craft, roaring in her ears. Colice bumped against the hull, headfirst. Her feet stuck out just as Arnoth said, like a flag.

Her eyes were wide saucers of terror. She'd expected Arnoth to cut her loose. She'd expected to die. For a second only, he hesitated. Sierra wondered if he would drop Colice "by accident." Maybe it had been too much to ask him to save a Tseir woman, after a Tseir woman had killed his wife.

But Arnoth reached from the shuttle, grabbed Colice's wrists, and hauled her through the door. He closed the door and met Sierra's gaze. What she saw in his eyes astonished her beyond words.

"Little alien, I owe you my soul."

He had saved his enemy. In doing so, Sierra knew he had freed his soul. "I love you so."

Arnoth smiled, the smile of a free man. "I know."

Colice lay facedown on the floor. She rose up on her hands and knees and looked between them. "You are lovers. Extrana was right."

Arnoth rolled his eyes and returned to the helm. Sierra offered Colice her hand. Colice eyed her hand doubtfully, then took it. Sierra pulled her to her feet. "Extrana was right before the fact, but, yes, I love him."

Colice noticed Koran. "You abducted Drakor?"

"It wasn't intentional." Sierra went to Arnoth and tapped his shoulder. "Can I remove Koran's gag now?"

"I guess so. But keep him bound, Sierra."

"I don't see the need. . . ."

"Woman, my 'soul' has limits. Do as I say. And bind her, too."

Sierra turned to Colice and made a face. "He's tense. I'm sure, when we're safe, you can go free."

Colice's brow furrowed. "It is unwise to allow prisoners freedom, Sierra. Had you made it to the Final Third, you would realize the dangers of anything less than full authority."

Sierra nodded as she tied a portion of the cape around Colice's wrists. "I found the elevation from Thirteenth to Twelfth particularly demanding, for that same reason. The discipline involved is tremendous."

"It was my most difficult assignment, too."

From the helm, Arnoth muttered under his breath. Sierra smiled and stood behind him, then kissed the back of his shoulder. "I was well on my way to the Final Third. Had it not been for you . . ."

He glanced back at her. "You'd still be a virgin."

Sierra blushed. "Arnoth! We are not alone."

Colice watched them, looking puzzled rather than shocked. "It was well done to disguise your passions.

253

The rutting desire between you is obviously strong."

Sierra drew a tight breath, then turned. "It's not 'rutting,' Colice. It's . . ." Arnoth cast a teasing look over his shoulder, waiting. "It's something you do when you love someone, and you want to be close to him more than anything."

Colice appeared skeptical. "It takes a firm thrust from a large male appendage to create sensation. Early graphics of the Ellowan's body indicate his proportion is substantial of girth and length, and capable of creating the necessary friction, which is why he is desirable as a mate."

Sierra's mouth opened, then closed. She peeked back at Arnoth, and felt sure he blushed now, too. "Are you that different from other men?"

He refused to look back, which convinced Sierra he really was blushing. "I don't know. I'm not in the habit of comparing myself to naked, aroused males."

"Our calculations indicated his aroused member would be on the largest end of the spectrum, the red column."

Sierra eyed Colice. "Calculations? You calculate the size of men's personal parts?"

"Of course. It is necessary when choosing one capable of causing sensation."

Sierra's brow puckered tight. "There's a 'spectrum'?"

"From insubstantial and thin to the massive varieties."

"I never heard about that!" Sierra paused. "Is this something reserved for the Final Third?"

"The spectrum information is available to any female desiring stimulation."

"Oh. I guess I never looked into the matter before." Sierra shook her head and sighed, while Arnoth cast an incredulous look over his shoulder. "You learn something every day."

"If we could alter the subject at hand, woman, we are

breaking free of the atmosphere. You mentioned a rescue code.''

''Nirvahda seven-nine. I'll do it.'' Sierra fiddled with the communications panel, then issued the code to the rescue ship. ''It's going to be close. The Tseir will send a pursuit. I don't think we can count on them wanting to secure us alive at this point.''

Colice looked over Sierra's shoulder as the shuttle rose through the final layer of atmosphere. ''The pursuit will engage double-quick. Your chances of escaping are remote.'' She turned her gaze to Arnoth. ''You wasted time retrieving me. It was a mistake. I am valueless as a hostage, and I bear no critical information.''

Arnoth adjusted the shuttle's trajectory, increased the speed, and the vessel surged from the atmosphere into black space. He sat back in his seat and cast a dark glance Colice's way. ''You don't have to tell me about the nature of this 'mistake,' Tseir. You owe your rescue to Sierra, not me. I would have been happy to let you burn up in space.''

Colice turned her attention to Sierra. ''What purpose does my rescue serve you?''

Sierra shrugged. ''None that I can think of offhand.''

''Then why did you do it?''

''I don't know, really. It's just that I saw you leaving the rehabilitation center . . .''

''My rehabilitation was successful. Tendencies toward nonconformity were subdued. I had parole as a guard but was expected to advance upward again from Sixth.'' Colice paused, then sighed. ''I doubt I would have made it back to the Final Third again, though.''

''No, it's unlikely. The Final Third is extremely strict.''

''This does not explain your decision to bring me onboard your escape vessel, rather than eliminating the question.''

" 'Eliminating the question' would mean killing you."

"We are enemies."

"True. I just know how it feels to be demoted, that's all. All that work, down the drain."

"What drain? Clarify."

"Figuratively speaking."

"I see. An analogy for the demotion. Understood."

Arnoth swiveled his seat to face them. "I hate to interrupt, but instruments record several vessels in pursuit. However, if your directions were correct, we can make it to the edge of the sector without being caught."

"They're correct. What's the problem?"

"What happens when we reach your rescue ship? We'll have to stop for docking, and the Tseir craft will catch up, with plenty of time to fire their fusion blasts."

"I don't think they'll risk engaging a Nirvahdi vessel yet, not unless they've mustered the whole fleet. They're not prepared to do that."

Sierra knelt beside Koran and removed his gag and ankle binding while Arnoth watched suspiciously. "What makes you think they won't blow away a Nirvahdi vessel just as easily as any other they've encountered?"

Koran took a breath. "Because one Nirvahdi flagship has as much power as the Tseir fleet, Ellowan. Didn't you know?"

Arnoth sat at the helm, staring into black space. *As much power as the Tseir fleet.* Sierra had shrugged off the Tseir's claim, without a satisfactory explanation. He sensed she hid something from him, but he wasn't sure why.

He glanced back at her. She sat beside Drakor, telling him of their friendship, which Arnoth gathered had begun at a school of some sort. She called him Koran, seeming to forget his cloned identity. As she spoke, gesturing, her small, beautiful face alive with expression, Drakor watched her intently, but Arnoth didn't think the clone was paying much attention to her speech.

"I am also in the red section of the spectrum."

Arnoth coughed, then swiveled his seat. He hopped up, seized Sierra's arm, and pulled her to the helm. "Woman, I can tolerate only so much." Sierra looked back at Koran, her brow puckered thoughtfully.

"Do you think he meant . . . ?"

"Yes."

"Why would he tell me that?"

Arnoth cast his gaze upward. "Oh, I don't know. . . . Maybe he wants to 'create sensation' in that adorable little body of yours."

Sierra's brow elevated. "Funny, I never would have thought Koran was at the red end." She paused. "I wonder what color code signifies the smaller varieties?"

Arnoth placed his hands on either side of her face. "Sierra. You're beginning to think like a Tseir."

She frowned. "I was simply curious."

"Too curious for your own good. Or mine."

Colice maneuvered across the ship. "The color code for the least bulky level is pale yellow."

Sierra considered this, then nodded. "That fits."

Arnoth clasped his hand to his forehead. "This is torture."

Colice ignored her captor and lowered her voice. "Drakor is exaggerating, as men often do. At best, he's an orange."

Sierra's face puckered in understanding. "Let's keep that to ourselves, shall we?"

Arnoth eased between Sierra and Colice. "Good idea. If it's never mentioned again, the men of this galaxy and every other will thank you."

Sierra chuckled. "Especially the 'pale yellows.' " She reached up and fingered the collar of his red shirt. "You reds have it better. I thought this shirt suited you particularly well.''

Arnoth's face heated while she watched in satisfaction. He'd endured more flashes of embarrassment in the last two days than ever in his life. Batty hopped to the viewport and issued a polite cough.

"In lingbats, the size of the reproductive organ is unimportant. It's the speed with which it's administered that counts.''

"Thank you for sharing that, Batty.'' Arnoth sank down into his seat and scanned the panel, hoping for something to alter the conversation's direction. A large blip appeared, too large for a vessel.

"There's something here. It appears to be moving toward us.''

Sierra leaned over his seat. "What is it?''

Arnoth indicated the blip. "By the size, I'd guess it's an asteroid. A good-sized one.''

She bit her lip and looked uncomfortable. "No . . . That's the rescue ship.''

"It can't be. Unless this scale is off.'' Arnoth tapped the panel, but the blip didn't alter. It grew larger as they neared. "It should be visible on the viewscreen soon.''

He magnified the port while Sierra waited beside him. She looked tense. Colice seated herself with the dull patience of a Tseir, but Koran rose to better his view. Batty issued a sudden piercing whistle.

"Whew! Is that it?''

High on the screen appeared an immense vessel. It was wide and long, appearing flat, though when Arnoth magnified the screen again, he realized it had many levels. His eyes widened in astonishment.

"That can't be . . . a flightship?''

Koran nodded. "It's one of the flagships of the Intersystem fleet. Does the size surprise you, Ellowan? Ah, but then, you're of a primitive race. Perhaps you are unable to comprehend the grandeur of the Nirvahdi.''

Arnoth realized his mouth was open and snapped it shut. Sierra was trying to look casual and not quite succeeding. ''It's really not that complicated.''

''Woman, that ship is as large as an Ellowan city from our most populous age. Maybe two cities.'' He gaped out the viewport again. ''A hundred Ellowan ships would fit inside that thing.''

Koran seemed to enjoy Arnoth's shock. Perhaps the clone found him competition for Sierra. Apparently, he desired more than life. ''The rescue ship is one of many, Ellowan. It has capacity for defense, and its speed would astonish a primitive such as yourself.''

Arnoth bit back his irritation. ''Would it?''

Sierra patted his arm. ''The military vessels are much smaller. Half the size.''

''Ah. Only fifty Ellowan vessels would fit inside those.''

Koran laughed, a rare sound for a clone. ''If this shocks you, Ellowan, you should see the colony ships.''

''One shock at a time, Tseir.''

Koran eyed him with a shade of challenge. ''Nirvahdi.''

Sierra beamed and hugged the clone while Arnoth glared. ''You do remember, don't you? Once you're home, it will come back to you. You will have a life again.''

Koran cast a triumphant glance at Arnoth, then hugged Sierra in return. ''I remember the life of another man, in shadows. It is a grief to me not to recall its entirety.''

Arnoth refrained from groaning loudly, but the boyish clone had already mastered garnering female sympathy. Colice watched without emotion. ''It takes several reproductions to erase the original's memories. Drakor is only a third-generation reproduction.'' She sighed faintly. ''He is still biologically functional.''

"Amply functional."

Arnoth could endure no more. He seized Sierra's arm and extracted her from the clone's overly amorous embrace. "Not with her, you're not. This is my woman, and mine only. Got it?"

Koran frowned, but Sierra gazed up at Arnoth with a smile of pure happiness. Batty hopped excitedly in the viewport. "Sir, we're really going to make it, aren't we? We're going home. She Who Leaps High will be waiting. I'll have the report for my Dane. That last part should please him. *This is my woman, and mine only.* Good phrasing, sir."

"Tell him and die, rodent."

Batty squeaked, but Sierra kissed Arnoth's shoulder. "A statement of obvious fact."

The giant vessel now filled the viewscreen. Arnoth reduced magnification, but the vessel hovered above the tiny Ellowan shuttle. "They've taken over the controls. I suppose this is standard procedure."

Sierra hesitated, looking uneasy. "I should open communications. Do you mind if I take the helm for a bit?"

Arnoth stood back. "Go ahead."

He watched as she seated herself, then flicked switches with deft, experienced fingers. She engaged a headset device, then spoke quickly to the other ship. "Vessel secured, awaiting entrance. Sierra Karian reporting in."

"Karian?"

She glanced up at him. "That's my full name."

"It's pretty."

She smiled, but the expression still seemed tense. "Thank you. I have always found Arnoth of Valenwood appealing, too."

"Umm."

Arnoth's gaze returned to the rescue ship. He'd never seen or imagined anything so vast. Yet created by human hands. Maybe. He looked at Sierra. She was listening to someone on the headset, nodding.

"No injuries. Four passengers . . ." She cast a quick glance at Batty. "Five, including one lingbat."

Sierra's brow rose and she looked up at Arnoth. "That's odd. I heard someone shout in the background." She shrugged and held the headset closer to her ear. A tiny smile formed on her soft lips. "Yes, the Ellowan prince is with me." Her smile grew. "There's the shout again. Someone's very glad you're here."

"I can't imagine why I'd be important to anyone on a vessel of that size."

"Size isn't everything, Arnoth." She cast her eyes deliberately down the length of his body. "And it doesn't preclude tenderness. When delivered in combination . . ." She issued a calculated sigh, distracting him from the shock of the Nirvahdi ship.

Sierra turned her attention back to the headset. "Request assistance for one Tseir and one cloned Nirvahdi, also."

Sierra listened a moment, and her expression changed. Arnoth knew she was listening to the voice of someone she loved. Her eyes misted with tears. "Yes, it's really me. I've come home."

Chapter Eight

Sierra stood by the door, waiting impatiently as the shuttle was taken onboard the rescue ship. Arnoth stood beside her, realizing he knew very little about the young woman he loved. It had certainly never occurred to him that her race might be so much more advanced than his own.

As the shuttle lowered into an interior docking bay, he considered how he'd spent four hundred years. Most of that time, he'd lived outside a swamp on a primitive world among amphibian warriors. Terrorizing an outpost of the Tseir, and accomplishing very little.

It hadn't seemed insignificant at the time. It was all he could do, and he'd done it well. He kept the Tseir from moving outward. He kept them off guard. And he'd helped the rightful ruler of Keir regain command of the planet. With a sudden pang, Arnoth missed the Keiroit leader, Rurthgar. He even missed the swamp.

Batty scrambled up his leg, and Arnoth helped him to his shoulder. "Can't believe it, sir. Home."

"This isn't home yet, Batty."

"As you say, sir. But it's a lot better than Dar-Krona."

The pressure in the interior atmosphere altered; noises changed outside the hull. "They're re-pressurizing the docking bay. It will only be a minute now."

"Wonderful." He actually felt nervous. Because he was seeing Sierra's world for the first time, and because he felt . . . primitive. Because he loved her and he didn't really know her, after all.

As if she sensed his thoughts, Sierra clasped his hand. She kissed his shoulder and closed her eyes. "We're really safe."

"For now."

"You can be so gloomy at times. We made it in time to warn the Council. They'll form a resistance, and the Tseir will have to change their plans to attack Nirvahda."

Colice stood behind her. "We have no such plans."

"Arnoth believes otherwise." Sierra looked to Koran. "Would you tell us if you knew?"

A slow, surprised expression grew on Koran's boyish face. "I believe that I would. But I know of no such plans. I was told we would attack the portion of the Intersystem fleet at Valenwood."

Arnoth eyed him scornfully. "Why should we take the word of a clone?"

Koran kept his attention on Sierra. "I have no reason to defend the Tseir. It's possible, although unlikely, that the Tseir plan as you say. If it was their intention, information would remain only in the First Command. Neither Colice nor I would hear even a rumor of such plans."

Colice nodded. "The First Command is impenetrable. I never aspired to their ranks. Only the clones of the original Tseir make it that far."

Sierra tapped her lip thoughtfully. "You mean, the clones of the original rebels?"

"That's right."

"Who were you cloned from, Colice?"

"From another clone."

"I meant the first one."

Colice hesitated. "I don't know. Her name was Colice."

A bell rang outside the shuttle. "Pressurization complete. Disembarkation mode."

Sierra drew a breath, then opened the shuttle door. Arnoth looked out at a huge docking bay, filled with narrow white vessels. They were sleek, trim, and obviously advanced. A large group of people hurried across the bay, and Sierra stepped out onto the elevated ramp, waving. A cheer rang out, as if a young queen returned to her throne.

Arnoth endured a stab of reluctance, then followed her. Batty quivered excitedly on his shoulder, clutching with small claws. Arnoth expected to see humans who resembled Sierra and Koran, but it wasn't the case. Some were tall and slender, with black skin, wearing long, multicolored robes. Some were tiny, to the height of his knee, and wore what looked like shimmering armor.

Several had bluish skin and white hair, with thin bones and large, long feet. Arnoth tried to restrain his astonishment and failed. "Blue people. The wonders of the galaxy are many."

"In a way, you've met them before. Those are the Zimdardri. They love music. You'll like them."

"What of the small ones?"

"Those are the Teradites. They are one of the most recent members of the Intersystem. Not long ago they were considered enemies because of their love of warfare. Hence, the armor that is grown into their bodies."

"Odd, but pretty."

Sierra chuckled. "They can be cantankerous and quarrelsome, but they now form the bulk of the Intersystem military." Sierra paused and sighed. "They've also designed fascinating games with which to satisfy their battle lust. Games that are played on small monitors." Sierra lowered her voice. "I also find their games enjoyable."

"I'm not surprised. Aggressive."

Sierra didn't argue. "For the Teradites, it is a problem, though. They become addicted to sport, and some will do nothing else."

"Yours is an odd world, little alien."

"The Zimdardri are overly fond of wine . . . and they play drums with their feet."

"The black-skinned ones are fair to look upon. What is their world?"

"They are . . ." Her words were cut short as a tall man with dark hair rushed toward her. Sierra clasped her hands over her breast, trembling, then jumped from the still-lowering platform and ran into his arms. He caught her and picked her up, kissing her cheek and weeping.

Arnoth followed her from the platform, but he stopped behind her, more uncertain now than he'd ever been in his life. The tall man stood back, and Arnoth assessed him carefully. He resembled Sierra and Koran, although he wore an aura of authority and wisdom that the youthful Koran lacked.

He had a sharp, intelligent face, an aquiline nose, and a high forehead. Nothing he wore indicated his rank. He looked casual but still commanding.

"Do you know him, Ellowan?"

Koran spoke beside Arnoth, a faint taunting note in his soft voice.

"No. Should I?"

"Only if you were a member of the Intersystem council. Before you stands Redor Karian."

"Karian? Then he's Sierra's father?"

265

"He is."

Arnoth noticed the unfriendly gleam in Koran's eyes and his patience shattered. "What of it?"

"What of it? You know little, Ellowan. Redor Karian is the prime representative of the Intersystem council. On your world, the highest official is the king, is it not?"

"It was."

"Well, Ellowan, a king isn't fit to clean the prime representative's feet."

Arnoth nodded. He'd suspected something like this. Batty chirped excitedly. "Think you'll have to clean his feet, sir? Oh, I wish my Dane could see that!"

A deep chuckle came from behind Arnoth. "Your Dane will take great delight in every winsome scrub."

Arnoth startled and whirled around. Dane Calydon grinned, then clasped Arnoth's shoulders, looking impossibly pleased with himself. Arnoth's mouth dropped in utter astonishment. "What are you doing here?"

Dane answered with a firm embrace, shocking Arnoth beyond words. "What do you think, you idiot? I came to rescue you." Dane released him and nodded at Sierra. "I see I came too late."

"As always." Arnoth shook his head, but a smile grew on his face. He wasn't alone. If Nirvahda's grandeur shocked him, Dane must have been on his knees in awe.

"It's something, isn't it?" Dane waved his arms, gesturing to the docking bay. "Wait until you see the rest of the ship!" No, he was wrong. Nothing shocked Dane Calydon. He adapted to his surroundings, be it a swamp or an empire of stardust.

Dane jerked and jumped back. "Ouch!" He yanked open his shirt, and a lingbat emerged. Dane seized the creature by the neck and pulled him to eye level. "You bit me. That will never happen again, *will it?*"

The lingbat scratched his way to Dane's shoulder. "Only if you neglect to allow me my moment. Creeping around the edge of this bay to sneak up on the prince was childish and silly. Typical of you.''

"Sire!" Batty hopped madly on Arnoth's shoulder as he addressed his father, the lingbat on Dane's shoulder "Sire! What are you doing here?''

"Came to rescue you, of course, lad. Heard the Tseir abducted you from Valenwood, and with your first litter on the way . . ." The lingbat issued a peculiar, clucking noise.

Dane nodded. "You may remember Carob from Candor. Or maybe you'd prefer to forget him. I know I would. Be that as it may, when we learned what happened to you, we decided to lend the Nirvahdi a hand in your rescue. They weren't optimistic, by the way. But the old man"—Dane gestured at Redor Karian, who Arnoth wouldn't have classified as old—"Karian was in a state over his little girl. . . ."

Dane paused, assessing Sierra. "For some reason, after hearing him talk, I pictured a child." He cast a slow, thoughtful glance at Arnoth. Arnoth squirmed uncomfortably as Dane's expression altered with a grin. "But that's no child.''

Batty coughed nervously. "Report secured, sir. No visuals available. Sorry, sir.''

Dane looked confused. "Report? What report?''

Arnoth reached to his shoulder and clamped his hand over the small lingbat. "Now would not be a good time for the issuing of reports, rodent.''

Dane's blue eyes widened with genuine surprise. "You're threatening a lingbat? Not that there's any lack of provocation . . . but you have changed, my friend.''

Batty chirped as he stretched his neck free of Arnoth's grasp. "You can say that again.''

Dane's grin intensified, creating dimples. "I'd be pleased to learn the details.''

Arnoth glared and Batty looked desperately between

267

them, probably wondering which human posed the greater threat. Arnoth quickly cleared it up. "I'm the one with the fingers around your neck."

"Right, sir."

Dane noticed Koran and Colice standing behind Arnoth. "You brought a Tseir?"

Arnoth sighed. "Her cape got caught in our door." He sighed again. "It's a long story."

"I'll bet."

Sierra was talking to her father. Arnoth noticed that both gestured, speaking rapidly. Dane followed his gaze. "Beautiful woman. Good length of leg, good hair." Arnoth's jaw clenched, and Dane chuckled. "Admirably formed, in fact. That little rear end is certainly worth a look. Even two."

Arnoth noted Dane's leading tone and ignored it. "Where is Aiyana? Did she accompany you?"

"She wanted to. But you'll see her soon enough, and our daughter. I left them on Nirvahda. Seneca and Nisa are there, too. Let me tell you, if this vessel shocks you, the Nirvahdi civilization will blow you away." Dane's eyes twinkled. "If it hasn't already."

Sierra turned toward them. She looked young and hopeful. Arnoth felt stiff and uncertain. Despite himself, he felt grateful for Dane's presence. Sierra took her father's hand and led him to Arnoth.

"Papa, this is Arnoth, the prince of the Ellowan." She seemed nervous, too. "Arnoth, this is my father, Redor Karian." Arnoth noticed that she gave her father no title. Probably sparing him the shock of learning her father was the most important man in the galaxy.

Arnoth bowed. "It is my honor and the honor of the Ellowan." It was the correct phrase for an Ellowan prince, but it sounded stilted and arrogant.

"Never seen an Ellowan before." In contrast to Arnoth, Redor Karian spoke casually, without any formality. "Thought your people were short and effeminate."

Dane laughed, then coughed to disguise his amusement. Sierra winced. "Not Arnoth."

"Guess not."

Dane cleared his throat. "My wife is also Ellowan. She's feminine, all right, and while I'd hesitate to call her short, she's not quite as tall as she thinks."

As always, Dane Calydon lightened what might have been an excruciating moment. Arnoth thanked his old nemesis silently.

Redor studied Arnoth with mild interest. "Your people will be alerted to your safe return. From here, we must first travel to Nirvahda. After that, you can go with the ambassador. . . ."

"That would be me." Dane had no qualms about interrupting the most important man in the galaxy, but Arnoth remained awkward and silent.

Redor didn't seem to mind the interruption. ". . . back to Valenwood. Although, as I understand it, you've got quite a few people waiting for you on Nirvahda."

Dane cleared his throat, interrupting again. He looked uneasy, an uncharacteristic mood, and Arnoth wondered why. "Aiyana and I went to both Keir and Valenwood. Rurthgar insisted on joining us, and so his mate insisted on going along, too." Dane patted Batty's head. "And there's another little surprise waiting with them."

"Sir?"

Carob growled. "You'll find out when you get there, lad." He cranked his head into Dane's face. "Wouldn't want to ruin the surprise, *would you?*" The lingbat snapped his teeth in warning.

"I wouldn't dream of it. As I was saying . . . the Intersystem fleet is secured around Valenwood. One of their ships took us to Nirvahda, and Carob and I hopped onto a transport coming here. As I understand it, Redor has been here on the rescue vessel for many cycles."

"I've been here since my little girl took off on a mission that she was forbidden to even *mention*."

Sierra patted her father's arm. "I did very well." She pointed at Colice. "This is First Commander Colice of the Third Division. She was my superior."

"You brought a Tseir? Does this mean you found a possibility of redemption?"

"Not exactly. Bringing Colice was something of an accident. But she's a very accomplished commander."

Redor turned his gaze to Koran. Arnoth saw the flash of bitter anguish. "And what of Koran? You say this is a clone."

"He's a third-generation clone. They called him Drakor. But he retains much of Koran's personality, Papa. I believe we can help him, and maybe preserve something of Koran, too."

Redor set his large hand on the clone's thin shoulder. "Koran was dear to me, like a son. We will do what we can to help you."

Redor seemed warmer to the clone than in his demeanor toward Arnoth. Arnoth wished he could be more like Dane Calydon, easy and cheerful, and with the capacity to endear himself to Sierra's father. Instead, he stood silently, unsmiling. The possibility of a personality clash seemed likely. For the first time in his life, Arnoth wished to be likable.

And had no idea how to do so.

"For now, it's probably best to keep a watch on the Tseir. Don't know what else to do with her. Koran can go to the medical station. What happened to his chest?"

Arnoth noticed the blood on the clone's chest and sighed. "I shot him."

"You shot Koran?"

The favored son. Arnoth contemplated offering a detailed explanation. His pride rose in defiance. "Yes."

Sierra drew a quick breath. "And he healed him, too. Koran is fine, Papa."

" 'Koran' is a clone." Arnoth felt Dane's warning gaze and knew he risked angering Redor. His pride was a dangerous thing.

"He's a living man. Doesn't that mean anything to you?"

"Considering the years I spent trying to annihilate the Tseir race, I can't claim otherwise."

Dane uttered a small sigh and Sierra closed her eyes tight. Arnoth held Redor's gaze and saw intense disapproval. "There is always an alternative to war."

"Is there? Well, you'd better come up with one fast. The Tseir intend to launch an assault on Nirvahda—with the weaponry they devised from your devoted Koran."

Koran huffed. "It wasn't my original, but the second copy who detailed the fusion lasers for the Tseir researchers."

Redor turned to Sierra. "Is this true? Do they have knowledge of fusion systems?"

"Yes, Papa. Arnoth is right. They have no real reason to attack Valenwood again. It's a ruse, so that the fleet will be separated, protecting Valenwood. That way, we'd be at less than half strength if they attack our planet. They aren't as advanced as we are, but they have many ships. If that is their intention, they could succeed."

"We'll return at once and bring the matter up at council." Redor cast a dark glance Arnoth's way. "It seems unlikely to me, but I will give it thought." He placed his arm protectively over Sierra's shoulder. "You've been through a lot, my dear girl. But you're safe now. There's a suite ready for you, and you can bathe, put on something more suitable, and we'll have your favorite dinner. How's that?"

"That would be nice, Papa. What about Arnoth?"

Redor's expression turned darker still. "He'll have quarters beside the ambassador's."

"I have promised him a Nirvahdi banquet."

Redor hesitated. "They will dine with us . . . of course. Koran, if you care to join us, I would be pleased to get reacquainted. Maybe tell you a little about the man you were."

Koran smiled, looking sweet. "I would like that, sir. My memories are vague but tender. It would please me to learn of my original."

Arnoth rolled his eyes, his lips curled to one side. Unfortunately, Redor caught his expression. Arnoth refused to alter it.

"I need to speak with my daughter in private. You . . ." Redor waved his hand in Arnoth's direction. "You can go with the ambassador. We will call you for dinner."

Sierra looked between them. Trapped. "There are some things we need to discuss, Papa." She paused. "Privacy might be a good thing." She met Arnoth's gaze. He knew she intended to tell Redor about their relationship, and he knew Redor wouldn't take it well. It wasn't rational, but he wanted her to tell the old devil here, in front of everyone, so that he could lay claim to her.

Until he'd seen this ship of the future, he hadn't questioned his claim. Now he wondered if he'd ever really had her in the first place.

"Well, I see you're still stubborn."

Arnoth watched Sierra leave with her father, then turned to Dane. "I was never stubborn."

Dane smiled. "Too stubborn to admit it." He placed his arm over Arnoth's shoulder. "Charm isn't your strong point, is it? Maybe I should teach you a few things."

Arnoth felt tired. He didn't argue. Right now, he'd give a lot to possess Dane's innate likability.

"Whether or not I endear myself to Redor Karian isn't important. He didn't take my warning seriously. The Tseir intend to invade Nirvahda. I feel it, Dane. I know it's true."

"We've got plenty of problems, my friend."

Arnoth sighed. "What else?"

Dane hesitated. "Nothing serious. When we went to Valenwood, Aiyana heard you were a night away from mating with Helayna." He paused, looking doubtful. "Were you?"

"I was."

Dane shook his head. "Somehow, I didn't think you'd go through with it. Oh, she's good looking enough. Just a little dull. And as for that spear . . ."

"I considered it my duty at the time."

"And now?"

"Now . . ." Arnoth's voice trailed and Dane glanced at Batty.

"I *could* wait for the official report."

"I didn't expect this. I didn't expect her."

"Redor's 'little girl'?"

"I suppose you're waiting for this. . . . You were right, Thorwalian. I fell, and I fell hard. And I have a feeling I haven't hit bottom yet."

Arnoth waited for Dane's inevitable gloating. But Dane just squeezed his shoulder, an act of male friendship and support. "That certainly explains your amazing effort to charm her father."

Arnoth frowned. "I'm not charming."

"No kidding."

A reluctant smile grew on Arnoth's face. Dane smiled, too. "I think he prefers the clone to you, my friend. Maybe you'd better clean up—the Nirvahdi have amazing cleansing units. I can't wait to stick Aiyana in one

273

and scrub that little body...." Dane paused and coughed. "Right. Let's get you changed out of the Tseir uniform, and maybe I'll give you a few pointers on charm. You'll get another chance at dinner."

"Papa, I love him."

Redor's face formed the darkest glower Sierra had ever seen. He exhaled a long, strained breath, then sat forward in his seat. Behind him, a large portal revealed the stars skidding by. He elevated a narrow goblet of wine to his lips, then sighed again.

"Do you know anything about the Ellowan race, Sierra?"

"I know all I need to know."

"Are you planning to be his wife, or to join his harem?"

"The Ellowan don't have harems. At least, Arnoth doesn't. That was in their past."

"And in their art, and in their music, and in the images of their mosaic walls. Which, incidentally, I've viewed on Candor. Amazingly graphic. I wonder if they've given up the public displays, too?"

"Of course!" Sierra paused. "What public displays?"

"You are too young and too innocent to know."

Sierra didn't argue, although she decided to question Arnoth on the matter later. "You were rude to him, Papa."

"And he was a model of good behavior, eloquence, and charm."

"Arnoth isn't the charming sort."

"You don't have to tell me that, girl. I met him."

Sierra glared at her father. She'd been through too much; Arnoth had been through too much. "I don't require your approval."

"Why did your mission fail?"

She puffed an exasperated breath. "Because they were

going to clone Arnoth, and kill him, and I couldn't let
them do it.''

"Uh-huh. So you saved him.''

"And he saved me.''

"And seduced you. Sierra, I'm no fool.''

"You are if you think that!''

Redor stood up and put his arm over her shoulder. "I
don't want to fight with you, my dear child. Maybe I was
wrong to forbid you to go on the mission. You were the
best candidate. But after what happened to Koran . . .''

"I know, Papa. I miss him, too.''

"Then why couldn't you have fallen in love with
him?'' Redor's voice boomed, but he caught himself and
shook his head. "I'm sorry. It's just that the Ellowan
have a . . . well, a reputation, shall we say. I shudder to
think how many wives he's had already.''

Sierra maintained a nervous silence and Redor's eyes
narrowed.

"Two . . . more or less.''

"More or less?''

"Well, the first one died, he gave the second one away,
and he didn't quite get a chance to marry the third. But
he didn't love that one, he just thought it was his duty.
And the second was more a friend . . .''

"Oh, curse the day I let you out of your room!''

Sierra cringed. "Papa, please . . . get to know him.
He's a wonderful man. And I love him, more than anything. Please . . . you seemed to like his friend.''

"If you mean Dane, yes, he's a good young man. Very
agreeable. I enjoyed the lingbat a great deal. But this
Arnoth . . . I don't know.''

Sierra clasped Redor's hand. "Papa, he lost his world
to the Tseir. Yet even though he thought I was a Tseir
woman, he saved my life.''

"I suppose you were injured because of him in the
first place.''

"He saved my life."

"Oh, very well. I'll give him a chance to prove he's something more than a ruthless, black-eyed warrior who'd be better suited to entertaining harem girls than my daughter."

"Thank you, Papa. I think."

Sierra made ample use of the cleansing unit. She washed her hair, then softened her skin with a light oil. She chose a long dinner gown rather than an onboard uniform and put soft satin slippers on her feet. She studied her reflection in a large mirror.

The dress was pale yellow, with white trim. The scooped neckline accentuated her throat and chest, and contrasted well with her long, curly hair. Sierra liked the effect. She hadn't looked this way in ages.

A tremor of excitement passed through her, tempered by the knowledge that they had to endure a dinner with her father before they could be alone. Sierra fluffed her hair and dabbed soft pink cream on her lips.

Her door panel buzzed and she caught her breath. Arnoth. Sierra hurried to the door and jabbed the panel, but it was Dane Calydon who stood in the doorway. The man who had stolen Arnoth's second wife, then engaged a lingbat to spy on him so he could gloat over Arnoth's weakness.

He looked innocent. He was definitely cute. Though tall and strong, she wouldn't call him *hulking*. He wore a pale blue uniform jacket with pale gold trim and a high white collar, and grayish-blue trousers with gold trim down the seam.

The "shaggy" blond hair was neat and just below his collar, and fell over one eyebrow in a boyish manner. He smiled. He had dimples. The man who had stolen Arnoth's wife *would* have dimples.

Dane was looking at her with the same scrutiny, although without her marked suspicion. His smile deepened and he bowed. "Your father requests your presence in the dining hall, lady."

Sierra clasped her arms around her waist. "He sent you?"

"Not exactly." Dane stepped into the room and held out his arm as if she was to take it. Sierra stiffened, and he lowered his arm to his side. "Actually, he sent for Arnoth earlier and requested that I join them . . . later."

Sierra puffed a breath of infuriated air. "He did *what?*"

"Your father wanted a private consultation."

"Oh, no!"

"Unfortunately, I didn't get much chance to brief my solemn friend on small talk."

Sierra braced, her eyes narrowed angrily. "Arnoth doesn't need small talk. It is a game for frivolous, and perhaps treacherous, individuals."

To her surprise, Dane laughed until his eyes watered. "I take it he briefed you on the circumstances of our meeting."

"I know you made off with his wife, and that he considers you a friend, which shows what a good and forgiving person he is."

Dane's laughter stilled, then started again. He pressed his lips together and contained himself. "I am guilty of all, lady." His blue eyes twinkled. "Be that as it may, I remain his friend. I'm not sure why, exactly, but I care for him." Dane paused. "Don't tell him that, though."

Sierra's mood softened. It was hard not to like Dane Calydon. No wonder Arnoth forgave him. "I will accompany you, but I won't take your arm."

Dane nodded, his expression serious, though his eyes twinkled devilishly. "That is fair. I wouldn't want Arnoth to think I'd made off with another one."

"What a reprehensible thought!"

"I know."

Dane stepped back and allowed her to pass. She cast a quick glance at him as she walked through the door. He seemed gentle. "Do you think they'll get along?"

"Do you want the truth, or a pleasant lie?"

"The truth!"

"I think if you want to see Arnoth after this dinner, I'll have to do some clever footwork."

"What do you mean?"

"Unless I miss my guess, your father will forbid you to see him before the final course is served."

"He has no such authority over me!"

"Maybe not, but his position gives him enough authority to have Arnoth confined or imprisoned, if only for the length of this trip."

"He wouldn't dare."

"Wouldn't he?"

Sierra's mouth curved to one side. "I don't understand why my father took such a violent dislike to him."

"Don't you?" Dane took Sierra's arm. She didn't resist. "When Arnoth of Valenwood stepped out of that shuttle, your father saw something he's never seen before."

Sierra looked up at Dane in wonder. "What?"

"A man stronger than himself."

"I'll bed your daughter whenever the urge strikes me!"

Sierra stopped outside the dining hall door, and Dane clasped his hand to his head. "I warned you . . ."

Sierra gripped Dane's arm. "I didn't think it would be this bad!"

"Ellowan, your audacity is astounding, and well beyond your power. You are on *my* vessel, and unless you want to be permanently confined, you'll stay on the far side of this ship!" Redor's voice quavered with rage, elevated higher than Arnoth's.

Dane sighed. "I have to admit, this is sooner and worse than I expected."

Sierra's eyes welled with tears. "What am I going to do?"

"Trust me."

"Why should I? You stole his wife. You're hardly a reliable person."

Dane grinned. "Because for reasons I'll never know, I love him. For the first time in four hundred years, he has a chance to find happiness. And because of you, Arnoth of Valenwood just insulted the most important man in the galaxy. I wouldn't have missed this for anything. Allow me to repay you both, hmm?"

She had no choice. She liked Dane. His vow of love seemed genuine. "What are you going to do?"

"Go in there and take over, of course. Use my charm to ease the situation. . . ."

Sierra's brow angled. "And I thought Arnoth was vain."

"I'm not vain. Now, do as I tell you. Agree with everything your father says."

"I will not!"

"You will if you want to see your lover tonight."

"You'd better be right."

"I'm right. I'm always right. Didn't you know?"

"I believe I've heard something to that effect. Very well. I'll do as you say."

Dane opened the door just as Redor hurled a goblet across the room. It shattered against the far wall. Arnoth stood like a regal statue, his face kindled with fury.

Redor rang a bell with shaking hands. "Guards!"

Dane eased Sierra aside. "I don't think that guards will be necessary. He's giving you trouble, too?" Dane paused to shake his head. "You have no idea what I endured at this Ellowan's hands."

Arnoth turned his dark gaze on Dane, but Dane just

smiled and positioned himself at Arnoth's side. "My wife is the same. Trouble, trouble, trouble. You've got to know how to handle them. Now, what's the problem, sir?"

"I want this black-eyed harem master as far away from my daughter as he can get!"

Dane nodded thoughtfully. "I can certainly understand that. He's a demon where women are concerned. No question."

Arnoth glared. "You would certainly know."

Dane nodded again. "I'm sure we can rectify the situation easily." He smacked his lips, reminding Sierra of Batty. "I'm sure once your daughter has gotten over the sensual delirium"—a tiny smile flickered on Dane's lips and he cleared his throat—"she'll see reason." He turned to Arnoth. " Let's see . . . You've bedded this innocent girl what . . . ten, twenty times?"

"Once, and it's none of your concern."

"Once?" Dane looked disappointed.

Sierra tapped her lip. "It depends on how you count it, actually. It was twice the first time, but that would count as once. We were interrupted the second time."

"I see. Well, once isn't really enough for him to fully ensnare you."

"I'm not . . ."

Dane shot her a look of warning, silencing her. "You are."

"I suppose so."

"It's simple, then. You need time apart, so you can come to your senses. I'm sure your father doesn't want to go so far as to forbid you from seeing him."

Redor's jaw assumed a stubborn posture. "I'm willing and able to shoot him into space."

Arnoth's lip curled. He radiated scorn. "It's been done. I survived that, and I'll survive whatever you throw my way, too."

"Without a capsule!"

Dane chuckled and slapped Arnoth's shoulder, too hard. "I don't think we need such drastic measures. I'm absolutely certain your little girl has seen the light and wants nothing further to do with this . . ." Dane paused and smiled. "What was it you called me when we engaged in a similar discussion before your tribunal?" He paused again, musing, while Arnoth fumed. "Ah, yes. I recall. 'Seducer.' "

Sierra caught Dane's look and she puffed a breath. "He's right, Papa. Arnoth is much too hotheaded and unreliable for me. I'll stay away from him."

"Good." Redor's entire demeanor altered and he smiled. "Dinner is served."

Arnoth lay on his back, glaring at the dark ceiling. They'd actually sat down to eat. All of them. Dane remarking on the quality of the wine, Sierra happily stuffing spicy rolls into her little, soft mouth. Redor, the devil, informing them that it had been a good season for Goyen fruit. Whatever that was.

Redor had called for the clone, Drakor, and given him the seat at his left hand. A position of honor. Redor called him Koran and "son," in the same breath. Unable to endure more, Arnoth had stormed from the dining hall, in the worst temper of his life.

Dane Calydon was more treacherous than he'd ever imagined. And Sierra . . . Arnoth couldn't bring himself to think about what she had done. Her father was the most abominable man alive. Most important man in the galaxy, indeed!

His world deserved destruction. Arnoth's fury gave way and he sat up in bed, raking his hands through his tangled hair. The old fool hadn't listened to a word he'd said about the Tseir invasion. He was certain Arnoth had if not raped, then seduced his daughter, and risked her life in the process.

He wasn't good enough for her. Redor made that perfectly clear. Sierra Karian was the smartest, best, most beautiful, adored Nirvahdi of all time. Advancing faster at the academy than any other, destined for glory in whatever she wanted.

She deserved something better than a bloodthirsty Ellowan whose people rejected real civilization for the presumed reason of keeping their sexual escapades secret. Arnoth had refused to defend his people, instead questioning how what his race did in bed was any of Redor's business.

Which was a fair question. And an unanswered one. Arnoth had the feeling it was just an excuse to get him out of Sierra's life, anyway. It was as if any man, including a clone, would be preferable to Redor as his daughter's lover.

Arnoth lay down again. True, he wasn't charming—unlike Dane, who could talk the stars out of the sky. But he wasn't loathsome, either. He was handsome, intelligent, strong. . . . Arnoth drummed his fingers on his chest. He imagined stuffing Redor into a cubicle and giving the amber whales a shot at him.

A prolonged shot. And this cubicle wouldn't have air.

The door opened and Dane stuck his head in the door. Arnoth considered which manner of death best suited his former friend, but Dane grinned, catching him off guard. "You owe me, my friend."

Dane stood back and guided Sierra through the door. She still wore the yellow gown that had taken his breath away in the dining hall. Her lips looked softer and pinker than usual. Her hair was coiled over her shoulder and one breast.

Dane chuckled. "Enjoy yourself. From what the bat has reported so far, you're quite capable of that."

Arnoth's mouth dropped, but Dane closed the door, leaving him alone with Sierra. She just stood with her hands clasped in front of her body.

"I thought I was too hotheaded and unreliable to interest you."

Sierra caught her lower lip between her teeth. "I have a debt to pay."

"What debt?"

"I made a mistake."

Arnoth eyed her suspiciously as she crossed the floor. His brow rose as she pulled up her skirt and seated herself astride his thighs. She slid her hand up her thigh, lifting the skirt to her hips.

She wore nothing underneath that beautiful dress. Arnoth's pulse surged. Her hand moved inward; her fingers played in her own soft curls. He hardened beneath the sheets, tenting the covers. Her gaze fixed on his arousal and she smiled.

Her fingers splayed out around the tip of his concealed erection and her legs curled closer around his. "Sierra, what are you doing in here? If your father discovers—"

"You'll be shot into space. But not before I get my fill of you, Ellowan. I am ensnared, and it creates such a craving. . . ." Her eyelids drifted shut, her lips parted, and she drew a sensual breath.

Suddenly Arnoth didn't care if he was shot into space, as long as it didn't happen now. "I know only one way to satisfy you, little alien."

"Umm."

She moved her hips higher, just below his arousal. She peeled back the covers, and the evidence of his desire sprang free. She caught it in her quick fingers, massaging in firm, greedy strokes. Arnoth groaned. "It's worth being shot into space."

"I'll make you forget where you are, who you are, Ellowan. You are mine."

Sierra squirmed lower so that she knelt between his legs. She looked up at him, still gripping him. The raw power of his full length contrasted with her sweet, delicate face. His blood turned to flame. She trailed one finger from his thick base to the rim, then circled his aching tip.

His sac tightened and she cupped it gently in her other palm. She kneaded his entire length until it seemed he could restrain himself no longer. She stopped, and he started to reach for her, but she pushed him back. "I've just begun, Ellowan. You've ensnared me. It's my right to ensnare you back."

His muscles went weak as she pressed her lips to the tip of his staff. Her little tongue flicked out to taste him, and a hoarse groan tore from his throat. "You can be as loud as you want, Ellowan. No one will hear. Nirvahdi walls are soundproof. In fact, scream if you want."

Arnoth stared down at her in amazement. She took the tip of him in her mouth, swirling her tongue around the blunt end, then taking him deeper. She suckled, then eased, then ran her tongue along the base of his shaft until he arched and thrust upward.

Her hair teased his groin; her breasts rested on his thigh. It was agonizing bliss, being teased to the edge of endurance—both forbidden and fully indulged. Sierra sat back and took a curling tendril of her long hair, lashing his heated flesh with its end.

He thought he would burst, engorged as he was, and filled beyond endurance. But she wasn't ready to offer relief. Instead, she seemed fixated on increasing her sweet torment.

She slithered up his body, teasing every portion of his flesh with her soft hair. She trailed lines over his stomach, his flat, male nipples, his throat, his chin. She followed the same trail back to his swollen length. The soft hair teased his inner thigh, then up his length again.

She released her hair and took him greedily in her mouth, delirious with her feminine power. Arnoth felt like a harp in her fingers, played as she wished, taken to heights he'd never imagined. She sent herself into an equal frenzy. Her face glowed her eyes blazed.

She sat up, a goddess of feminine strength. She freed her round breasts from the snug bodice, cupping them in delicate hands. He braced himself up on his arms, and she bent forward for his attention.

He caught the firm little peak between his teeth, lashing it with his tongue until her cries echoed his. He suckled and teased, and she positioned herself over his length.

He felt the damp curls, the pulsating, hot need of her body. She grasped his shoulders, then lowered himself over him. Arnoth thrust upward, deep inside her. She gasped and cried out, then moved in sweet rhythm above him. Her head tipped back, her eyes drifted shut as she focused on her pleasure.

His restraint was long gone. His culmination started in pounding waves, milked and urged by her inner spasms. His whole body quaked; he called out her name and his body bucked upward as he poured himself inside her, through her.

Sierra twisted above him as her own convulsions rippled through her lush body. She collapsed on his chest, gasping for air, her skin damp from her passion. Arnoth wrapped his arms around her and kissed her forehead. "I will never let you go."

She kissed his chest, then his neck. "I love you. You knew that, didn't you?"

"I know it now."

Sierra moved from his body and curled into his arms. Arnoth cradled her head on his shoulder. "I'm sorry about my father. I don't know what's wrong with him."

"Power has gone to his head."

"Well, if that's it, it waited a very long time to happen.

He's usually quite reasonable and tolerant.''

"Those are the last two descriptions I would apply to your father, woman."

"Dane says he'll get over it."

"Oh, does he? With that treacherous Thorwalian's 'help,' I'm likely to be cast into space as bloody bits of debris."

"Dane won't let anything happen to you."

Arnoth adjusted his position to look at her sleepy face. "That man has some kind of secret charm over women."

"No. He's just cute. As you said."

"I never said that."

"By tomorrow, he'll have my father begging you to be his son."

"There's a fanciful notion, if ever there was one."

"Did you get enough to eat?"

"I didn't get anything to eat at all."

Sierra kissed his shoulder. "We could call for something."

"What? And risk having me shot into space?"

"We'll have a big breakfast, then."

"If I survive the night, little alien, there's only one thing I want for breakfast. You."

Something cold and sharp probed at his neck. Arnoth emerged reluctantly from the heavy blanket of sleep and lifted his hand to push it away. It returned, pricking his flesh.

"Awake to battle, Ellowan. Your doom is at hand, and this deed will not go unpunished."

Arnoth opened his eyes and blinked. Dane stood beside his bed, holding what looked like . . . a fork. He was grinning from ear to ear. He flipped the fork onto a cart, then seated himself on the bed beside Arnoth.

"Do you know how long I've dreamt of doing that?"

"You, Thorwalian, are a troubled man."

Dane chuckled. "Vengeance is mine. Of course, I'd be happier if I could have you hauled before a tribunal and enlist your lovely Sierra to explain in detail what the two of you spent the night doing."

Arnoth tried not to smile and failed. "Thorwalian, my tribunal was merciful compared to that Intersystem tyrant."

"You may be right."

Dane waved his arm at the cart beside the bed. "When I first entertained Aiyana thus, you treated me to breakfast. Thought I'd do the same for you."

"Generous." Arnoth's stomach churned. Dane passed him a roll, which Arnoth ate. It crumbled deliciously and tasted sweet and substantial. "Thank you."

"My pleasure."

Dane crossed one leg over the other, in no hurry to leave. Arnoth eyed the Thorwalian's elaborate pale blue attire. "What are you wearing? I don't remember any such uniform on Candor."

"There isn't one." Dane fiddled with the gold braiding. "The Nirvahdi can create any kind of garment in the blink of an eye. I thought I'd conjure up something suitable to my station." He looked proud.

"Vain as always."

"I requested a gown for Aiyana that shows every curve of her precious little body, and a good portion of those shapely legs, too." He paused and sighed. "She'll only wear it in private." His eyes twinkled. "Which is the best place to make use of it, anyway."

Dane peered over Arnoth's shoulder at Sierra. "If you use your limited imagination, you should be able to dress that sexy body in something suitable."

Arnoth eased the blanket higher over Sierra's bare shoulder. Dane beamed with pleasure at the possessive gesture. "Ah, yes. I found that part of the bat's report interesting. *'The woman is mine, and mine only. Got it?'*"

"Your abundant interest in my personal affairs is indeed flattering."

"Actually, I'd forgotten telling the rodent to keep an eye on you. Lingbats have superior memories, you know."

"So I've been told." Arnoth finished the roll, then reached for another. He realized his last meal had consisted of a few berries and three nuts. He drained a goblet of a flavorful, tart nectar, then tried a round pink fruit. The fruit was good, too. Ripe and sweet.

Dane rubbed his hands together in undisguised glee. "Now, I'd like a few clarifications. The bat has amply described your fall, but there is a point or two I'd like cleared up."

"I knew I'd have to face your demonic inquiry sooner or later." Arnoth sighed and lay back beside Sierra, his hands clasped over his chest.

"Couldn't let it pass, you understand. Batty assures me you were *on your knees,* humbled beyond my wildest dreams. But I've got to know . . ." Dane was enjoying Arnoth's discomfort beyond his usual capacity. Arnoth waited stoically. "Was it before or after?"

Sierra stirred beside Arnoth, snuggling against his shoulder. She yawned and stretched, then slid her leg over his. Dane noticed the sensual gesture and his blue eyes widened almost imperceptibly.

A languid smile formed on Sierra's pink, thoroughly kissed lips. "During."

Dane's mouth opened, then closed. He looked suddenly . . . tense. Arnoth couldn't restrain a grin of masculine pride. Sierra opened one eye and peeked at their uninvited guest. "I wouldn't say he was exactly humbled, though." Sierra paused. "Because, you see, I spent some time on my knees, too."

Dane hopped up from the bed and cleared his throat. Twice. "I see. Too clearly for comfort." He drew a tight breath, then headed for the door. "Warm in here, isn't it? We're arriving on Nirvahda in a few hours. And not a minute too soon. Aiyana had better be waiting. . . ."

Dane left the room in a hurry. Sierra chuckled and slid her arm over Arnoth's chest. "I think he deserved that, don't you?"

Arnoth touched her chin and kissed her mouth. "Little alien, you please me."

Dane poked his head back in the door. "Sorry to interrupt. Forgot to mention, Redor requests the honor of your presence, both of you, at his . . ." Dane paused, snapping his fingers as if to stir his memory. "What did he call it? Something like 'tribunal.' "

Arnoth jerked upright, and Dane laughed. "You've got just enough time for breakfast and to dress. Keep the red shirt, Arnoth. It looks good on you. But those tight leggings of yours must go."

Dane cackled like a lingbat, then disappeared. Arnoth sighed and shook his head. "Well, it was a good night. I hope the last face I see before I'm shot into space is yours."

Sierra and Arnoth stood outside the door of Redor's office. She held his hand; they looked into each other's eyes. "I can't believe, after all we've faced, that the worst enemy is my father."

"The Tseir were merciful comparatively. But I will not let you go, Sierra. He'll have to shoot me into space first."

The door slid open and they entered together. Redor sat at the center of a circular table, with Dane at his right hand. Dane looked more smug than Arnoth had ever seen him. *A tribunal*. His blue eyes gleamed with pleasure.

Stobie Piel

Redor fixed his dark gaze on Arnoth, then Sierra. "I ordered you two to stay apart."

Sierra's chin lifted. "We didn't. And we won't."

Redor nodded. "I see."

"I love your daughter, Nirvahdi. . . ." Arnoth hesitated. He suspected no one ever referred to the prime representative as "Nirvahdi." "Your orders mean nothing. I will not let her go."

"This situation needs to be rectified before we reach Nirvahda. Sierra's mother is sensitive to these matters."

Arnoth wondered how anyone could be more "sensitive" than Redor, but he made no comment.

Sierra's eyes narrowed. "How do you want it rectified?"

Dane cleared his throat. "I'm sure we'll come up with something."

Arnoth eyed the devious Thorwalian. "If it's up to you, I'll end up as space debris."

"Worse. You'll be mated through all eternity, and I will be able to issue the words 'I told you so.' The presence of children might rectify the situation between us, I might add."

A slow smile grew on Arnoth's face. Somehow, Dane Calydon had convinced Sierra's furious father that the only solution was marriage.

Redor sighed. "It seems the only way. I expect a vow from you that Sierra will be your only mate, that you will treat her with respect, and do nothing peculiar to her in public."

Arnoth's brow angled, and Dane looked away to hide laughter. "I agree to those terms. Restraining myself in public *may* be a hardship, but I'll give it my best effort."

Sierra looked up at him doubtfully. "I meant to ask you about that."

"I'll tell you later, little alien." He noticed Redor's suspicious frown. "Much later."

290

* * *

Arnoth stood with Sierra at the end of a long ramp, waiting for the shuttle transport to the surface of Nirvahda. The Nirvahdi flagship remained in space and passengers were transported to the surface of their planet in smaller shuttles.

Small, compared to the flagship. Arnoth estimated only fifteen Ellowan vessels could fit in one Nirvahdi shuttle. "Woman, I'm almost afraid to see your world."

"I wish we had time to explore. I want to show you everything."

"When we've convinced your crazy father that he needs to form a resistance, and form it now, you can show me everything there is to see. Maybe we'll even leave your bedchamber."

Redor joined them as Arnoth spoke. The man glared. Arnoth cringed inwardly, but he kept his expression solemn and proud. "You will restrain your vulgarities before my wife, Ellowan. Understood?"

"If a vulgarity happens into my thoughts, I might choose to keep it to myself. Since it's never happened before . . ."

Dane bounded down the platform and assumed position between the angry father and Arnoth. The two lingbats sat on Dane's wide shoulders, looking like ornamental epaulets on an odd, young king.

"They match your uniform, Thorwalian. Impressive."

Carob straightened on Dane's shoulder. "His uniform suits us well. It was necessary to clothe the human in a way befitting our station."

On Dane's other shoulder, Batty puffed with pride. "The gold braids are particularly useful for gripping."

Arnoth chuckled. "Meaning he's a lingbat perch."

Neither Carob nor Batty argued, though Dane looked a little deflated. He eyed Arnoth's red shirt. "Still dressed as a Tseir, are you? Well, Arnoth, prince of Valenwood, seducer of . . .''

Arnoth's threatening frown stopped Dane's words. Dane issued a smile of satisfied vengeance. ''It suits you.''

Sierra nodded. ''That's what I told him.''

Two alien men with black skin and bright robes led Koran and Colice down the ramp. Redor brightened when the clone approached and ushered him in front of Arnoth, which Arnoth suspected was a deliberate action. Colice stood beside Sierra, expressionless as always.

Sierra smiled at Colice. ''Did you sleep well, Colice?''

''There is no structure for rest duties. I am used to the monitor system of waking up.''

''You'll get used to it. You can sleep whenever you want here.''

Colice eyed her doubtfully. Sierra seemed so hopeful, so intent on giving others freedom and joy. But Arnoth guessed that the Tseir might prefer their structure.

''What about consumptives? Are you enjoying our meals?''

Sierra's question confused Colice further still. ''Nirvahdi consumptives are unusual. They require administration in strange ways, rather than directly to the mouth.''

''That's the beauty of it. And the taste . . . Didn't you notice the difference in flavor? I don't mean to be ungrateful, but Tseir consumptives have almost no flavor at all.''

''I noticed no difference.''

Arnoth tapped Sierra's shoulder. ''She's a clone, Sierra. They've lost the subtler elements of the senses.''

''I see. Their reduced capacity to feel explains the need for the red section, doesn't it?''

''Not in front of your father, woman!''

Sierra bit her lip and nodded. ''Maybe she'd taste

something very spicy. We'll try that at dinner.'' Sierra eyed her father. "I assume we're having a full banquet tonight, and that *everyone* will attend."

Redor frowned tightly, but he shrugged. "Your return warrants a banquet. Your mother would be disappointed with anything less, naturally. Of course, she'll probably be too stunned to make an appearance." He cast a long, dark look Arnoth's way. "I may have to break this news to her in private, so that she has time to contain her grief."

Sierra stepped in front of her father, seized one of the tall, black-skinned aliens, and pulled him to Arnoth. "You didn't get a chance to meet Garian last night at dinner. Garian, this is Arnoth."

The tall black man bowed. "It is my great honor." He spoke with an accent, low and musical.

Arnoth bowed, too. "And mine, Garian. What is your world?"

Garian looked puzzled and glanced at Sierra. "Nirvahda is my world."

Another error. Arnoth suspected Dane would never have asked, but Garian didn't seem offended. Sierra seemed to understand his discomfort. She slipped her hand onto his arm and squeezed gently. "Garian is married to my oldest sister."

"You have a sister?"

"I have three sisters and two brothers. I am the youngest."

Redor nodded. "And the least manageable."

Arnoth touched Sierra's soft cheek. "We have much to learn about each other."

Redor issued a low growl. "In private."

Arnoth glared behind Sierra at Redor. "Unless you want me to start here and now, you'll dispense with the orders, Nirvahdi."

Garian's mouth dropped and he eased back. "Interesting to meet you, Arnoth.'' His tone gave every indication that he didn't expect Arnoth to live through the day.

Sierra sighed, then rested her forehead on Arnoth's shoulder. ''Garian is a cloning specialist. He's been searching for a solution to the Tseir problem. My oldest sister is also a scientist. The others are at work on other planets. I couldn't tell you much about my family while we were imprisoned because I didn't want the Tseir to learn my identity.''

Colice nodded. ''That is correct. The First Commanders made an unfounded assumption that the Nirvahdi leader wouldn't send a member of his family on such a mission.''

Redor thumped his fist into his palm. ''And he wouldn't!''

''We didn't consider that she might have acted in defiance of your orders.''

''And not for the first time.''

''Prisoner Sierra made an impressive commander.''

''That's true, Papa, I did. I was closing in on the Final Third before I met Arnoth.''

Redor's brow furrowed and he glanced at Arnoth. For the first time, his expression revealed something short of intense dislike. He seemed to be seeking an explanation of his daughter's behaviour from the one person who might know.

''Your daughter has spent too much time with the Tseir. She's taken their numerical titles and references to heart.'' Arnoth stopped and sighed. ''Unfortunately, she's taken their system of color coding to heart, also.''

''Color coding?''

''You don't want to know. I don't want to know.''

Dane looked between them. ''What color coding?''

Arnoth cast a dubious glance at Dane's elaborate uniform. ''Never mind. Suffice to say that pale blue is probably the best color for you.''

Dane's eyes wandered to one side. He obviously sensed a veiled insult but couldn't quite pin it down. Arnoth relished the moment.

The doors at the end of the ramp parted, opening into a shuttle that locked onto the hull of the giant flagship. Redor led his group into the smaller craft and seated himself beside Koran. Arnoth went to the opposite end of the vessel, followed by Dane and Sierra.

Dane looked out the long, low window behind their seats. The shuttle dislodged from the larger vessel, then eased smoothly away. "Impressive, isn't it? When I left Nirvahda, Nisa was hard at work studying their technical prints." Dane looked around Arnoth to Sierra. "Nisa is my sister. Like myself, she's a technician."

"You're a technician?" Sierra cast an incredulous glance at Arnoth. Arnoth didn't respond. "I thought you said he was some kind of barbarian warrior."

"No. I only said he looks like one."

Dane appeared flattered. "I am both."

Carob issued a long whistle. "Ha! What's your weapon, boy? A smile?"

Dane frowned, but Batty nodded earnestly. "He uses it well, sire. No mistake."

Dane brightened. "I do, at that."

Arnoth winked at Sierra. "As you've spent too much time with the Tseir, our Thorwalian friend is beginning to take on lingbat traits."

"I noticed that."

Dane bristled, but he didn't argue. Carob looked proud. "We've taught him well."

Despite being seated at the far end of the vessel, seemingly engaged in conversation with Koran, Redor overheard their comments. "Every representative should have a lingbat or two, to offer guidance and wisdom. Do us all good."

Arnoth and Dane exchanged a pained glance. Dane

bowed his head in defeat. "I've feared this for years. First they're 'advisors.' Next thing you know, lingbats are seated on thrones, ruling the galaxy."

Carob tangled a wingtip in Dane's hair and yanked. "Galaxy, indeed! Universe, boy. Universe."

Chapter Nine

A huge blue and green planet came into view through the shuttle window. "This shouldn't surprise me. At least ten Valenwoods would fit inside Nirvahda." Arnoth sat back in his seat and sighed.

Dane slapped his knee. "And five Thorwals. It shocked me, too." Dane paused. "Well, I'm not bedding one of the natives, so it wasn't such a *personal* shock, but still . . ."

"You're enjoying this, aren't you?"

"Every minute."

"I'm happy for you."

Dane gazed out the window at the swelling planet and his expression changed. "There's something I should probably tell you before we land."

"What?"

"Just a small problem, I'm sure. Nothing we can't

handle. You've dealt with the Tseir, the father . . . This should be nothing.''

Dane spoke as if the worst was yet to come, and Arnoth steeled himself. "Thorwalian, speak plainer. The way this shuttle moves, we'll be on the surface in seconds. If I need warning, I'd like it before the fact."

"Aiyana."

"What about her?"

Dane glanced at Sierra and offered a weak smile. "My wife."

"Yes, I know. Arnoth has told me about her. I'm looking forward to meeting her."

Her response seemed to trouble Dane. He looked pained, though Arnoth had no idea why. "The thing is, when Aiyana gets something into her head, it's hard to get it out again, if you understand my meaning."

"No."

Carob snorted. "No one would understand your meaning, boy. You're as clear as fog."

Batty adjusted his position on Dane's shoulder. "Didn't follow, either, sir."

"If I was explaining to a lingbat, I would use simpler terms. I trust my Ellowan friend will understand."

"No."

Dane rolled his eyes, then cast a quick look at Sierra. There was something he didn't want to say in front of her. Arnoth's patience wore thin. "What is it, Thorwalian? I can't imagine Aiyana causing any trouble."

Dane's brow angled doubtfully. "You lived with her for four hundred years, didn't you?" He paused and shook his head. "You don't know that little woman the way I do."

"I know she's never caused me a speck of the trouble you've caused."

"Not yet."

Arnoth's eyes narrowed. "Thorwalian . . ."

"Oh, all right. . . . She's never accepted her sister's death, Arnoth. Not really. She keeps something of Elena alive, and she does it through you."

"What are you talking about?"

Sierra touched his arm. "I think I know. As long as you remain unbonded, it's as if her sister were still alive."

Dane nodded, looking more solemn than usual. "That's right."

Arnoth considered this. "She had no objections to my mating with Helayna. In fact, she encouraged it, if not downright forced it on me."

"Aiyana has never seen Helayna for what she is. Which is, quite frankly, a rather dull, unimaginative young woman with an attractive body and a pretty face. Too even and uninteresting for beauty, in my opinion."

Sierra frowned. "If she's so dull, why does your wife prefer her?"

A gentle smile formed on Dane's mouth. "Whatever happens, Sierra, don't take it personally. It may take a while for Aiyana to accept you. She loved her sister very much. Helayna resembles Elena quite closely, or so I'm told."

"Actually, Elena looked more like your sister." Arnoth sighed. "But Nisa is what Elena should have been, not what she was."

"Did Elena pilot like a madwoman, too?"

Arnoth hesitated, confused. "Pilot . . . ? No, not that I recall."

"You've never seen Nisa at the helm of anything, have you?"

"No."

Dane shook his head. "And you don't want to, my friend. When I left, her husband Seneca was trying to talk her out of flying a Nirvahdi hovercraft."

Sierra giggled at Dane's representation of his sister. "She sounds rather endearing."

"You'll have no trouble with Nisa. Since Arnoth healed her, she's considered him some sort of hero. Never understood why—the Ellowan healing technique is simply biological, but she thinks he's beyond reproach."

"Maybe I can convince her to speak to Redor Karian on my behalf."

Dane dismissed the tension with Redor with a wave of his hand. "That was nothing I couldn't handle. This—" Dane scrunched his shoulders and grimaced. Both lingbats teetered, then dug their claws in unison.

"Watch it, boy!"

The shuttle dropped through into the Nirvahdi atmosphere, then lowered toward the surface of the planet. Arnoth looked out the window, and a vast green and blue world came into view. He saw rivers and oceans quickly brought into view as the shuttle neared the surface.

As they lowered, he saw white cities, interspersed with green forests. Dane chuckled. "Wait 'til you see . . ."

They drew closer, and the white cities were revealed as high, slender towers of intricate shape, some with rims, some with wide bases, some in reverse. The entire city seemed designed as one enormous work of art. The white shimmered like crystal, almost translucent.

White hovercrafts buzzed from building to building; some darted outward toward the forest.

"Your mouth is hanging open, *prince*."

Arnoth closed his mouth and cast a dark look Dane's way. Dane sat back in his seat, grinning. "Not quite the Swamp of Keir, is it?"

Arnoth shook his head, but he wasn't sure what to say. Dane's grin eased and he laid his hand on Arnoth's shoulder. "You never did belong on Keir."

Dane's gentle words implied that Arnoth belonged on

300

Nirvahda. An unlikely assessment, if ever there was one. Batty cranked his small head to look out the window, seeming to find the forest of more interest than the glorious city.

"If there's green, there are bugs."

"That's a truism, lad. Bugs the like of which you've never seen or imagined in your wildest dreams. Bugs that crunch and pop and melt in your mouth, too fat to put up much of a struggle."

Dane groaned as the two lingbats leaned toward each other—in front of his face. Arnoth enjoyed the posture. "Tell me, Thorwalian, it was your own technical genius that gave these formidable creatures speech, wasn't it?"

"It was." Dane's voice was a tortured groan.

"Ah. So when they're running the galaxy, and you're busy cleaning their feet, you have only yourself to blame."

Dane held his hand over his heart. "That was, and has been, and always will be, my greatest torment."

Sierra held Arnoth's hand in hers as the shuttle landed. For a while, she'd been nothing more than a woman. A woman who intrigued Arnoth for what she was, and nothing else. She had been just Sierra. As her father aimed for the door, Koran close beside him, she remembered who she had been before.

Sierra Karian, Redor's favored child, beloved daughter of Nirvahda, the pride of the Intersystem academy. A low ache centered around her heart. She'd never liked the role. No one had teased her, groaned, or rolled their eyes when she spoke rashly. She glanced up at Arnoth. If he changed . . .

No, his manner toward her wouldn't change. He'd never become agonizingly respectful of her station, never worshipful of her. But he might withdraw; he might find it more comfortable to live without her. Dane was chattering about something—

"The doors, Arnoth . . . They glide open as if they're not really there, just . . . whoosh! Unbelievable!"

Arnoth looked down at her. She heard his voice in her head. *"I assume Nirvahdi doors open swiftly so as not to get in your way. Your race would never survive otherwise."* Sierra held her breath, hoping his brown eyes would twinkle and he'd tease her.

But Arnoth said nothing, and Sierra's heart fell. It wasn't important. Maybe he was just being polite because Redor stood beside them. No, that wasn't likely. Why would he start now?

Carob leaned against Dane's head. It made a strange picture: the tall, broad-shouldered Thorwalian in his decorated uniform, and the chubby lingbat, casually leaning against Dane's blond hair. Batty sat stiff and alert on the other shoulder, excited, enthusiastic.

"The thing that impressed me, lad, was that the Nirvahdi doors opened for me, on their own, without assistance from a human. Detected my presence despite my lack of vertical dimension."

Dane coughed. "Meaning *height*."

Carob ignored him. "I've seen very diminutive humanoids, a few on the ship. As I understand it, they're the Intersystem's best soldiers. Size, lad . . . it's important only to those who have it." He cranked his head to look into Dane's face. Dane just sighed.

Sierra's heart warmed and constricted at once. She liked Dane Calydon and his lingbats. She liked the way he both tormented Arnoth and admired him, even loved him. She liked the way Arnoth suffered his presence and loved every minute of their banter.

She loved it, too. Yet as the shuttle door slid open, revealing the warm sun and golden earth of Nirvahda, she feared his reaction to a world so much more powerful than his own, and to the woman he thought he knew.

Sierra kept her gaze on Arnoth as he stepped from the shuttle. A warm, temperate breeze tousled his long hair; he breathed the air and smiled faintly. "It's a far cry from the air of Dar-Krona, I'll say that."

Colice stepped out beside Sierra and took a deep breath. "I detect no difference."

Sierra touched the Tseir's shoulder. Colice looked at Sierra's hand suspiciously. "If you close your eyes, Colice, you might focus your senses on the smell in the air. It's from flower petals." Sierra pointed to a large, flowering Karva bush, its bright orange blossoms sending sweet aroma through the air. Tiny pink birds sipped at its nectar.

Colice closed her eyes and sniffed. "Nothing."

"We'll have our medical persons check you over. Maybe something can be done to elevate sensitivity."

Redor stepped out beside her. "Good idea. Garian, take the Tseir to the med lab. See what you can do for her. And keep her under some kind of guard, too, would you?"

Garian took Colice's arm. She looked to Sierra, who nodded helpfully. "You'll be fine, Colice. Once you've adjusted, we can research your original, if you're interested."

"My original? For what purpose?"

"It might be interesting to you."

Colice appeared skeptical. "I can't think why."

Colice left with Garian, and Sierra sighed. "This is going to be harder than I thought."

Arnoth folded his arms over his chest. "If you're attempting to humanize that Tseir, it's going to be impossible." He looked around, then back at the shuttle. "What is this place? It's not a docking bay."

"The shuttle has dropped us off near the Intersystem capital." As Sierra spoke, the shuttle lifted silently behind them and eased from the planet's surface. "We keep them in space so they don't clutter our landscape."

"Good idea."

A wide, geometrically designed garden stretched around the city, greeting those who landed on Nirvahda with sweet aroma and beauty. The vast garden was her father's pride. Sierra hoped Arnoth would compliment it lavishly, and please Redor in the process.

"Who would plant a garden around a docking bay?"

"I would, Ellowan."

Arnoth sighed faintly. "I should have known."

Sierra sighed, too. "It's beautiful, don't you think?"

"Yes."

"He certainly has a way with words, daughter." Redor passed by, leading Koran protectively by the arm. "You'll stay with my family, son."

Sierra caught Arnoth's frown and she patted his arm. "My father cared very much for Koran."

"I see that."

"Koran worshipped my father, and he was eager and cheerful and handled matters my father disliked, such as formal pleasantries."

"You mean, matters he was incapable of handling."

"That, too."

"Now what?"

"My father has called a council session, and we'll be asked to speak. That will be your chance to convince them the Tseir plan to attack our planet rather than the fleet at Valenwood."

"If the Intersystem representatives are as thick-skulled as your father, we won't get far."

Sierra bit her lip and looked quickly around, but Redor was in conversation with Koran and didn't notice Arnoth's comment. "Behave."

Dane elbowed Arnoth in the ribs. "Good idea."

A ground craft buzzed toward them at an unusual

speed. Much faster than normal. It elevated suddenly, then dropped, spun, and whipped past their group. It circled back, then jerked to a stop. Dane Calydon laughed and shook his head, though Sierra had no idea why the near collision amused him.

The side doors of the ground craft opened and a powerful-looking dark man leapt out. He whirled to face the craft, pointing his finger. "I am *never* entering another vessel of any size, shape, or form with you again. Never. Do you understand? From now on, I'm walking!"

Dane howled with laughter, but Sierra glanced up at Arnoth for an explanation. He shrugged, but he was smiling, too. The dark man walked to Dane, grumbling. As he drew near, Sierra saw that he resembled Arnoth as closely as a brother. Blue shells decorated a braid of his hair, and his clothing resembled a hunter's garment, well worn and crafted by hand.

A blond woman stuck her head out of the craft and looked around. Even from a distance, Sierra could see a wild gleam in her eyes. She hopped down from the craft, glanced fondly at the vessel, patted its smooth, white surface, then headed after the man.

The woman wore a soft-looking uniform of white with gold trim. The contrast between her and the dark man had the odd effect of making them seem like two halves of a whole.

"Do you know these people?"

"This would be Dane's sister, Nisa, and her mate, Seneca."

Sierra studied them as they approached. Nisa's shoulders stiffened as Seneca shook his fist at her. "I had the impression they were a happy couple."

"I had that impression, too. When I first met them, they seemed to me what I might have had with Elena." Arnoth stopped and sighed. "It is possible we never had their depth of feeling."

305

Sierra eyed him skeptically. "He looks like he might kill her."

Dane slapped Seneca's shoulder in a friendly manner, then hugged his sister. He was still laughing. He approached the craft, then held out his hand. Sierra watched as Dane's expression changed. His smile turned sensual, teasing.

A delicate black-haired woman left the craft. She puffed a breath of relief, then placed her hand in Dane's. He kissed her cheek, then her mouth. Dane Calydon was obviously a man in love.

"Is that Aiyana?"

"It is."

"She's very pretty." Sierra found herself hoping Aiyana would like her despite Dane's prediction. Aiyana turned from Dane and saw Arnoth. Her small hands clasped over her heart and she closed her eyes. Arnoth took a step toward her, and she ran to him, her black hair flying like a shining curtain.

He caught her in his arms and picked her up. She wrapped her arms around his neck and kissed his cheek. She was crying. Arnoth set her upon her feet and she patted his cheek fondly. "You're all right. Arnoth . . ."

"I'm all right, *damanai*. Or I was until you sent your crazed mate after me."

"Sent him, indeed! I told him he couldn't do anything the Nirvahdi hadn't tried." Aiyana waved her arms, gesturing vaguely at the city spires. "Isn't this amazing? Only Dane would think he could better these people. When he heard you were taken captive, he left everything, summoned everyone he knew, and headed off after you."

Arnoth turned a slow, satisfied gaze to Dane, who looked uncomfortable. "Indeed. I am flattered by your concern."

"She exaggerates."

"Ha! He couldn't sleep, he barely ate . . ." Aiyana scratched behind Batty's ears. "He was equally distraught over your disappearance, Batty."

"Were you, sir?" Batty seemed deeply moved, and touched Dane's head fondly.

Aiyana nodded vigorously. "He neared tears whenever you were mentioned."

"Quiet, woman."

Sierra listened happily. Aiyana took equal delight teasing Dane. A fit mate. Arnoth's friends were interesting people. Fun. In their company, she could be herself.

Nisa noticed her and smiled pleasantly. Sierra smiled back. Nisa looked like a feminine version of Dane, tall and cheerful and beautiful. Mischief sparkled in her eyes. Seneca looked her way, too, then turned his penetrating gaze to Arnoth. A smile flickered on his lips, as if he naturally guessed the situation between them.

Aiyana moved back from Arnoth, a bright smile on her face. "There's someone else who's been waiting for you, my friend."

"Who?"

Dane hopped forward, coughing. "Rurthgar!" He turned toward the shuttle. "Is he in there?"

Aiyana shook her head, looking irritated. "I didn't mean Rurthgar, Dane. He's back at our quarters. He . . ." She paused, hesitant.

Seneca turned a meaningful gaze his wife's way. "He'd seen Nisa at the helm before and flatly, and wisely, refused to travel with her. He's waiting back at our quarters."

Dane positioned himself in front of the ground craft and splayed his arms over the exit, blocking it. "Let's walk, shall we? This garden wraps around the whole city. We'll take the lingbats hunting for the more interesting, crunchy, winged varieties of mothdom."

Aiyana placed her fists on her hips and glared. "Dane,

307

remove yourself from the door. Arnoth's 'surprise' is waiting.''

Batty looked from Dane's shoulder into the craft, then whistled. ''He'll be surprised, all right. Sire, didn't you mention a surprise for me? It's not like this one, is it?''

Dane cranked his head around and looked Batty in the eye. ''Your surprise is back at the guest quarters, rodent.''

Aiyana marched to Dane's side, shoved him aside, and motioned to someone in the craft. A slender, lovely young woman appeared. Arnoth breathed a muted groan. ''Oh, no.''

Sierra's eyes narrowed. The girl wore a loincloth and a narrow binding twisted over her breasts. Her flat stomach showed fully. She wore a string of ceramic beads, and bracelets decorated her bare arms. Her dark blond hair fell straight over both shoulders. She looked like a warrior princess.

The kind of princess who carried a spear. ''That's the girl in the cave of Valenwood, isn't it?'' Helayna, the woman who was supposed to become Arnoth's third wife.

Arnoth nodded, looking pained, but he didn't comment. Dane threw up his hands and hurried to reach Arnoth before Helayna. Redor studied the young woman, an expression of the utmost suspicion on his face.

''Who is that?''

Dane's face paled. He looked at Redor, then back at Arnoth. As if she saw his mind working, Sierra knew Dane was selecting the lesser of evils. He seized Redor's arm and pulled him away from the others. Only Dane Calydon had enough charm to haul her father around this way.

''The gardens, sir. You mentioned a walk . . .''

''Did I?''

''I'm looking forward to it.''

Dane cast a final, apologetic glance toward Arnoth, then shrugged. "You're on your own with this one."

Sierra heard Carob's high chirp as Dane disappeared with her father. "It's about time, too. You, boy, have bungled things mightily."

"Not another word, rodent."

Koran positioned himself beside Sierra. "I sense . . . tension."

Arnoth glared at the clone. "I'm not surprised. You're fairly well versed at causing it."

Sierra waited uncomfortably while Aiyana brought the Ellowan woman to Arnoth. Aiyana beamed. She held Helayna's arm like a sister. Helayna looked neither nervous nor shy. In fact, very little expression showed on her face. Koran nodded his approval. "She'd make an admirable Tseir."

"I was just thinking the same thing."

Aiyana seemed far more excited than either Helayna or Arnoth. She stood back, hands clasped over her breast, waiting. "I knew it would happen. The moment I met Helayna, I knew she was the woman for you."

Sierra braced herself. Her affection for Aiyana dwindled rapidly. She started forward, but Koran caught her arm. "This is his choice . . . isn't it?"

Koran's soft, knowing voice shocked her from motion. "I suppose so."

Helayna studied Arnoth dispassionately. "You freed yourself from the Tseir?"

"With help."

"Not by battle?"

Koran stepped forward, leaving Sierra. "Well, he shot me."

Helayna's gaze shifted to the clone. "Not very effectively, I would say."

"Effectively enough." Koran gestured to Sierra. "Sierra convinced him to heal me."

309

"Who are you?"

"I am Koran, known among the Tseir as Drakor, third-generational clone and former military commander, First Level."

"That is an impressive title."

Aiyana watched with a puzzled expression on her face, then tapped Helayna's shoulder. "He's a clone, dear. They're not exactly . . . real."

"I am real."

"You're not! And be quiet. You're interrupting Arnoth's reunion with his mate."

Koran shook his head. "The prime representative was right about you, Ellowan. How many mates do you have, anyway?"

Aiyana's face knit in indignation. "Arnoth has no mate anymore, clone. I wasn't really his mate in the first place, and he never got the chance with Helayna."

Koran pointed at Sierra. "What about that one?"

Aiyana turned her attention slowly to Sierra. Sierra realized that the small woman hadn't actually looked at her until now. Her avoidance had been purposeful. Dane Calydon was right: Aiyana didn't want to see. Her expression altered, her bright, green eyes narrowed to slits, then returned to Arnoth.

"That one?" Her soft, controlled voice indicated disbelief and potential outrage. Sierra cringed.

Arnoth drew a long breath, glanced to where Dane led Redor around the garden, muttered what sounded like a curse, then turned to Sierra. He held out his hand, a reassuring expression on his face that didn't quite meet his eyes. Sierra swallowed hard, then went to his side.

Arnoth took her hand, which Aiyana watched intently and without pleasure. "Aiyana, this is Sierra. My wife."

"Your *what?*" Aiyana's calm voice shattered and burst. Across the garden, Sierra saw Dane tense and cringe, then yank Redor down a path farther from view.

310

Helayna seemed thoroughly unaffected by Arnoth's announcement. "If he's taken another one, does this mean I still have to become a breeder?"

Aiyana clasped her hand to her forehead, probably fighting for self-control. She ignored Helayna's question, which made Sierra suspect Dane was right. There was no genuine friendship between the two women. Aiyana's affection for Helayna came from her resemblance to Elena, and perhaps in her pliability.

"You can't possibly have mated, Arnoth. There is ritual, ceremony. It is a sacred act."

"It took you approximately two minutes to become Dane's mate. He said he wanted to, you agreed. That's it, Aiyana. That's all it takes."

"Not for our prince!"

Arnoth smiled gently and touched Aiyana's chin. "The prince allowed himself an exception."

Aiyana nodded stoically. "Of course, any informal agreements, *formed under duress,* aren't really binding. You've been imprisoned by clones. You've had to endure . . . stars know what." Aiyana shot a pained glance at Sierra, then looked away. "What did she do to you? Threaten you? Promise you something?"

Sierra clenched her fist. She was taller than Aiyana: she could probably best the woman. . . . But Arnoth touched Aiyana's pretty face, then kissed her forehead. "She gave me life."

"I knew it! Sex!" Aiyana's voice blasted at a higher volume than her size would seem to allow. Sierra wanted the ground to open and swallow her whole. Better yet, she wanted it to swallow Aiyana.

From somewhere in the garden, Sierra heard loud, forced laughter. She heard Dane's voice, raised in a panicked tone. "No, no. I'm sure that's not what she said, sir."

Sierra's chin formed a furious ball. "I suppose you

311

were relieved from dormancy by soft speech and smiles?''

Aiyana's brow elevated into ripe indignation. ''That is none of your affair, young woman!''

''After your comments, I gathered these matters were up for public debate.''

Nisa eased herself between Sierra and Aiyana. ''Perhaps we should discuss this at another time. I'm sure Arnoth knows what he's doing.'' Nisa turned to Sierra. ''Sierra, am I right in guessing that you are the prime representative's daughter?''

''I am.''

Aiyana huffed. ''That's it. She threatened you with Nirvahda's power.''

''Actually, she failed to mention that little detail.''

Aiyana ignored Arnoth's remark. ''You were vulnerable—''

Nisa coughed loudly, in a manner similar to Dane. ''We've heard a lot about you since visiting Nirvahda, Sierra. You've been missed terribly. This whole planet has been on edge, waiting for news of you. And we've met your mother. A wonderful woman. She looks a lot like you, doesn't she? Aren't family resemblances amazing? I've been told I look like Dane. Now our son, Ananda, looks like Seneca. Our daughter does, too. But Aiyana's little girl looks like me.''

Nisa paused to draw a quick breath. Aiyana opened her mouth to speak, but Nisa didn't give her the chance. ''Do you like children, Sierra?''

Sierra nodded, her face still twisted with anger. Tears burned in her eyes, but she refused to cry. What Arnoth's second mate thought of her was unimportant. Infuriating, but meaningless.

''I wanted to bring the children to greet you, but Seneca wouldn't let them in a shuttle I was piloting. He's

Dakotan, you see, and Dakotans are nervous, *irrational* persons.''

Seneca chuckled. "With a strong sense of self-preservation. You neglected to mention the banquet, maiden.'' He took up where his wife left off. Seneca placed his arm over Arnoth's shoulder. "You'll like Nir-vahdi food. It's healthful and satisfying, a rare combination. There's a lot we can grow on Dakota. Which reminds me, we were discussing a manner of speeding up agriculture on Valenwood. . . .''

Aiyana pressed her small body between Seneca and Nisa, then glared at Sierra. "Valenwood needs a prince *and* a priestess. The Nidawi line hasn't been sundered in a thousand years. Until now.''

Nisa looked to Seneca, who shrugged as he considered the matter. "You have a daughter, Aiyana. With luck, Arnoth will have a son; you can betroth them. . . .''

"I am *not* forcing my daughter into marriage!''

Sierra quivered in fury. "Oh, no? You seem willing enough to force Arnoth into it.''

"I didn't get the chance! You insinuated yourself and applied whatever tactics you could think of, and . . . and thoroughly disrupted everything!''

Aiyana straightened, shoved past Seneca, and marched toward the garden. Sierra watched the little woman storm away. Dane abandoned Redor and caught up with her, leaving Redor bent over a bush, still talking to the vanished Thorwalian.

Arnoth sighed heavily, then took Sierra's hand. "I guess he knows her better than I do. I'm sorry, Sierra. I've never seen Aiyana angry. Not like this. Not even at Dane.''

Nisa sighed, too. "And there's provocation in Dane, to be sure.'' Nisa touched Sierra's shoulder. "It's not you, Sierra. Most of us have something in our past that's too painful to touch.'' She glanced at Seneca. "We all have to face it sometime. For me, facing it meant getting it back again. For Aiyana, it means letting go."

Seneca plucked an orange blossom from the Karva bush and placed it carefully in Nisa's hair. "Maiden, you astound me. Just when I think you're the craziest, most dangerous woman alive, you speak words of such wisdom. . . ."

Nisa turned her twinkling gaze to Seneca and fingered his beaded braid. "Is that so? Then perhaps you'll let me pilot you back to the city?"

"There is no chance of that, maiden."

Nisa's bright face formed a tight, fierce pout. "I am eminently capable . . ."

"Of destroying Nirvahda from within, one collision at a time."

Nisa cast an apologetic glance at Sierra. "He exaggerates, as Dakotans often do. A skilled pilot doesn't hesitate—"

"Or brake."

"A skilled pilot has instantaneous reflexes—"

"Which plaster the passengers onto the viewport."

Sierra's tears eased into a reluctant smile. "Nirvahdi vessels are sturdy."

Nisa pointed her finger into Seneca's face. "See!"

"Not that sturdy, maiden. Nothing is *that* sturdy."

"One more chance?"

He rolled his eyes. He groaned. And then he nodded. "If we could infect the Tseir with your piloting 'skills,' we could eliminate their threat forever after."

Nisa clapped her hands and started for the ground craft. Seneca gave a final look of a doomed man to Sierra and Arnoth. "I suggest you two walk. It's not far and you've been through enough."

Seneca disappeared into the craft after his wife, and it jerked forward into motion. Then back. Then straight up

314

with a roar. "That's odd. I never heard a ground craft make that noise before."

"This is typical." Helayna stood at Sierra's side, shaking her head. "They've forgotten me. And not for the first time, I might add."

Sierra endured a pang of fierce, feminine guilt. She'd taken Helayna's intended mate. It must have been a cruel shock. But Helayna didn't look particularly upset. "You can walk with us, Helayna."

"At least this day has turned out better than I expected. You have no idea what a relief it is to know I am spared becoming a breeder." Helayna eyed Arnoth without apology. "Aiyana convinced me it was my duty, but it is a revolting image."

Sierra restrained an outburst of laughter, but Arnoth frowned. "It wasn't an appealing notion to me, either."

Helayna seemed unoffended by his remark. "After the Tseir hauled you off, I studied the subject of reproduction. The old seers provided graphic images of male appendages, which I can only assume are exaggerated for clearer viewing. Why any woman of courage and merit would allow such a vulgar unit into her body is well beyond me."

Koran eased to Helayna's side. "You were obviously scrutinizing specimens from the red end of the spectrum. Perhaps something a little closer to . . . oh, say . . . *orange* would suit you. I'm not sure how much memory I retain of Nirvahda, but I'd be happy to escort you back to your quarters. Or possibly mine."

"You are odd, clone. But I do need direction to find the correct habitation."

Sierra's mouth dropped in unison with Arnoth's as Helayna and Koran headed off toward the city. Sierra looked up at Arnoth. "Is it possible we're dreaming this?"

Arnoth started to smile, then frowned and rolled his

eyes. "No, it's not possible. Your father is approaching."

Redor plucked a thistle from his gray trousers and tossed it aside. He looked around, puzzled. "Where is everyone? That young Thorwalian seemed so interested in gardening—and you know it's my special interest. I turned around, and he was gone. Just like that."

"He went with his wife, Papa."

"What about Koran?"

"He went with Helayna. I'm not sure where exactly, but they seemed to make friends."

"Well, well." Redor stretched his arms behind his back. "I see the ground speeder took off without us. Again. You'd think the prime representative would get better transport around this city, wouldn't you?"

Sierra smiled and patted her father's hand. "Where's Mother?"

"I sent word to her that I'd bring you home, so you could have your reunion in private. Make it quick, though. I want you both speaking at the council session. You can make your case to them, Ellowan. I don't know that they'll believe you, but we'll see."

"I will tell you what I believe to be true. It is your choice to take action or not."

Redor sneered. "Thank you for allowing me that."

Arnoth met Redor's glower without wavering. He even smiled slightly. "My pleasure."

"Your warnings are . . . interesting, Prince of Valenwood." Redor sat at the head of a long table, casually reclining in his high-backed chair, a faint smirk on his lips. Koran sat beside him, admitted to the assembly despite the fact that he was cloned by the Tseir.

Arnoth contained his anger, but it wasn't easy. The other Intersystem representatives had listened to his report on Dar-Krona, yet when the time for choice arrived, their gazes turned to Redor. The most important man in the galaxy had ultimate say, whether he claimed the role or not.

"If you find my warnings 'interesting,' you would do well to act on them, Karian."

A low murmur emanated from the far side of the table. The small humanoids, the Teradites, whispered among themselves, their pink eyes wide in astonishment. Arnoth looked around at the alien beings. He'd never realized how many advanced races populated the galaxy. And every one looked to Redor Karian for guidance.

The blue-skinned Zimdardri representative rose to her feet and bowed. "If I may, Prime Representative . . ."

Redor waved his arms casually. Apparently, the highest council in the galaxy operated on a far more informal level than an Ellowan tribunal. "Go ahead."

The Zimdardri faced Arnoth. "I share your concern, Prince. The Tseir are aggressive, as they revealed when they swarmed my world. I understand your bitterness over the destruction of your planet. . . ."

Arnoth guessed where this was leading. The Zimdardri's soft, musical voice held a faintly patronizing tone. "Yes, yes, I'm bitter. And I'd prefer to spare Nirvahda the same result. Which may be possible, if you'll recall your fleet from Valenwood and . . ."

The tiny Teradite hopped to his feet and banged the table with an iron-gloved fist. "What? You expect us to withdraw the fleet? Oh, *that's* good thinking!"

"You're a cantankerous little person, aren't you?"

The entire assembly gasped. Beside him, Sierra clasped her hand to her forehead and groaned. Her elegant, beautiful mother chuckled. Arnoth hadn't been formally introduced to the woman who Redor claimed would enter grieving over Sierra's marriage to a "harem master," but she seemed much less upset than the old devil had claimed.

The Teradite was speechless with fury. Arnoth waited

317

patiently for the repercussions of his latest rash statement. He glanced toward Redor, who seemed to be repressing a grin. Redor rose to his feet and tapped the table.

"Since this Ellowan isn't an Intersystem council member, and his race refused our communications, I don't think we can hold him responsible for his lack of tact."

Across the table, Dane sat with Seneca. They both looked stiff and uneasy. Neither had been in the Intersystem long enough to have a voice in its proceedings and were only present on behalf of their respective worlds.

The two lingbats sat on the back of Dane's chair, looking more at ease than any of the humans. Here, as Dane feared, was their rightful assignment.

Arnoth turned his attention back to Redor. "Karian, the Tseir will invade your world. They want more than domination of a few minor planets. They want the people who created them." Arnoth turned his gaze to Koran. "Ask him what it is to be a clone, what they've lost by becoming shades of real people."

A slow, mocking smile grew on Koran's boyish face. "I wouldn't know the answer to that, Ellowan. For, you see, I am not a clone."

Sierra's jaw dropped; she squeaked and hopped to her feet beside Arnoth. "What are you talking about? Of course you're a clone!"

Redor didn't appear shocked, and Arnoth realized this secret was known to more than Koran. "Just what are you, then?"

"I'm Koran Darvana, Nirvahdi spy. Who else?"

"Koran! You let me think you were dead, you . . ."

Redor tapped the table with a gavel. "Calm yourself, girl, and sit down. Standing at assembly is forbidden until you're called upon. You're out of turn."

"I'll sit when I'm good and ready! What's going on here? Why didn't you tell me?"

318

"Because, oh obedient daughter of mine, I didn't know until Koran and I talked on the rescue ship, and we had a few details to assess before it became common knowledge."

Sierra thumped back into her seat, but Arnoth remained standing. "I see. Is it the manner of spies to teach the Tseir their most powerful weaponry?"

Koran beamed with pleasure. "Only if those weapons won't work right when the time comes."

Arnoth felt oddly deflated, and yet . . . something burned beneath the surface, something wrong. The Nirvahdi were too sure of themselves. "I would see your claim verified before accepting it, Koran."

The Teradite banged his fist again. "It's been 'verified,' Ellowan. Our fleet has completely surrounded the Tseir at Valenwood and established their surrender . . ."

The Teradite launched into a grumbling diatribe in a guttural language, then shook his head. Arnoth guessed he would have preferred the annihilation of his enemies to surrender. "The Intersystem fleet was successful in their mission, as always. Your minor system is protected, the Tseir are defeated, and I don't know why we're wasting our time at this assembly. I've got alien worms to pop."

"What?"

Sierra tugged at Arnoth's shirt. "He's referring to a monitor game."

"Ah."

Sierra fixed her gaze on Koran. "If you're real, why did you let us think you were dead? And why did you allow the Tseir to hunt me down, and nearly kill Arnoth, and . . ."

Koran's expression softened immediately. "I didn't know you were on Dar-Krona until you were captured, Sierra. When I realized what you'd done, I was terrified for you, naturally."

Arnoth eyed the young Nirvahdi in growing dislike. "That doesn't explain how you managed to fool the Tseir into thinking you'd been killed and cloned."

Sierra nodded. "From what I saw of the Tseir, that would be impossible."

Good. Sierra sounded suspicious, too.

Koran seemed unperturbed by their question. "Actually, it turned out to be a simple matter. I went to Dar-Krona with the intention of infiltrating their ranks, as you did, Sierra. I learned immediately that men don't rise to anything over guard. I made a few well-placed slipups, they discovered my identity . . ."

Arnoth frowned, ripe with suspicion. He wasn't sure why, but something about Koran's story didn't ring true. Redor wanted to believe that Koran survived. Sierra wanted that, too. But something wasn't right.

"With some amazingly quick work, I managed to be coming out of the cloning unit, supposedly for the third time, when the technician arrived. He thought another had done his work, and I made a great show of where 'my' body was dumped."

Arnoth rolled his eyes. "I don't recall any such 'quick work' at my own near-cloning."

"Quite frankly, Ellowan, you weren't of major importance in my plans. It hardly seemed worth the risk to save you when we had the fate of the Intersystem at stake. Unfortunately, Sierra thought differently. I can only speculate about what you did to persuade her."

"You don't have the necessary imagination to envision what I did."

Redor growled. "Ellowan . . ."

Sierra's mother leaned toward Sierra. "He . . . is magnificent." Arnoth overheard her soft words and eyed her doubtfully. She couldn't mean Koran; but then, Redor seemed to consider the fragile boy heroic in the extreme. Maybe the mother did, too.

Sierra sighed. "I know."

Koran bowed his head. "I do understand Sierra's choice. When you abducted her from the Tseir confinement . . ."

"Abducted her?" Arnoth clenched his fist, but Koran paid no attention.

"I had no choice but to send the guards after you. I had to work quickly when I realized that the two of you were stealing a shuttle. I sent them off in the wrong direction, then followed her myself."

Sierra's brow furrowed in doubt. "How did you recognize me in that uniform?"

Koran grinned, and Arnoth seethed with dislike. "Well . . . you have an . . . identifiable backside, to be honest."

Arnoth cast a pertinent glance at Redor, waiting for the father to rightfully explode. But Redor just nodded. Sierra's mother tapped her long, slender fingers on the table. "Watch yourself, boy."

Arnoth quivered. "Or die."

The Teradite threw back his small head and issued a peculiar howl. The two lingbats looked in unison at the alien, then at each other. Arnoth felt sure they shrugged. The Teradite banged both fists. "This assembly has deteriorated beneath anything I've witnessed since joining the Intersystem. If the prime representative will approve the motion, I suggest we make war on the Ellowan and remove what's left of their civilization."

Dane's head sank into his palms and Seneca patted his shoulder. "It had to come to this. I knew it, I knew it. What am I going to tell Aiyana?" The Teradite turned his angry pink eyes toward Dane, and Dane held up one hand, his face still buried in the other. "I know, I know. I spoke out of turn. Forgive me."

Redor rose from his seat and braced his arms on the table. "If the ambassador from Candor wishes to speak, it is permitted. We're not going to annihilate anyone."

321

He eyed Arnoth. "As powerful as the temptation might be."

Dane looked up, tipped his head back, and drew a long breath. He didn't bother to stand. "You people need to remember that Arnoth of Valenwood has been alive twice as long as any of you."

The Teradite issued a moan. "Our lifespan is seven hundred years."

"All right, most of you. Be that as it may, Arnoth's senses are amazingly well developed. If he says you're in danger, sir, you are. Don't discount his word because you're angry that he's made love to your daughter."

Arnoth dropped into his seat. "Well, that was worse than anything I could have said. Thank you, Thorwalian. Maybe we can face execution together."

Amid the astonished hush, Seneca laughed. "Life was so much simpler when I lived among the Akandans. . . . If the prime representative will permit me . . ."

Redor shrugged. "Why not?"

Seneca rose and bowed. "You say the fleet has overcome the Tseir. Yet Arnoth tells us their power is spread upon many colonies. Isn't it possible their forces at Valenwood were only a fraction of their power? If they intend to assail Nirvahda, they won't do it as a frontal assault. Their only hope is in surprise."

The assembly doors burst open and a robed, squat figure charged into the room. "Sorry I'm late. I was making use of the city central lake. You people could use a bog or two, but it was adequate."

Arnoth's heart moved with affection. "Rurthgar."

The Keiroit ambled to his side, seized a seat, and placed it next to Arnoth's. He shoved the Zimdardri ambassador aside, then nodded politely. "Needed more room, you understand."

Rurthgar seated himself, belched, and looked around at the representatives. "So, what's going on here?"

322

"We're attempting to convince the Intersystem assembly that the Tseir's easy defeat . . . ."

The Teradite interrupted with another howl. "Who says it was easy?"

Arnoth sighed. "You won; it was easy. If I may continue . . ." He didn't wait for permission. "The Tseir surrendered. What do you make of that, Rurthgar?"

"Tseir don't surrender. You know that. I know it. We've seen it plenty of times on Keir. So, they don't want to take your warning seriously, eh?" Rurthgar shoved himself up from his seat and belched again. "So, let's get out of here, head on back to the swamp, and let the Tseir have at them."

"I can't do that, my friend."

Rurthgar waved a concealed paw. "The prime representative is a thick-headed glob of flesh and bones. Why fret yourself over his fate?"

"Because I love his daughter."

Rurthgar bellowed in dismay. "Sex, sex, sex! With humans, it's always the same story."

Sierra's mother sighed, her hands over her breast as she gazed lovingly at her daughter. "That was beautiful." She sniffed. Arnoth wondered if she meant his declaration of love or Rurthgar's subsequent assessment.

Sierra took Arnoth's hand. "Papa, I've never known you to make a mistake. I've always believed it was because you saw all sides of every issue, because when you look at the whole, you see its parts and know how it works. Please understand, Arnoth is the same. But he has a capacity you don't. When Arnoth sees one small sliver, one part, he sees the whole that lies beyond."

"Babble. Girl, you're under some kind of spell. Assembly adjourned." Redor's face contorted in anger. "Curse the day that Ellowan crawled out of his crib!"

"Ellowan don't have cribs, Karian. We're carried on cradleboards, and on our parents' backs."

Stobie Piel

"You're spoiled. That doesn't surprise me. As I was saying before your latest interruption, Ellowan . . . I don't believe a word of your story. I think you're crazy and devoid of any kind of scruples, but here's what I'll do. I'll send out flagship patrols and recall the fleet from Valenwood. That way, if any Tseir comes into this sector, we'll be alerted."

Sierra sighed in happiness, but Arnoth's frown didn't waver. "Likely too little, and too late. But something is better than nothing."

"To think, I used to consider council meetings boring!" Sierra smiled as her mother watched the representatives file out of the hall. Redor left with Koran, saying nothing to either Arnoth or Sierra, but Sierra knew his last words were an indication that he valued Arnoth's opinion, whether he wanted to or not. Arnoth wouldn't see it that way, but Sierra recognized a concession when she saw one.

"Arnoth, you haven't really met my mother yet. This is Natassja Karian. Mother . . ."

Natassja didn't wait for Sierra's introduction. She patted Arnoth's cheek in a fond, motherly gesture while he watched, as if questioning the reality of the moment. "You were magnificent, Arnoth. I've never seen anything like it."

Arnoth's expression turned even more puzzled. "I failed."

"What? Oh, not at all! Redor changed his mind. You may not realize the significance of it, but he did. True, he was clever about it, adjourning the session first, *then* rearranging the fleet, but it was a weak tactic to cover the fact that he thinks you may be right."

Arnoth glanced at Sierra. "I must have missed something."

"And not for the first time."

His face flushed slightly and Sierra chuckled. Seneca joined them, but Dane remained in his seat. "What's the matter with Dane?"

Seneca smiled and shook his head. "His charm ran out. Dane has spent his whole life being agreeable, pleasing everyone. Today, he spoke in defiance of the most powerful union in the galaxy. . . ." Seneca chuckled. "I didn't realize you meant that much to him, Arnoth."

Dane overheard Seneca's teasing comments, groaned, and lowered his head to the table. The two lingbats seized the opportunity to jump onto his bowed shoulders. "Well, boy, you've done it now. I *think* I can persuade the prime rep to overlook your . . ." Carob made a smacking noise. "*Defiance,* but it won't be easy."

Batty placed a commiserating wingtip in Dane's hair. "The smile finally gave out, did it, sir? Never thought I'd see the day." Batty's wingtip entangled in Dane's hair and he hopped frantically to free himself.

Dane didn't move.

Arnoth went around the table and seated himself by Dane. "No man ever had a better friend than you."

Rurthgar belched and coughed. "Is that so?"

"Except for Rurthgar."

Sierra eyed the wrapped Keiroit, wondering what he looked like beneath his cumbersome robes. "We haven't met."

"No. We haven't." Rurthgar made no motion to introduce himself, and Sierra endured a pang of sorrow. Another of Arnoth's companions who didn't accept her. Probably he'd been talking to Aiyana.

Rurthgar turned her way, looked her up and down, then belched again. He waved toward Arnoth. "This one should drop a fine set of hatchlings."

Sierra and her mother exchanged a doubtful look. "Hatchlings?"

Batty squeaked from his position on Dane's head.

"That reminds me, sir. There's something I'd like the prince and Mistress Sierra to see. . . . If you don't mind getting up and perhaps escorting us to your guest chambers."

Dane groaned, but he didn't move.

Carob puffed his chest, seized Dane by the hair, and pulled. "Move, boy! Or else."

Dane rose slowly, haggard and defeated. He looked cuter than ever. He gazed mournfully at Arnoth, then at Seneca. Natassja's brow angled. "That young man has a flair for drama. But he's certainly handsome."

Dane must have overheard Natassja's quiet comment, because his eyes brightened despite his downcast appearance. He sighed deliberately. "The work of friendship is never done. Come along, rodents. I believe Batty wants to share his 'surprise' with our noble prince and his sexy beloved."

"They're the cutest things I've ever seen, ever in my life."

Sierra bent over a large, golden box and studied twelve minuscule lingbats. They squirmed around their nest, eyes just open, tiny wings tight to their chubby little bodies. One tripped and fell flat, and another stepped on its head.

Sierra seized Arnoth's hand. "Have you ever seen anything so cute?"

"Well . . ." Arnoth glanced at Batty, who was puffed up with insurmountable pride. "They're handsome, no question." Sierra beamed.

She noticed one baby lingbat apart from the others. It didn't move, just watched the others with what looked like . . . Sierra bent closer to examine the lingbat's face. . . . Yes, a frown. A condescending expression formed on the tiny, scrunched face.

"What's the matter with that one, Batty?"

Batty peeked in at his litter. "That would be Valued Descendent of Greatness. My sire named that one. That's my firstborn, or so She Who Leaps High told me. I missed the birthing, mistress, but they're beauties, aren't they? Twelve!" Batty whistled and puffed still more. "Only a very *potent* lingbat sires that many in his first litter. Of course, they're the first of their kind, a hybrid between the Ling and Dwindle Bats."

Sierra reached in and touched one of the little bats. "You could call them 'Lingle Bats.' "

Dane stood at the back of the room, hands on his hips. " 'Dwindling Bats' sounds better to me."

Carob oversaw the litter from the edge of the box, an imperious expression on his peculiar face. She Who Leaps High sat beside him, an even smaller bat than Batty. She was delicate and had blacker fur than her mate, and her wings looked capable of flight.

"I think Dane should teach your mate to speak, too, Batty. And every one of those adorable little babies."

At Sierra's suggestion, Dane flopped back onto a long, low bed and uttered a groan of pure misery. "The suggestion has already been made. Nay, let us not call it a suggestion. It was a command, issued by the proud grandsire of these tiny rodents. My life is over."

Arnoth ambled to the side of the bed, his arms folded over his chest. "I wonder if there's a little one named 'He Who Walks With Dane?' "

Batty whistled. "What a good idea, sir! There's one little fellow . . . There, on the bottom. The one that keeps tripping and getting stomped. We haven't found a suitable name for him yet."

Sierra pressed her lips together to contain laughter. She watched Arnoth and her heart filled with joy. He looked happy, strong. He had attained every level of his power, he owned his life. And she would share that life . . .

327

A splash distracted her. "Oh, dear! He Who Walks With Dane just fell into the water dish."

A small blond girl raced into the room and jumped onto Dane's stomach. "Ling-dings, Papa!"

Dane laughed and caught his daughter in his arms. He picked her up and brought her to Arnoth. "This is your . . ." Dane sighed, resigned. "Uncle Arnoth, Elena."

The little girl studied Arnoth's dark face with a serious expression. She looked little more than a year old, but she seemed advanced, thoughtful. Sierra's eyes filled with tears. Elena resembled Dane and Nisa, which meant she also resembled her dead aunt.

Arnoth touched the child's head. "She's a beautiful child, Dane."

"I know. She takes after me."

Both Elena and Arnoth eyed Dane doubtfully, then looked back at each other. The child reached out a chubby hand and touched Arnoth's face, a comforting gesture. "I'm sorry, Uncle."

Sierra's breath caught. Arnoth glanced at Dane, whose brow angled. Elena smiled at Arnoth, unaffected by their shock. "Are you happy now, Uncle?"

Arnoth hesitated, then nodded. "I am."

"I am, too." The small face formed an earnest expression. "I am not afraid anymore, because I have Papa and Mama."

Chills ran along Sierra's spine at the child's calm words. She remembered that Arnoth's Elena had lost her parents as a small child. Perhaps that explained the fear that consumed her life. But this Elena's attention wavered to the nest of baby lingbats. "Ling-dings, Papa."

Dane stared at his daughter as if she might transform before his eyes. "The Ellowan are peculiar beyond comprehension."

328

Arnoth shook his head. "Not this peculiar, Thorwalian."

Sierra touched his shoulder gently. "The Zimdardri say that at the moment of death, the spirit passes from the body and seeks out the World Beyond. There arriving, it finds rest, and learns from the life it departed. When the spirit is ready, it seeks out a new form and begins again."

Dane looked into his daughter's eyes with new wonder. But Elena kicked her feet, more demanding this time. "Papa. Ling-dings."

Sierra tapped Dane's shoulder. "I think she wants to see the babies, Dane."

"Babies? The rodents. Yes, of course." Dane shook his head, banishing what he couldn't understand, and carried Elena to the nest box. "Look well, Elena. By the time you're grown, these little winged rodents will be running the universe."

Despite himself, Dane Calydon couldn't restrain his interest. He studied the lingbat babies with a solemn expression, then winced. "That must be Valued Descendent of Greatness . . . the one who just stepped on He Who Walks With Dane's head."

Carob leaned in, reached down with his frail wingtip, and smacked at the weaker rodent. It braced itself and struggled from beneath its larger brother.

Dane's mouth dropped, aghast. "What did you smack He Who Walks With Dane for? It was that bruiser-rodent—named for yourself, I might add—who did the dirty deed."

"When you've sired as many young as I have, boy, you'll learn that you've got to show the smallest you respect them. I honored He Who Walks With Dane by expecting him to brace up."

Sierra studied the small bat. "He has a point, Dane.

Look! The little fellow's chest is puffed up. Just like yours.''

Sierra bit her lip, and Dane leveled a meaningful gaze in her direction. Arnoth was right: Dane Calydon was becoming more and more like one of his lingbats.

As if he realized this, too, Dane smiled weakly and drew back from the nest. Two more children burst into the room, followed by Nisa and Seneca. "Are they up yet? Can we play with them, Carob?"

"No, you cannot." Carob flared his fragile wings in warning, but the children ignored him. Both had dark brown hair and wore beaded braids. They were beautiful, strong children, and Sierra found herself wondering if Arnoth's children would resemble them. *Her* children. She looked up at him, and saw the same expression of wonder in his eyes.

We will have children, you and I. Tears filled Sierra's eyes. Surrounded by babies, by happiness, it seemed impossible that anything could go wrong. The Tseir threat faded from her thoughts. *It can't happen. Life is too good to lose it now.*

The boy picked up a lingbat baby and presented it to Seneca. "We must bring a linglebat to Dakota, Father, and teach him TiKay."

Carob bobbed his head. "An honorable apprenticeship for my grandyoung."

Nisa beamed, though Seneca looked a little weary. "Apprenticing a linglebat . . ."

Dane shook his head in warning. "My friends, this is how it begins. They insinuate themselves into the ruling households of our galaxy. One will find its way to Valenwood. Another will worm its way into the prime representative's home. Simple. Innocent. They're on their way."

Arnoth wrapped a supportive arm over Dane's shoulder. "And you have only yourself to blame."

Chapter Ten

"We don't have time for a banquet, woman. Something's wrong."

Arnoth watched Sierra twirling before her bedroom mirror, admiring herself in a long white and yellow dress. It was snug around her waist, full over her hips, and brushed the floor with white lace. Her curly brown hair shimmered with gold and amber highlights, loose over her shoulders.

She tossed a flirtatious glance over her shoulder. "You are the gloomiest man alive." She dampened her lips as she sauntered toward him. "We will have to see what can be done to ease your tension."

His body responded despite his uneasy premonitions. "You take much for granted, little alien."

"Do I?" Her gaze raked over him, then centered on his breeches. "Dane is right. Your leggings are too tight.

Sometimes." She reached one finger to his concealed excitement and traced its line.

Arnoth grabbed her hand. "If you don't mind, I'd rather not prove your father's worst fears true. At least, not today."

"What worst fears?"

"About my losing control and taking you in public."

"Is that what he meant about public displays?"

"There was a time when Ellowan were uninhibited in their pursuit of pleasure. We were a sensual race."

"You are a sensual race."

Arnoth's brow angled. "Tell that to Helayna."

"I suspect she's an exception."

"I hope so." Arnoth drew Sierra's hand to his lips and kissed the backs of her fingers.

"What troubles you, my sweet prince? If you tell me now, perhaps it won't prey on your thoughts at the banquet. My sister will be there, and Garian. And my mother adores you, despite what my father said. True, Aiyana will be there, too, but we'll sit far apart, and Dane can restrain her. Your Rurthgar requested live fish for dinner, which was a bit of a problem, but he settled for raw samples, so you'll have all your friends."

"Your capacity for rapid speech astounds me, woman."

Sierra nodded, waiting. "What's bothering you? Father did what you wanted, didn't he?"

"More or less. Sierra, I don't believe the Tseir are as obtuse as your people seem to think. They know what they're doing. Don't you see? Their 'surrender' at Valenwood might have been a tactic. A brilliant tactic, to set the Intersystem off guard. And Sierra, it worked. No one is expecting an attack, despite your father's precautions."

"Is that what Seneca was saying before Rurthgar interrupted?"

"It was. And another thing: Koran. There's something wrong about his story, about him."

Sierra's expression darkened. "I thought that, too. It's almost too much to hope that he survived. He made it seem casual, easy. It couldn't have been easy. For one thing, the monitor in the reproduction facility is always attended. As it was when I rescued you."

"I thought that, too. Your father wasn't in the mood for listening. Perhaps I should have pressed the subject."

"Is it possible Koran is still allied with the Tseir?"

"I don't know. He might be. It worries me, because I don't see the whole." Arnoth paused, smiling. "I liked that part, incidentally. About my amazing capacity to see the whole from its parts. And it's true, too. When I first saw your body, I knew those massive breasts didn't fit."

"That's not exactly how I meant it, Arnoth."

"I know."

"I suppose we should go. If we're late—"

Arnoth stopped her words with a finger. "You are beautiful, little alien. You are sweet, and when I look at you, I feel things I didn't know existed. I love you, and no matter what happens, my life is blessed for finding you."

Her eyes widened, then misted with sudden tears. "Arnoth . . . Why are you telling me this?"

"Because it's possible I won't get another chance."

Sierra seated herself beside Arnoth, quiet amid the din of the banquet hall. The giant room sang with activity as representatives from every world bustled and conversed. The lingbats had left the litter and sat perched on Dane's shoulders. Both the Thorwalian and bat appeared equally proud.

Aiyana stood close beside Dane, holding her daughter's hand. Sierra couldn't help a surge of affection when she noticed the tiny She Who Leaps High on Aiyana's shoulder. Helayna walked behind Aiyana, looking more like a disoriented servant than a friend.

Seneca carried his daughter on his shoulders, and his son stood proud and strong beside him. The Teradite stomped past them, and the little boy took Nisa's hand for silent support.

Rurthgar shoved his way through the crowd, knocking representatives aside as he entered and apparently not noticing the dark looks cast his way afterwards. A smaller Keiroit accompanied him, presumably his mate. Both were robed from head to toe.

"What do the Keiroits look like under the wrappings?"

"I'm not sure you want to know. They're green, with quite beautiful scales, actually, if you can get used to the bulgy left eye and the enormous mouth. They're amphibians, more or less. Webbed feet . . . They wear metal support shoes when out of the marshes. They've got environmental controls beneath their wrapping, to keep them moist."

"You're fond of them."

"I am."

"They're fond of you, too."

Rurthgar walked to the table, hopped up on it—sending platters dangerously close to the edge along with teetering goblets—then jumped down beside Arnoth. His mate paused, shook her concealed head, then did likewise. Arnoth's eyes sparkled, but he didn't laugh.

"Well, Prince, you're a fool to stick around. I'm a fool to stick around. But they promised raw fish, so I thought I'd take the risk and wait with you."

Sierra leaned around Arnoth to look at Rurthgar. "You expect the Tseir to attack, too, don't you?"

"Don't you?"

"I'm not sure. Once the fleet returns, they won't stand a chance. And the fleet will be here by tomorrow."

334

"Then they'll attack tonight, little human."

Sierra sat back and chewed her lip. "There's a comforting thought." She paused, considering the Keiroit's gloomy prediction. "You've lived with this species for four hundred years, Arnoth?"

"Approximately."

"I can see where you get the gloom. . . . Dane and lingbats, you and amphibians."

The large group assembled, taking their respective seats in a disorderly fashion. "There are many representatives on Nirvahda today, more than usual."

Arnoth nodded. "Making it an even better time for the Tseir to wage an assault."

"How would they know who's here?"

Arnoth didn't answer, but his eyes shifted to Koran and Redor. Sierra followed his gaze, and fidgeted uncomfortably. Her father loved Koran. Maybe Rurthgar was right. Love could be blind.

"Even if the Tseir attacked . . . what good would it do? The fleet would return and annihilate them."

Arnoth took a long breath. "I don't know, Sierra. I've considered that, too. Yet my heart tells me that is their intention. If the Tseir held your people captive here, rather than destroying them, wouldn't that be provocation enough to hold your fleet at bay?"

Sierra's heart chilled. "It would. Arnoth . . ."

Dane and Aiyana sat across from Sierra and Arnoth, a position Sierra considered excruciating. Aiyana's pretty face was marked by disapproval, although Helayna actually smiled at Sierra. Nisa and Seneca sat farther down, and seemed to be bickering.

"We *need* speeder crafts on Dakota, Seneca."

"Why? One good reason, maiden."

"Because they're fast!"

"I said *good* reason. In your hands, speed is a decidedly negative factor."

335

"You are difficult and tiresome at times, Akandan. Primitive, primitive, primitive. Dakota needs to advance!"

"And you think dangerous speeds will advance us?"

"Yes!"

Seneca's daughter reached down from his shoulders and tugged at his hair. "Father, I would like to learn to pilot like Mother."

Seneca lowered his head and cursed.

Sierra spotted her sister and Garian entering the hall. Colice walked beside them, looking confused and a little lost. Sierra rose and waved to them. "That's my sister behind Garian. They've been working with Colice to see what might be done to help the Tseir."

Arnoth rolled his eyes. " 'Help the Tseir'? You'd be wiser to use her to find out how to stop them."

Garian led Colice around the table, and she sat beside Sierra. "Colice asked to sit with you, if that's all right, Sierra."

Sierra patted Colice's hand. "Of course. I was hoping you would."

Sierra's sister eased in front of Garian, studying Arnoth with undisguised glee. She winked and Sierra blushed. "Arnoth, this is my sister, Sofia."

Arnoth rose and bowed. "It is my honor."

Sofia grinned. "You are *so* cute. I should have known Sierra would find someone who looked like you." She elbowed Garian in the ribs. "Isn't he cute?"

Garian shrugged. "He's still alive, which is more than I expected after the way he talked to your father." A grin appeared on Garian's face, too. "If you're going to do it again, Arnoth, warn me so I can maintain a safe distance. But please, let me hear it, all the same."

Arnoth bowed again. "Should the occasion arise, I will."

Sofia patted Sierra's shoulder. "We'll see you later.

Father wants us to sit with Koran, to get reacquainted.'' Sofia paused to groan. "I never liked him when he was fully human. He's even more of a pain now. Oh, I forget, he was faking. Either way . . ." She and Garian gave nods and moved off toward where Redor was seated.

Arnoth seated himself, looking pleased. "I like your sister."

"I thought you might. Cute, indeed!"

Arnoth didn't argue the assessment. He glanced across the table at Dane, who sneered in an exaggerated fashion. "Did you happen to overhear that, Thorwalian?"

"I did, and it destroyed my appetite entirely."

"Good."

Sierra looked between them, then shook her head. "You're always trying to one-up each other, aren't you? Behave!" She turned to Colice. "Was Garian able to help you, Colice?"

Colice bowed her head and closed her eyes before answering, a surprising gesture for a Tseir. "I have learned of my original."

"Who was she?"

Colice looked up and stared across the banquet hall. "She was taken in battle by the Tseir and cloned against her will. Before that . . ." Colice paused and swallowed, as if collecting herself. "She was a mother. She studied no other profession. She had seven children. The Tseir killed them all before cloning her."

Tears filled Sierra's eyes; her heart went out to the woman.

"Sierra . . . I am no longer Tseir."

Sierra took Colice's hand and squeezed it tightly. "Colice, you never were."

Arnoth watched their exchange, a strange expression on his face. "Forgive me, Colice. I wronged you in thought and in action. I believed humanity could be destroyed. I was wrong."

Sierra angrily brushed her tears away. "What about the Tseir that killed Colice's family?"

"Ah, Sierra, they were human. Too human. The dark side of humanity is bitter and strong. It is in us all. In Aiyana as she glares at you, in your father when he glares at me. In Elena's fear and, most of all, in me. I would have annihilated their race in vengeance; my hatred knew no bounds. Until you."

"I love you, Arnoth of Valenwood. And your dark side gives you strength, because you own it now. It doesn't control you."

"No longer." Arnoth drew a long, deep breath. "No longer."

"If you're right . . . then Koran can't be bad, even if he's a clone."

"Sierra, what is in him, whoever he is, was there before he traveled to Dar-Krona. You can't know another's heart. We hope, and tonight, hope is all we have."

The feast began: food of every planet moved slowly around the table, delivered on hovering, robotic trays. Rurthgar seized his raw fish and stuffed the whole thing beneath his hood. Across the table, Aiyana avoided looking at Sierra, but Sierra's own anger faded and disappeared. It was Aiyana's darkness, and Aiyana had to contend with it.

No longer.

Dane appeared uncomfortable beside his small, angry wife, but it didn't stop him from conversing cheerfully with the nearest representatives. The lingbats sat on the table, and Carob took bites from everything that passed by. He stuck his head in a goblet and drank while the Zimdardri representative watched in horror.

She Who Leaps High remained on Aiyana's shoulder, but Batty carried portions of food in his mouth and devotedly delivered them to his mate.

Koran laughed loudly at the end of the table, and Redor patted his shoulder. Sierra frowned. "Sofia is right. Koran is becoming obnoxious."

Helayna leaned forward and set aside her fork. "You are correct in that assessment, Sierra. Do you know what 'walking me' meant to him?"

Sierra glanced at Arnoth, who shrugged. "No . . . what?"

"He wanted to place what he referred to as 'his orange' into my female reproductive center." Helayna sat back, disgusted. She didn't bother to lower her voice, and the nearest representatives choked and coughed.

"In fact, he informed me that I was fortunate to be spared Arnoth as a mate, because the bulk of a 'red' was too cumbersome to stimulate pleasure. It was the most disgusting conversation of my life. I struck him, of course, and laid him out in a stunned posture."

Aiyana and Dane turned in unison to stare at Helayna. Dane looked to Arnoth, whose face had turned a satisfying shade of deep pink. Sierra contained her amusement, then nodded stoically as she patted his shoulder.

"The oranges can be that way. They're threatened by you reds."

Dane's shocked expression reverted to his former indignation as he guessed the true meaning of the Tseir color coding. "Pale blue? *Pale blue,* Ellowan?"

Aiyana's face knit suspiciously. "What are you two talking about? What's all this about red and orange and pale blue?"

Batty hopped away from She Who Leaps High to perch on the edge of Dane's plate. "Don't worry, sir. It's not the size that counts, it's the speed of the thrust."

"Thank you, rodent. A comforting word in this time of need. . . . Seneca, send that robot plate down here. I want wine."

* * *

Arnoth appeared to like Nirvahda's spicy food, too. Sierra watched in satisfaction as he summoned the robotic tray and seized another *teeya*. He swirled it around with professional ease in the cool, green dip, then ate it by hand.

"Well done!"

Arnoth nodded, his mouth full. "Good." He swallowed, and his eyes widened, then watered. "Hot."

Sierra passed him a carafe of goyen juice and he drained the goblet. "This is your third helping. Save room for dessert."

Arnoth looked brightly around as another robotic tray eased his way. "What's that?"

"You have a choice, my beloved. Flaky cakes are lighter. There's chilled cream pudding, and nut cakes. I favor the heavy cake that is doused in Zimdardri liquor." Sierra lowered her voice and spoke close in his ear. "As you can see, the Zimdardri know liquor and wine."

The Zimdardri representatives had already abandoned their dinner in favor of a large carafe of bluish-green liquid. Both looked bleary, smiles on their faces.

"Ah, yes. You mentioned they tend to overimbibe."

The robot tray stopped in front of Arnoth. To Sierra's delight, he took a sampling of each dessert, then gave the tray a shove toward Rurthgar. Rurthgar didn't react. He leaned back in his seat, snoring. Beside him, his smaller mate sat in the same posture.

Dane noticed the Keiroits and turned his teasing smile to Aiyana. "My sweet, they sound just like you."

Aiyana glared. "I do not snore."

"You do." Dane began a low, rumbling mimic of a soft snore while Aiyana fumed. Apparently, the lavish meal hadn't softened her spirits. Sierra suspected Dane's teasing was meant to cheer her mood, but it failed.

Dane's smile faded, replaced by an expression of resignation. "The dinner seems to be ending. I guess it's time. . . ."

Aiyana peered up at him suspiciously. "For what?"

Dane sighed, looking doomed. "Rurthgar, do you have it?" No response. "Keiroit!"

Rurthgar startled, sat forward, then nodded. "Got it here, Thorwalian." He reached beneath his massive robes and pulled out a small, golden harp. "I brought this along for you, Prince, figuring you'd bust free from the Tseir."

Arnoth smiled, and Sierra saw unshed tears glittering in his brown eyes. The Keiroit carried Arnoth's harp on faith, for the sake of love and friendship. Rather than give the instrument to Arnoth, Rurthgar passed the harp to Dane, who rose and turned toward Redor.

Natassja nodded at Dane, then brought a Nirvahdi lyre to Sierra. Her mother's eyes glittered, and Sierra realized this moment had been carefully orchestrated between the nosy Thorwalian and her mother. Natassja placed the harp in Sierra's hands, a wide smile on her mischievous face.

"I told Dane you'd won two awards for this, my dear, and it gave him a rather insightful idea. I hope you remember what you've learned."

Natassja backed away, beaming, and Sierra glanced at Arnoth. "I was just thinking the same thing."

Sierra blushed. "Yes, but Arnoth . . . the way I learned. I don't remember much about the first part."

"They're one and the same, little alien. That is what you need to remember."

Redor glared at his wife, and Aiyana glared at Dane. Redor drummed his fingers on the tabletop. "What's the meaning of this, Ambassador? I haven't finished dessert yet."

"If I may, Prime Representative . . ."

"You're not going to make any more announcements concerning my daughter, are you?" A smile flickered on

341

Redor's lips despite his serious expression.

"No, sir." Dane shifted his weight from one foot to the other. Aiyana frowned.

"He'd better not."

"Not exactly, sir. Most certainly *not* . . ." A look of absolute horror formed on Dane's face, and he clapped his hand to his forehead. "I'm beginning to talk like one, too."

Redor's brow angled. "One what?"

Dane shook his head, banishing the thought. "Nothing, sir. Here's the thing . . . Every man has something within him that offers a glimpse of his soul. I wouldn't have believed it, but Arnoth's offers poignant beauty. If you would permit it, sir, I will hereby force him to show you what your daughter saw."

Redor hopped up from his seat, overturning a goblet of wine. "Over my dead body!"

Dane winced and scrunched his shoulders like a ling-bat. "Not that . . ." He rolled his eyes, sucked in a desperate breath, then thrust the harp across the table at Arnoth. "Play, and play your heart out, Ellowan. If you don't do me proud, and make me look like the wisest man in the galaxy, I'll rip your lungs out."

"With that sweet request, how could I refuse?"

Arnoth pushed his seat back from the table and set the harp between his knees. His eyes met Sierra's, and her heart took wing. She positioned her lyre and set her fingers to the strings. She glanced again at Arnoth and he smiled. "I will never let you go."

His long, magical fingers touched the harp, and it sang. Sierra listened for a moment as it rose and flew, and she knew where he was going. His joyous music seized life, and gave it beauty and meaning. Sierra touched the strings of her childhood lyre, and she followed.

Where Arnoth went, Sierra went, too. And when she reached the sweetest heights, she led him to new places.

The passion between them soared, then soothed, then leapt again like flame across dried fields. It rushed like flood water, then eased like an ocean at peace.

When at last they reached a fathomless plain, Sierra knew neither would have found that bliss alone. What he was, she would be, and what she carried within, she shared with him. His music ended on a final, sweet note, and there was hope beyond. Sierra's music echoed his, then faded to silence.

No one spoke. Silence filled the banquet hall. Sierra stared up into Arnoth's beautiful face and saw tears in his eyes. She knew they were tears of joy.

Arnoth set his harp aside, and Sierra placed her lyre by her feet. Redor stood slowly, still silent. For a long while, he held Arnoth's gaze. Neither man wavered or looked away. A smile formed on her father's lips.

"I have looked my own blindness in its eye and realized a man's dearest treasure is the one he gives away. Ellowan, my daughter is yours, and you have my blessing on your union." Redor paused as Sierra's tears fell to her cheeks. "Except in public."

"And I will give her all my soul, and all my love, and all she wishes will be hers." Arnoth smiled, then chuckled. "Except in public."

A short, stilted cry burst from Aiyana, startling Sierra. She Who Leaps High squealed and tumbled from Aiyana's shoulder, then skittered across the table in fright. Aiyana leapt from her seat, staring at Arnoth and Sierra. Her small, beautiful face was stricken with tears, her green eyes wide with shock.

She looked at them as if—Sierra's heart moved in unwilling sympathy—as if she looked at death. Aiyana shook her head back and forth in denial, then spun away and fled from the room.

Dane started to get up, to follow her, then stopped and drew a long breath. "She needs this time alone." He

343

picked up Elena and spoke softly to her, reassuring her after her mother's outburst. Whatever he said worked. Elena relaxed, then turned her covetous gaze back to the sweets.

"One more?"

Dane shrugged, then gave his daughter another flaky cake. "Just keep it between us."

Arnoth gazed at the door, after Aiyana's hurried departure. "I thank you, Thorwalian, for what you did for me. But for Aiyana . . ."

"I didn't do it for you, my friend. You and Sierra already have all you need. What I did, I did for Aiyana. She must see, and face her loss. It is I who thank you."

Sierra stared at Dane in astonishment. Until now, she'd seen him as charming and amusing. But beneath his light-hearted surface, she saw a wise and powerful man. It seemed Arnoth chose his friends well.

Redor rang a bell on the nearest robotic tray. The guests rose, turned toward him, and bowed. It was the only formal moment of the banquet, yet it was performed in solemn honor. Sierra's heart warmed when Arnoth bowed, too.

Redor bowed in return, then held up his hand. "I thank you, all of you, most honored representatives of distant worlds. Such beauty you have brought to Nirvahda, such wonder. . . . It is my honor to serve you."

An alarm rang, desperate and shrill, silencing Redor's speech. It blared through the banquet hall and across all Nirvahda. Sierra froze, then seized Arnoth's hand. "We are under attack."

Redor didn't panic. "Assume stations, commanders. All civilian persons to shelters. That means you, Natassja."

"I am not leaving you."

"Not so fast." Koran assumed position beside her father. Sierra's heart chilled. Beside her, Arnoth stiffened, tense.

Redor turned, slowly. "Koran? What is the meaning of this?"

Koran was smiling, but it wasn't a pleasant expression. "Anyone who leaves this hall, dies."

"What?" Redor's voice was a growl.

"You are under attack, Redor. I will permit the Teradite commander to check his monitor." Koran turned his mocking gaze to the small Teradite representative. "I assume you carry the instrument with you?"

The Teradite said nothing but pulled a little screen from his pocket.

"Check this sector, Teradite. What do you see?"

"Sir, this sector has been invaded. The Ellowan was right. They're stationed in the outer atmosphere already."

Koran laughed. "He guessed right, but too late. The Tseir fleet surrounds Nirvahda, Redor. Your feeble home defenses have moved too late, and have been destroyed. While you sat celebrating, feasting, your patrols were annihilated."

"The Tseir fleet can never stand against the Intersystem."

"We won't have to. We surround you now, and unless they want Nirvahda to face the same ending as so many other lesser worlds, they will do nothing."

Redor sank into his seat. "I have been such a fool. You are a clone."

"Rise, and stand before me, old man. I am no clone. I am Koran Dirvana, Nirvahdi 'spy,' and lord commander of the legion of Tseir."

Sierra's mouth dropped. "What? This is crazy. Extrana is the supreme commander, not you. And you have to be a clone. Koran would never . . ."

Koran's face darkened, his boyish face disfigured by arrogance. "Ah, Sierra." Koran left Redor and walked around the table toward Sierra. Arnoth moved in front of her, his dark face burning with anger.

"Come near her and die, Tseir."

Koran hesitated, then laughed. "Ellowan, your feeble attempt amuses me. You do realize, don't you, that I have ultimate control over what happens to everyone in this world, everyone in this galaxy? I am in communication with the fleet, even now. They await my orders. In the event of any harm to myself, this world will be destroyed before your fleet returns."

"But you want something else."

"I want the rule of the galaxy, and I will have it." Koran's eyes fixed on Sierra. "And more. I will have all that I desire, all that is power. My plans have worked perfectly. The one unforeseen instant was when your Ellowan lover shot me. Somehow, I overlooked that possibility. But not your affection for your dear 'friend,' Sierra. You convinced him to heal me, and my plans moved in perfect accord."

Sierra's heart palpitated with terror. "What did they do to you?"

"Do to me? Ah, Sierra, you overestimate the Tseir. They were empty, operating on fear, on the base desire to control, to subdue. Yet it is effective, isn't it, Ellowan? Zimdardri? I, on the other hand, have goals. Desires. It took an amazingly brief time to convince Extrana to follow my wishes. Sensation is something the Tseir crave, and I provided it. My ambition fueled her emptiness, and all the power of the Tseir is now mine."

Sierra's terror turned to disgust. "And now that you have it, what will you do?"

"I will take what I've always wanted, Sierra. You."

Arnoth drew her into his arms. "Never, Tseir."

"You'll let her go, Ellowan, or watch every person in this room be destroyed. Is your lust worth their deaths?" Koran pointed toward Dane and Seneca. Their children

346

clung to their parents, too terrified to cry. "We will dispose of the young ones first."

"We? I see you and no other."

Koran drew up his sleeve, exposing a wrist band device. He pressed a button and the banquet hall doors burst open. Tseir guards poured into the room and took position along the wall, their actions more robotic than the food trays. Sierra squeezed her eyes shut, forcing herself to fight her rising terror, to remain calm.

"Your planet has been subdued in the space of an instant. You see, we have increased the cloning facilities not only on Dar-Krona, but on every colony we dominate. Soldiers fill our largest vessels, and have swarmed Nirvahda like flies."

A guard entered, dragging Aiyana by the hair. "This little one tried to shoot at me, Lord Commander."

Dane passed his daughter to Nisa, then started toward Aiyana. A guard knocked him back, and three more surrounded him, holding him from his struggling mate. Aiyana didn't relent. She kicked and bit. The guard slammed the back of his fist into her face and she cried out.

"Another troublesome Ellowan. Kill her."

"No!" Sierra drew away from Arnoth. "If you start killing people, Koran, we have no reason to obey you."

"I expected you to offer yourself for another, my precious Sierra. . . . But for her? The woman insulted you. It is my intention to use your lover for this task."

Arnoth gripped her shoulder. "Sierra, don't. There is another way."

Sierra wanted to believe him, but the Tseir filled the room, they filled the sky. "What do you want with me?"

"It would be unwise for me to remain on Nirvahda until your fleet is disabled and our control complete. For this reason, I will return to the First Vessel and take my rightful position as leader. And I will have you with me,

Sierra, because neither your doting father nor your lover will challenge me while your life is in my hands.''

"If I go with you—"

Arnoth's hands clenched. "No . . . Sierra, no.''

Sierra closed her eyes and drew a painful breath. "What is to stop you from killing these people?''

"I want your continuing cooperation, Sierra.'' Koran touched her cheek, and her flesh recoiled. "I want you. But I'm no fool. Unless I have people you value, I have no power over you. Who would have thought it would come to this? That the price of taking a lover would mean surrendering to me?''

Sierra turned and gazed up into Arnoth's face. "Nothing that happens can touch us. . . .''

"I will never let you go.''

"Guards! Restrain the Ellowan.''

Colice stepped forward and seized Sierra's arm. For an instant, Sierra hoped the Tseir woman had come to her defense. "Prisoner secured, Lord Commander.''

Sierra whirled and tried to yank free of Colice's grip. "Colice, no! What about your children?''

Colice's eyes remained black and fathomless. "My children? I have no children, Nirvahdi. I am a clone.''

"That was a lie, too.''

Colice nodded, still expressionless. Koran hesitated. "Your capture was not part of my scheme, Colice. The Sixth Command was not alerted to my status until the assault began.''

"It was accidental but fortuitous, Lord Commander.''

"For us both it appears Colice. Rank restored to Third. Bring the prisoner to my ship.''

Koran took a short rifle from a guard. Sierra watched as he set the rifle on stun force, then aimed it toward her. Arnoth leapt forward, and Koran shot. Sierra screamed as he fell to the floor. She crumpled beside him. She heard the second blast, but she didn't see it. The blow

348

struck her like a bludgeon, then spread across her body like ice. . . .

"Wake up! Prince . . ."

Arnoth felt someone shaking him, tugging at his forearm. His body felt like lead, numb, refusing motion.

"This is what happens when a race isn't conditioned by proper rest duties."

Rest duties. Colice was trying to wake him. She sounded desperate, frightened. As if surging upward through black water, Arnoth forced himself into consciousness and opened his heavy eyelids. Colice bent over him, holding a cup. A cup she was about to empty onto his face.

Arnoth jerked away just as she splashed water in his direction. "What are you doing, woman?"

Colice clasped her hands over her large chest and breathed a sigh of relief. Arnoth stared, slow comprehension wending its way into his brain. Colice hadn't betrayed Sierra, and she was no longer Tseir.

"Where are we?"

"We're on the lord commander's vessel, in orbit around Nirvahda."

"Sierra . . ."

"She is still unconscious, in a guarded cell on the lower level. The lord commander wants to engage the fleet before reviving her."

"Then she's all right."

"For now. He plans to celebrate his victory with a public spectacle of her surrender. That means sexual union. Apparently, he got the idea from the prime representative's distaste for Ellowan practices."

"I've got to get her out of here. But how?"

"That is why I woke you. I have been promoted to my former station of Third Command. No one will question my assignment. I will take you to the lower deck, to the cloning chamber.''

"They have cloning chambers onboard vessels?"

"They do now. Koran has accelerated the procedure. The decks are crammed with Tseir. So many . . . cloned to the hundredth level, empty, without memory or feeling. One hand can produce twenty Tseir, yet the last in that cycle are weak and survive no more than a few months. During Extrana's rule, we never reproduced more than three on one hand."

Arnoth grimaced. "A gruesome procedure."

"To those who feel pain, perhaps. Do you know what it is to be Tseir? To be alive, yet have little power to feel?"

"I know what you are remains, Colice."

"As a shadow, yes . . . For these new clones, there is nothing. Even the base lust and savagery of the old guards is missing. They move like machines, and Koran taunts them as they pass."

"He is mad."

"A living man, a Nirvahdi, from the most powerful race in the galaxy . . ." Colice paused and shook her head. "I do not understand. Even as Drakor, he seemed weak."

"He is weak, Colice. Only a weak man seeks to control others."

"And in the weakness of the Tseir, in our fear of emptiness, we did the same. How many of us come from beings such as my original? How many were enslaved, tormented? Prince, if I do not survive this evil day, one thing I ask of you. . . ." Colice paused, her black eyes penetrating. "The Nirvahdi, Garian, believes some humanity might be restored, some method of aiding Tseir to regain a portion of their lives. Please, see that it is done. Let them make Dar-Krona not a prison, but a home."

Arnoth clasped Colice's hand. "I will."

"I thank you. Whatever comes, my original's soul will know peace."

Arnoth gazed into her face, then drew her pale hand to his lips. Very gently, with infinite tenderness, he kissed her hand. "Colice, you bear your original's soul with honor."

A mist of tears shrouded her black eyes; a tiny smile formed on her pale lips. "Forgiveness, Prince, will make you a wise king. Now come, we must save Prisoner Sierra."

"Colice of the Third, bringing Prisoner Arnoth to reproduction device one."

Two guards blocked the narrow passage which led to the cloning chambers. "Did the lord commander order it, Third Commander?"

"You have questioned inappropriately, Guard Two-hundred-ninety-four."

"In error, Third Commander. Proceed."

Colice lifted her head and shoved Arnoth forward with the butt of her canister, and he tripped forward down the hall. "Look your last, Ellowan. The man who returns down these corridors will be your clone."

Arnoth didn't answer, though Colice's harsh voice impressed the guards. When they rounded a bend, Colice lowered the canister. "It was necessary I display brutality before them. They were Dar-Krona clones, still in possession of savagery. The lord commander has sent the most diluted models into the fore ships, where they are likely to perish in battle."

"He plays them like toys, like game pieces."

"And they do not resist. Perhaps it is because all that is left to these diluted beings is a desire for ending. For death. I can not blame them for what they do."

Arnoth glanced at Colice, but her expression didn't

change. She pressed a grid sequence and the cloning chamber door opened. A technician stood by the unit, and a Tseir guard emerged from the cell. He walked past Colice and Arnoth, blankly, somnambalent, then left for duties he had no heart to question.

"This is the prisoner, scheduled for cloning in chamber one."

The technician eyed Colice doubtfully. "I have no instructions for this, Commander."

"No, I know. I'm a traitor." Before the technician could react, Colice aimed her canister and fired. He dropped, stunned. "It gives me pleasure to stun rather than kill."

Arnoth chuckled. "Now what?"

Colice assessed him. "You still wear a Tseir shirt, but the tight leggings must go. Remove them."

Arnoth hesitated, then tore off his leggings. Colice assessed him like a scientist, from his waist to his feet and back. Arnoth glared. "Should you be tempted to make any reference to color coding . . ."

"The thought never crossed my mind."

"Good."

The new Tseir trousers were red, probably to differentiate the diluted from the Dar-Krona Tseir. Their fit was looser than the others, a simpler weave. Arnoth tugged them on and fastened the waistband.

Colice clucked her tongue in a decidedly non-Tseir fashion. "Red, all over . . . It suits you, Ellowan."

He blushed. The words of a Tseir had made him blush. Arnoth stared at her in astonishment. She smiled. The world moved on. . . .

"Sierra, wake up." It was Arnoth's voice, whispering. Almost a hiss. Sierra tried to move, to roll over and snuggle into his arms. Her body felt heavy, weighted with sleep. "Get the water, Colice."

Water? Why would he want . . . ? Cold fluid splashed into her face. Sierra squealed and flung herself upright. Water dripped from her cheeks, down her neck.

"What did you do . . . ?"

He clamped his hand over her mouth. "Quiet, woman. We're rescuing you."

He released her, and she flung her arms around his neck. "Arnoth." She kissed his face feverishly, crying. "You're all right. I thought he killed you."

"Just stunned. Colice snapped me out of it." Arnoth drew back to dry her face with his sleeve. "She didn't have to go to this extreme, fortunately."

"You might have spoken once more, Arnoth. I was hearing you, you know."

"No time for that, little alien. We have to get you out of here."

Sierra leaned on his shoulder and he helped her from the narrow bunk. Colice took her other arm, and Sierra leaned over quickly to kiss her cheek. "Thank you, Colice. I knew you would help me."

"Had you said anything, Koran's suspicions would have been aroused. Your instruction at Twelfth Command taught you admirable restraint."

"It did, didn't it?" Sierra puffed up with pride, and Arnoth shook his head. "Where are we going now?"

Arnoth glanced at Colice, who seemed to have a plan ready. "The shuttle bay is near here. Shuttles are moving constantly to and from the surface. You will not be detected."

Sierra hesitated. "But what happens then? Koran still controls the Tseir, and they control Nirvahda. Even when our fleet arrives, they can do nothing while the people of our planet are held hostage. Should we engage them in battle, Koran will signal his ground-based guards to kill."

Arnoth didn't respond. His expression changed, but he

said nothing as he put on a Tseir helmet. Colice's brow furrowed as she considered a solution. "I do not know a way to stop the lord commander. But freeing you is most important now."

Guards moved like robots to and from shuttles. Arnoth had clamped an oversized helmet over Sierra's head and dressed her in an ill-fitting uniform, but no one noticed her unkempt appearance as she made her way to the shuttle. It almost seemed too easy when Colice opened the door and directed Sierra inside.

Sierra seated herself at the helm and puffed a breath of relief. Colice climbed in after her, and Sierra turned to Arnoth. He didn't follow. "What are you doing? Hurry up! We have to get out of here."

Arnoth reached into the craft and took her hand. "Sierra, I love you."

"Oh, no!"

"I think I can stop Koran. If I can reconfigure their communications, it may be possible to end this madness."

"If you're in the middle of battle, Arnoth of Valenwood, how will you escape?"

"Sierra, I will find a way. Please, understand. I lost my world. I will not lose yours."

Sierra's throat tightened, cutting off speech. She started to extract herself from the helm, but Arnoth aimed a stun pistol at the controls. Sierra's mind flashed to their attempted escape from the cloning chamber on Dar-Krona. "No!"

The shuttle surged and lifted, knocking Sierra backwards. Colice leapt through the door and tumbled out beside Arnoth. Sierra scrambled to her feet and tried to follow, but the door ground shut as the shuttle surged toward the exit. She screamed, banging on the hull, but the shuttle was sucked into the exit tube. She raced to the rear viewport as the tube closed behind her vessel. Before it shut tight, she saw Arnoth standing with Colice.

Trapped onboard a ship doomed for destruction.

Sierra's craft was set on automatic pilot. The tube opened into space and spewed the small vessel away from the mother ship. Away from Arnoth. Sierra stood shaking in the empty shuttle, stunned by his action. For the first time since she'd met him, his life was beyond the reach of her help.

"I do not wish to speak with anyone."

Sierra stood alone in the rear chamber of the assembly hall, staring through her window at the spires of Nirvahda. She'd returned with no problem, but now Tseir vessels hovered in the sky, motionless. On perpetual guard. Above, beyond sight, the Intersystem fleet drew closer, and the Tseir formed their battle line of defense.

The door monitor buzzed again, but she ignored it. The Tseir had confined the representatives to the banquet hall, though Nisa had taken the children into a side room. They slept now, perhaps freed of their terror by sleep. For a while.

Disguised as a guard, Sierra had returned to the hall to report to her father. She told Redor how Arnoth had rescued her, how he'd remained behind, sacrificing his life for Nirvahda. No other words would come. Redor sent her into the rear chamber and ordered her to sleep.

Instead, she stared out the window, knowing that if Arnoth died, she would die, too. The monitor buzzed again, and Sierra grit her teeth. Why couldn't they understand? She couldn't talk to anyone now, when all her attention, all her heart was focused on him.

Time seemed to lengthen with his absence. Each heartbeat forced fear and pain through her veins, every pulse was labored with the knowledge that her beloved was alone and she couldn't reach him. "Please, Arnoth, don't leave me."

"He will never leave you."

Sierra jumped and spun around. Aiyana stood in the doorway, the last person Sierra wanted to see. "I wish to be alone."

Aiyana nodded, but she stepped into the room and the door closed behind her. Sierra frowned and wrapped her arms tight around her waist. "What do you want?"

It was, perhaps, unkind to snap. After all, Aiyana cared for Arnoth, too. But Sierra couldn't bring herself to alter her mood.

Aiyana crossed the room, her eyes on the ground as she approached Sierra. For a long while, they both stood silently, Sierra glaring at the top of the woman's dark, shiny head. Aiyana was staring at her feet. Very slowly, Aiyana lifted her head and met Sierra's eyes.

"I have known him all my life. I have seen him furious; I have seen him so deep in concentration that he didn't hear my voice. I've seen him afraid, and proud, and so lost in grief that my own was no more than a pale reflection."

Sierra wasn't sure where this was leading, but Aiyana spoke with such deep feeling that she couldn't bring herself to interrupt.

"But I have never seen Arnoth content, or his eyes filled with bliss. I have never truly seen him in love." Aiyana's green eyes shimmered with tears, but she didn't cry. "He loves you more than he loved Elena. He is happy."

Sierra's breath came short and labored, her eyes filled with hot tears.

"When I met Dane, all my life sang with bliss. I cannot tell you how it felt, to feel life in its fullest measure. When I look at him, I see myself, and I think if he asked me, I could fly. In one instant, Arnoth saw this, and

356

wanted for me what I dared not want for myself. Yet when his time came . . .'' Aiyana's voice cracked and her tears dripped onto her cheeks. "When his time came, I could not do the same for him.''

"I think I understand why.''

Aiyana's head tilted to one side. She smiled faintly. "Do you? I did not. I saw you beside him, and I saw all the things Arnoth of Valenwood might have been if not for our planet's destruction. He had become those things, and I knew you were the reason. I knew, because I had been transformed thus when I fell in love with Dane.''

Aiyana stopped and sighed. "My heart seized in such terror, in such anger, I didn't know why. It felt such a betrayal. It felt like murder.''

"Your sister's murder.''

"It was nearly four hundred years ago. I saw her die in Arnoth's arms. The truth of that moment has eluded me ever since.''

"What truth?''

"In that moment of death, Arnoth released Elena. I never did. As long as he remained in grief, she survived to me.''

Sierra's grip on her waist eased. Aiyana's darkness had passed, leaving only a grieving sister. "Why did you want him to marry Helayna?''

"Helayna carried a spear. You may have noticed.'' Aiyana sighed. "She never lets it out of her sight.''

Sierra's brow furrowed at Aiyana's explanation. "Then she would carry it even . . .''

"To the bedchamber, yes.'' A tiny smile formed on Aiyana's lips. "I do not think a man would find much tenderness in Helayna. I didn't realize what I was doing at the time. Dane knew, but I wouldn't hear his warnings. So long as Arnoth mated for duty, my memory of Elena was safe. Even if he had children, her memory would remain intact. But you . . . you gave him more than life.''

357

Sierra chewed her lip uncertainly and said nothing.

"It is Dane's fault, of course. Most things that happen perfectly are. He orchestrated the harps at the banquet, knowing I would be forced to see the reality of your love, and what it meant to Arnoth. On Valenwood, it was said if a man and woman played music well together, they would be well matched. If not, the match was doomed to fail. Music is something Elena never mastered. She broke several harps, and nearly destroyed my grandfather's flute."

Aiyana drew a long breath. "It is odd, but for all the time I knew my sister, I was blind to so much. I loved her, and thought she could do no wrong. Dane has made me see that my love is as true even when I see her for what she truly was."

"When I first met your mate, I thought he was vain and amusing. His wisdom is a source of surprise to me."

Aiyana didn't seem offended on Dane's behalf. "That is because he *is* vain and amusing. And he is the wisest man in all the galaxy. He is rooted to no concept, no belief. He sees what is, just as Seneca sees what can be. But Arnoth . . . Arnoth sees what always was."

Sierra closed her eyes to stop tears. "I love him so."

"I know that now. It is my deepest shame that I didn't honor it from the start, for the man who deserves happiness more than any other. And for you, Sierra, because you must be a kind and open soul to look beneath the armor he wore to the heart beneath."

Sierra's tears eased from beneath her lashes onto her cheek. "I'm so afraid he won't come back."

"From our earliest days, the Ellowan believed if a man truly desires life, he will have life. For nearly four hundred years, I lived in fear of the moment Arnoth would have to choose. I feared he would turn it aside when the time came. But I have no doubt today." Aiyana reached out very gently and touched Sierra's cheek. "Arnoth of Valenwood desires life. And he will come back to you."

Arnoth lay hidden beneath the circuit panels of the Tseir command vessel, while Colice stood guard. He twisted a blue and green wire together with a red cord, then drew a quick breath. "All clear, Prince. Are you done?"

"Almost. Just one . . ."

"Attention! Lord commander on deck!"

Arnoth froze, easing himself farther beneath the panel. If Koran came around to this side, if he looked down . . . Arnoth closed his eyes.

"Colice. The Third Command station is below, running navigation schemes."

"Reporting, sir. Mishap at Navigation Central one-forty-five."

Arnoth held his breath. Koran walked toward Colice. "I have heard no such reports. Navigation commands report positive." Suspicion rang in Koran's soft voice.

"Minor glitch, Lord Commander."

"You lie."

"No! No, Lord Commander."

"Stand aside from the console, Colice."

Arnoth's muscles drew taut as he waited. Colice hesitated, then moved aside. Koran walked slowly. Arnoth imagined a smile on the boyish face, now turned mocking and cruel. One boot, then the other appeared. Arnoth rolled from beneath the console, and Koran stumbled.

"Guards!"

The door burst open as Arnoth leapt to his feet. He had no weapon, and Koran aimed his short rifle, a mocking smile on his lips. "Seize him. But do not kill him. Leave that to me."

The guards charged forward and surrounded Arnoth. He backed up against the central console, every muscle taut. The guards ignored Colice as they moved in around him, their heavy canisters aimed, their motion like crouched robots. Arnoth didn't fight.

Two guards grabbed his arms and he stood motionless as Koran walked toward him. "Remove his helmet."

The guard obeyed and the helmet clattered to the floor and rolled away. Koran's eyes darkened with hatred, but he laughed with evil delight. "Ellowan, I guessed as much. Freed by Colice? Is this possible?"

Colice stepped forward, fearless and without passion, yet sure. "It is possible, Lord Commander. You used our lust for control to control us. For that, we have ourselves to blame. Yet what of the dilutes? They are no more than children, children with no future, no capacity to grow. You have created misery from misery, and simply for your own power."

Koran's smile deepened. "Do you expect to elicit pity for a clone, Colice? You, indeed, require dilution to become useful. When I am finished with the Ellowan, we will see you reduced from this pitiful condition."

Koran turned his back on her, returning to Arnoth. "Do you know, Ellowan, that had Sierra accepted my proposal, years ago, none of this would have been necessary?"

"Don't attribute your act to love, Koran."

Koran laughed again. "Love? A desire to view that firm backside in the flesh, perhaps. Sierra is now, and always has been, Redor's favored child. By establishing a friendship with her at the academy, I established contact with the doting father. It wasn't difficult. When I met her, she was nothing more than a lonely child, immersed in study, determined to prove herself 'worthy.' Her position separated her from others at the academy. Befriending her was simple."

"And profitable."

"Redor approved the match at once. He admitted me to the council, took me on as a clerk. All because I doted on his sweet daughter, yet never challenged his authority.''

''But Sierra had a mind of her own, and a heart you couldn't tarnish, or ever hope to reach.''

Koran sneered and rolled his eyes. ''Ellowan, your penchant for sensual imagination astounds me. I didn't care about her heart, and she was too cerebral to do much for my body, either. She was all grace and poise, not a woman to stimulate the flesh.''

Arnoth kept his expression impassive, though several questions leapt to his mind. Grace and poise clearly had another meaning on Nirvahda, and as far as stimulating the flesh . . .

''While this conversation is surely fascinating, it might please you to draw your attention outward.''

''Why?''

''The Intersystem fleet is upon you, Koran. The direction of the 'lord commander' may be needed.''

Koran glanced over his shoulder toward the giant viewscreen. In the foreground, Tseir ships waited in a wedge formation. Farther beyond, the vast and seemingly endless Intersystem craft came into view.

Koran shrugged, then turned his attention back to Arnoth. ''They already know the situation, Ellowan. In essence, I hold their planet hostage. They will not attack. I will summon their commanders, and send Dar-Krona commanders to each Intersystem vessel. Soon, not only the Tseir fleet, but the entire Intersystem fleet, will be mine to command. A bold plan, don't you agree?''

''An unlikely plan. It will be interesting to watch the events unfold.''

''A shame you won't be alive to see it, Ellowan.''

The guard clutched Arnoth's arm. ''To the reproduction chamber, Lord Commander?''

''While an Ellowan clone might be amusing, he is too

361

proficient at escape. I doubt you'd get him there. No, I will kill him here and now."

Koran poised his short rifle, then slowly and deliberately set the switch to full force. Arnoth tensed. He'd counted on being sent to the chambers. *Sierra. I will not let you go . . .*

"Know before you die, Ellowan, that Sierra is mine. I will use her to keep her father in line, and to torment him with my power. I will use her in revenge for her denial of me, and I will use her for my pleasure."

Koran took aim, then stepped closer to Arnoth, probably to be certain he didn't miss. "It may shock you to learn this, but I didn't travel to Dar-Krona to betray Nirvahda. I thought to arrive, then make a quick escape to the rescue ship, to be rewarded by Redor's relief, and utilize stories of my brutal captivity to convince Sierra to offer her own reward."

Arnoth drew a tight breath. He had to keep Koran talking. The man had no end of conceit. Perhaps the diluted clones weren't much for conversation. "What changed your mind?"

"An accident, a twist of fate; I was summoned to Extrana's chambers. You can guess what she wanted, I think."

Arnoth grimaced. "It is an ugly image."

"I thought so, too. At first. Tseir women require no tenderness, Ellowan. They want pure, brutal masculinity."

Despite the situation, Arnoth fought a sudden desire to laugh. "And Extrana found this in you?"

"And more. I could have gone on for hours, feeling the power, knowing the power I had over her. She called herself supreme commander, yet she crawled at my feet if I asked it. Because I gave her sensation, and she thrilled to every second of it."

"So you found true love with a clone. A tender story,

Koran. Perhaps you and your large-breasted mistress should build a happy home on Dar-Krona and leave the rest of the galaxy in peace.''

''Your levity in this moment before your death is amusing, Ellowan. It will please me to bring your body to Sierra, after the guards have added a few choice touches to your corpse. A slit throat; perhaps a gash to mar your face.''

Arnoth's heart went cold, his limbs heavy. ''Koran, you shame even the Tseir with the ugliness of your soul. You cannot take or tarnish what is truly pure. While you destroy my body, my soul will hover beside her, and she will have what eludes you through eternity.''

Koran frowned in disgust. ''Nothing eludes me now, Ellowan. I have everything. Power, control.''

''You're wrong, Koran. You lost everything in the pursuit of power. Can't you see that? You reach for what you don't have. Power is within.''

A desperate hatred glittered in Koran's eyes. ''For one such as yourself, Ellowan, that may be true. But I had nothing. . . .''

''You had Redor's devotion, and Sierra's.''

''Devotion? Ha! I was nothing more than a pleasing flower in a garden to Redor Karian. Nothing more than a doting fool to Sierra.''

Arnoth stared at Koran and knew he looked at true evil. Yet worse than what he saw was the knowledge that it hadn't always been so. It took a long path of many wrong turns to bring Koran Dirvana to this dark place. ''Sierra truly cared for you, Koran.''

''Maybe so, but I couldn't inspire her affection as you have, because I had no power. But I have made myself a powerful force now, Ellowan. Even you can't deny that.''

''I don't deny it. But I see what you do not. As a living creature, you were always a 'force,' Koran. You're free to choose, and by the choice, earn Redor and Sierra's forgiveness.''

Koran sneered. "I don't want their forgiveness, Ellowan. I saw Redor's fear, and I will have Sierra at my mercy. I have power they *must* acknowledge now.''

"I was sure of my life's route once, too. I was wrong. Koran, you are free to choose another path.''

Arnoth's words made no impact. Backing up a step, Koran aimed his rifle at Arnoth's face and pulled the trigger. Colice flung herself in front of Arnoth as Koran fired. Her body hurtled backwards, into Arnoth, then fell into a lump at his feet.

Arnoth jerked to the side, knocking the closest guard to his knees. He whirled, and the other guard's canister spun, then dropped. Two more leapt toward him. He leapt forward, caught them by the collars of their red shirts, then slammed their helmeted heads together. They dropped in unison, stunned.

"Well done, Ellowan. But too late . . .''

He turned just as Koran retrieved his rifle and took aim.

A shot fired, a blast of blue plasma that streaked upward from the floor and pierced Koran's heart. The Nirvahdi wailed, then crumpled, his eyes glazed it wide with the suddenness of death.

Arnoth turned and saw Colice on her side, clutching a canister in her bloodstained hands. "Colice." He knelt beside her. He could heal her. She was Tseir, and he had no doubt—he could heal her.

"Koran . . . Is he dead?''

"He is.''

"Did you break communications . . .'' Colice broke into a harsh cough. "Between the fleet and the ground troops?''

"It is done.''

"The Intersystem fleet will attack, then. Without Ko-

ran to threaten them, they will move quickly. You must
go swiftly. There is no time. The Tseir fleet cannot withstand an attack, it will be over in minutes. But they will
not surrender, Prince. You know that."

"Some may, Colice. I wouldn't have believed it once,
but I do now. The Nirvahdi will provide that chance."

"As you provided to me. You are a good man." Colice's eyes closed and she sucked in a tortured breath.
"Go now, before it's too late."

"I can heal you, Colice. You can help your people
find life again."

"They will find it on their own. Life is strong. But
Arnoth, understand . . . I do not desire life. I desire peace,
and rest. My soul is a remnant of hers, and she is so
tired . . ."

Colice's voice trailed off. Arnoth set his hand to her
forehead, then drew it away. "Rest, then. And find
peace."

Colice opened her eyes and looked at him. A tiny smile
formed on her white lips. "Tell Sierra . . ." Arnoth took
her hand.

"I will tell her goodbye, and that you care for her."

A faint expression of confusion formed on Colice's
pale face. "No. Tell her I feel certain she would have
made it to . . ." Her voice trailed into a whisper, but the
smile remained. "The Final Third."

The assembly hall was deadly silent. All eyes turned toward the giant viewscreen, gazing upward. Redor Karian
stood at a podium, his back to the amassed crowd of
Nirvahdi and Intersystem representatives. Above his
head, the satellite images portrayed the events transpiring
outside Nirvahda's orbit.

The Intersystem fleet formed a double line, facing the
Tseir wedge. Neither moved, a standoff reached only because the Tseir Commander held their planet hostage.

Sierra stood at the rear of the auditorium. Aiyana gripped her hand. "I am afraid to watch this, Aiyana. He is still there, with the Tseir."

"Arnoth entered many Tseir outposts and vessels when we formed our resistance on the planet of Keir, Sierra. Every time, I was sure he'd never return. Trust me when I tell you, he knows what he's doing. It would not surprise me to see the entire Tseir fleet explode in one blast, triggered by Arnoth."

Sierra gulped air. "But he is still onboard their vessel!"

Aiyana's grip on her hand tightened. "He won't be."

Sierra forced calm over her shaking nerves. Together, she and Aiyana pushed their way through the crowd. The representatives stepped back, allowing them passage to the forefront of the auditorium.

Seneca was speaking with the Teradite commander. Nisa waved her hands and seemed to be giving orders, while Seneca patiently assessed the situation. Dane paced back and forth between Redor and the Teradite, alive with helpless frustration. Batty and Carob perched on his shoulder, Batty tense and straight, Carob hunched as if in thought.

The Keiroit, Rurthgar, stood motionless, staring up at the screen.

Sierra stopped, and tears filled her eyes, then dripped slowly down her cheeks. "I hope he feels them."

"He does." Aiyana was crying, too. "And he feels you most of all."

"I hope so."

They joined the others, and Dane stopped his pacing. "Arnoth would find a way. What way? If we can foresee it, we might be able to aid him." Dane seized Aiyana's arm and drew her to face him. "What would he do, Aiyana? The two of you terrorized the Tseir for centuries. What would he do?"

Aiyana puffed a tight breath, her brow furrowed as she considered Dane's question. "Arnoth is logical. . . ."

"That point is up for debate, but go on. . . ."

Sierra's mind cleared; her heart expanded. "He sees the whole . . . Dane, he sees the whole."

Dane turned toward her. "What?"

She fought to restrain emotion, to think. "Our fleet can't attack while Koran's troops hold us hostage. Arnoth knows we can't break free on our own, not quickly. Koran must be controlling them from his ship. If our fleet attacks, he will order them to annihilate us here."

"Thank you for stating the obvious, Sierra." Dane groaned and rolled his eyes.

"It is obvious. Don't you see? To annihilate us, Koran must *give the order.*"

Dane's eyes narrowed to slits. Seneca overheard Sierra's words and nodded. "Arnoth will prevent that possibility, and the fleet can engage the Tseir."

Dane's whole face brightened. "Of course! The professional saboteur, like my sweet mate. If anyone could do it, it's Arnoth. Unless he's been caught . . ."

Aiyana patted his arm. "They won't catch him."

Dane spun in a circle, waving his arms. "So how do we know if he's done it or not? If it worked? It seems an awful risk—a whole planet."

Rurthgar turned, nodded, then marched to the rear of the hall. He shoved open the door, seized an unsuspecting guard, and yanked him into the room. He closed the door again, then pinned the guard to the wall. He held his elbow at the guard's throat and ripped a communication device from the guard's uniform.

He bumped the guard's head against the wall, and the guard crumpled, unconscious. Rurthgar carried the device to Dane. "You do a fair Tseir, boy. Do it now."

Sierra held her breath as Dane fiddled with the device. "Guard . . ." He glanced at Rurthgar.

"Nine-hundred-eleven."

"Guard Nine-hundred-eleven reporting to command vessel. All secure below. Request response on matter of tightening security."

Dane waited, but no answer came but the static of dead space. He tried again. "Guard Nine-hundred-eleven, reporting. Request immediate response."

He paused, and again no answer came. "Guard Two and a half, trouble below. Anybody out there?"

No answer. Dane's brow elevated. "It would seem our brave and noble prince has succeeded in his attempt. Now what?"

Redor slapped the Teradite. "Get hopping, my cantankerous little friend."

The Teradite rose onto his toes in excitement, then bowed. He whipped his small monitor from his chest plate and punched in a code, signaling the Intersystem fleet that it was safe to engage the enemy.

"Done, my cantankerous prime representative!"

Sierra started to smile, then realized what this meant. "Arnoth . . . If the fleet engages. . . ."

Redor hesitated, then shook his head. "He knows, girl. If our fleet doesn't move now, the Tseir might discover his sabotage. And Arnoth will return to a dead planet."

"What if the Tseir down here are monitoring the sky, too?"

Dane chewed his lip in agitation. "The ground forces are all in the city, or hovering just above. We need to provide a distraction."

Redor slapped his shoulder. "What do you have in mind?"

Dane Calydon smiled until his cheeks dimpled. He took his wife's hand and kissed it, then nodded to Rurthgar. "We've got two of the best terrorists in the galaxy. I'm sure my little Ellowan can come up with something to trouble the Tseir."

* * *

The first explosion rocked the assembly hall until the robot trays shuddered and overturned. Sierra held her breath, her heart pounding as the Tseir alarm rang out. She opened the door, and the representatives gathered around, watching as Tseir guards raced back and forth, seeking the source of the explosion.

The second explosion wasn't as great, but it was followed in close succession by a third. And then created chaos among the Tseir.

Aiyana and Rurthgar had slipped from the auditorium while Dane provided a distraction. Apparently, they knew what they were doing.

Sierra turned her attention back to the wide screen. The Teradite howled, then stomped his small, armored feet. "There she goes!"

The Intersystem fleet moved in perfect unison, spreading out, circling the startled Tseir. Sierra's pulse moved cold and slowly, her limbs numb, as if she drifted from her body, out toward the black sky to reach him.

The Tseir fired first, obviously shocked by the sudden advance of their enemy. Sierra knew the procedure. It had been argued between Teradite and Nirvahdi when Intersystem battle tactics were approved. The fleet would offer the chance for surrender, then fire the first round. Then offer surrender again. Few enemies refused after that first, deadly round.

But Tseir don't surrender. Arnoth had said so. Rurthgar had agreed. Sierra closed her eyes as the Tseir launched another round of blue plasma from their small craft. The Intersystem vessels fired as one. Not blue, but white, their energy shattering the hulls of the first line of Tseir spacecraft.

Sierra's heart stopped its beat. The largest Tseir vessel was in the next line. Koran's vessel. "Arnoth . . ."

There was an agonizing wait while the fleet commanders silently offered a second chance to surrender. The second line of Tseir delayed, and below, time seemed to stop as they watched for the Tseir's decision. A blue sheet of energy spewed forth, and Sierra crumpled to her knees.

Natassja stood beside her, weeping, too. The Intersystem vessels fired again. The second line of Tseir ships burst and shattered, brilliant implosions against the black void of space. Sierra looked up just as the command vessel burst into a thousand sparkling shards.

The hall fell deadly quiet. The Intersystem fleet had victory, but was it at the cost of Arnoth's life? Sierra went numb; her tears stopped, frozen as if in death. She bowed her head and stared at the white floor, her thoughts blank, drained of all hope, all life.

Again the pause between salvos, between life and death. She knew what would happen. The Tseir would fire again, and die. Dimly, she realized the first line had been the most diluted clones, those farthest removed from humanity. At the rear were the oldest clones, the commanders, those with the most individuality.

But still she had no hope. She had never known what it meant to be hopeless, but she knew now. She closed her eyes and remembered when she'd first seen Arnoth of Valenwood. His brown eyes, so heart-piercingly beautiful, devoid of hope, yet still shinning. . . .

"Sir, it appears they're surrendering." Batty spoke, a high chirp in the silence. A gasp emanated through the crowd. "Don't believe it, sir, but there they go. They're backing off. That means surrender, doesn't it?"

"Of course it means surrender, lad! You don't back off from a bug unless you're meaning to spit him out, do you?"

In her empty heart beat a tremor of life. Sierra looked up and watched as the last line of Tseir pulled back. Arnoth had won. No matter what happened, no matter

370

how much she hurt, he had won. He was free, and he had saved a world, her world.

"I love you so," she murmured softly.

Aiyana burst into the hall, followed by Rurthgar. "You're never going to believe this! Dane!"

Dane turned, smiling, though tears sparkled in his eyes. "What, love?"

"The ground forces. They surrendered! All of them. Rurthgar tore off his hood, just for a second—you know Keiroits need to be in moisture to survive—anyway, they just gave up! Threw down their arms. I don't know why the sight of a Keiroit would bother them, but for some reason, it's as if they didn't really want to be here."

"Perhaps they were disheartened by loss of communication with the fleet." Redor spoke quietly, and Aiyana's bright face darkened. Victory is ours, on all fronts."

"What is wrong?"

Dane took her hand. "The Intersystem fleet was also successful."

Aiyana puffed a breath of relief. "Those Tseir surrendered, too?"

"They did. But not before—"

Aiyana's face went white and she looked to Sierra. "No . . ."

Sierra rose to her feet, her heartbeat slow and without force. "He is gone."

"Little alien, you underestimate my desire to see you again."

Sierra turned, slowly, shocked. He entered the hall, smiling, his dark hair falling loosely around his face, past his wide shoulders. He was clothed all in red, and he was smiling.

"Arnoth . . ." She mouthed his name, but her voice wouldn't come.

"Didn't I tell you I would never let you go? A dead man can't hold such a promise."

She moved as if born by wings. The crowd parted, forming an aisle, and she raced toward him. He caught her and lifted her, kissing her mouth with the sweetest tenderness, with the full heart of an eternal love.

Arnoth of Valenwood had returned.

Epilogue

"After all that glory, after ships the size of small moons, after the hovering food dishes . . . we've come to this." Dane Calydon sat hunched beside Arnoth. He cast a mournful, depressed glance at Arnoth, then bowed his head in misery. "My friend, we're in a swamp. A stinking, stagnant, cursed . . . swamp."

Arnoth felt as low as Dane. Lower. The pungent swamp air filled his nostrils; quagmire fumes rose all around their rotting-log bench, forming tendrils in the air.

"At least it's summer on Keir, Thorwalian. Be thankful for that."

"Thankful? You forget, Ellowan, my race evolved in snow. This disgusting, dank, putrid heat is more than I can bear." Dane straightened. "And do you know why we're here? Because of the most evil, fiendish, demonic species in the galaxy."

Arnoth nodded, his expression grim. "Women."

Dane nodded, too. "Exactly."

Arnoth's frown imbedded into his face until it ached. He, king of the Ellowan, ruler of Valenwood, was sitting in a swamp. Not even on his own planet. No. He was in the swamp of Keir. At least Rurthgar had cooked his fish before serving it. After Dane had gagged and retched and complained about the still-twitching breakfast they were served.

Dane turned his face upward, gazing through the high canopy of gray-green trees. The sky above darkened as nightfall moved over the swamp. "This is the most depressing day of my life."

Arnoth didn't argue. He'd defeated the Tseir; he'd saved Sierra's planet. From that point, their love affair was supposed to progress into eternal happiness.

Instead, it had progressed into a swamp.

Splashing footsteps caused both Dane and Arnoth to turn. Seneca appeared amid the swirling tendrils of swamp fog, his dark face tight with fury. There could only be one reason.

"Rurthgar told me I'd find you two here."

Dane and Arnoth slid down the log, giving Seneca room to sit. They all stared into the fog, over the green and brown marsh. Fat, winged insects darted over the surface, humming.

Dane leaned forward and looked around Arnoth to Seneca. "So . . . what brings you here? As if I have to ask."

Seneca's frown deepened. "She took one apart and smuggled it onto the ship."

Arnoth glanced at Dane, who sighed. "A Nirvahdi shuttle?"

"Worse. One of their small speeders." Seneca turned his face to the sky. "Do you know what that woman can do with a speeder?"

Arnoth and Dane shuddered, then nodded in unison.

"Well, she's doing it on Valenwood, my friends. Alone. I was forced to abandon our children, with the hope that she would have to tend them, instead of reassembling the speeder. It is" ... Seneca paused to sigh ... "a faint hope."

Neither Dane nor Arnoth argued. "Women." They said it together.

A small squeak interrupted their conversation. Batty bounded out of the misty alder branches, out of breath. Dane's brow furrowed. "What's the matter with you, Batty? Nothing's chasing you, is it?"

"The demon of the swamp." Batty hurled himself upon Dane's shoulder. His small, scrunched face revealed not terror, but fury. One reason.

Arnoth sighed. "Women."

"That is a truism, and no mistake, sir. She Who Leaps High and I have parted company for the entirety of our lives."

Dane crossed one leg over the other. "Then you've come to the right place."

"Thought so, sir."

Arnoth studied the furious lingbat. "What happened, Batty? I thought lingbats mate for life."

"No longer, sir." A tremor infected the bat's high voice. Arnoth couldn't tell whether it came from grief or fury. Probably both. "The prime representative of Nirvahda requested that I send one of my young back to his world, as an apprentice."

Dane caught his breath. "I knew it!"

"I suggested Valued Descendent of Greatness, naturally."

Dane frowned, insulted. "What about He Who Walks With Dane?"

"I couldn't possibly send him, sir."

"Why not?"

"He's going with you."

Dane bowed his head, but he didn't argue. Arnoth repressed a smile, knowing Dane couldn't wait to get the little bat under his tutelage. "Redor grew fond of your species, Batty. That seems an honorable request. What's the problem?"

"She Who Leaps High doesn't see it as such. She feels our young are not ready to leave the nest. She thinks . . ." Batty closed his eyes and braced in an imperious posture. "She thinks I am hastening their departure in order to . . . beget another litter."

Dane eyed the bat doubtfully. "Are you?"

"Of course not, sir! Certainly not! Not in the *least*."

Dane glanced at Arnoth, and Arnoth nodded. "He is."

Batty hopped up and down on Dane's shoulder. "It is my right! Lingbats have powerful reproductive instincts!"

Dane held up his hand. "Say no more."

Batty cranked his head to look into Dane's face. "So . . . why are *you* here, sir?"

Dane stiffened, his chest puffed. He looked utterly sure of himself. "I am here, rodent, because that demon in a woman's body . . ."

Arnoth chuckled at Batty's confused expression. "He means Aiyana."

Dane nodded, refusing to say her name. "Indeed. She has tested my patience to its limits and beyond. As soon as we landed on Valenwood, she informed me of a small oversight. She neglected to mention that while on Nirvahda, she casually and *without asking her mate,* accepted a position as advisor on criminal affairs and explosives."

Seneca sighed. "She's certainly good at it."

"Indeed." Dane glowered in seething annoyance. "It will mean frequent ventures to out-of-the-way worlds, stars know where."

Arnoth considered the matter. Aiyana *was* good at ex-

ploding things. And she liked it, too. During their time
together, she'd booby-trapped countless Tseir outposts,
with dazzling effect. "Can't you travel with her?"

"Yes, I can travel with her . . . She is pregnant, you
know, with my second child. But did that stop her? No.
She feels her 'skills' must be shared with the Intersystem.
Skills, indeed. She'll probably blow up a planet and herself with it before she's through."

Seneca's face set in a grim expression. "I wonder if
she'd consider starting with a speeder?"

The marsh water gurgled and bubbled. Rurthgar's head
emerged and he hoisted himself onto the relatively dry
ground in front of their log. "It is the male's right to sire
hatchlings on any female in season."

Arnoth watched as Rurthgar shook mud from his body
and stomped back and forth in front of their seat. "I take
it your mate feels otherwise."

"An ultimatum has been delivered. I sire hatchlings
on her only."

"Rurthgar . . . You sired seventy-two eggs this year.
Thirty hatched. A record, if I'm not mistaken. How many
more can you fertilize, anyway?"

Rurthgar waved his webbed foot. "That is not the issue. It is my *right,* as a male. As ruler of Keir." He
hesitated, glanced around, then lowered his voice. "I
have not done so as yet, nor did I plan it, necessarily. I
simply want the female to accept my position of authority."

"And she hasn't."

"She hasn't, and she won't. For that reason I am above
water, and I will stay above water for the duration of my
reign. Which could be five hundred years."

Dane made a fist and lifted it above his head like a
barbarian warrior. "Then it's settled. By the strength of
our conviction, we will subdue the females to our will.
We will remain here, despite the stench and the heat and

377

the utter unpleasantness of it all. . . . Nothing they say
will sway the steadfastness of our resolve. Until they
crawl, begging . . . dressed in stimulating attire . . . we remain adamant and aloof.''

Arnoth straightened. ''Yes.''

Seneca straightened, too. ''It is the only way.''

Batty chirped. ''She Who Leaps High will bow to my
will.''

A booming, screeching squawk startled all. Dane's
eyes opened like saucers. ''By the stars, what was that
noise?''

Rurthgar edged back toward the swamp. ''Just a female.''

Arnoth's brow angled. ''Any particular female?''

Rurthgar shrugged and dabbed one foot in the marshy
water. ''Oh, none in particular.''

Batty squeaked. ''It sounded like your mate, Rurthgar.
Her squawk is higher . . .''

Rurthgar dove beneath the marsh water and disappeared. Seneca, Dane, and Arnoth sat back, shaking their
heads. Dane frowned in disgust. ''Well, *that* was awe-
inspiring.'' He drew himself up, undaunted by Rurthgar's
hasty departure. ''Rurthgar wasn't really one of us.''

A tiny peep sounded from the alders at the edge of the
water. Dane sat forward. Batty tensed on his shoulder.
''What was that?''

The peep came again, no louder, but clear. Batty eased
down Dane's arm and hopped casually to the ground.
''Oh, well, sir . . . just a bug, I think. A juicy one.''

Dane eyed the lingbat suspiciously, but Arnoth
laughed. ''I lived on Keir for nearly four hundred years,
Batty. I know the call of a Dwindle Bat when I hear
one.''

Dane grimaced in disgust. ''Rodent, you should be
ashamed. Wait! Where are you going?''

Batty hopped, backwards, toward the alders. ''Nowhere, sir. Nowhere at *all*.'' The lingbat turned, took three, giant leaps, and flung himself into the alder. The peep came again, doubled by two.

Seneca shook his head and Dane held up his hands. "He caved."

Arnoth sighed. "He caved."

Dane straightened again. "That's a lingbat for you."

Seneca dug a hole in the mud with the heel of his boot. "They don't understand the need to remain steadfast."

"Akandan . . ."

They turned. Nisa stood at the edge of the swamp path, half concealed in the mists. Seneca swallowed and Dane rolled his eyes. "Oh, no . . ."

Nisa stepped out of the fog, and Arnoth choked back a burst of laughter. One eye was entirely surrounded by a huge purple bruise, and swollen nearly shut. Dane coughed. "What happened to you?"

She kept her tragic gaze on Seneca. "My speeder . . . it worked like magic, Akandan. So fast, beyond my wildest dreams." She cast a quick, apologetic glance at Arnoth. "I'm sorry about your new bridge, Arnoth. I thought I'd given it enough leeway, and they were almost finished building it to the white city. . . . It would have been a beauty. It still will, I'm certain . . . when they rebuild it."

Dane sighed. "You crashed into the bridge? It's obvious what happened to you. What about the speeder?"

Nisa sniffed, fighting tears. "It's in tiny pieces, Dane. I'll never rebuild it now."

Dane sat back. Arnoth sat back, too. Waiting for Seneca to alert his mate to the error of her ways. To make her crawl.

Seneca rose slowly. He went to her and took her hands. Not quite the way Arnoth would have handled it, but perhaps his words would be suitably stern. A slow, loving smile formed on Seneca's lips. "Maiden, I love you.

If we ask it, the Nirvahdi will give us the details of the speeder, and we'll build another."

Dane groaned and covered his face. Arnoth just stared.

Nisa's one healthy eye brightened. "Do you mean it? You'll help me?"

"I will . . . on one condition."

"What?"

"We'll add a full set of bumpers to the design."

She hesitated. "Bumpers might slow the aerodynamic thrust, Akandan."

"Maiden . . ."

"Oh, very well."

Seneca stooped and kissed her forehead. He took her hand, and he didn't look back. Arnoth suspected he didn't dare. They walked away, hand in hand, and disappeared into the mist.

"That was pathetic." Dane straightened, but his expression revealed utter shame on Seneca's behalf.

Arnoth found it hard to argue. "Well, she followed him here, she agreed to the bumpers . . . That's something."

Dane leveled a lingbat look at Arnoth. They both shook their heads.

"A disgrace. The male of the species must set an example for the female, lead her by the strength of his will . . ."

A woman appeared in the mist. Aiyana. Arnoth gestured toward her. "Now's your chance."

She stood exactly where Nisa had when she admitted the wreckage of her prized speeder. But Aiyana didn't talk. *Good*. Without a pleading apology, Dane might stand a chance.

She looked at her feet. Shy. She glanced up, just a little. The tiniest of smiles touched her lips. Arnoth glanced at Dane. Dane's lips curved slightly, then widened. Aiyana glanced to the side and bit her lip. Dane rose to his feet. Arnoth felt sure she batted her eyelashes, though it was hard to see, obscured by fog.

She must have, because Dane went to her and took her little hands in his. They looked at each other. Her shy smile widened, *in victory*. Dane Calydon, barbarian warrior and technical genius, glanced back at Arnoth and shrugged. Without a single word, he turned, and Aiyana led him into the mist.

Arnoth sat alone. Alone. He waited a while, half expecting Sierra to come to him. And he would remind her that he was king, and she was his mate, and what he said was law on Valenwood. He would tell her, as he had the first time, and from the beginning, that Ellowan do not join. So there was no way he would become the Intersystem representative from Valenwood, even if she was right in her ridiculous assumption that Redor was grooming him for the prime representative's chair.

Redor wanted to "travel." He wanted to take his beautiful wife and toss aside his responsibilities, visit his children and grandchildren. The man even planned to go to Dar-Krona, where Helayna had marshaled the Tseir into an odd but effective regiment of disciplined accountants. The Tseir were good with numbers, no question, so it made sense. They liked handling the various currencies of the Intersystem. Helayna liked the authority of issuing rules and regulations, and she still hadn't set aside that spear.

Everything was perfect. Or would be, except Sierra had reacted irrationally—which shouldn't have surprised him, but had—to his refusal to join the Intersystem. She said it didn't mean giving up independence, and that Garian could help him rebuild Valenwood, and the Nirvahdi would assist in developing the old cities to their former glory, and beyond.

Arnoth preferred the swamp. He wasn't sure why. The

Nirvahdi might do better at rebuilding. But it was the principle of the issue.

Someone moved behind him. Arnoth jumped, his heart pounding. He whirled. And no one was there. His heart fell so fast that it hurt.

"Message for you, sir."

Arnoth looked down, Carob.

"I thought you were on Valenwood."

"I was. Came with the females, sir."

"Is Sierra with you?" *What a pathetic, mournful question!* He shamed himself with the wistful query.

"No, sir."

Arnoth sighed, his spirits at their lowest ebb. "Oh." He thumped back down on the log. "What do you want, Carob? What message?"

"You're to report to Valenwood immediately. Troubles, sir."

Arnoth stiffened. "Troubles? What troubles?"

"Message broke up before I got it clearly, sir. It sounded like some quarrelsome, difficult ambassador had arrived on your planet, and had something to offer. Not sure what, sir."

Arnoth hesitated. "Was Sierra's name in the message?"

"No, sir."

"She probably returned to Nirvahda."

"Had a quarrel, did you, sir?"

"We did."

"Bad one, sir?"

"I'm in a swamp, rodent."

"Thought you might be vacationing, sir."

"No."

"Sometimes, sir, it's hard to be king. I'll just return the message and tell them to handle it on their own."

The lingbat started away, but Arnoth rose wearily to his feet. "No, Carob. It is my duty. I will go."

382

Arnoth sighed heavily, his heart like lead in his chest. He looked up into the misty sky, then down at the ling-bat. "Tell the others that I have returned to Valenwood. I'd tell them myself, but I assume they're all . . . busy."

Arnoth of Valenwood disappeared into the swamp mists, heading for his shuttle. Back to Valenwood. Carob gazed across the brown and green swamp as the sky turned purple in the last light of evening. "Humans . . . the most innocent species in the galaxy."

Carob knew human nature better than any lingbat, although He Who Flames With Courage was learning. But even Carob hadn't expected Arnoth to submit so easily. The female of the species was craftier, no question. Arnoth hadn't even questioned the purpose of the message, hadn't pressed for Sierra's influence in the matter. He deserved whatever came.

Carob sighed, feeling the evening air cool and lighten. A plump darter-fly hovered over the swamp, dangerously close to the path's edge. Oblivious. The wings quivered as it consumed yet another tiny swamp vit. Swamp vits didn't interest Carob. But plump darter-flies did.

Stupid creature. No sense whatsoever. It fluttered over the path, toward the log. It was obviously thinking to add to its fat stomach with the vits that spun mindlessly around the rotting bark. Carob waited, almost sorry that it came so easily. No challenge.

It darted back and forth, then toward its doom. Carob froze, evening his breath to perfection. *Balance. Focus. Aim.*

He sprang. The darter-fly didn't stand a chance. One crunch, and the feast began. Carob lingered over the last bites, fully satisfied. Another darter-fly made the same mistake and fluttered stupidly close to the log.

Carob hesitated. He was full. Then again, it might be a joy to bring this juicy specimen to Dane. He'd become more and more a lingbat, began to talk like one, to think like one. Maybe it was time he ate like one, too. . . .

Arnoth walked along the tiled corridors of his recon-structed palace. He was tired, because nothing had gone his way. He'd eaten, alone. Sierra hadn't come to greet his shuttle. He hadn't dared ask where she was, and no one had offered the information. Probably afraid of his reaction if he learned she'd returned to Nirvahda.

At least there was one pleasant surprise upon his return to Valenwood. The tiled city overlooking the golden ocean was well on its way to completion. The palace villa was finished, and more beautiful than he remembered.

Thanks to Nirvahdi builders he didn't remember au-thorizing. . . .

The design of the villa was similar to his memory, although larger and perhaps brighter, with larger win-dows to let in the sun. The corridor to his bedroom, how-ever, hadn't changed.

Bright tiles decorated the walls; crystal light fixtures lined the hall. He went to his door, the door to the king's chamber. He reached to open it, but it was already ajar. Arnoth sighed and walked in.

The bedchamber opened wide before him. He saw his long, low bed beneath a kingly canopy. It was a room built for sex.

She stood by the bed, young and sweet and innocent, wearing a soft gown the color of fruit nectar. Her skin was freshly bathed and softened with scented oil. Her long, dark hair curled over her shoulders like a sensual cloud. Her gray eyes glittered, and her soft lips curved in a smile.

A smile that threatened to bring him to his knees.

"It is said to create union between our people, an of-fering is required. . . ." Sierra moved toward him, then stopped. Arnoth's heart throbbed, but he couldn't speak; he couldn't move.

"Such an offering as you require, my king, is a temptation."

The sound of her voice sent tremors down his spine. His manhood hardened so fast that his knees threatened to buckle. She trailed her slender finger along her low neckline, drawing his gaze over her soft, warm skin. Her lips parted; her eyelids lowered.

The gift of an alien lord, and his dream. "Little alien . . ." She smiled, and his words caught.

"It is the Ellowan way, is it not? An alliance formed through pleasure, and through love." She stepped closer, her eyes smoldering. "I will give you pleasure, and all my love, my sweet king. And whatever you wish of me, I will do." As she spoke, she drew nearer, until she nearly touched him. He couldn't move. "Whatever you want is yours, because I am yours."

She looked up at him, her face aglow with love. Arnoth's pulse raged like fire. "Little alien, I want only you."

She reached her arms to him, tears glistening in her eyes. "I want you, too."

He caught her and drew her close. She quivered with desire as he pressed his lips against her cheek. Her arms wrapped around his waist, but he drew back. "I have dreamt this, my love, I have dreamt of you. But I never imagined that this love you offer could ease the weight of my soul, nor bear the full force of desire throughout time."

"I long for it, for every second with you."

He ran his hands down her arms; she tipped her beautiful head back, and he kissed her throat. He felt her swift pulse racing beneath his lips, and he knew her desire was equal to his.

The sight of her, ripe from his dream, an offering of

385

passion, sent hot, demanding pulses into his loins. She leaned toward him, and he cupped her face in his hands. He kissed her gently, but her lips parted, and his restraint shattered. He tasted her lips, the sweet nectar of her mouth, and her tongue brushed seductively over his.

"I will take you slowly and show you every sweet pleasure, and I will never let you go."

She drew back, holding him at arm's length. "You will take me over and over, and show me everything, and I will show you...." She backed away, drawing him with her to their bed. "And you will fill this ache in me, because my desire has grown to such feverish heights without you that I think I can't stand the torment of waiting."

She drew him closer and parted his white tunic. She pressed her warm mouth against his bare skin, teasing his flesh with small licks. Arnoth ran his hands along her sides, down her back, and over the flare of her firm bottom. He tugged up her silken skirt, feeling the soft skin beneath. She wore nothing beneath the gown.

His pulse raced to a frenzied speed. She tore apart his tunic, then pulled it away and tossed it aside. Her deft, quick fingers slid beneath the waistband of his leggings, reaching.

His excited flesh strained to his navel, full and hot and near bursting with need. Her fingers reached its tip, circling and teasing as he pulled her gown over her head. It slithered to the floor at their feet, leaving her bare skin warm and full to his sight.

"You are beautiful, little alien. I would love you slowly, for hours."

She smiled, though her breaths came in quick, short gasps. "We have hours, Arnoth. We have forever. You will make love to me over and over, but if you don't start now, I will die."

He lowered her to the bed beneath him and positioned

his aching staff between her thighs. His blunt tip met her soft curls, dampened from her desire. She wrapped her long, slender legs around his waist and lay back before him.

He cupped her round, pink breasts in his hands, teasing the tips until they formed hard buds. She arched beneath him, her legs tightening as she urged him closer. He delayed, holding his staff against her woman's center until he felt her pulse against his own, until she moaned and squirmed.

His blunt, hard tip pressed there, against her moist opening, and he groaned with primal lust. She angled her firm bottom for his entry, and reached to grab his hair. He felt himself pulsate and hesitated, prolonging his pleasure. She pulled him fiercely toward her.

"Arnoth, I do not wish to wait."

He moved against her, stopping her words with a quick, shuddering gasp.

"Hours, little alien."

"No! Now!"

He chuckled at her fierce insistence, then inched slowly inside her. A low, rumbly growl emanated from deep in her throat. She pulled his head down to hers and kissed him hungrily. What his lust sought, he found. She twisted around the tip of him, and he drove deeply inside her. She moaned his name, her arms wrapped tight around his shoulders.

He would love her to sweet exhaustion, then love her again. The first surge of desire would be repeated, longer. He thrust and she answered, her head tipped back, her hair splayed across his bed, rippling as he drove inside her. Her soft, inner flesh contracted around his length, urging him to join her as she shuddered beneath him in waves of rapture.

His control shattered, his desire erupted and poured into her, through her . . . She was his.

* * *

"Does this mean you accept my father's offering?"

Arnoth turned lazily to look into Sierra's face. She snuggled close beside him, one leg over his. "I will toy with the notion for a while longer, sample all your pleasures, then, yes. . . . You may call me representative of Valenwood. It is a fair exchange."

Sierra smiled and yawned. "Our alliance is formed. Such alliances must be renewed continually, you know."

"Over and over."

His desire returned already; his flesh hardened. Sierra ran her palm over its shape and murmured, "As you wish."

"I missed you, little alien."

"Good. But while you were in the swamp, grumping, I spent my days more profitably."

Arnoth kissed her and drew her closer into his arms. She rested her head on the expanse of his shoulder, and he sifted her dark hair across his chest. "I see that. Nirvahdi builders work wonders. When I left, the palace was no more than a shell."

"Do you like the balcony over the ocean? That wasn't in the plans. I made that part up myself."

"It's a strange thing, but when I dreamt of Valenwood, a balcony just like that existed. It never existed before, outside my dreams. But then, neither did you."

"Dreams are real, Arnoth. They are in the air, waiting for you to build the reality."

"The tiled city will be grander than it was. The forest leaps to life again, the desert blooms with life. . . ." His voice trailed off as an unknown sorrow tinged his bliss.

"There's one other thing I did while you were away." Sierra sat up and hopped up from the bed. She put on a silken white robe and tossed her hair loose around her shoulders. She reached for his hand and tugged.

"Woman, I'm in no mood to explore my new city. Tomorrow . . ."

"You don't have to leave the bedroom. We have a balcony, too. And you can wobble that far."

"Wobble, indeed." Arnoth rose reluctantly, and she handed him his new, dark red robe. He pulled it on, leaving it open, then joined her as she pushed open a wide doorway. Outside their room stretched the sea, vast and forever. The fading sun cast sparkling gold across the surface. Gold that rose and disappeared . . . almost as if the amber whales had returned.

His sorrow found its roots. The whales . . .

"You can make them out. There, I think. Yes! There's one!"

Arnoth eyed her doubtfully. "One what?"

Sierra turned, beaming. "A baby whale."

"It can't be."

"Garian is here, you remember. I showed him where the bones of the whales were imbedded in rock. He was able to extract enough—"

"Sierra only living things can be cloned."

"Well, not exactly. To make an exact replica of a being, it requires living tissue. To instigate regrowth of a species, it is possible. If you cloned a dead person in this fashion, you wouldn't get the same person, but a new person, if you follow me so far."

"No, but go on."

"So these whales aren't the whales you knew. I don't know if they'll sing. But they are of the same formation as your amber whales. Garian says many such species might be returned to Valenwood. There are only two so far, and for some reason, they haven't met, or seem to want to. Garian is working on more, and one day the sea will be filled with life."

Arnoth drew her into his arms as evening drifted over the sea and the tiled city. Her long hair ruffled and entwined with his as she rested her head on his shoulder. Across the ocean, he saw them. Small, golden whales that breached and splashed.

The golden sunlight faded beyond the western horizon, and the ocean disappeared slowly from view. Sierra's brow knit thoughtfully. "Wait here!"

She disappeared into their room, then emerged bearing his old harp. Arnoth's brow angled. "Now? Little alien, I had something else in mind."

"Play."

Arnoth propped his leg up on the balcony and set the harp to his knee. He touched the strings, sending strands of simple, pure music out across the sea. He stopped and set the harp aside, waiting.

Nothing. "Maybe it's too soon. But it's enough they're alive, Sierra."

Sierra sighed. "I just thought . . . well, you said the amber whales taught your people to sing at the dawn of your existence. I thought maybe you could teach them at the dawn of theirs."

Arnoth kissed her cheek. "It was a sweet thought, my love, from the sweetest heart. . . ."

And then it began. Low, primal music rose from the invisible sea, and his heart leapt, beyond shock, beyond hope. A tentative song of rebirth filled the air.

The lone keening echoed over the tiled city. Sierra hugged him, crying softly as the hauntingly beautiful song fell into silence. Then, farther away, another voice rose in song.

The whale songs drew nearer as the creatures sought each other out. The music grew in strength and confidence, then blended into one exquisite chorus.

All along the shoreline, the Ellowan emerged, silent, in awe as they listened to the whale song. On a balcony below, Arnoth saw Morvin standing with his new bride.

Children ran to the new bridge, like shadows of the future beneath the arched lampway.

Arnoth listened to the whale's rebirth until his heart overflowed with bliss. The bliss of his people, of his world. And of his own future with the woman who gave him life.

The wind turned cool, and his thoughts turned back to the present. "Come, little alien. The night is just beginning for us as well."

"The bliss of this night will never end, my love. But maybe I'm wrong. It began the moment I saw your face, and it will last forever after."

Arnoth kissed her hand, then led her back to their bed. He engaged a soft, warm light that set her hair sparkling like the dark sea. Sierra's face remained knit in a thoughtful expression.

"You seem lost in thought, little alien. What troubles you? I have plans for this night with you, and I wouldn't have you distracted by anything."

"When Batty and She Who Leaps High mated, they called their babies Linglebats. . . ."

Arnoth's gaze wandered to the side. "An interesting observation." He paused. "Why do you mention it?"

"Well, you and I are of a different race, you being Ellowan and me, Nirvahdi. I was just wondering what we'd call our young."

"Nirv-owans?" Arnoth chuckled. "El-vahdis?" Neither sounded quite right. "Elves? Well, we'll worry about it when the time comes."

She looked up at him, her eyes twinkling with mischief. "That's the point, Ellowan. The time is on its way."

His jaw dropped, and his heart took an odd leap. "Is it?"

"I felt a bit ill, after you left. Quite frankly, I think that's what made me so grumpy, when we argued. Anyway, I asked Aiyana to use her Ellowan technique and check me, in case I'd caught something, maybe from the Tseir. They seemed healthy enough, but you never know. . . ."

Arnoth seized her shoulders. "Sierra . . . rapid speech . . . Draw a breath and tell me that you bear my child."

She looked puzzled. "I think I just did."

"Say it."

"Very well. I bear your child. Aiyana says it is a boy, so we have a prince on the way. We discussed the matter quite thoroughly—before she had to go to retrieve Dane and make him see reason, and after she healed most of Nisa, leaving, of course, just the bruise around her eye so Seneca—" Sierra stopped, cleared her throat, and offered a tense smile. "Anyway, Aiyana and I decided that we shouldn't formally arrange a betrothal, but if we perhaps visit frequently, bringing our son and Elena together, ever-so-casually . . ."

Arnoth sank down onto the edge of the bed, his eyes wide with shock. "You're pregnant. A son."

She sat beside him and patted his thigh. "Aiyana is having a son, too. They're going to name him Hakon, after her grandfather."

"You're pregnant."

"We'll have to have several lingbats in our home, to instruct him."

"A son."

Sierra sighed happily. Her hand slid higher up his thigh, then beneath his dark red robe. "You keep saying that. I will have to think of something to distract you."

And she did.

AUTHOR'S NOTE

I hope you enjoyed *The White Sun*. I loved writing it. The cultures and history, and especially the people, have become so real to me. I picture this galaxy when these three men, Seneca, Dane and Arnoth, with their lingbats and their wild, lovely wives, come to the ultimate leadership of their world. Arnoth will follow his father-in-law, of course, as "Prime Rep," with Seneca and Dane at his side. I see Dane as an old sage, surrounded by lingbats, and Seneca as the spiritual leader, all the while trying to keep his wife from a still-faster vehicle. Their world is dear to me, and I hope one day to journey to his place again.

I hope you'll look for my next Love Spell romance. *Free Falling* sends two ex-lovers back into Apache territory, Arizona, where an awkward, eccentric woman learns to be a hero to the man who saved her one too many times.

You can write to me at: P.O. Box 1305, Suite 194, Brunswick, ME 04011, or E-mail stobie@ime.net. Visit my web page at http://w3.ime.net/~stobie. I look forward to hearing from you!

The Midnight Moon

STOBIE PIEL

Dane Calydon knows there is more to the mysterious Aiyana than meets the eye, but when he removes her protective wrappings, he is unprepared for what he uncovers: a woman beautiful beyond his wildest imaginings. Though she claimed to be an amphibious creature, he was seduced by her sweet voice, and now, with her standing before him, he is powerless to resist her perfect form. Yet he knows she is more than a mere enchantress, for he has glimpsed her healing, caring side. But as secrets from her past overshadow their happiness, Dane realizes he must lift the veil of darkness surrounding her before she can surrender both body and soul to his tender kisses.

___52268-3 $5.50 US/$6.50 CAN

Dorchester Publishing Co., Inc.
P.O. Box 6640
Wayne, PA 19087-8640

Please add $1.75 for shipping and handling for the first book and $.50 for each book thereafter. NY, NYC, and PA residents, please add appropriate sales tax. No cash, stamps, or C.O.D.s. All orders shipped within 6 weeks via postal service book rate. Canadian orders require $2.00 extra postage and must be paid in U.S. dollars through a U.S. banking facility.

Name_____
Address_____
City_____State_____Zip_____
I have enclosed $_____ in payment for the checked book(s).
Payment <u>must</u> accompany all orders. ☐ Please send a free catalog.
    CHECK OUT OUR WEBSITE! www.dorchesterpub.com

STOBIE PIEL

"An exciting new voice!" —*Romantic Times*

Sheep, sheep, sheep. Ach! The bumbling boobs are everywhere, and as far as Molly is concerned, the stupid beasts are better off mutton. But Molly is a sheepdog, a Scottish Border collie, and unless she finds some other means of livelihood for her lovely mistress, Miren, she'll be doomed to chase after the frustrating flock forever. That's why she is tickled pink when handsome Nathan MacCallum comes into Miren's life. Sure, Nathan seems to have issues of his own to resolve—although why people are so concerned about righting family wrongs is beyond Molly—but she knows from his scent he'll be a good catch. And she knows from Miren's pink cheeks and distracted gaze that his hot kisses are something special. Now she'll simply have to herd the spirited Scottish lass and brooding American together, and show the silly humans that true love—and a faithful house pet—are all they'll ever need.

_52193-8 $5.99 US/$6.99 CAN

Futuristic Romance

Love in another time, another place.

Don't miss these tantalizing futuristic romances set on faraway worlds where passion is the lifeblood of every man and woman.

Warrior Moon by Marilyn Jordan. Dedicated to upholding the ancient ways of her race, Phada is loath to mix with the men of her world—but the young Keeper can't understand her burning attraction for virile and courageous Sarak. On a perilous quest to save her people from utter destruction, Phada must trust her very life to Sarak. And if she isn't careful, she'll find love, devotion, and ecstasy without end beneath a warrior moon.

_52083-4 $5.50 US/$7.50 CAN

Keeper Of The Rings by Nancy Cane. With a commanding presence and an impressive temper, Taurin is the obvious choice to be Leena's protector on her quest for a stolen sacred artifact. Curious about his mysterious background, and increasingly tempted by his tantalizing touch, Leena can only pray that their dangerous journey will be a success. If not, explosive secrets will be revealed and a passion unleashed that will forever change their world.

_52077-X $5.50 US/$7.50 CAN

Futuristic Romance

Star-Crossed

Saranne Dawson

Bestselling Author Of *Crystal Enchantment*

Rowena is a master artisan, a weaver of enchanted tapestries that whisper of past glories. Yet not even magic can help her foresee that she will be sent to assassinate an enemy leader. Her duty is clear—until the seductive beauty falls under the spell of the man she must kill.

His reputation says that he is a warmongering barbarian. But Zachary MacTavesh prefers conquering damsels' hearts over pillaging fallen cities. One look at Rowena tells him to gird his loins and prepare for the battle of his life. And if he has his way, his stunningly passionate rival will reign victorious as the mistress of his heart.

_51982-8 $4.99 US/$5.99 CAN

Dorchester Publishing Co., Inc.
P.O. Box 6640
Wayne, PA 19087-8640

Please add $1.75 for shipping and handling for the first book and $.50 for each book thereafter. NY, NYC, and PA residents, please add appropriate sales tax. No cash, stamps, or C.O.D.s. All orders shipped within 6 weeks via postal service book rate. Canadian orders require $2.00 extra postage and must be paid in U.S. dollars through a U.S. banking facility.

Name_____
Address_____
City_____ State_____ Zip_____
I have enclosed $_____ in payment for the checked book(s).
Payment <u>must</u> accompany all orders. ❏ Please send a free catalog.

ATTENTION ROMANCE CUSTOMERS!

SPECIAL TOLL-FREE NUMBER
1-800-481-9191

Call Monday through Friday
10 a.m. to 9 p.m.
Eastern Time
Get a free catalogue,
join the Romance Book Club,
and order books using your
Visa, MasterCard,
or Discover®

Leisure
Books